No Smoke

Without Fire

Paul Gitsham

ONE PLACE. MANY STORIES

HQ
An imprint of HarperCollins*Publishers* Ltd
1 London Bridge Street
London SE1 9GF

This paperback edition 2020

1
First published in Great Britain by
HQ, an imprint of HarperCollins*Publishers* Ltd 2020

Copyright © Paul Gitsham 2020

Paul Gitsham asserts the moral right to be
identified as the author of this work.
A catalogue record for this book is
available from the British Library.

ISBN: 9780008389154

MIX
Paper from
responsible sources
FSC
www.fsc.org   FSC™ C007454

This book is produced from independently certified FSC™ paper
to ensure responsible forest management.

For more information visit: www.harpercollins.co.uk/green

This book is set in 11/15.5 pt. Minion

Printed and bound in Great Britain by
CPI Group (UK) Ltd, Melksham, SN12 6TR

To Mum and Dad. Thanks for everything.

DECEMBER 2010

Prologue

The old man shuffles through the gate, blinking as if he hasn't seen the sun in years. In many ways, he hasn't. Not really. He's dressed in a shabby grey suit that's a size too small and a once expensive shirt, open at the neck. A simple crucifix on a thin metal chain is just visible, partly hidden by curling grey hair. The leather of his shoes creaks, having stiffened over time. In his right hand he clutches a blue plastic carrier bag — it contains all that he has owned for the last twelve years.

Behind him the guard stops, still inside. One more step and his authority evaporates; inside he is as a god, his jurisdiction absolute — outside he is no more than an ordinary man.

"I'm sure we'll be seeing you again. Your kind never change. I just hope they catch you next time before you ruin any more lives." His voice is muted, his cruel taunt only audible to the old man.

For his part, the old man keeps on walking as if he hasn't heard a word; a few more paces as if to guarantee he is truly outside and he stops. Turning slowly to survey the place he has called home for over a decade, he looks slowly at the guard and fingers the crucifix.

"No, you won't. I'm never coming back. I will never spend another day in that hellhole." His voice, quiet, raspy, damaged by too many cigarettes, is nevertheless resolute.

The guard scowls, disappointed that the prisoner — former prisoner — doesn't rise to the bait. Sometimes they do; sometimes they start the first day of their new life in a bad mood, as he manages to turn a joyous occasion for the prisoner and his family into a nasty confrontation. Prisoners dream of the moment they step through those gates free men. They idolise it, constructing fantasies about how perfect it will be — as if they are soldiers returning from a far distant front line; conquering heroes, not the dregs of humanity finally released back into society, more often than not to pick up where they left off. The guard always does his best to spoil that moment — his final gift to his former charges. If he had his way, people like the old man would never leave. They'd serve time until their dying breaths, and then they'd be buried in unmarked graves in an inaccessible and overlooked part of the prison grounds.

Finally, the old man breaks his gaze and turns back towards the road, starting his shuffle again. He seems to notice the chill December wind for the first time and shivers. It was spring when he was driven through the gates that last time; the lightweight suit that he wore in his final court appearance was more than adequate. Now it's winter and he almost wishes he'd put on his prison-issue sweater. But no, he could never do that. He only has it in his bag so that he can light a bonfire with it and start to expunge the legacy of his recent incarceration. To have put the sweater back on would have been to surrender his freedom again. Never.

He waits on the side of the kerb, not quite sure what to do, his teeth starting to chatter. How ironic, he thinks, to have survived all of these years, only to freeze to death because his lift is late. Behind him he hears the whine of an electric motor, then the heavy thunk as the huge door closes, shutting him off from the nearest source of warmth for miles around. Never mind, he long ago made a promise

4

to himself: even if the snow was three feet deep and the temperature twenty below freezing he would never step inside a prison again, either by choice or by compulsion. He'd rather die of exposure.

Finally, he hears the purr of a well-tuned engine. Looking up, he sees a dark blue Jaguar driving slowly towards him. Instinctively he knows it's for him. The car, an unfamiliar model sporting the new type of licence plate that means nothing to him — yet another small detail that slipped past as he languished inside — eases to a halt. The driver reaches across and opens the passenger door. He remains leaning across the seat, looking up at the old man.

"Hello, Dad. You survived, I see."

TWELVE MONTHS LATER

FRIDAY 2ND DECEMBER

Chapter 1

The young woman stepped into the ice-cold December air. It was 6 p.m. and already it had been fully dark for two hours. She operated her mobile phone with one hand, fumbling in her handbag with the other. Wrapped up tightly against the cold, with a long red woollen coat, a dark, knitted scarf and matching hat, she nevertheless had yet to put her gloves on, in deference to the touchscreen on her phone.

Activating it, she saw that it was precisely one minute past six. Selecting the text icon, she read the short message:

On my way babes. C U soon. X

She smiled as she finally located her cigarettes and lighter. Darren was on time as always. The couple had developed a well-oiled routine over the year that they had lived together. Darren would leave the tyre fitters where he worked at six on the dot and drive across town to pick her up. A devious little rat-run let him avoid Middlesbury's one-way system in the rush hour and arrive in the side street behind her office building at about ten past six, giving her just enough time to enjoy a well-earned cigarette. Unfortunately, the only place he refused to allow her to smoke was in the passenger seat of his well-loved and heavily customised Vauxhall Astra.

Truth be told, she thought the Astra was a bit much. A man in his mid-twenties really ought to have grown out of motoring magazines and "pimping his ride" as he liked to call it. It seemed ludicrous to her that a grown man couldn't see the folly of spending thousands of pounds customising a car worth less than five hundred. Then again, he couldn't understand why she insisted on buying more shoes and handbags when she had a wardrobe full already. In the end they had agreed to disagree. Besides which, it beat catching two buses to and from work every day.

She took a long drag on her cigarette and was surprised to hear the sound of an engine entering the far end of the road. That was quick, she thought as she took another hit, anticipating the need to stub it out at any moment. It had to be Darren — the narrow side street was little more than an alleyway and she couldn't remember ever seeing anyone else using it in the past year. The local businesses put their recycle bins out for the council to collect on a Monday morning, but as far as she knew the bin lorries didn't even come up there; the refuse collectors just dragged them around the corner to the main road.

At that moment her phone beeped; a short note from her best friend, confirming that she was coming around at eight with a bottle of rosé and a DVD.

Despite the distraction, her subconscious had spotted something was not quite right; the engine sounded wrong. Rather than the throaty growl of Darren's twin exhausts, it was the grumbly rattle of a diesel engine that made her look up. She blinked in surprise at the unexpected sight, then mentally shrugged. The vehicle was a common enough sight in other parts of town; she wouldn't have even noticed it if she hadn't been expecting Darren. She turned her attention back to her mobile, already ignoring the vehicle as it pulled up to the kerb a few metres past her. Out of the corner of her eye she saw the driver get out and start to walk towards her.

The driver was only a few paces away from her when she finally paid attention. What alerted her she would never know. Was it the purposeful stride in her direction? The fact that the vehicle shouldn't be here at this time of the evening, let alone stationary with its driver out? Or was it the smell, sweet yet slightly acrid, even at this distance? A scarf covered his mouth against the cold, while a woolen cap pulled low hid most of the rest of his features. With a jolt of surprise, she realised he was wearing one of those rubber masks that you could buy in a joke shop.

She opened her mouth to scream, but it was too late. The driver covered the last three paces impossibly fast, his right hand blurring upward towards her face. Suddenly her nose was filled with a solvent smell that reminded her of her mother cleaning paintbrushes in turpentine. She struggled to breathe, her eyes filling with tears, but the driver's hand was clamped tightly across her face. The world was already starting to spin; a sudden feeling of lightness swept through her body and a rushing noise filled her ears. Her legs weakened and before she knew it she was slumping downwards as if trying to sit on the kerb.

The world was now turning a fuzzy light grey, like an old-fashioned TV set when you pulled the aerial lead out, followed by a dark grey, then finally black. Her last memory was the clatter of plastic on concrete as her mobile phone hit the pavement.

THREE DAYS LATER

MONDAY 5TH DECEMBER

Chapter 2

The strident ring of a mobile phone sang out in the silenced hall. Three hundred pairs of eyes swivelled immediately towards the back row and Susan Jones cringed in embarrassment, trying to disappear from view. Beside her, her husband, Detective Chief Inspector Warren Jones, fumbled frantically for the offending gadget, trying in vain to silence it. On stage, the earnest fourteen-year-old girl started to sing the opening notes of "Silent Night", before stumbling and losing her place as the phone rang for a second time. The teacher accompanying her on the piano stopped playing and turned around, glaring at the audience.

A chorus of tuts and hisses sounded from around the auditorium as Jones got to his feet and tried to leave the darkened room as unobtrusively as a six-foot man holding a ringing, glowing mobile phone, seated in the middle of a row of interlocked school chairs, could manage.

Mumbling his apologies, Warren stumbled into the centre aisle, knocking over at least two handbags and a pair of precariously balanced crutches. Resisting the urge to break into a run, he strode with as much dignity as he could muster to the rear exit. As he slipped through the double doors into the hallway outside, he heard the piano start up again and the opening notes of the young soloist. The phone continued to ring. Giving up on trying to silence the damned thing using its touchscreen, Warren simply answered it.

"One moment, Tony, I can't talk now." Although he had whispered into the handset, his voice seemed to echo down the hallway. The two white-haired ladies setting up the coffee urn and interval biscuits scowled at him. As he hurried towards the front of the school, he prayed that nobody had recognised him. The last thing he wanted was for the school's new Head of Biology to become known to the Parent Teacher Association and other gossips as "that science teacher with the really rude husband".

Finally finding himself alone in the school's reception area, he was able to answer the call. "OK, Tony, what have you got?"

The booming Essex voice on the end of the phone sounded amused. "Caught you at a bad time, guv?"

"You could say that. Let's just say that 'Silent Night' was suddenly no longer silent. What's happened?"

All traces of humour immediately left the other man's voice. "You'd better get over here, boss. We've got a body."

* * *

Less than thirty minutes later, Warren carefully manoeuvred his dark blue Ford Mondeo up a sodden dirt track. The cold December night was pitch black, the dark and threatening rain clouds blotting out the nearly full moon and stars. The only lights visible were the flashing blue strobe from the police patrol car blocking the road and the interior lights of the empty ambulance parked next to it.

To his left, Warren saw several parked vehicles. He made out the familiar white outline of Detective Inspector Tony Sutton's sports car, a Scenes of Crime incident van and a few others that he didn't recognise.

A middle-aged uniformed sergeant with a clipboard stepped out to greet him.

"DCI Jones?"

He scribbled Warren's name and time of arrival on the scene log and directed Warren to park up next to Sutton's Audi.

"DI Sutton is at the scene, sir, along with the paramedics and the members of the public that found the body. A Scenes of Crime manager is on site and others are on their way; they should be here within the hour."

"Thank you, Sergeant. Where is the body?"

The officer pointed ahead, up the dirt track.

"A couple of hundred yards up there. Apparently it was found by a group of dog-walkers. They were pretty on the ball, by the sounds of it. They stood still and phoned for us; didn't trample all over the scene. They swear that they only walked on the footpath, so we've made that the main access route."

Warren nodded his approval; the sergeant seemed pretty on the ball himself. It never ceased to amaze him the way that despite all of the pleas and warnings from the crime scene specialists, many police officers — detectives included — insisted on poking around the site of a suspicious death, potentially destroying any evidence before it could be collected. By designating the already forensically compromised footpath as the only access route to the crime scene, the sergeant had ensured that any evidence in the surrounding area would be left undisturbed.

Pulling out his mobile again, Warren called Tony Sutton. The detective inspector answered immediately.

"I'm down at the main gate," Warren informed him. "I have a paper suit in the boot of the car. I'll come and join you."

With the aid of the sergeant's powerful Maglite torch, Warren perched on the edge of his open car boot as he squirmed into a white "Teletubby" suit made out of plastic-coated paper. The last thing he wanted to do was contaminate the scene with any trace evidence from his own clothes; he could destroy valuable clues, or, worse, he could give the murderer's legal team the tools necessary to raise reasonable doubt and secure an acquittal.

Finally, suited and booted and feeling faintly ridiculous, he clumsily started up the path. Even without the large torch, he could have found his way; the designated path was wide and well-established and somebody had stuck metre-high sticks in the ground with police tape around them to act as a guideline.

As he walked Warren felt himself shiver, and not just because of the crisp air. The path cut through a small stretch of woodland and the trees loomed forbiddingly on either side of him. The rustle of his paper suit and the sound of his breathing weren't quite enough to hide the haunting hoot of an owl, hunting in the distance. A sudden rustle to his right betrayed the presence of some small animal, spooked by the powerful beam of his torch. It was at times like this that Warren was reminded of the fact that, despite enjoying a country walk on a summer's afternoon as much as the next man — especially if it involved a pub or two — he really was a city-dweller.

Continuing his slow trudge, he became more accustomed to his surroundings: the damp smell of the woodland, the faint pull against each footstep from the muddy path. It had rained a bit the day before, he recalled. Depending on when the body had been dumped, the scene was either preserved with nice footprints in the damp soil and the victim covered in fibres and other forensic gifts, or nature had done her best to cleanse the area and make the Scenes of Crime team's job harder.

Finally a glow started to appear through the trees. The shiny, plastic crime tape that led the way curved sharply to the right. Warren was grudgingly impressed; the spot was well hidden from the road, suggesting that the killer — assuming the victim was murdered — knew the area and had probably chosen the site with some care. He filed that away for future consideration.

Ahead, a small clearing was brightly lit with a bank of powerful battery lights and criss-crossed with blue and white tape, designating which areas had already been walked upon and which might still yield some clues.

Standing huddled together against the night air were four late-middle-aged people: two men and two women, comprising two couples, judging by the way they were paired off. A chocolate-brown Labrador sat alert at the feet of the shorter of the two men, watching everything going on with great interest; a fat, golden lump of indeterminate breed lay slumped as if dead next to the other.

A rather less-well-wrapped police constable looked as if he would dearly love to swap the ramblers' Gore-Tex and fleeces for his own fluorescent police jacket. On his feet, he wore a pair of muddy white booties, stopping him from contaminating the crime scene with outside material. At least he wouldn't have to clean his boots before his next shift.

The couples were also wearing the white booties, but this time to stop them losing any trace evidence that they might have picked up as the first on scene. It was an elegant solution, Warren decided, given that it was impractical to have them walk all the way back to the front gate in their socks. He wondered if anybody had told them that their walking boots would be spending at least a couple of days at Hertfordshire and Bedfordshire's Forensic Science Unit at Welwyn Garden City.

He glanced at the two dogs and couldn't help a smile as he realised that in a perfect world they would also be wearing plastic booties. Depending on what the Crime Scene Manager decided was necessary, both of those dogs might just find themselves undergoing a very thorough grooming in Welwyn.

After introducing himself to the shivering PC, Warren was told that Tony Sutton was with the CSM, Andy Harrison, examining the body. Two other Scenes of Crime officers were with him, starting a preliminary search and setting up a tent to protect the body from further degradation from the elements. The paramedics had been told to stand down as the body would be left in situ overnight. They looked relieved to be going, but agreed to wait to escort the couples back to the waiting SOC van after Warren heard their story.

Finally, Warren met the walkers. Thanking them for their patience and apologising for the wait, he soon ascertained that they were two recently retired couples out on a regular walk. Apparently, they got together about three times a week and went for a three- or four-mile ramble with their dogs, before retiring to their local pub. They had a number of favoured routes, with this one being preferred on colder evenings, since the trees sheltered them from the wind somewhat. Their last walk through these woods had been four nights previously. That might or might not give a time frame on the dumping of the body, Warren decided, since a very fresh corpse might not have attracted the attention of the dogs.

As Warren had guessed, it was Peanut, the chocolate-brown Labrador, who had found the body. As was their custom, both dogs were off their leads with Peanut romping through the trees on the edge of the pathway. Susie, the golden lump, was getting on a bit now and preferred to trot alongside her owners. At the mention of her name, one of Susie's ears pricked up, before flopping down again. The poor thing looked knackered, thought Warren.

The walkers had been alerted by a sudden urgent barking from Peanut.

"He's a sensible one, is Peanut. He's not given to silliness, so I thought I best go and see what got him all excited." The oldest of the four retirees was a short man, with a trim grey beard and gentle accent that might once upon a time have been West Country.

Leaving his wife with the other couple, he'd entered the trees to find Peanut sitting on his haunches barking and whining, clearly distressed.

"It was the smell that gave it away, see. I knew that there was something dead in there as soon as I got near. And I figured that if it had been a deer or something else, Peanut wouldn't have been acting up like he did, he'd have been straight in there sniffing around. Far as I can tell, he never went within ten feet of the body.

"Anyway, it was pretty dark in there, but I've got one of those little wind-up torches on my key ring and as soon as I shone it on the body I could see she was dead." The man's voice cracked slightly. "Poor thing. I took a couple of paces closer, figuring I should at least take her pulse, but I didn't. You don't smell like that if you're still alive. Then I remembered all of those crime dramas that Marie watches and I figured I best leave well alone."

At the mention of her name, his wife slipped a comforting arm around his waist.

"Ben here has a mobile phone and so I got him to phone 999 and then we waited for you lot to arrive." The other man, taller and still sporting a full head of dark hair, waved an old, brick-like phone in the air as if to prove his friend's point.

After asking them a few more questions and making sure that the CSM had taken everything he needed, Warren thanked them again and sent them back down the path with the paramedics.

Now it was just him and the police constable. If anything, the bright lights made the woods seem more oppressive, blotting out what little natural moonlight could make it through the clouds, enveloping the two men in a white bubble, surrounded by inky blackness. There could be absolutely anyone or anything standing outside that little cocoon and neither man would know…

Jesus, Warren, get a grip. You're in bloody Hertfordshire, five miles from Middlesbury, not two hundred miles up the Amazon River. There aren't jaguars waiting in the trees or crocodiles lurking under the river; we've probably scared off every rabbit or fox for miles around.

Still, he was relieved when he saw the flash of white light coming from the woods and, a few seconds later, the slightly comical shape of Tony Sutton waddling towards him.

"Stop smirking, guv, you look just as bloody silly."

Warren, glad that his smile of relief had been mistaken for mirth, responded in kind. "What have we got, Detective Inspector Tinky Winky?"

A snort of laughter was quickly suppressed by the presence of the uniformed constable, then the brief moment of levity was gone, neither man feeling it appropriate now. Sutton's face turned sombre.

"I think you'd better come and see for yourself, Chief. It's not a nice one."

Chapter 3

Sutton led Jones deeper into the woods, between two strands of police marker tape. About thirty metres in, a large white crime scene tent loomed into view. Another bank of lights illuminated the scene. Opening the flap on the tent, Warren recognised the shape of Crime Scene Manager, Andy Harrison, bent over.

"That you, DCI Jones?" he asked, without turning around.

"Yes, it's me, Andy. Good to see you again."

Warren had worked with Harrison at a couple of scenes since joining Middlesbury CID in the summer. The short, portly man was located at the Serious Crime headquarters in Welwyn Garden City, but lived in Middlesbury. For that reason, he usually managed to get himself assigned to any major crimes in the Middlesbury area. Warren was pleased to see him; the man was a safe, competent pair of hands.

Looking over the man's shoulder, Warren felt a wave of sadness. As Tony had told him over the phone on the way in, the body belonged to a young woman. It was important not to draw too many conclusions at such an early stage — as his former mentor in the West Midlands Police had been so fond of saying, 'When you Assume, it makes an Ass out of U and Me'. Nevertheless, a few things were immediately apparent.

First, the body had almost certainly been there more than twenty-four hours. Even at this time of the year, a body started to decay rapidly when left to the mercy of the elements. The smell in the small tent was pretty rancid — thank goodness it wasn't summer, Warren thought. No wonder Peanut had homed in on her so quickly.

The young woman was dressed in a smart black knee-length skirt that had been raised up above her waist. A pair of white panties were pulled down to just above her knees along with her thick black stockings, exposing her pubic region. First order of the day when she was finally moved to the pathologist's lab would be a full rape kit. Hopefully, whoever had done this to her had left traces of his semen or other DNA sources behind.

The victim had been wearing a red woollen coat, now open to expose a smart white blouse. The blouse had been partially unbuttoned, showing a sensible bra, pulled to one side, exposing her left breast. Wrapped tightly around her neck was a charcoal knitted scarf.

Without wanting to prejudice any future conclusions too much, Warren was already thinking: work clothes, possibly an office worker or similar. He noted her shoes, shiny black with substantial heels, and decided that she probably had a fairly sedentary job. He knew that his wife, Susan, a science teacher who spent most of her day on her feet, always wore flats or modest heels.

"My preliminary observation is a white Caucasian female between the ages of twenty-five and thirty of average build. Possibly raped. Judging by the smell, she's been dead for at least twenty-four hours, probably more. The body and clothes are wet, suggesting it has rained since she was left here, which gives us a time frame of some time prior to yesterday morning. The scarf

24

is certainly tied in a manner consistent with a ligature, although I can't determine cause of death here. That's up to the pathologist."

"What about the scene?"

"Not much yet. I suspect that the killer carried her here down the same path that the walkers and we have used; that and the rain have probably obliterated any footprints from there, but there looks to be a couple of boot prints around the body." Harrison motioned towards the small squares of white plastic pinned to the ground around the victim's head, protecting the imprints until casts could be made.

"The bloke that found her claims not to have approached the body, so hopefully they can be linked to the killer."

"You said 'carried'. Was she killed elsewhere and dumped here?"

Harrison shrugged, his suit rustling. "That I can't tell you yet, but I'm pretty sure she didn't walk here." He pointed at the woman's shoes. "Look, almost spotless. Her heels in particular would be caked in mud if she had walked here under her own steam."

Warren eyed the young woman again. She was of average build, he judged, certainly no heavyweight, but even if she was dead or otherwise incapacitated it would have taken a fairly strong man or more than one person to have carried her down the path.

"Anything else?"

Harrison shook his head. "Nothing but speculation at the moment. I wouldn't want to put any wrong ideas in your head at this stage. We'll secure the site and get a full team up here in the morning. I'll email you a clear headshot for ID purposes; her face is probably OK to show to relatives — I'll leave that up to your judgement."

Warren glanced at the young woman's face again. She looked almost serene, with no visible cuts and bruises. Mercifully it didn't look as if anything had taken a nibble of her face whilst she'd lain waiting to be discovered. Only the waxy pallor suggested she was anything other than asleep. Warren decided to run the photo by Family Liaison; they might even add a little pink in Photoshop to soften the blow.

With nothing more to be done, Sutton and Jones trudged back to the clearing, before continuing back to their cars. Neither man said anything, each lost in his own thoughts.

It was the beginning of December and somewhere a family would never look forward to the festive season in the same way again.

TUESDAY 6TH DECEMBER

Chapter 4

"Sally Evans, twenty-six. Reported missing four nights ago by her boyfriend when she failed to meet him at their usual pick-up point in the side street behind Far and Away travel agents, where she worked."

It was 8.30 a.m. and Warren was holding a team briefing in the conference room at Middlesbury's small CID unit. Behind him a projector showed a close-up photograph of the body taken at the scene by Andy Harrison and beside it a much happier image, taken that summer on holiday. The victim had shoulder-length light brown hair; the smiling young woman in the holiday snap had longer, sun-kissed blonde hair, but it was clearly the same person.

"We have a positive ID from the victim's boyfriend, with whom she lived, and her mother and best friend. Family Liaison broke the news last night."

"The body is still in situ up at Beaconsfield Woods, where it was found by a group of dog-walkers at approximately 6.30 p.m. yesterday evening. The body will be moved to the morgue at midday and a PM is scheduled for early afternoon. Preliminary indications are that she may have been sexually assaulted; cause of death is unknown at this time, but her scarf was wrapped around her throat and may have served as a ligature. Her body was almost certainly carried to the woods, but we don't know if she was dead or alive, or when and where any assault took place."

The atmosphere was sombre. Everybody in the room knew that the three days between Sally Evans' disappearance and the discovery of her body could prove to be a major hindrance to the investigation. Valuable trace evidence from the site could have been lost, contaminated or destroyed; similarly, the killer or killers had had over eighty hours to cover their tracks. The team couldn't afford to lose any more time.

Reading from the list he had prepared before the meeting, Warren started to assign jobs to the officers present. "DS Kent, can you set up an incident desk and get HOLMES up and running, please? I want you to start entering everything as it comes in, especially the particulars from the autopsy. I want to see if the MO matches any known cases. See if we can find links to any previous attacks. DC Hastings, I want you to assist." The older sergeant was the unit's expert on HOLMES2, the Home Office's crime management database. Used across the country, the system employed a degree of computer intelligence to link cases together and manage all of the documents relating to a crime. Although all officers used the system to some extent, it was experts like Kent who could really make the system work for them.

Working with him would be Detective Constable Gary Hastings. Newly returned from several months' sick leave after being stabbed in the summer, the young officer was on light duties whilst he continued to recuperate. He was keen to learn and quick-thinking, and Warren had assigned him to the older sergeant's care, having decided that putting the young man back into the heart of a major investigation was probably the best way to help him exorcise any demons remaining from the summer's horrors. Besides which, it hadn't escaped Warren's notice that DS Kent was approaching retirement age. He had no idea what the older man's plans were — and the new age-discrimination laws made him wary about asking — but training up other officers seemed prudent to Warren.

Of course, as with any system, HOLMES2 was only as good as the information put into it and the next stage was to gather that information.

"DI Sutton, I want you and DS Khan to co-ordinate the interviewing of all of Ms Evans' known associates. Start with her workmates, then her friends. Let's see if we can find any witnesses. Use the missing person file as a jumping-off point, but remember it isn't a crime for a twenty-something not to come home of an evening, so there probably won't be much in there."

Sutton and Khan nodded, already casting their eyes around the room at the various other officers they would second to their teams.

"DS Richardson, speak to Traffic and any CCTV operators in the area. Let's see if we can find any useful images from around the time that she went missing. I doubt that there will be much in the way of CCTV footage up near Beaconsfield Woods, but you never know, we might get lucky and pick up something on the speed cameras on the main road.

"In the meantime, I'm going to speak to her family again and see what her boyfriend has to say for himself."

* * *

Warren chose Detective Constable Karen Hardwick to accompany him to interview Sally Evans' family. The young woman was relatively new to CID, but had shown a lot of promise. Warren firmly believed that a small unit such as Middlesbury should be careful to ensure that more junior colleagues received the full range of learning experiences, and so he regularly took detective constables and sergeants out with him to interview witnesses or suspects.

It was almost a cliché that whenever a murder occurred, the first place the police headed for was the victim's home. However, as Warren's first mentor, Bob Windermere, would often remind him, clichés and stereotypes only become such because there was more than a grain of truth to them. The vast majority of murders were committed by someone known to the victim and so when a young woman was killed the first people the police investigated were her husband, partner or any exes that might still be on the scene. Consequently, the first person that they questioned was Darren Blackheath, Sally Evans' boyfriend.

The two had been together for almost three years and had been renting a small third-floor flat for the past eleven months, the young man explained as the two police officers sat on the small sofa opposite him.

Darren Blackheath was a twenty-four-year-old tyre fitter with no previous convictions. A Middlesbury resident all of his life, he'd lived with his parents until moving in with Sally Evans. Similarly, Sally was also in her first serious relationship, although she had shared flats with housemates and lived in student accommodation when studying for a degree in tourism management.

The couple had met in a bar one night, exchanged phone numbers and started dating "officially", as he put it, a month later. A bit of delicate probing revealed that the relationship had been going well, according to Blackheath. So well in fact that he had been planning on proposing to her on Christmas morning. With reddened eyes, he showed the two police officers the diamond ring with which he had hoped to seal the deal.

The night that Sally had disappeared had been unremarkable. He'd left work at his usual time, sending her a text message to let her know that he was on his way. Crossing town had taken no longer than normal and he'd pulled up outside the rear entrance to her workplace at a few minutes past six. As usual the street was deserted, but unusually his girlfriend was not waiting for him.

"She usually comes out on the dot of six and has a fag whilst she's waiting for me to pick her up. I don't mind her smoking in the flat, but I draw the line at me car." His eyes grew moist again. "She promised she were going to quit in the new year. It's one of the reasons I decided to propose. She always said she'd quit before she got married, 'cos she wanted a white wedding and she said there were nothing worse than a bride with a fag in 'er mouth. Nearly as bad as tattoos." He looked embarrassed for a moment. "No offence if you have tattoos. But I figured it would give her an extra incentive, you know?"

"So what happened then, Darren?"

"Well, I checked me mobile, but there was no message. Normally she's out the door on the dot, so she doesn't bother replying. But if she's going to be late she always texts me so I don't worry.

"I waited for about five minutes before I rang her mobile but it rang out and went to voicemail. So I locked the car and tried the back door to her place, but it's a fire door and it was locked from the inside. So I walked around the front and saw that the shop was closed. The front door was locked and no one was in."

"Was that unusual? It was only just after six."

"No, not really. The shop actually closes at five-thirty. They spend the last half an hour cashing up and finishing the paperwork. They all leave together at six o'clock. Most of them leave by the front door. Sal is the only one to leave by the back. The manager checks the door locks behind Sal then bolts the front door and I guess sets the alarm."

Warren jotted this down. So far the story matched that given by Blackheath four days before when he reported her missing. Now, however, it was important to make certain that no details were missing or different — no matter how small they might seem.

"Do you know who was working that night?"

Blackheath recited a list of office staff that matched the list already supplied to the missing persons team. The office was small and on a typical weekday four of the six permanent members of staff would be in. Warren made a note to have them all questioned again to make sure their stories corroborated Blackheath's.

"What did you do next?"

"I went back to the car, to see if she'd reappeared, and tried her mobile again. Then I phoned her boss Kelli. She said that Sal had left at the usual time and that she'd locked the door behind her.

"I was getting worried, so I phoned her mum and her best friend, Cheryl. Neither had seen her. Cheryl had sent a text message just after six saying that she was coming around for a girlie night, but Sal didn't reply." His voice broke slightly.

"What did you do then?"

"I drove home and started phoning all of her friends. Cheryl and Sal's mum came around about half-seven. By midnight we couldn't think of anyone else to call and figured that if she had gone to the pub with some other mate, she'd be back by now. That's when we called the police and reported her missing."

By now, Warren's gut was telling him that Blackheath was not their man. However, if his timing was to be believed, there was a ninety-minute window between Sally Evans leaving work and her mother and best friend arriving at the flat — potentially long enough for him to have taken Sally Evans to Beaconsfield Woods, raped her, dumped her body, then returned home. Warren made a note to check with neighbours what time Blackheath's car had arrived back at the flat.

In order to eliminate him fully, Warren arranged for Blackheath to be escorted to the police station for fingerprinting, DNA typing and a formal statement. He also arranged for Forensics to go over his car and the flat.

With Blackheath dispatched to the station and a forensic unit on its way to look for evidence, Jones and Hardwick drove the short distance to the home of Cheryl Davenport, Sally Evans' best friend.

The young woman that answered the door was a short, slightly plump girl with bottle-blonde, permed hair. Her make-up, though expertly applied, couldn't conceal the dark rings under her eyes and their swollen redness. The tears came back within moments of the two police officers entering her small kitchen. She offered her visitors a coffee, which they both accepted, less to quench their thirst than to give the grieving woman a few moments to compose herself.

As she fiddled with the kettle Warren took stock of the tiny room. It was pretty much what he expected of a twenty-something, single woman. Tidy and compact, the sink was already full of mugs but no other cutlery; the overloaded ashtray spoke of a person whose world had been turned upside down and who had spent the past three days living on caffeine, nicotine and worry.

The kitchen units were clearly the cheap MDF beloved of low-rent landlords. A washing machine took up the only space under the counter, forcing the tall, fridge-freezer to stand awkwardly in the corner, half hidden by the open door. Stuck to its white front were the usual Post-it notes and postcards. In pride of place were a half-dozen photographs of Cheryl and her best friend Sally, mostly arm in arm, taken on beaches or foreign-looking nightclubs.

Noticing his gaze, Cheryl started to cry again. "We've been going on holiday ever since we left school. The last couple of years we've been to Greece, Turkey, Egypt, you name it — Sally kept an eye out for cheap deals when she was at work and she usually managed to wangle us some sort of discount or upgrade." She sniffed loudly. "Even when she started seeing Darren, we still went off on our girlie trips. That doesn't always happen you know. Some girls get hooked up and that's it, they only go away with their blokes. But Darren was all right about it — he was pretty cool. He said she could have her week in the sun with me, as long as he could go on his footie tour."

It was another point in Blackheath's favour, Warren decided. Men who killed their partners often turned out to be domineering and controlling types; hardly the sort of man who'd let his girlfriend disappear for a week of fun in the sun without him. Nevertheless, they needed to pursue every lead to its conclusion. He glanced at Karen Hardwick, who picked up on his subtle cue.

"We're sorry to put you through this, Cheryl — it must be an awful time for you — but we need to ask some questions. Will you help us?"

Cheryl nodded; underneath the tears, Warren could see a strong resolve to help in any way that she could to find her best friend's killer.

The story she told was much the same as that of Blackheath. She'd texted Evans at about 6 p.m., inviting herself over with a DVD and a bottle of wine. She hadn't received a reply, but about six-thirty Darren had called, asking if she'd seen her. After he'd hung up, she'd put it out of her mind as she made herself something to eat and got ready to go out. Apparently Sally could be a bit forgetful when it came to charging her mobile phone and so she hadn't been worried. By seven-thirty, Sally hadn't phoned or responded to her text message and she had been just about to try her landline when Darren had called again, sounding worried.

Picking up her address book, she'd set off for their flat, arriving about the same time as Sally's mother, who Darren had also called. At first they'd been a bit jokey, trying to convince Darren that it was nothing, but as they finished calling all of her usual friends the worry had set in. Finally, at about midnight, they'd called the police to report her missing.

"If only we'd called sooner, maybe they'd have found her before… before…" She dissolved in a flood of tears, her carefully constructed façade collapsing completely.

Hardwick leant over and took her hands and Warren was again glad that he'd decided to bring the young detective constable along with him. The two women were roughly the same age and some jobs needed a special touch that Warren, try as he might, would never possess.

"You don't know that. It's unlikely that we'd have found her any sooner — we wouldn't have known where to start looking." Karen didn't mention, of course, that with no evidence of foul play a young woman missing for less than six hours — before the clubs even closed — wouldn't merit much more than a few details in the duty log and a sympathetic, but firm, "wait and see if she turns up in the morning, then call again".

After a few moments, the young woman regained her composure. Warren took over now. "Tell me about Darren. I believe they'd been together a while?"

Cheryl nodded. "Nearly three years. They'd been in the flat for almost a year. He's been good to her. He has a heart of gold." For the first time since they arrived, she smiled. "I teased her when they first started dating. He's a right skinny one is Darren and he isn't the sharpest tool in the box, but he really loves her and he'd do anything for you. He's never really been one for nightclubbing or that, he prefers a quiet night in, but he always insists on picking us up if we've been out on the town. 'No smoking and no puking', he always says whenever he turns up in that car of his. Sally used to joke that she never worried about him having an affair, because, between looking after her and polishing his car, he hasn't got enough energy." The smile faded as the reality of the past few days came flooding back.

"So you would say that they had a strong relationship?"

Cheryl nodded vigorously, before her expression turned conspiratorial. "He was going to ask her to marry him."

Warren blinked. It seemed a little odd that he would share his intentions with his girlfriend's best friend. He said as much.

Cheryl laughed slightly. "Oh, he never said a word. Sal told me. The silly sod hid the ring in his underwear drawer — she found it one day when she was hunting for a missing sock. She knew exactly what he was planning but didn't have the heart to let him know the cat was out of the bag. She was going to act all surprised when he asked her. She swore me to secrecy." The brief moment of happiness passed and Cheryl's face crumpled again. "I don't suppose it matters now."

The feeling in Warren's gut was even stronger. Mentally he crossed Sally Evans' boyfriend off his suspect list. Moving on, he asked Cheryl if Sally had mentioned anything strange over the past few days. Had any ex-boyfriends turned up on the scene or had she mentioned any disagreements with friends or co-workers?

To every question, Cheryl shook her head firmly, insisting that Sally told her everything.

"She didn't have much of a history before Darren. He was her first really serious boyfriend. She dated a couple of lads at university, but never for more than a few months and I think they are all happy and married now." She blushed slightly. "She wasn't… inexperienced before she met Darren, you know, but she didn't put it about and she's been faithful to Darren ever since she met him — I'm absolutely sure of that."

"What about co-workers? Is there anybody who could have perhaps mistaken friendliness for a bit more and got jealous?" Warren was grasping at straws now. The statistics showed that so-called "stranger attacks" were far rarer than the public feared. Almost all victims had had some prior contact with their murderer, no matter how slight. Attacks by a total stranger were not only rare, they were also inherently more difficult to solve, because so many of the leads that the police would normally follow were absent.

In answer to his question, Cheryl was again equally firm. Almost the entire company was composed of females, varying in age from twenty-something to late fifties. Warren wasn't quite ready to dismiss them yet; he'd interview them first. He couldn't rule out that they were working a partnership with a male accomplice, but he knew it was unlikely, given that Sally Evans had probably been sexually assaulted as well as murdered.

The two male employees were added to the interview list,

but again Warren's instinct told him that, based on Cheryl's description, Kevin the seventeen-year-old Saturday boy and Angus the openly gay former flight attendant, who lived in a civil partnership and took care of his elderly mother, were unlikely to be responsible.

Finally, Warren could think of no more questions. As they left, he heard the sound of the kettle being filled again and smelt the first wisps of tobacco smoke. Sally Evans' best friend settled down again with her grief.

Chapter 5

The final visit of the morning, before returning to the station to take stock, was to Sally Evans' parents.

The small house where Sally Evans had spent most of her childhood was filled with mourners. Grandparents, aunts and uncles occupied every chair. The air was thick with cigarette smoke and every surface held an ashtray, a teacup or both. The atmosphere was one of grief but also mutual support. Warren couldn't help contrasting that with the loneliness of her boyfriend — why wasn't he here?

Don't judge, he chided himself. For all he knew, Blackheath could have spent the last two days here and only returned to the flat to get changed. He'd probably have found the smoky atmosphere hard going as well. Warren remembered that when the law changed to outlaw smoking in enclosed public spaces, some bright spark with more legal sense than common sense had noted that when a police officer visited a person in their house, it could be argued the house was now a "place of work" and so the occupants should be asked to refrain from lighting up whilst the visitor was present. Needless to say, as much as Warren and his colleagues might dislike sitting in a cloud of fumes when they did their job, it would be regarded as rather poor taste to ask a grieving family if they'd mind stubbing out their cigarettes before the police could interview them.

After expressing their condolences to the many family members, Jones and Hardwick were led into the kitchen where Sally Evans' parents were sitting. The similarity between mother and daughter was immediately apparent, even through the tears and running make-up. The two even sported a similar haircut, although Jane Evans' hair was running to ash-blonde, rather than the dark blonde of her late daughter.

Bill Evans bore only the most superficial of similarities to his daughter. A tall, craggy man of late middle-age, he had steel-grey hair and a slight paunch. Behind rimless reading glasses, his eyes were also puffy.

After declining a cup of coffee — there was a limit to how much he could drink in one morning — Warren turned to the matter in hand. Focusing first on Mrs Evans, he asked her to recount the events of the night Sally went missing. Again, the details matched exactly those told to the missing persons team and most recently to Jones and Hardwick by Cheryl and Darren.

Moving on to the subject of Darren, Warren asked about the relationship between the two young lovers. Suddenly, Bill Evans surged to his feet, his face reddening. "Don't speak to me about that man in this house — if it hadn't been for him, our girl would be sitting here safe and sound, not dead and lying on some…" His voice choked off and, brushing away his wife's hand, he raced out of the room.

Warren rocked back in surprise at the man's sudden outburst. Everything they had heard about Darren Blackheath had been good so far, so why the animosity from Sally Evans' father?

He turned to Jane Evans, who looked as if she was about to

start crying again. Visibly pulling herself together, she waved a hand in the air as if to ward off their concern.

"Don't read too much into that, Detective," she started. "He doesn't mean it really. He's just upset."

"I'm a little surprised," admitted Warren. "I thought Darren was popular with Sally's friends and family?"

"Oh, he is, just not with her father."

"Why is that?" Warren had been all but certain that Blackheath was in the clear, but obviously at least one person wasn't so sure.

Jane Evans sighed and took a long sip of her tea.

"Sally has always been a daddy's girl and she was the apple of Bill's eye. She's our only child and he worshipped her from the moment she was born. Truth be told, I don't think that any man would ever be good enough for her in his eyes, least of all Darren."

Warren waited silently as she composed her thoughts.

"Sally was a slow developer at school and she was finally diagnosed as dyslexic. That was a real blow for Bill as he is dyslexic also. It's silly, I know, but he always felt guilty that he'd passed on some gene. Anyway, the school were fantastic and, with lots of support from them and us, Sally started to pick up the ground that she'd lost. By secondary school, she was scoring average grades and her reading and writing was almost normal for her age. She worked so hard and when she finally got the A levels to go to university we were both so proud. Nobody in our family had ever been before."

As the topic of conversation switched from her dead daughter to her husband, Jane Evans visibly softened. Warren wasn't certain where her long, rambling tale about her husband's achievements in spite of a disability that forty years previously had seen him dismissed as thick and lazy was headed, but he let her talk at her own pace.

"The thing is, Sally may have got the dyslexia from her father, but she also got his work ethic and determination. Despite joining the company straight from school, with no qualifications, Bill is now national sales manager. He's based in Cambridge, but travels all over the country."

As the conversation wound its way back to her murdered child, Jane Evans' eyes filled with tears again. Nevertheless, she forced the words past her trembling lips.

"Sally graduated with a two-one from university. We were both so proud." She smiled at the memory. "Bill can be a bit abrupt and stern if you don't know him, but he cried all the way through her graduation ceremony. He truly believed that she could accomplish anything now and I think he wanted her to do all of the things he never got the chance to do. Anyway, she moved back here with us and got a job at the travel agents Far and Away."

She paused for a moment, before continuing, "At first I think Bill was a little disappointed, but Sally convinced him it was only temporary — she wanted to learn the ropes somewhere small where she could get a lot of experience, before joining one of the big companies and maybe becoming senior management. That was the plan at least, but she's been there for years now and seems comfortable. Lately, Bill has been pushing her to move on, but she claims that the time isn't right with the recession. Bill thinks that this is exactly the time to move as he doesn't think that there will be a future for small independents. They argued about it a lot." She shrugged. "Sally says her dad doesn't know anything about travel agents, since he's only ever worked in sports clothing. Bill says that business is business and an outside perspective is important." She wiped her eyes with another tissue. "Maybe they're both right, but they kept on going around in circles and I stopped getting involved."

"So where does Darren fit into this?"

Mrs Evans sighed. "He's a tyre fitter and a lovely boy, he really is, but he has zero ambition and isn't very well-educated at all. Bill always felt that Sally should marry a doctor or a lawyer or a dentist — not a tyre fitter. It was something else to argue about."

"So what was his reaction when Sally moved in with Darren?"

Mrs Evans looked even more sad. "He was really angry. He told her she was wasting her life and tried to make her feel guilty, claiming that she was throwing away all of her years of hard work. He implied that he wouldn't contribute to any wedding plans and told her not to turn up on the doorstep pregnant and homeless."

Warren could feel the pain in the room and struggled to find the words to ask her the questions he needed to without upsetting the poor woman further. Again, it was Karen Hardwick who saved the day.

"It sounds as if he really loved her and was afraid of losing her."

Mrs Evans smiled through the tears. "That's exactly right. He loves her to bits. I think that with a little more time he'd have come around and everything would have been all right." Her voice choked slightly. "I guess we'll never know."

Taking over from Hardwick, Warren tried to be as sensitive as possible. "I imagine he was worried when she didn't come home that night. Where was he?"

If Mrs Evans realised that the question was about establishing Bill Evans' alibi, she gave no sign.

"I called Bill just before we called the police. He was working away in Leeds that night. He's been doing that quite a bit lately. They have a new branch up there and Bill has been going up to iron out the teething troubles. He stays in a Travelodge hotel near the airport. He came back immediately, made it in record time — he was here by 3 a.m."

Warren jotted down the company's details and made a note to get his alibi checked out. It could just be that this wasn't a stranger murder after all.

In the car on the way back to the station, Warren praised Hardwick's questioning technique before asking her opinion on what they had heard so far.

"I can't see Darren Blackheath being guilty. He doesn't seem the type."

"I tend to agree," admitted Warren, "but we can't rule him out just yet. It's possible that he had a motive — what if he popped the question early and Sally decided to turn down his proposal because of her relationship with her father? Maybe he flew into a jealous rage and killed her?"

Hardwick looked doubtful. "Anything's possible, sir, but again I don't think he seems the type. And if her upcoming wedding was the catalyst, what about her father? Could he have had an argument with her about it?"

Warren shook his head slowly. "I don't see how the timing would work. If, as Mrs Evans claims, her father loved her, then if he did kill her it would almost certainly be a crime of passion. The sequence of events as we know them suggests that Sally Evans left work at her usual time of 6 p.m. If Blackheath is in the clear and telling the truth, then she disappeared some time in the next ten minutes. Could her father have dropped by unexpectedly to offer her a lift home — and she forgot to text Blackheath — then they get into a row and he kills her and dumps her, before pretending to be all concerned when his wife phones late that night?"

Hardwick pursed her lips. "I agree, it seems a bit farfetched. I guess we'll just have to see if their alibis check out and what Forensics have to say."

In other words, hurry up and wait — sometimes Warren thought that should be the motto of the police.

Chapter 6

By the time they returned to the station it was more or less lunchtime. Warren scheduled a team briefing in a half-hour, insisting his officers got at least a short break and something to eat. Warren's gut told him that this investigation might run for some time and he wanted his team to take care of themselves.

Karen Hardwick stopped by her desk and picked up her lunchbox, before heading out for some fresh air. Almost exactly a minute later, Gary Hastings grabbed his lunch and followed her out of the door.

Tony Sutton sidled up to Warren.

"Do you reckon they think nobody's noticed?"

Warren nodded, a small smile forming on his lips.

"Yup. They haven't a clue."

Sutton sighed theatrically.

"Young love, eh, boss. Is there any better kind?"

Warren chuckled, glad for a moment of brightness in an otherwise bleak day.

"Yeah. I think they make a sweet couple. I wonder how long it'll be until they stop trying to hide it."

* * *

Warren held the team meeting in the largest of the unit's briefing rooms. Detective Superintendent John Grayson had formally delegated the lead investigator role to Warren; nevertheless, he was present, since part of the agenda would be to discuss the upcoming press conference.

Grayson was a small, dapper man, with a steel-grey moustache, in his early fifties. Common consensus was that he was more interested in securing his next promotion and thus a more generous final-salary pension than actively heading up investigations. Whether that was a fair assessment or not, Warren had yet to decide, but it was certainly true that he spent more time meeting with senior colleagues at the Hertfordshire and Bedfordshire Major Crime Unit in Welwyn Garden City than he did at his desk in Middlesbury CID.

The man was certainly a crafty politician. Warren still remembered his first serious case at Middlesbury during the summer, when Grayson had made it clear that it was sink or swim for the newly promoted DCI. To make things worse, Tony Sutton had been extremely vocal in his opposition to Warren's handling of the case and the two had almost come to blows. Sutton had finally confided in Warren that he was worried that the future of Middlesbury CID was under threat, with its unique role as a small, first-response CID unit outside the main Major Crime Unit in Welwyn a source of tension in a time of budget cutbacks. Sutton had been convinced that Jones had been sent to close them down.

Matters were further complicated by the fact that the strongest proponent for maintaining Middlesbury's unique status had been Gavin Sheehy, Warren's predecessor and Sutton's mentor, who was currently awaiting trial later in the new year for corruption. Grayson had yet to make his views clear on whether he thought

Middlesbury had a future or should be absorbed into the main unit and so Sutton and now Warren, who had grown to value Middlesbury CID's independence and unique place in the local community, were careful around him. Both men had a strong suspicion that Grayson would happily see Middlesbury CID closed if it meant that he would be moved to a more senior role within Welwyn Garden City.

One plus, as far as Warren was concerned, was that Grayson was always willing to talk to the press. Warren, on the other hand, regarded press conferences as a necessary evil and was happy to let Grayson enjoy his fifteen minutes of fame, whilst he stayed in the background and answered the odd question. Grayson had already decided that there would be a press conference to announce the finding of Sally Evans' body that evening, just in time for the late-night news bulletins and later editions of the next day's newspapers; therefore he was jotting down notes and ideas as the meeting progressed.

Calling for quiet, Warren brought the team up to speed on the various interviews conducted that morning. All those present agreed that Darren Blackheath was probably not guilty of his girlfriend's murder, although her father's outburst couldn't be dismissed entirely. Warren moved his name to the unlikely column on the whiteboard, until the results of the house-to-house enquiries and forensics came back.

As for her father, his behaviour was certainly strange and Warren made a note to pull him in for questioning after he'd had a few hours to cool off.

A second team, headed by DI Tony Sutton, had focused on Evans' workmates, using the initial investigation from the missing person enquiry as a starting point. The travel agency had been closed and the entire staff, including those not working on the day that she went missing, had been questioned. By the end of the morning, Sutton and his team had built a far more detailed profile of Sally Evans' last day and largely ruled out all of her former colleagues as realistic suspects. Confirmation of a couple of alibis were outstanding but they didn't expect much from Maureen the obese sixty-something grandmother with an arthritic hip.

Evans had arrived at work as usual at about eight-twenty, dropped off in the same alleyway her boyfriend picked her up from after work. After smoking a cigarette, she had knocked on the fire door and had been admitted by her boss, Kelli Somerton. This was confirmed by Somerton, who said that there was still a cloud of smoke around the bin and that Evans smelled strongly of it.

The shop didn't open until 9 a.m. and at this time of the year they weren't expecting many customers, so the staff had logged onto the computers, put the kettle on and sat around gossiping until opening time. No customers had appeared until almost midday, so the staff had spent the day preparing for the expected post-Christmas sales. Sally Evans had occupied her time unpacking boxes of promotional material and catalogues.

The weather had been cold and Evans had stayed in for her lunch of homemade tuna sandwiches, nipping out on her own for a cigarette. Evans had been described by everyone interviewed as "her usual cheerful self", looking forward to Christmas. Nobody could recall her mentioning any worries or strange people that she'd met.

The shop closed at five-thirty and Evans had helped lock up, before exiting via the back door at her usual time, ready to get picked up by her boyfriend, Darren Blackheath.

Warren rubbed his eyes, his hopes of an easy collar slowly fading. He still believed that killings by a total stranger were very rare; however, if Evans and her killer had crossed paths, he didn't seem to be in her immediate circle of acquaintances.

He said as much to the team.

"OK, let's start to shake the trees a little harder." He turned to Gary Hastings. "Use the PNC and HOLMES to see what we can find out about all of her acquaintances. Let's also scan a list of recent customers and see if anybody interesting turns up." He turned to Karen Hardwick. "You built a pretty good rapport with her friend Cheryl. She mentioned past boyfriends. See if you can get a list of friends — try and get as many as possible, right back to university if you can. We'll chuck them all in the pot and see what comes out."

He turned to DS Khan.

"Mo, can you continue co-ordinating the house-to-house enquiries with the neighbours? Make sure the evening shift pick up those who were out earlier in the day."

With the jobs assigned, Warren glanced at his watch: ten to three. "I'm due at a briefing on the autopsy in a few minutes. Keep feeding back to the incident desk and we'll meet again tomorrow morning 8 a.m."

The room emptied quickly, everyone eager to complete their given tasks, hoping to be the one that found the vital link. Human nature, mused Warren, just as it's human nature to lose energy and become frustrated as time wears on with no new leads. They were less than twenty-four hours in and already Warren had a bad feeling about the case. If it was a true stranger murder then they were probably in for the long haul. And it would be up to him to keep his team engaged and focused all that time.

Chapter 7

Warren had never been a big fan of autopsies. Some of his colleagues were happy to go into the morgue and see firsthand with their own eyes the clues teased out by the pathologist. Warren privately accused them of having a lack of imagination and a touch of voyeurism. He had no problem visualising everything he needed in his mind's eye using a few colour photographs and a well-written report. He could see nothing to be gained by looking at the corpse on a table. Truth be told, he wouldn't know what he was looking for. Far better that a practised expert describe what he was observing.

The expert today was Professor Ryan Jordan, a fifty-something, American-born, Home Office Certified pathologist, and he was happy to meet with Warren at Middlesbury CID rather than calling Warren down to look at the body in the morgue.

He read from his notes.

"The body is that of a Caucasian woman, mid-twenties. One hundred and sixty-one centimetres tall, weighing sixty-four kilograms. Average build, with no distinguishing scars or body decoration. Medically, she appeared to be of average to below average fitness, with limited muscular development and lungs consistent with that of a pack-per-day smoker of about ten years — some evidence of early cardiovascular disease. Her liver was again consistent with somebody who drank more than she should, showing early signs of inflammation. It is my opinion, however, that none of these conditions contributed to her death." He glanced up. "Give it a few more years and I reckon she'd have had a hard time climbing the stairs though. You see a lot of young women like this in the UK. It's a ticking time bomb and I don't see how the NHS will cope."

Warren nodded politely, not really interested in the American's opinions on Britain's binge-drinking and smoking culture. "How did she die, then, do you think?" he asked, steering the conversation back to the matter in hand.

"It's largely as Andy Harrison guessed at the scene. She was killed Friday evening, judging from her stomach contents, which are consistent with a tuna sandwich and a banana eaten at about 1 p.m. Cause of death was strangulation with her scarf. Prior to death she underwent very rough intercourse, probably penile. Bruising confirms that she was alive; however, we can find no signs of any struggle, suggesting that she was either compliant or unconscious."

Warren raised a sceptical eyebrow and Jordan raised his hands in surrender. "I'm just saying it as I see it, Chief. Or, more importantly, how the defence will try and portray it. Consensual sex gone wrong."

"So we have no evidence of rape."

"I wouldn't say that." He pushed a photograph across the table.

"Look how smeared her make-up is. Assuming it's the same lipstick that she had in her handbag, it's waterproof and long-lasting. It shouldn't really smear like that. Unless it was dissolved in solvent."

Warren was one step ahead. "You're suggesting that she was subdued by some sort of solvent, like chloroform, which smeared her make-up? That's a bit Agatha Christie, isn't it?"

Again, the American pathologist raised his hands. "As I said before, I say it as I see it. We've sent off for blood toxicology reports to see if she was sedated, but they'll be a few weeks. There is no evidence of irritation to her respiratory passages, which rules out some solvents, but not chloroform."

"What else have you got?"

"Not a lot really, although that in itself may be interesting. We can hardly find any trace evidence from the attacker."

"So he wore a condom?"

"More than that, I would say. With this sort of rough penetration, I would expect some genital-to-genital contact. It would be hard to avoid. We've looked under the microscope and combed her pubic area, but we haven't found a single alien pubic hair, or skin flake. The only thing we've found are traces of lubricant, consistent with that used on pretty much all of the major brands of condom, some tiny chemical traces that the mass-spec machine suggest is dry latex powder, and a commercial adhesive, usually found on rolls of sticky-tape."

"I thought dry latex powder was discouraged in condoms because it causes allergies?"

"It is, but you can still find it in some cheap rubber gloves. If I were a betting man, I would suggest that our killer wore a couple of condoms at least, in case of accidents, has a shaved pubic area and used a cut-up rubber glove and sticky tape to ensure that he left no trace where he made contact with her."

Warren winced. This was a sick person and, it would seem, clever and well prepared.

"Anything else on her?"

"We have found some fine powder on her coat that seems to come from brown cardboard and a couple of fibres that may or may not be significant. We'll look at the database and see if the fibres are interesting."

"She spent the day unpacking cardboard boxes," offered Warren.

"That could account for the cardboard powder," mused Jordan.

"Was she murdered and raped in situ?" asked Warren.

"It looks that way. Skin lividity indicates that she died in that position and wasn't moved post-mortem — gravity pooled her blood just the way we'd expect. Her coat has two muddy patches that line up with indentations on the forest floor, suggesting that he knelt on her coat as he penetrated her. As I said before, the bruising indicates that she was alive at the time, but probably unconscious or compliant. I couldn't say whether she died during or after the rape. Hopefully the toxicology tests will show that she was unconscious throughout."

Warren nodded soberly. It was a small mercy, but he'd take it, he decided.

Chapter 8

Next stop for Warren was the office of Detective Superintendent Grayson to discuss their plans for the upcoming press conference. As always, Grayson had his dress uniform hanging on the back of his office door and Warren knew that he wouldn't miss an opportunity to wear it in front of the cameras. Looking closely, Warren thought the man's jowls seemed suspiciously shiny and his hair seemed even smarter than normal. *The bugger's had time for a bloody shave and haircut,* Warren realised. For a second, he felt self-conscious — he hadn't had a haircut for over a month and his early morning shave was some hours behind him — but then he shrugged mentally. If past form was anything to go by, he would barely say a word anyway and would almost certainly be edited out of the bulletin that was broadcast. He was only there because he was the named officer in charge of the investigation. One or two of his answers to more technical questions might be quoted in the broadsheets, space permitting.

The press conference would be a fairly formal, by-the-book affair. Since the family had informed everyone that needed to know about Sally's fate, she would be named and her parents would both be present to make a plea for information. It had been decided that details of her death would be kept to a minimum to stop cranks and lunatics from wasting the police's time with seemingly plausible stories full of authentic detail. No mention would be made of the rape. At the end of the conference, Detective Superintendent Grayson would attempt to remind young women about being vigilant at night without sounding overly alarmist.

The conference was scheduled for 6 p.m — just early enough for the editors of the six-thirty local news to squeeze it into the end of their bulletin. Depending on what else was happening in the world, the story might make it onto the 7 p.m. national broadcasts. It was a definite for the late-night news and the next day's papers.

Grayson had ordered a police car to take them down to the main headquarters at Welwyn and they had a few minutes to spare. Truth be told, Warren would far rather have driven himself. It might not be strictly legal, but Grayson had enough pull for the police driver to put the lights and siren on. Previous jaunts down the A1(M) with the detective superintendent had left Warren feeling decidedly shaken. Lights or no lights, one hundred miles per hour plus in rush-hour traffic was far outside Warren's comfort zone and it was all he could do to stop his feet trying to stomp on an imaginary brake pedal. Grayson usually read the newspaper or fiddled with his BlackBerry smartphone.

As Grayson used his mirror to check his appearance Warren enjoyed the last few mouthfuls of his coffee. One benefit of being called to the boss's office was his expensive filter-coffee machine and selection of fine roasts.

"I've got a bad feeling about this one, Warren," mused Grayson.

Warren was forced to agree. "It's looking more and more like a stranger killing. That immediately rules out half of our usual lines of investigation."

"Worse, it increases the chance of him striking again."

Again, Warren had to concur. Most murders had a reason, the victim or victims killed for a purpose or as a consequence of an event. That reason might not be fathomable to normal-minded people, but it did mean that the murders were limited. Once the perceived slight had been avenged or the goal accomplished, the killings stopped. With a stranger killing that might not be the case; the act of killing might be the reason and didn't necessarily lead to a resolution for the killer.

As he returned his empty mug to its saucer and grabbed his coat off the chair back, Warren felt a heavy weight settle onto his shoulders. A slight ache started in his stomach. They were signs he'd grown to understand — this case was going to be a nasty one.

Chapter 9

Warren and Grayson survived the headlong dash along the motorway and were soon in the room Herts and Beds used for major press conferences. An announcement earlier in the day about the finding of the body ensured that the room was pretty much full.

The aim of the conference was to formally identify the victim as Sally Evans and to appeal for help from the public, although as usual the press had managed to identify and name Evans some hours before. Mercifully her family and key friends had been notified before the press spilled the beans, but Warren always worried that one day some over-eager journalist was going to cause a lot of distress by breaking such news on air.

Key to the conference would be the presence of Sally Evans' parents and her best friend, Cheryl. Between them, they would deliver a carefully written direct plea to the murderer or those that might know him to search their consciences and contact the police. Darren Blackheath was too upset to attend the conference — or maybe he was avoiding Sally's father. There was definitely more to that story, Warren mused. Hovering in the background were the force's press officer and a trio of family liaison officers, there to support the victim's family and friends during the coming months.

Sally Evans' parents had insisted on delivering a direct appeal to the public for information but after Bill Evans and then his wife choked up it fell to Cheryl Davenport to finish reading out the moving tribute to the murdered woman. Although it saddened him, Warren knew that the added drama had probably bought them a few extra seconds on the news and a couple of extra lines in the newspaper, which could only be a good thing. The press briefing packs included an uncropped version of the main picture that they were using, with Sally and Cheryl both laughing at the camera. No doubt at least one picture editor would use this to emphasise the human tragedy.

As he'd predicted, Warren had been introduced then promptly forgotten about. This early on in the investigation, he had little to offer the press and so a well-groomed John Grayson had answered the few perfunctory questions.

Finally, barely two hours after leaving Middlesbury, the two officers were back at the station. Grayson didn't even enter the lobby, practically stepping from the back seat of the police car into the driver's seat of his Mercedes, muttering something about his golf club's awards ceremony. He left with a squeak of tyres and not so much as a backward glance. Warren sighed and glanced at his watch. Ten past seven. Turning, he headed back inside.

Chapter 10

Warren had barely taken his coat off, when an excited Gary Hastings appeared at his door. He waved him in.

"Got something interesting for you, sir. I was checking out Bill Evans' alibi like you said and it seems that he wasn't in Leeds the night of the murder. Better still, he hasn't been up there for months. And a check of the PNC shows that he has previous convictions."

* * *

Fifteen minutes after Hastings' shock discovery, Warren called a short briefing in his office.

The team decided to bring in Evans for formal questioning. Why had Evans lied about his whereabouts on the night of his daughter's disappearance? Was her upcoming marriage to a man he clearly disliked enough for him to lose his temper with murderous consequences? And, even worse than that, after killing his daughter, had Bill Evans defiled her body? Perhaps most alarmingly, according to the pathology report, the rape had been carried out with such care to avoid leaving evidence behind that it had to have been pre-planned to some degree. And what about his previous conviction?

According to the report, Evans had been arrested drunk outside a primary school twelve years previously, after exposing himself to a couple of mothers waiting to pick up their children. He had been hit with a raft of charges, but had eventually been convicted of being drunk and disorderly and public indecency and fined accordingly.

Conscious that every second they wasted was another second that the killer had to cover his tracks, the team headed straight for the Evanses' house. As before, the house was full of family and friends giving comfort to the grieving couple, both of whom were still dressed smartly from the press conference.

Warren was acutely aware that in circumstances like this he would be judged as much for his tact and sensitivity as his deductive abilities. For that reason, Warren had decided not to flash an arrest warrant; rather, he would ask Evans to accompany them voluntarily to the police station to answer some additional questions.

However, despite Warren's best efforts, they left the house with their ears burning. As far as the relatives were concerned, Bill Evans was supposed to have been in Leeds the night that Sally Evans went missing — so why were the police taking him away for further questioning? Maybe what he'd said about Darren Blackheath was true, they thought. Already, as Warren glanced back through the front windows, he could see at least two people on their mobile phones.

Passing Evans' BMW estate, Warren made a note to have Forensics impound the car. As he opened the back door of the police car for Evans to enter Warren instinctively placed his hand on Evans' head as the man climbed in, immediately regretting the action. The gesture was purely Health and Safety and CYA (Cover

Your Arse) — it stopped passengers bumping their heads on the door frame and then trying to make something of it in court. Unfortunately to Joe Public, brought up on a diet of police shows, it screamed "you are under arrest" as loudly as a pair of handcuffs. Warren's ears burned even more hotly.

* * *

In the interview room, Warren finished advising Bill Evans that he was not under arrest and that he was there to answer questions on a purely voluntary basis. The man nodded wearily. He had aged in the past hours, Warren saw, looking even more haggard than he had during the press conference. Was it grief? Guilt? A mixture of the two? Warren's gut was sending him conflicting signals. Bill Evans had something to hide; he was certain of that. But what? The scenario and timing just didn't seem right to Warren. Everything pointed to a planned, premeditated kidnapping and attack but the only scenario under which Warren could see Bill Evans killing his beloved daughter was anything but that.

Beside him sat Tony Sutton. It was the first time that the detective inspector had met Evans and he stared at him with barely concealed fascination, the way one might look at a strange and dangerous creature in the zoo. Of course, it was all part of the act. Sutton's role in this was to keep Evans on edge, making it more likely that he would slip up and reveal something that he didn't want to.

With all of the legal requirements fulfilled, Warren decided to open with a quick, hard question designed to rattle the man's cage.

"Tell me, Mr Evans, why did you lie to us about your whereabouts on the night of your daughter's disappearance?"

Evans blinked in surprise. "I didn't."

"Come on, Bill, we're not idiots. You claimed to have been up in Leeds overseeing one of your new branches. We phoned head office and they said that you hadn't been in Leeds for months and that you had been working exclusively in the Cambridge office since the summer."

Evans continued to look bewildered. "I never said any such thing. I hardly said two words to you before I left."

Suddenly a cold feeling of dread went through Jones, followed by a flush of embarrassment. The man was right. He had said no such thing. It was Jane Evans who had claimed that her husband had been working away in Leeds; he had not even discussed his whereabouts that night. Shit! What a stupid mistake! And worse, he'd potentially squandered any opportunity of a "perverting the course of justice" charge that would have at least given them a pretext to release him on police bail whilst they continued their enquiries.

Well, no use crying over spilt milk, Warren quickly decided.

"Well, your wife seems to think you have been working there — what are you doing there each month?"

As if sensing that Warren was on the back foot, Evans sneered, "I don't see what that has to do with anything, Detective Chief Inspector. My private life is just that."

"Be that as it may, Mr Evans. Perhaps we should confine ourselves to the night Sally went missing. Your wife appears to be under the impression that you were in Leeds. Your company claims otherwise. This gives you the perfect window of opportunity to take your daughter away from work, kill her and dump her body, before appearing at 3 a.m. to help with the hunt for her. We know all about the arguments that you had with Sally about her job and her boyfriend. What was it that caused you to snap, Mr Evans?"

There was silence in the room, before the father in front of them started to cry — great wracking sobs that shook his shoulders and sent tears coursing down his face. Finally, he regained his composure enough to speak.

"You're right, but not about killing Sally. I could never hurt my darling daughter." He paused for a moment, then continued.

"I haven't been to Leeds for months. It's just an excuse. I've been seeing someone I met on the Internet. I think she's married as well. I use the excuse of staying overnight in Leeds to spend time with her. She does the same." He started to cry again. "I'm such a fucking coward. On the night that Sally went missing, Jane phoned me. I was supposed to be in Leeds. My little girl was missing and yet I stayed in bed with my lover in a bloody Cambridge hotel for two and a half hours before driving home to my family, just so I wouldn't arouse suspicion. My place was with my wife…" He stopped, unable to continue.

Warren waited for the man to compose himself.

"You realise that we are going to have to check out your story, don't you? We'll need to contact this woman and get her to back you up. We'll also need details of the hotel."

The man nodded miserably. "I can get you the details of the hotel. I use my credit card — it just comes up as a Travelodge, doesn't say where it is. The problem is, I don't know the name of the woman."

Warren blinked in surprise. "How does that work?"

Evans stared at the tabletop, his voice now rough with embarrassment. "We met on the Internet. It's a special, discreet site for people wanting affairs. No names, no details, just anonymous sex.

If you want something more regular they supply an untraceable private email account and mobile phone SIM cards. We arrange to meet online."

"Well, you must call her something." Sutton struggled to hide the incredulity in his voice.

The man's voice was barely audible. "Boadicea."

"As in the ancient queen of the Britons? What are you called?"

"Arthur," he mumbled.

"But that's two completely different legends…"

Warren placed a hand on Sutton's shoulder and cleared his throat. "I'm sure we can discuss the details later if necessary. In the meantime, how can we get hold of this… woman?"

Evans looked helpless.

"I don't know. We arrange to meet up the first weekend of each month. I log on a couple of days before and she leaves me a message telling me when to keep my mobile phone switched on for her to call. Then she tells me when we are going to meet up. I book the room on my credit card."

"Send her an email and ask to see her sooner."

"It doesn't work that way. We keep to the arrangement to avoid getting caught. She probably won't read her email."

"Can't you phone her?"

"I don't have her number — she blocks it when she calls me. Besides, I think she uses a separate SIM card — I know that I do. I don't even put it in until I need to and I've never had a missed call. I think she does the same."

Warren sighed in frustration. "You aren't being much help here, Bill."

The other man gestured helplessly. "The whole point of this set-up is not to make it easy to track each other down."

Again, he started to look tearful. "The thing is, I love my wife very much. She really is the one I want to grow old with and I know that she feels the same, 'till death us do part' and all that…"

"Isn't the next line, 'forsaking all others'?" interjected Sutton.

A brief flash of anger crossed the man's face.

"Don't be so fast to judge, Detective. My wife is not a well woman — we haven't been intimate for years. A man has needs…" He broke off. "Anyway, I don't need to explain myself to you." With that he folded his arms and stared at a spot above both men's heads.

Needing to get the interview back on track, Warren spoke softly.

"You are right, Mr Evans, the details of your private life are none of our concern. However, we are in the middle of a murder investigation and it is our job to eliminate suspects. For that, we need your co-operation."

After a few moments, Evans grunted softly and agreed to hand over what details he had of his mysterious lover and the mobile phone that he used to Welwyn's IT specialists.

With the interview back on track, Warren steered it around to the sensitive subject of Darren Blackheath. Immediately, Evans' eyes flashed with anger.

"I can't understand what she sees in that man. I really can't. She was so beautiful and she had so much going for her… Why would she waste herself on that loser?"

Neither detective said anything; the question was clearly rhetorical.

"He was just leaching off her. I know for a fact that Sally paid most of the bills on the flat. She earned more than he did. And, of course, Jane was slipping her money each month. She thought I didn't know but I'm not daft."

"I believe that you had a big row with Sally and issued an ultimatum when she moved out?"

Again, Evans' face crumpled, but he managed to speak. "I had to. I had to make her see sense. She'd come round eventually, I knew that. It would just take time." He paused, reaching for the necessary words. "But she didn't have that time, did she?"

Warren paused a few moments respectfully before continuing again. "Tell me, Bill. You said that it was Darren Blackheath's fault that she was dead. Why do you think that?"

"She was going to break it off with him. We met up the day before… you know. She told me that she thought Darren was going to propose and suddenly it wasn't a game anymore. She didn't say as much, but I think she was worried about what sort of husband he would be. Those holidays that she went on with Cheryl? I reckon that he thought they gave him a green light to go and sleep around on his football tours. I've heard the rumours: wild parties, drugs and hookers.

"When she married him that would be it — before you know it, she'd be pregnant and trapped. She'd be one of those women you see down on the estate, three kids, working full-time, whilst the husband pisses all their money up the wall of the local pub.

"He had it bloody good with Sally. If she left him, he would end up living with his mum and dad and fitting tyres for the rest of his life — where was he going to find a girl like Sally again?"

* * *

The two detectives decided to take a break for a few minutes to process what they had just heard. Evans was not under arrest, so

69

they arranged for the custody sergeant to take coffee in for him and see if he needed the bathroom.

"Well, I'm confused now," confessed Warren. "This morning, Karen Hardwick and I heard nothing but praise for Darren Blackheath. I'd pretty much crossed him off the list. Now, we have the victim's father spelling out quite plausible reasons why he thinks he's a murderer."

Sutton gulped his coffee before answering. "He makes a good case, I'll give him that. We'll have to check the forensics out. But then what about him? He's admitted he was angry with her and he clearly hates Blackheath. It's not impossible to imagine a scenario where he kills his daughter and tries to pin the blame on her boyfriend. If they were from the Asian community, we'd call it an 'honour killing', but human nature is universal."

"I tend to agree. What's the betting that when they met the day before the killing he picked her up in his car? That'd put the kibosh on any trace evidence."

"What doesn't fit is that Cheryl claimed she was excited that Darren was going to propose and her workmates said that she was her 'usual cheerful self'. That doesn't fit with what her father said."

"I figure that leaves two possibilities — either he's completely misjudged her attitude and is seeing what he wants to see, or he's lying about Blackheath. It could be that she revealed to him that she knew he was going to propose and that made him mad enough to kill her."

Sutton nodded his agreement. "If so, then he is a sick bastard. From what we know of the crime it was well planned and of course he raped his own daughter. There is one other possibility though. He could be right. He might be the only one to have seen through

Blackheath. We'll need forensics and eyewitnesses that can place Blackheath's car outside his house when he says it was."

"So it seems that in both cases it comes down to forensics and alibis. Great. Well, we have one more thing to try him on. Let's see his reaction when we bring up his priors."

Sutton looked sceptical. "It's a hell of a jump, don't you think, from some alleged willy-waving over a decade ago to strangling and raping your daughter?"

"These perverts have to start somewhere."

* * *

Sutton's scepticism seemed well founded. When confronted with the conviction and all that it implied, Evans was contemptuous, with no hint that he was at all concerned.

"Ancient history and total bullshit anyway. All that happened was I got very drunk at lunchtime after we won a big contract at work. I decided to walk home to clear my head and got caught short. I was in the middle of pissing in a big bush when I heard two women yelling and I realised I was next to a bloody primary school. I should have done a runner, but I decided to stick around and try to explain. They called the police and I was arrested for indecently exposing myself. Unfortunately, it was raining so there was no piss to back up my story.

"When it got to court, they decided that since the pupils were all inside with no realistic way they could see me or I could see them, they'd drop the more serious charges. In the end they fined me for being drunk and disorderly, urinating in a public place and indecent exposure. If those two women hadn't made such a bloody song and dance about it, it wouldn't have even gone that far. Like I said, ancient history. Now, if you want to drag up relevant past history, ask Darren Blackheath about Kim Bradshaw. See if you still think he's Mr Bloody Perfect after you hear what he did to her."

Chapter 11

It was nearly eleven by the time Warren and Sutton finished at the station. Bill Evans had been picked up by his wife after handing over the keys to his BMW. The car was now on a flatbed truck, heading towards the vehicle crime specialists where it would join Darren Blackheath's pride and joy.

As he walked across the car park the icy wind did little to lift the fatigue that settled around Warren like a blanket. It was always the same. The first few days of any murder investigation were necessarily frenetic. At this stage, the passage of hours mattered. The perpetrators had time to cover their tracks, witnesses' memories started to fade and delicate evidence would degrade or disappear.

Climbing into his car, he caught the reflection of the station's lights in the wing mirrors. Almost every window was brightly lit, shadowy forms moving around inside. Grayson's office and his were the only dark windows.

A brief stab of guilt was quickly repressed. He could go back in and easily work through the night, but experience had taught him his limits. There was a whole team following the leads that had already been generated; he would just be getting in the way. Besides, he needed the rest to lead effectively. It was far better to get a good night's sleep and hit the ground running early the next morning. If anything urgent turned up, he trusted his team's judgement to decide if he should be called or if it could be added to his morning task list.

Waving goodbye to Sutton, Warren drove the short distance home. Letting himself in, he found Susan sound asleep on the sofa, two piles of red exercise books next to her, another book open on her lap. One pile was much taller than the other — Warren sincerely hoped that was the completed set. The TV played quietly in the background: some dreadful-looking "reality" show that he knew his wife would have immediately turned over if she had been awake.

The slight draft from the open door caused Susan to stir. "What time is it?" she mumbled, her voice thick with sleep.

"Late," replied Warren, bending over to kiss her forehead. She smiled, before glancing down at the pile of books.

"Oh, no. I promised 9D2 I'd mark their books before the lesson tomorrow." She groaned. "I shouldn't have sat on the sofa to mark. I knew I'd fall asleep." She picked up her red pen again. "I'll be another hour at least."

Warren knew better than to argue with her. If there was one profession that could engineer spurious guilty feelings from never doing enough work, it was teaching, he mused. He'd been with Susan long enough to know that, just like detectives, teachers could never do too much. There was always another job that could be done.

Warren felt a debt to the victims and families to turn over every stone; Susan felt the same way about her pupils. If she wasn't marking their work, she was preparing lessons or devising new ways to teach difficult concepts, all in the hope that what she taught next lesson might be instrumental to them fulfilling their future dreams.

Warren kissed her again before heading upstairs to bed. Often, if one or the other was working late, they used the guest bedroom so as not to wake the sleeping partner. Warren vowed that he wouldn't let Susan go to sleep alone tonight and so, after cleaning his teeth and getting ready for bed, he picked up the David Baldacci novel he was currently reading.

The plot was as gripping and suspenseful as ever, with ingenious twists and turns. So good that when his eyes closed of their own accord barely thirty pages in, his dreams were a riot of unconnected facts and strange occurrences.

An hour later Susan switched off the bedside reading light, carefully closed the book and carried her nightdress into the guest bedroom.

WEDNESDAY 7ᵀᴴ DECEMBER

Chapter 12

The arrival of Wednesday was announced by the insistent ringing of Warren's mobile phone, which pulled double duty as his alarm clock. Somehow, he managed to locate it and perform the complicated swiping gesture necessary to silence it. A few moments later, a similar sound emanated from the guest bedroom. He groaned as he glanced over, noticing for the first time that Susan's side of the bed hadn't been slept in.

Despite the couple waking up in different rooms, their morning routine was pretty well established. Susan would jump in the shower first, whilst Warren put the kettle on and got breakfast ready. Although he wasn't much of a breakfast person, Susan was and he dished up cereal — sultana bran, this month — with another handful of dried fruit on top and a chopped banana. He left the skimmed milk to one side, not wanting the cereal to get soggy, and poured a generous glass of apple juice.

As he waited for the kettle to boil, he made their lunches. Susan got bored with sandwiches very quickly and was always on the lookout for new combinations. This week was some sort of fishy, Greek paste that she'd found in the supermarket. The smell alone was enough to turn Warren's stomach as he spread a generous helping on top of some sesame-seeded bread and buried it under lettuce and tomato. The odour reminded him of the time he'd been left to feed his best friend's cat when he went away on holiday.

After a moment's thought, he added a bit more spread to the sandwich. Susan would appreciate the extra filling, whilst Warren hoped that it would accelerate the pot's emptying. He doubted her next discovery could smell any worse.

Carefully discarding the knife and selecting a new, uncontaminated utensil, Warren constructed his own sandwich. Mature Cheddar cheese on brown bread. No margarine — he couldn't see the point. A banana, a fistful of grapes and a bag of unsalted cashew nuts apiece filled the rest of their plastic boxes. He poured both coffees and, leaving them to cool, he headed back upstairs, just in time to meet his wife coming out of the bathroom.

Her citrus-scented shampoo smelled lovely and the taste of mint toothpaste as they kissed good morning was delicious. Unfortunately, their cuddle was all too brief and Warren had to ignore the allure of the soft curves that he knew lay beneath the fluffy bathrobe.

By the time Warren had showered, shaved and dressed, Susan was fully dressed, her breakfast dishes were in the sink and she was cramming exercise books into a hemp bag-for-life; the sturdy, £1 eco-bag was one of the best ways yet invented to carry heavy books to and from school.

Downing his slightly too hot coffee in one go, Warren grabbed his briefcase and sandwiches and headed for the door, Susan following, book bag in one hand and keys in the other. The burglar alarm was set and the door closed behind them. A perfunctory, coffee-tasting kiss on the front doorstep and seconds later the couple's cars were heading in opposite directions.

Seven a.m. — another day started.

The office was quiet when Warren arrived a few minutes later. The phones were silent and the quiet working buzz of the office had yet to get going. Even in policing, seven-fifteen wasn't considered "office hours" and phoning witnesses or calling colleagues in other departments was discouraged unless it was an emergency. Even the most helpful eyewitness was unlikely to be entirely co-operative if you woke them up in the early hours of the morning or the middle of the night.

Nevertheless, those pulling the night shift had been busy and a glut of new reports sat in Warren's in-tray and his computer's inbox. It was an encouraging start to the day, he decided, gauging the thickness of the pile, but he doubted there was anything too exciting in there otherwise he'd have been called at home. By a quarter to eight he had a couple of pages of notes and had planned out the next few hours' worth of activities for him and his team.

First order of the day was to revisit Darren Blackheath and question him about Kim Bradshaw. After Bill Evans' outburst the previous evening he had requested details of the incident. The report sat in his tray, waiting to be read fully.

The results of more tests from Sally Evans' PM were expected soon and he was going to ask that they be run through HOLMES. Ideally, they'd pick up some matches later in the day.

In the meantime, different teams of officers would be trying to catch up with witnesses and pinpoint Darren Blackheath's whereabouts on the night of the murder. Warren still felt that the young man was innocent, but there was work to be done before he could be discounted entirely.

Similarly, Bill Evans also needed his alibi corroborated and specialists in Welwyn would be trying to track down his mistress. Warren's gut was giving him conflicting signals about the man. On the one hand, the man's distress seemed genuine but on the other hand, he seemed shifty. Whether that was just a result of Warren's personal distaste towards the man's private life, he couldn't be sure. He was only human after all; try as he might, his feelings could be influenced by his personal prejudices as much as anybody's.

Chapter 13

As soon as the morning briefing concluded, Warren snared Tony Sutton and Karen Hardwick and the three officers drove to the flat where Sally Evans and Darren Blackheath had lived. Tony Sutton had yet to meet Blackheath and, if he was in the frame, Warren wanted his second-in-charge to get a good look. On the other hand, DC Hardwick had been with Warren for the initial interview. If there was any change in the man's demeanour he hoped that the insightful young officer would pick it up.

After ringing the doorbell twice and receiving no reply, Warren knocked on the neighbour's door. A few moments later, it opened slowly and a gnarled, weather-beaten face appeared.

"Whatcha want?"

The voice was so gravelly and the face so wrinkled that only the pink dressing gown hinted at the occupant's gender. A cloud of stale cigarette smoke drifted out.

Warren held his warrant card open. "DCI Warren Jones, madam. I wonder if you could tell me the whereabouts of your next-door neighbour, Mr Blackheath."

"I already spoke to the police. I was at me club on the night the poor girl was murdered, God bless 'er soul. I didn't see nothing and have no idea if that young fella of hers and his silly car were around."

The old lady either hadn't heard or had misunderstood Warren's question. He raised his voice and enunciated his words more clearly. "No ma'am. I wondered if you knew where he is this morning. We've knocked on the door and there was no reply."

"Well, he's gone to work, in't he? When you towed that car of his away, I'd hoped that'd be the end of all the noise first thing in the morning. The bloody thing makes such a racket, especially the way he revs the engine. But the lad who picked him up made even more noise. I reckon he must have loosened that exhaust pipe 'specially, just to annoy folks like me in bed."

"So you're saying he's returned to work?"

"Yeah, he went in yesterday. I spoke to him last night, just to pass on my condolences, like, and he said he needed the company." For the first time, the fierce visage softened slightly. "Poor lad. He might be a bit noisy and he won't be gettin' a Nobel prize any time soon but he was nice enough and he helped me no end when I was burgled last autumn. Now he's all alone. I remember what that's like from when my Stan died… Maybe I'll take him round something to eat. He's hardly had a single visitor 'cept the police and you don't count. No offence."

Warren was getting the feeling that the elderly lady didn't get too many visitors herself and might just welcome a bit of a gossip. She might not have been here the night that Sally Evans disappeared — which explained why she hadn't been flagged as "of interest" by the door knockers — but with the right questions, she might provide insights into the couple's private life. Time for a little charm, he decided.

"Please forgive my bad manners — I haven't asked your name.

This is Detective Inspector Tony Sutton and Detective Constable Karen Hardwick and you must be getting chilled with this door open."

"Maeve Cunningham." She stepped back as Warren had hoped she would. "Why don't you come in out of the cold?"

The three officers stepped over the threshold into the house, the stale fug of tobacco hitting them hard. At least it was warm. Up close, the woman was even older than Warren had first guessed. She was bending over a metal walking stick with a bird-like frame, and her hands were twisted, the knuckles swollen with arthritis. The fingertips on her right hand were stained the dark yellow that only a truly dedicated smoker could achieve. Her teeth and even the fringe of her thinning white hair were similarly affected, almost as if she had started to dye her hair blonde, before giving up.

After slowly leading the three officers into her living room, she carefully sat down on what was clearly her favourite chair. A bag of knitting lay next to an open newspaper and a TV remote control. A packet of Marlboro Red cigarettes and a lighter sat next to an overflowing ashtray, although much to Warren's relief she made no move to light one.

After clearing her throat a few times, a wet, wheezy sound that made Warren wince inwardly, she was settled.

"So you were saying that Darren has had very few visitors since Sally's disappearance? What about his parents? Or her parents?"

The old lady shook her head. "I don't like to gossip, you understand, but I heard that he doesn't get on very well with his parents anymore. Not since the incident with that Kim Bradshaw. He thinks that they betrayed him."

There was clearly much to this story, Warren was beginning to realise, and it seemed to be common local knowledge.

Unfortunately, Mrs Cunningham knew, or was willing to admit to knowing, few details and so he dropped the discussion.

"Tell me, how well did they get on as a couple, do you think?"

"They always seemed happy, whenever I saw them. Dead close. But then I suppose that you have to be, when both of you have been practically disowned by your parents. I suppose it's romantic in a way — bit like Romeo 'n' Juliet."

"So you were aware that Ms Evans' parents didn't like Darren Blackheath?"

The old woman cackled, her eyes suddenly dancing with amusement. "I'll bloody say I did. A few weeks after they started living here, her dad turned up, didn't he? He was drunk and he started shouting at Darren to come out. It was late at night, so I got up to see what was going on. Anyway, he starts banging on the flat door. Well, the original doors in these flats are cheap and flimsy and it popped open. I had mine replaced after I was broken into but they haven't yet.

"I heard shouting and came back in here to call the police, but it stopped. A few seconds later, what do I see but Darren Blackheath, wearing nothing but a bath towel, climbing down the fire escape!"

The old woman burst out laughing, before subsiding into a coughing fit. She leant forward, patted Karen Hardwick's knee and winked.

"I can't say he was the finest specimen I've ever seen — boy needs a good feeding — but when you get to my age you take what you can."

Warren couldn't help smiling; the old woman's good cheer was infectious. Sutton was grinning from ear to ear.

"Do you have any idea why her father disliked Darren so much?"

The old lady paused, thinking. "Obviously, I can only tell as what I hear down the club, but Mr Evans is a bit of a snob. He looks down on us working-class types. He forgets that a generation ago his parents worked in the factory. Then there was the whole Kim Bradshaw incident. He figured his little girl was better than all that."

She shook her head. "But they were in love. And they were happy. Seems a shame he couldn't deal with that."

After a few more questions, it soon became obvious that Maeve Cunningham had little more to say. Besides which, she kept on glancing at her cigarettes. Finally, standing up, the three detectives took their leave of the elderly lady.

"Thank you very much for your time, Mrs Cunningham. Can I leave you my card in case you remember anything else?"

"Of course. But it's Miss Cunningham. Why did you think I was married?"

Warren blinked, completely nonplussed. "Sorry, I shouldn't have assumed. You mentioned how lonely you were after Stan died and, well, you know, I thought he was your husband."

"Well, I'd heard about how strange folks were in Birmingham, but I didn't realise they married their dogs."

The three officers could still hear her laughter as they turned the corner of the corridor.

Chapter 14

Back in the car, Hardwick and Sutton unsuccessfully tried to hide their smirks.

Warren sighed. "OK, you two, be honest, do I really sound like a Brummie? I'm from Coventry and I only worked in Birmingham for a few years."

The two more junior officers glanced at each other before Sutton took the lead, clearing his throat. "Well, sometimes. You know, certain words and phrases."

"It's more of a general West Midlands twang," supplied Karen Hardwick helpfully from the back seat. "You know, a bit like Lenny Henry."

"Lenny Henry! He's from bloody Dudley! No way do I sound like that." Warren was amazed, how could they not hear the difference?

"It's just a regional thing, guv," Sutton interjected quickly. "You know the way most English folks can't tell the difference between Northern and Southern Irish, or different parts of the North East. You have to live somewhere ages to tell the difference."

"I imagine the local accents down here are a bit difficult to distinguish for you as well, sir."

A fair point, Warren acknowledged grudgingly. He had lived

here for six months and, although he was slowly starting to recognise the difference between Eastern accents and London, this whole corner of England sounded remarkably homogenous. He was sure that there must be a difference between an Essex and a Hertfordshire accent, but he had yet to figure it out. He admitted as much, even letting slip that he couldn't distinguish between the Cockney accents on *Eastenders* and Essex accents. His two colleagues shook their heads in disbelief.

Warren grunted and scowled. Truth be told, though, he was enjoying the banter. The atmosphere had been heavy the previous twenty-four hours, with only the darkest humour glimmering. He was confident that details of the conversation would circulate the office in record time. Hopefully a little good-natured teasing would improve morale and even make him seem a bit more human.

The time for levity soon passed though, as the car pulled into the customer parking bay of the tyre fitters that Darren Blackheath worked for. The three officers made their way into the small, glass-walled customer waiting area. At one end of the room was a small desk with a computer. A middle-aged man with greying hair was busy pecking away, two fingers at a time, on a battered keyboard, as he grunted and 'uh-huh'ed into the mouthpiece of the phone clamped between his shoulder and ear. A small name badge identified him as 'Jack Bradley — Manager'.

As they waited, they gazed through the window into the garage beyond. Blue-overalled mechanics worked away on four different vehicles, Along the far side of the space were literally hundreds of different tyres, forming an almost seamless wall of black, shiny rubber, broken only by brightly coloured advertising posters urging customers to ready their car for winter. Warren counted four mechanics, but no Darren Blackheath.

Finally, the man on the phone finished. Looking up, his eyes narrowed. It was clear that the three visitors weren't customers. Still, Warren showed his warrant card and asked if Blackheath was working.

The man nodded his head, wearily. "Yeah, out the back in the stockroom for all the good he's doing, poor sod. He turned up yesterday morning unexpectedly." He gestured towards the garage. "I'd already covered his shift and promised the overtime to somebody else, but I couldn't turn him away. He clearly needs the company. Of course, he's not said two words to anyone since he turned up, but what can you do?"

Warren nodded sympathetically and asked if they could speak to him.

"Sure, you can use the kitchen. I'll tell the lads to give you some privacy." Rounding the desk, the man led them through a door marked "Staff Only". "He's a liability at the moment," the man whispered quietly. "I don't trust him to do MOTs or change tyres — he's too distracted. I don't want to think about what would happen if he accidentally forgot to tighten something... Fortunately, we've just received a big parts delivery that needs putting away and Ken our store man is off with a bad back. Worst that'll happen is we spend a bit longer than usual trying to find things."

He glanced over at Warren, unable to contain his curiosity.

"Have you any idea who did it? She was a lovely girl, and Darren was well loved-up. He'd be out the door six on the dot every day to collect her. Had to get permission to come out for a pint, you know. Some of the boys used to take the piss a bit, like. Said he was under the thumb. He just smiled and said she had lovely thumbs."

Warren smiled politely.

"We're actively pursuing a number of lines of enquiry, but as you can appreciate we aren't in a position to elaborate." So Sally Evans wore the trousers in that relationship, then. Was that significant? He wouldn't be the first man to snap under the pressure of a domineering woman — or was he truly as smitten as everyone, her father aside, seemed to think? A brief image of his own in-laws leapt to mind and he quickly suppressed it.

The short corridor that they stood in had four doors, not including the one that they had just walked through. Two doors on the left had signs bearing "Toilet" and "Kitchen" respectively. The single door on the right said "Parts" and the door at the end labelled "Garage" was covered in bright warning signs, including that for a fire exit.

Pushing open the door marked "Parts", Bradley called out Blackheath's name and stepped aside to let Jones enter the room. The room smelled of rubber, oil and lubricants and transported Warren back to childhood Saturdays waiting for his dad in Halfords as he picked up a replacement for whatever component had failed that week on his mother's ageing Mini.

Blackheath was sitting on the floor, surrounded by small cardboard boxes, some empty, others still sealed. A plastic drawer marked "5 Watt bulbs — clear" was half filled by individually packaged small bulbs. Warren winced; he'd once spent over two hours trying to change just such a bulb on his old Citroën. Finally admitting defeat, he'd eventually paid a small fortune for his local dealer to replace it for him. He still had the scars on his knuckles.

Looking at Blackheath, Warren could see that the man was not doing well. He looked gaunt, his skin a pale, sallow colour. His eyes were bloodshot and Warren was sure that he could smell the faintest whiff of alcohol over his strong aftershave.

"Darren? DCI Jones, we spoke yesterday."

The young tyre fitter looked up and nodded slowly. "I remember. Have you any news?"

"We're pursuing a number of different leads, but we need to clarify a few things with you. Would you be willing to accompany us to the police station?"

The young man's eyes widened slightly. "Am I under arrest?" He looked nervous. Warren filed away the man's reaction for future consideration; however, in his experience, most people were uncomfortable when asked to go to the police station. Furthermore, unless he was completely naïve and never watched TV, Blackheath had to know that the police routinely suspected the boyfriend in cases such as these. On the other hand, perhaps Blackheath had something to be afraid of?

"No, nothing like that. I'd just rather we got the facts down on tape. At this stage you are simply accompanying us voluntarily to help us with our enquiries."

The young man nodded his agreement, clearly not registering the caveat that Warren had slipped into the start of the third sentence. As he got to his feet Warren reminded him who Karen Hardwick was and introduced Tony Sutton. As agreed, Hardwick was sympathetic and asked how he was coping; Sutton said nothing, remaining a dark, brooding presence.

* * *

Jack Bradley had been visibly relieved when Blackheath had asked to take a break and the three police officers and the grieving youth arrived back at the station barely twenty minutes later. After being reminded that he wasn't under arrest and advised of his rights, Blackheath was given a cup of coffee and led into Interview Suite One.

The team of detectives knocking doors on Blackheath and Evans' estate had yet to find a witness who could positively place Blackheath or his car outside his flat at the time he claimed and so Warren started the interview by confirming the timings claimed by Blackheath the previous day, looking for any discrepancies that might indicate the man was lying. He repeated everything precisely for the tape.

Now for the hard part.

"Darren, how would you describe your relationship with Sally's father?"

Blackheath sighed. "Me and Bill never got on well. He doesn't think I'm good enough for his little girl." He shook his head bitterly. "Sally is… was a really bright girl. And ambitious. She went to university and dreamed of becoming a senior manager in one of the major travel companies one day. Whereas me… Well, you've seen where I work. I don't even have a college certificate."

"So that was it? He just thought you were a bit beneath her?"

"It was more than that. He thinks I'm lazy and lack ambition and he thinks I've made Sally the same way." Blackheath's eyes flashed; he was clearly angry about Evans' perception of him.

"Why would he think that? From what we've heard, Sally was a strong, independent-minded young woman, with lots of plans for the future."

"Exactly. The thing is, her old man never really understood what she did at Far and Away. He thought she was just sitting at the desk, checking the computers for cut-price deals. He thought she was stuck in a rut and needed to move on. But she did much more than that. She was unofficially deputy store manager.

Kelli, her boss, took her under her wing and was letting her sit in on meetings and try her hand at running the business. Her dad wanted her to leave Far and Away and join one of the big companies as a trainee manager. But Sally reckoned she was getting more experience with Kelli than she'd have got in any of the bigger companies. Besides which, her job at Far and Away was secure — the company was bucking the trend and holding its own against the online companies. If she started fresh at one of the big travel agents, there's no guarantee they wouldn't sack her the moment they hit a tough patch." He smiled sadly, clearly remembering a conversation. "She always said that she should be grateful to have a job in the current climate and she'd be mad to risk it. She planned to stay put until the economy picks up."

"You were going to propose to Sally at Christmas. What do you think her father's reaction would have been? Were you going to ask his permission?"

Blackheath snorted, his face darkening.

"No way. He'd have turned me down flat. Me and Sally are grown adults. I've been putting away a little money and Sally had some savings. We were going to pay for the wedding ourselves, do it our own way."

"You seem pretty confident, considering that you hadn't yet proposed and she hadn't accepted. How did you know she would say yes?"

Blackheath shrugged and his eyes turned moist. "I've known ever since we moved in together. We've talked about having kids but we're both a little old-fashioned and wanted to get married first. We had plans for the future." He sniffed loudly, wiping his eyes with the cuff of his overall. "It was never a question of if we'd get married, but when we'd get married."

There was a few moments' silence, whilst Blackheath composed himself.

"What about your parents? How did they feel about Sally? What did they think about you moving in with her?"

Blackheath's face darkened. "I'd rather not talk about that. I haven't spoken to my parents since before I met Sally."

Warren raised an eyebrow as if surprised. "How is that so? I thought that you were living with your parents until you moved in with Sally? That was less than a year ago and you'd been dating for, what, two years before then? How can you live with your parents and not discuss Sally with them?"

"My parents' house is very large and I had the use of the granny flat. It was quite possible to live day to day and not speak to them."

"I see. Why don't you get on with your parents, if you don't mind me asking?"

"I do mind you asking and I'd rather not talk about it."

"I'm sorry, Mr Blackheath. I didn't mean to intrude." Warren backtracked slightly, careful not to upset the young man. That was Sutton's job.

"I don't see why you didn't just move out if you weren't speaking to your mum and dad." Sutton spoke up, right on cue.

"I couldn't afford to. Not on my own, with the money I earn. Mum and Dad let me have the granny flat for free. Felt guilty, I suppose."

"What did they feel guilty about? Is it why you don't talk?" Sutton pressed.

Blackheath scowled. "Like I said, it's private. I don't want to talk about it. It's got nothing to do with Sally's death."

"I heard it was to do with the Kim Bradshaw affair."

Blackheath stared at Sutton in stunned silence for a few seconds, before shaking his head slowly from side to side.

"It's never going to leave me alone, is it?" he asked no one in particular. "Everywhere I go. Everything I do. It's never going to be forgotten." He sank forward, burying his head in his hands.

"Tell us what happened, Darren," suggested Hardwick, kindly.

Blackheath's voice was muffled, but clear enough for the tape. He started slowly.

"The whole thing ruined my life. Just one foolish accident and that was it. I was happy until then; life was good."

He sat up and looked the three officers squarely in the eyes, one at a time.

"You know, I never planned on working in a tyre fitters all my life. In fact, if you'd asked when I was sixteen I'd have laughed at you. I wanted to be a mechanic, not a 'technician'." He mimed quote marks in the air. "I wanted to run my own garage. Do real repairs. I wanted customers to drive in with a weird noise under the bonnet first thing in the morning and drive out good as new that afternoon. Instead I spend all day changing fucking tyres and exhausts. If we do an MOT and the car fails on anything more complicated than a dodgy windscreen wiper, we have to get one of the local garages to fix it for us. It's bloody embarrassing. They barely hide their contempt for us when we drop off the car. They write down what they did on a piece of paper so that we can read it to the customer, as if we don't know one end of a spanner from the other."

"So what happened?" Hardwick repeated softly.

"It was a few years ago. I was about halfway through a motor mechanics course at college, studying two days a week and working the rest of the week as an apprentice at my dad's mate's garage. Everything was going fantastic. Then I met Kim Bradshaw."

He paused, taking a deep breath. "She was the boss' daughter.

Nothing dodgy, you understand," he added hastily. "She's the same age as me. Anyway, it was just a bit of fun, you know. We went out a few times, nothing serious. But one night we got drunk at a party and ended up around the back of the garage." He grimaced at the memory. "Not terribly romantic. Anyhow, I forgot about it for a few weeks — we sort of avoided each other, I guess. Then one day she texts me out of the blue asking to come over and see me. She was pregnant."

"What did you do?"

"Well, I shit myself. I didn't know what to say. I was nineteen, in college, earning bugger all. I didn't even love her. She was in the same position. She worked two days a week in the small parts shop attached to the garage and spent the rest of the time studying hair and beauty at the tech college.

"I said we couldn't keep it, but she refused to consider an abortion. Her family are strict Catholics. My parents are too. So in the end I proposed."

Warren raised an eyebrow. "I thought Sally was your first serious relationship."

Blackheath blushed. "She was. Kim meant nothing to me. I was just panicking. Getting married seemed to be the right thing to do. Fortunately, Kim turned me down. Called me a bloody idiot. Either way, we knew we had to tell our parents, which neither of us was looking forward to.

"So she went home to tell her old man—" Blackheath's voice started to shake "—but I was too scared to go with her. I wish I had now, then maybe she wouldn't have done what she did.

"I knew I should tell Mum and Dad, but I couldn't figure out how to, so I went to bed, praying the phone wouldn't ring, promising myself I'd tell them in the morning.

"I never got the chance. At 2 a.m., the doorbell rang. It was the police."

Blackheath's voice was getting quieter and quieter. "They arrested me on suspicion of rape. I'll never forget it. Mum was in tears and Dad was demanding to know who I was supposed to have done it with."

Blackheath's eyes were looking watery again, but this time his voice was tight with anger. "They took me straight down the police station. I was fingerprinted and a DNA sample taken, then I was strip-searched and they photographed me." His lip curled in disgust. "It was the most humiliating experience of my life."

Warren ignored the faint feeling of sympathy, knowing that whatever indignities Blackheath had suffered were nothing compared to the violations heaped upon rape victims.

"Anyway, I was charged and spent the weekend in jail before being bailed on the Monday morning, pending trial in six months."

"It says in the file that the case was dropped. The prosecution changed their case at the last moment. What happened?"

Blackheath shook his head, slowly as if he still couldn't believe it.

"It was all part of the plan. It's obvious now. She got what she wanted. If her old man knew she was pregnant because of a drunken one-night stand he'd have disowned her. As things stood, she was the victim. The fact was, the prosecution case was really weak. We had a really strong defence and we knew that we were going to win. There were holes in her story and her credibility was poor. We had the texts that she sent to me the morning after the night we did it and the text she sent me asking to meet up when she told me about the pregnancy. If I really had raped her, why would she have wanted to meet me again?"

The question was clearly rhetorical and Blackheath continued without prompting. "Anyway, you know how this country works. Rape victims are granted anonymity, of course, but the accused is dragged through the mud, his life laid out for everyone to see. Obviously I lost my job, I couldn't carry on working for Kim's dad, and college suspended me indefinitely — in reality, they kicked me out. I couldn't continue there.

"And the anonymity thing is a joke. They couldn't report Kim's story in the papers obviously, but she made sure that everyone in the community knew. And her old man made sure every business in the area knew the story. I couldn't go for a pint without people pointing or staring. Some places wouldn't even let me through the door. I was attacked twice and my parents' house was spray-painted and the tyres slashed on their car.

"Anyway, finally the day comes for her to testify. It was a Monday and I turn up and after hanging around all day I'm told that the prosecution have requested a delay because Kim is ill.

"'The next day I turn up and she isn't there. I'm told that the prosecution case has been dropped and I'm free to go.'"

"Well, surely that was a good thing?" Karen Hardwick looked confused. Warren said nothing, letting Blackheath explain.

"No! That was the worst thing that could happen, other than being convicted of something I didn't do. I wasn't acquitted or cleared of any wrongdoing. Everyone reckons I 'got away with it'. The story Bradshaw and her family put out was that the stress was so bad she had a miscarriage and they decided that it wasn't worth putting her through the ordeal and dropped the case.

"It's bollocks, of course. Everyone knows that she got a late abortion and that her case was so weak it shouldn't have made it to court. But you lot are under pressure to solve more rapes. They must have figured they were going to lose this one, so they didn't raise a stink when she said she wanted to drop it." The bitterness was strong in his voice and he stared the three police officers straight in the eyes, as if he held them personally responsible for his ordeal.

"So what happened next?"

Blackheath snorted derisively. "Well, you know what they say — 'no smoke without fire'. Obviously I couldn't get my job back and those bastards in the college admissions department refused to enrol me again, so I spent the next nine months on the dole. Nobody was interested in employing me.

"Eventually, I got a call from Jack Bradley." Here, Blackheath's expression softened slightly. "He's a good bloke. He needed a tyre fitter and he knew I had enough training for the job. He's a Methodist preacher and he believes in giving people a second chance. He said that in the eyes of the law I'm an innocent man and if Jesus could forgive convicted criminals, then the least he could do was give someone like me a helping hand." Blackheath shook his head. "Twelve months previously, I'd have called him a patronising bastard and told him to stick his job, but I was desperate."

He paused for a moment. "He really is a good man. Everyone who works for him has been in trouble of some kind. Two lads have been in jail and Joe is a recovering alcoholic. Ken, our store man, had a nervous breakdown when his wife left him and ended up on the street. Jack took him in, gave him a job and ten years later he's got a new wife and two kids."

"Sounds as if it all worked out, then," said Sutton crassly, still playing the role of "bad cop".

Blackheath's eyes flashed. "Well, I was getting by. I had a job at least and over time people were starting to forget about the court case."

"Is all this why you don't speak to your parents?" Hardwick asked softly.

Blackheath glared at her for a few seconds, then sighed. "Yeah. They stood by me and all that and I know they don't believe I did it, but it cost them. Dad said I had been bloody stupid to get mixed up with the boss' daughter, let alone get her pregnant. They said they thought I'd been better brought up than that."

"What do you mean it cost them?"

"Kim Bradshaw's old man is a big name in the local community. My dad was a painter and decorator with a really good reputation. He never had to advertise — he had more work than he needed just by word of mouth. That all dried up. He had to let his three lads go. They'd worked with him for over twenty years. They were like family. We stopped going to church. Mum couldn't stand the whispering and the pointing. And then Nan died. She took the court case really hard. She was terrified I'd go to prison. She had a heart attack just before the trial. I know Mum and Dad blame me.

"Anyway, I couldn't afford to move out and Mum and Dad wouldn't let their son go homeless, so I moved into the annexe where Nan used to live."

The tears were back and Blackheath did nothing to stop them. "I hated it. Even though I'd emptied it all out, it was still Nan's flat. It had its own separate entrance, so I locked the connecting door and that was it. I never set foot in Mum and Dad's house again. I spent Christmas at a mate's."

"And then you met Sally?"

Blackheath nodded. "She was the best thing that happened to me."

"And she knew about the Bradshaw affair?"

"Who bloody didn't? Her father certainly did. At first, I think she was attracted by the bad-boy image — she was going through a bit of a rebellious streak — but pretty soon she got over it and we fell in love. At least living with Mum and Dad was free. I got a pay rise at work after Jack arranged for me to qualify to do MOTs and we managed to scrape together enough to rent the flat and start saving for the future."

He looked into space, a sad, wistful expression on his face. "Finally, things were going well, you know. We were going to get married and when things picked up we were going to move away. Sally would try for a management position in a travel agent — she'd get a great reference from Far and Away — and I'd try and get another apprenticeship, maybe even start college again. Jack has already said he'd write me letters of introduction or anything I need."

After a few seconds, Warren started again.

"We know that Sally and her father disagreed over you. Were you aware that the day before she disappeared, she met her father and told him that she thought you were going to propose?"

Blackheath looked thunderstruck.

"What? I don't understand. How could she have known? I never said anything."

Warren shrugged slightly.

"You didn't hide the ring as well as you thought. Regardless, she spoke to her dad about it. He claims that she was having cold feet, that getting married seemed like a big step. He thinks she was going to leave you and come back to live with them." This last bit was probably a bit of an exaggeration, but Warren was keen to see Blackheath's reaction.

"No! No way!"

Blackheath shook his head violently, his voice rising. "We were in love. We'd planned our future out together — she wanted to get married. She wanted kids. He's lying."

"Why would he lie to us, Darren? He was her father. He just wanted what was best for his little girl. No offence, son, but you're hardly a prize catch, are you? A poorly paid tyre fitter with a questionable police record hanging over you. And what about those football trips, eh? Whilst Sally was away with her mates in the sun, you'd be off with the lads doing drugs and shagging birds. I hope at least you learnt from your last mistake and you use a condom."

Blackheath recoiled from Sutton's accusation as if he'd been physically slapped. "How dare you? I've never so much as looked at another woman since I met Sally. And as for drugs, I've never touched them. Those football tours are hard work, five games in five days. We're aiming to top our league — coach won't let us have more than two beers in the evening and we have to be in bed by midnight. Who told you this bullshit?"

Sutton shrugged. "Not important. The thing is, I can't help wondering what your response might have been if she decided she didn't want to get married. You've told us repeatedly how great life was with Sally, how finally things were moving forward and how you had plans for the future. Well, what if you suddenly find out that isn't going to happen? You said yourself how she was going through a rebellious streak when she met you. Maybe she didn't 'get over it'. Talking about getting married and having kids — it was just a fantasy. One in the eye for her old man. Maybe he was right and she was coasting, then when she realised you were serious and really did want to get married she got cold feet.

It wasn't a game anymore. And who would she turn to, to rescue her? Well, Dad, of course."

Blackheath was shaking his head violently. He was gripping the edge of the table, and his knuckles had turned bone white. "No. Why would you say that? We loved each other." His voice was strangled, whether with grief or anger Sutton couldn't be sure. Regardless, he pressed on.

"We're just brainstorming, son. It's just that I can't help asking myself what your response would be. I know that if I was in your position, I'd be pretty pissed off. Everything is finally rosy. All that shit about Bradshaw is in the past and the future is looking great. Then 'wham!' it all comes crashing down. She finds the ring — in your sock drawer, come on, lad! — and tells you it's over, she can't get married." Sutton leant forward, his expression looking for all the world like a bad actor trying to look sympathetic towards someone he despised. "I bet she even did the whole 'it's not you, it's me' thing. Did she tell you that she'd always love you and you'd remain friends?" Sutton shook his head and looked at Warren. "I hate it when they do that, don't you, sir?"

Warren nodded. "I wish they'd just be honest. I reckon it's a way of feeling less guilty for treating you so badly."

Sutton turned back. "Doesn't make you feel any better though, does it? Makes you feel even more humiliated. And how do you tell your mates? Or the blokes at work? And what about your mum and dad? If she leaves you can you afford the rent on your own? It's back to the granny flat with your tail between your legs. And what about the whispering? I'll bet there's a few crass enough to tell her it's for the best and bring up the whole Kim Bradshaw thing. No wonder you were so angry."

Blackheath was now crying. "No, never. It never happened like that. I know what you're saying, that I was so angry about being dumped by Sally that I killed her. But I didn't. I couldn't do that to her. She never said anything about finding the ring. And even if she had, I'd never lay a finger on her. I love her too much."

For the next few moments, the room was silent, save for Blackheath's sobbing. Eventually, he wiped his eyes and sniffed loudly. "I'm not going to say another word without a lawyer." He nodded towards the tape machine. "I was stupid to say anything without one."

Warren shrugged. "No need for a lawyer. Like I said, you aren't under arrest and are free to leave at any time. We have no more questions. Interview terminated at witness' request." Stating the time, he leant forward and turned off the tape recorder.

"Thank you for your time, Mr Blackheath. Would you like a lift back to work, or can we arrange for a cab to take you home?"

Blackheath could only look on with surprise. "I'll walk," he mumbled.

With that, Warren called the duty sergeant. Within a minute, the young man was out on the street, breathing in the icy December air.

* * *

Back in the interview room, Warren polled his fellow officers. "Thoughts?"

"I think he's genuine. I rattled his cage good and hard but his story never changed. My gut tells me he didn't do it." Sutton shrugged apologetically as if sorry that he hadn't been able to wring a confession out of the young man.

"I have to agree with DI Sutton, sir. He seemed genuine when we saw him yesterday and he hasn't changed a single detail since then. I think he really did love her. I also think her father was wrong and that she was going to marry him."

Warren agreed with both Sutton and Hardwick. "My gut feeling is exactly the same. But we can't completely rule him out without eyewitness evidence or forensics—" he glanced at his watch "—which I am expecting any minute. Tell you what, why don't you two go and have an early lunch? We'll get the rest of the team together and have a meeting at 1 p.m."

"Yes, sir," both officers replied as Warren left the room.

Karen Hardwick turned to Sutton. "How do you do it, sir?"

Sutton knew what she was asking about. "You just have to put aside your feelings. It doesn't matter if you feel sorry for them or not. Policing isn't a popularity contest. Sometimes you have to be harsh and nasty, because it's a harsh and nasty world." He grimaced slightly. "Even if it does leave an unpleasant taste in your mouth."

"Well, when we find the real killer, hopefully he'll understand."

Sutton shrugged. "Time will tell."

Suddenly the door opened again and the desk sergeant poked his head around the door. "DCI Jones says don't be late back from lunch. Blackheath's off the hook and you've got a new suspect."

Chapter 15

After a revelation like that, lunch was the last thing on Sutton's and Hardwick's minds and both raced upstairs to the CID main office. One o'clock was nearly an hour away and detectives by their very nature were insatiably curious; there was no way that the two officers were going to wait to find out what had been discovered. Unfortunately, the door to Warren's office was closed. The DCI's rules were very clear — if the door was open, they could knock and enter. If the door was closed, they shouldn't knock unless it was an emergency. Sutton looked at Carol, Warren's unofficial PA. She shrugged apologetically and pointed at the highly complex telephone unit that sat on her desk. "He's in there with DC Hastings on a conference call."

"Any idea who he's talking to?" blurted Karen Hardwick, without thinking.

Carol pursed her lips in disapproval. "I'm sure that if DCI Jones wants you to know who he is talking to on his private line, he will tell you himself, *Detective Constable.*"

Hardwick blushed and stared at her shoes.

Sutton thanked Carol for her assistance and led the embarrassed constable away.

"OK, plan B. When Gary comes out of there and you two disappear off for lunch together, you find out what he's got."

Hardwick turned even redder. "What do you mean 'disappear off for lunch together'?"

Sutton looked at her in amusement. "You're working with a team of trained observers, Karen. How long did you two think you'd keep it quiet?"

Karen covered her face with her hands. "Oh, no. We were so careful, trying to be professional at work."

Belatedly Sutton realised why she was so uncomfortable. "Don't worry, lass. Nobody thinks otherwise. So long as you keep your private life at home, nobody cares." He patted her awkwardly on the shoulder. "If anything, the guv thinks you make a sweet couple."

Karen moaned as if in pain.

"I'm not really helping, am I?" asked Sutton.

"No, sir, not really."

* * *

The briefing room was packed with team members, all eager to hear the latest developments. Warren called for quiet and the buzz of conversation settled down. Neither Karen nor Tony Sutton had managed to speak to DCI Jones or DC Hastings, so they were still in the dark about the new suspect.

Warren decided to address the question of Darren Blackheath first, handing over to Gary Hastings.

The DC shuffled the piece of paper in front of him. "I have the remaining results from the house-to-house inquiries conducted with Sally Evans' neighbours. We've finally spoken to everyone on the estate. It's the usual story: half the neighbours didn't recognise her photo and most of the rest couldn't remember what they were doing that evening. Those that knew the couple said that they seemed 'nice enough' and never had any bother. There was no evidence that there were any problems.

"The night she went missing, most couldn't recall if Blackheath's car had been present earlier in the evening, before her mother and Cheryl came around. However, we finally found one eyewitness who claims to be certain that he saw Blackheath's car about six-thirty, before he went out to join his wife at the local bingo hall. I showed him a picture of the car and he said he recognised it immediately." He gestured towards a picture of the car projected on the far wall. "Let's face it, he's hardly going to be mistaken."

A polite titter went around the room. Darren Blackheath's pride and joy was nothing if not distinctive. It had started life as a dark purple Vauxhall Astra. Its year of manufacture was unclear as the personalised number plate suggested the owner was a "Bad Boy", rather than giving a registration date.

The vanity plate was the least personalised element of the car. The car's tyres had been replaced with what appeared to be little more than black elastic bands wrapped around gold alloy disks. The suspension was lowered to make anything higher than a few centimetres a hazard to the fat twin exhaust pipes that protruded from the rear, and graffiti-style electric-blue decals covered the vehicle, contrasting jarringly with the paint job. An unnecessarily large spoiler on the back made the whole thing look like a toy. The blacked-out windows, fluorescent-pink windscreen wipers and double bank of headlamps completed the whole garish ensemble.

"Thanks, Gary. Anything from Forensics?"

"No evidence of any foul play in either Blackheath's car or their apartment. The car has been cleaned very thoroughly recently, which may have removed traces of mud, but that in itself isn't suspicious. Blackheath is known to be obsessive about his car and he polished it most weekends. There is plenty of Sally Evans' DNA inside the car and some fibres matching the coat she was wearing the night she was killed, but that is to be expected. She didn't drive so Blackheath ferried her around a lot. However, there was none in the boot, or the back seat where you'd expect him to have forced her to sit."

"He could have propped her up in the passenger seat. It was dark," suggested Sutton, although he was clearly playing devil's advocate.

Hastings shrugged. "Anything's possible, I suppose." He didn't sound convinced.

"What about traffic and surveillance?" Warren asked, eager to move the conversation on.

"There are no surveillance or traffic cameras near the back alley where she was presumably abducted from. However, traffic cameras a couple of junctions away caught his licence number both just before six, when he should have been about to arrive and pick her up, and about fifteen minutes later when he claims to have left. We can't tell what he did in that fifteen-minute window, but the timings are consistent with his version of events. Unfortunately, we have no other sightings of the car, so only the eyewitness report ties him to the apartment and rules out him driving her to the woods."

Warren tapped a pencil thoughtfully. "So it seems that this witness, what CCTV we have and the forensics back up his story of what took place. I'd suggest that he's no longer a suspect." Heads nodded around the briefing table.

"OK, next up, where are we on Bill Evans' alibi?"

DC Annabel Willis, a new probationary constable who had been assigned to follow up on that lead, spoke up. "Not much yet, I'm afraid. Travelodge have been very helpful. They confirm that his credit card was used in the Cambridge branch that evening. We're looking at CCTV to see if we can piece together his comings and goings, but by their own admission it'd be easy enough to leave the hotel for a few hours without being picked up if you really wanted to."

"What about this mysterious woman he claims to be having an affair with?"

This time it was DS Johnson who addressed the team. "Not a lot yet. As he suggested, her mobile phone is switched off. They aren't due to meet up for another month — more if they skip the New Year weekend. We're trying to trace ownership of her phone, but it doesn't look helpful. We contacted the dating agency to see if she paid by credit card and to ask what records they have on the two of them, but they've insisted on a court order. However, the woman I spoke to hinted that they hold very little useful data. They might not even use credit cards, rather an Internet-based payment system that isn't located in this country."

"So verifying his alibi is going to be very difficult," summarised Sutton.

"Well, keep at him. Something about him doesn't quite ring true." The two officers nodded their assent.

"With those two out of the way, perhaps we should turn our attention to new suspects. Gary, why don't you take us through what you and DS Kent have found?"

Hastings removed the picture of Blackheath's car from the screen.

"DS Kent and I have been putting all of the forensic and scene evidence into the HOLMES database to see what comes up. It's been quite tricky as the most striking characteristic of this case has been the *lack* of evidence at the scene. Anyhow, we finally figured out the correct search terms to use, uploaded what information we had and we've started getting interesting results."

He clicked on the screen.

"We have five potential hits. Rapes where very little forensic evidence was gathered and the CSIs speculate that the perpetrator went to great lengths to avoid leaving trace behind. In all five cases the victims followed a very set routine and were kidnapped, subdued with solvent, bound then taken to a secluded spot to be raped. They were then left and found by a member of the public. However, none of the five were killed. If it's the same guy, either he's changed his MO or Sally Evans' death was an accident.

"Working backwards in time, the most recent was that of a jogger in June 2006 in Reading. The case was unsolved. Four years earlier a similar attack took place in Bristol — again the case is unsolved. We know these two cases are separate to the first three cases, because those were solved and the attacker was behind bars when the later two took place."

"So we believe that the person responsible for the attacks in Bristol and Reading has struck again?" suggested Tony Sutton.

"Actually, we suspect not. The other three attacks took place in June, August and November of 1997."

"It seems a long time between attacks. Why would he suddenly resurface?" asked Karen Hardwick.

"The attacker was convicted in May 1998 and sent down for eighteen years. The attacks occurred in and around the village of Stennfield, a couple of miles north of here."

Tony Sutton, who had been at Middlesbury CID longer than anyone in the room, gasped audibly. "You're kidding? You're talking about Richard Cameron? That case was ongoing when I was a rookie DC. He'd be due parole pretty soon, I'd have thought."

Hastings nodded. "Released on licence this time last year. Bloody big coincidence, don't you think?"

Chapter 16

With the name of a potential suspect on the table a strategy was needed to bring the man in for questioning. Richard Cameron was a convicted serial rapist living on licence in a tiny village to the north of Middlesbury. Like all such ex-offenders he was required to report his current address to the police and maintain contact with a probation officer. Current police records on Cameron were sketchy and largely out of date, with interest in him minimal in the almost thirteen years since he'd been sent to prison. Prior to his release, the files had been updated with a more recent mugshot and details of his current whereabouts, but for the most part he was the responsibility of the probation service.

Sam Pargeter was a no-nonsense ex-submariner. A gruff, bullish Yorkshire man with a salt and pepper haircut, he was candid about why he'd joined the service as he helped himself to a cup of jet-black coffee from the CID urn.

"I got meself a reputation in the Navy as a bit of a hard bastard. Hard but fair. They stuck me in charge of whipping the less responsive boys into shape. Some of them see it all as a bit of a laugh when they're training. 'Course, as soon as they come aboard a boat, and it finally dawns on them that they won't even see daylight for the next six months, some of them start to play up. That's where I came in."

After loading his cup with several heaped spoons of sugar he followed the two detectives back to Warren's office, where he continued his story.

"They called it 'Pargeter's detail' and the kids were named 'Pargies'. I don't take bullshit from nobody, but I also don't give it out. They stuck them with me for a week. For most of that week, they hated me — some of the names they called me when they thought I wasn't listening would make your hair curl. Of course, by the end of the week, they thought the sun shone out of my arse. They realised that I was right and they was wrong — simple as. Some of them still write to me, letting me know about their latest promotions. Wouldn't want to name names, of course, but there's more than one flag officer who still sends me a Christmas card and a bottle of rum each year and calls himself a 'Pargie'.

"Anyhow, eventually it was time to leave the service. A mate of mine asked if I fancied helping out in one of those places out in the sticks where they hide out-of-control teenagers. I did about twelve months there, but found it too depressing. Everybody's just marking time until the kids turn sixteen, get turfed out then stab their way into an adult prison. Then I saw a programme one night about the National Offender Management Service. It talked about how their job was to stop reoffending — by any means necessary — and try and get some of these folks back into doing something useful in society.

"So I contacted them, went for an interview and here I am. They found out that I'm good with young lads and so I tend to specialise. A lot of these boys never really had a father figure, or if they did, he was a drunk or an abuser. I keep an eye on them.

If they don't do what they're told I'll come around unannounced and smack 'em round the ear. If they've got a job interview and I'm free, I'll turn up and hammer on the door until they get out of bed. I'll even throw them in the shower and turn the water on them fully clothed if I have to."

Pargeter shrugged and took a large swig of his coffee. "Some of them don't like it and neither do some of the more liberal-minded folk in the office, but my re-offending rates are 30 to 40 per cent lower than the average and I have a wall full of pictures from my former boys showing me what they're up to now. Can't argue with results like that."

Warren eyed the man closely. Coming from most people, Sam Pargeter's little speech would have sounded self-serving. Yet there was something about the way that he said it — calmly and matter-of-factly in a no-nonsense northern burr that seemed to invite trust in the man. Warren thought he could see why so many wayward youths responded to his methods.

Sutton also seemed impressed, or at least as impressed as he ever did. "So why did you end up with Richard Cameron? He hardly seems to fit your usual profile."

"Well, ultimately, we have to deal with what comes our way. Cameron was released last year and I had space on my list, so I got him. He's unusual and that's why I've come to speak to you. Your call surprised the hell out of me."

Warren glanced at Sutton.

"Why so surprised? Repeat offending in these cases is pretty high — we've all seen the stats."

Pargeter nodded. "Normally I'd agree with you, Chief Inspector, but I thought Cameron was different."

Warren's face must have betrayed his scepticism.

"Look, Richard Cameron was sentenced to eighteen years for three rapes back in 1998. He did nearly twelve years and was released on licence this time last year. When he entered the system he was a dangerous man, no question, with priors for drink-driving, domestic violence and petty theft. When the rapes occurred he lived with his wife, Angie, and teenage son, Michael, in a small farmstead about three miles north of Middlesbury, just outside the village of Stennfield. It isn't much, a couple of acres of potatoes, a handful of pigs and a few chickens. He wasn't a farmer by any stretch; he just inherited it from his old man, who inherited it from his old man et cetera.

"He basically left school at fifteen and drifted in and out of odd jobs before meeting Angie in about 1980. They had Michael in 1982. The farm was paid off by his father and he owns the land, so even when he didn't have a job they always had a roof over their heads. Anyway, he wasn't really on the radar as far as the police were concerned; he had a file, like I said, and Michael's school raised warning flags with social services but nothing ever happened.

"And then the rapes occurred. You're familiar with the details; suffice to say, it was luck as much as detective work that nailed him in the end. Michael was barely sixteen when Cameron was sentenced. The girls were all local and everyone knew who his dad was. In the end he finished his GCSEs, changed his name by deed poll to his mother's maiden name and switched schools for sixth form. By all accounts, the move was successful and he went on to get a decent set of A levels and go to university.

"Angie divorced Cameron and reclaimed her maiden name but stayed at the farm with Michael. Cameron apparently signed over the lease without much fuss. He told me when I first met him it was his first step in trying to repair the damage done to his family."

Sutton looked pointedly at the clock on the wall. Where was all this going?

Warren tried to be a little more discreet. Pargeter got the hint. "The thing is, Cameron didn't kill those three girls. He raped them and beat them, but he isn't a murderer. That was his downfall. One of the girls gave a description of the mask that he was wearing, which ultimately led to his arrest."

"You said it yourself, that was his downfall; he left a witness behind. Maybe he's learnt his lesson — dead bodies can't testify in court." Sutton's tone was getting decidedly impatient; he knew that Detective Superintendent Grayson would probably be appearing any moment with an arrest warrant, to be served should Cameron decline to attend the police station voluntarily.

Pargeter ignored Sutton's tetchiness. "You're right. I think he has learnt his lesson. When inside, he worked hard to complete the schooling he should have done thirty years earlier and became a lay preacher, and volunteer counsellor to other prisoners."

Sutton was unable to resist a snort of derision. In his opinion, the fabled prison conversion, especially amongst dangerous sex offenders, was just that. Nevertheless, an outside observer sitting in on parole-board hearings could be forgiven for thinking that a spell in prison was the making of a man and that HM Prison Service was singlehandedly doing more to arrest the decline in active church-going than any number of evangelical outreach programmes. All nonsense, of course. Prisoners had a lot of time to try and figure out what it was the parole board wanted to hear and would do their best to oblige them.

For the first time since arriving at Middlesbury's little CID unit, Sam Pargeter showed the briefest flash of irritation. "Look, I'm not a bloody idiot. I've been in this game far too long to be fooled by the old 'I've found Jesus' defence; besides, whether he truly has found God or it's just enlightened self-interest, I don't think Richard Cameron would do anything that could get him put back inside. He barely survived the place. He attempted suicide three times — and I mean really attempted it. He's made it quite clear to me and anyone else that will listen that he'll kill himself before he sets foot inside another prison."

Sutton looked at Warren. "Better make certain everyone knows that, guv. Last thing we need is a bloody suicide or death-by-cop."

Pargeter scowled. "I doubt it will come to that." He settled back into his chair and struck a more reasonable tone. "Look, make the appropriate preparations, but I don't think it's him."

Warren shrugged non-committally. "Well, let's see if we can rule him out. I'm telling you this in the strictest confidence, you understand." He locked eyes with Pargeter, who nodded briskly and professionally. "We believe that the victim was carried several hundred yards, possibly dead, almost certainly unconscious. We've found no evidence that there was more than one person involved. Do you think that Cameron is capable of carrying the body of a young woman of average build and weight that distance?"

Pargeter's brow furrowed and he pinched his bottom lip between his thumb and forefinger, before, finally, taking his glasses off and rubbing them on his sleeve.

"I honestly don't know. Twelve months ago I'd have said no chance. He was a physical wreck. He was overweight and smoked like a chimney. He could walk that distance, but he'd have struggled if he had to carry a shopping bag, let alone a body.

"But since then he's been working on the farm, trying to make a business of it with Michael. He's lost about three stone and cut right back on the fags. Last time I dropped in, he was wrestling hay bales off the back of a truck. He must have shifted a dozen whilst I was there; he was out of breath but didn't look in danger of a coronary. If he slung her across his shoulders in a fireman's lift, then I reckon he might be able to do it."

Warren made a note, before changing tack. "Tell me a bit more about his current situation. You said he's back at the farm, but I thought his family had disowned him."

"They did at first. His ex-wife never got over what he did and died a few years ago. Michael hated him at first, but after his mum died he realised that his father was the only family he had left. He received counselling and eventually started going to church himself. A couple of years ago, he visited his father in prison for the first time and was convinced that the old man wanted to change his life. They bought a bit more land from their neighbour and resurrected the farm. Michael has a good job and so they get by OK."

"What about the local community? Twelve years isn't that long."

"The two of them largely keep themselves to themselves. When word first got around that Cameron was back a few things were sprayed on the front of the house and neither of them are welcome in the village pub, but it's mostly died down. They tend to travel to Cambridge or Stevenage if they fancy a pint.

"The only place they are cautiously welcomed is at the village church. I've met the local vicar a few times and he's taken it upon himself to help me keep Cameron on the straight and narrow. Nobody has invited them to join the choir, like, but they don't get any bother."

Warren looked at Sutton. Much of what Pargeter had said was of little relevance, he decided. Richard Cameron had been a very dangerous sexual predator and, as far as Warren was concerned, men like that had something fundamentally wrong with them. The urges that drove them were unlikely to ever disappear entirely. The question was, did Richard Cameron control those urges or did those urges still control him?

Chapter 17

Warren and Sutton drove to Cameron's farm in a tense silence. Behind them, two police cars, each with a pair of uniformed constables, followed, lights and sirens off. Detective Superintendent Grayson had drafted an arrest warrant, but Warren hoped to bring in the former convict voluntarily. Although the killing had now been reported in the local and national press, the details were scanty and it was possible that they would arrive before he caught the news.

Delaying any arrest would buy the police valuable time for questioning. The rules governing arrest were strict; the moment that a person was formally arrested, the clock started ticking. They would have twenty-four hours to either charge or release their suspect, on bail if necessary. A further twelve hours could be authorised by Detective Superintendent Grayson, but beyond that a magistrate would need to be consulted. If Warren could get a few questions in before Cameron started making noises about legal representation and detention limits, so much the better.

The farm was at the end of a long, winding, single-track lane. Parked in front of the house were a vintage Land Rover and a far smarter Jaguar, presumably belonging to Cameron's son.

The farmhouse was an old and weather-beaten affair. Two

storeys in height, it looked as though it would need serious renova-
tion in the next few years to survive the elements. Next door an
even more rickety barn had its doors partially open. Parking the
car so that it couldn't be seen directly from the barn, Warren and
Sutton stepped out into the chilly air. It was now late afternoon
and Warren doubted they had much more than an hour's daylight
left. They'd have to move quickly.

Speaking quietly to the accompanying officers, Warren
instructed them to spread out around the house to stop
Cameron if he decided to make a run for it. With the officers
in place, the two detectives walked cautiously towards the open
barn. From inside they could make out the sound of a radio
playing. Radio 4 by the sound of the presenter, Warren decided.
There was a good chance he had heard the news, then. Warren
stepped into the doorway, his eyes quickly adjusting to the
gloom inside.

The barn was pretty much what he expected. Hay bales stacked
against one half of the building made an improvised open
enclosure amongst which a few hens — or were they chickens?
Warren had no idea — strutted and pecked at the straw-covered
floor. On the other side of the barn a wooden enclosure housed
what looked — and smelt — like a few pigs. In the middle of the
barn sat an old, rusty Massey Ferguson tractor. Two legs clad in
dirty grey corduroy trousers tucked into well-worn, muddy leather
boots poked out from under the engine. The tractor had probably
been assembled in part by one of his schoolmates' fathers, Warren
realised, back when Massey Ferguson was a major employer in
his hometown of Coventry. He shook off the feeling of sadness
that passed through him. He'd been young at the time, but the
closing of that plant had turned upside down the lives of many of

the children he'd gone to school with. Some families never really recovered. The factory was a housing estate now.

"Richard Cameron?"

The legs jerked in surprise.

"It's the police. We'd like to speak to you."

There was a long pause, before finally the legs moved again. With a grunt, the body of a late middle-aged man slid out from under the vehicle. In his hand, he held a large steel spanner.

"Could you put that down, please?" asked Warren carefully.

Sutton had found the radio and switched it off at the wall socket; the clatter of the metal tool against the concrete floor echoed loudly through the shed.

"What do you want? I'm not due a visit until next week."

"We're not with the Probation Service. We're here to ask you some questions in connection with an ongoing enquiry."

"Am I under arrest? I ain't going back to prison." The man's eyes darted wildly around the barn as his voice started to rise. His hands started to shake and his foot tapped. The man was clearly terrified at the prospect of prison. Were his fears justified?

Warren appraised the man standing before him. According to his file, Richard Cameron was days shy of his sixtieth birthday. The photograph in his file, taken just before his release, could have been of a man ten years older. Greying and stooped, the face in the picture was creased and lined. The man in front of him could pass for fifty. The green wax jacket that he wore was loose around the waist, suggesting recent weight loss, and his back was straightened. His face, though still craggy and battered, had more definition. His complexion had lost the greyish pallor of the long-term smoker and inmate and was instead pink, with a ruddiness to the cheeks that spoke of time outdoors. His beard, although grey and tinged with yellow around the mouth, was neatly trimmed. The man's hands, he noted, were dirty and scabbed, but underneath the oil were the faint remnants of a summer tan. Life on the outside clearly agreed with Richard Cameron far more than life on the inside.

Warren spoke carefully. "At the moment, we just want you to answer some questions. However, I remind you that you are required to co-operate with the police under the terms of your parole. I have a warrant here for your arrest if necessary."

"What's going on here?"

The voice came from behind the officers and belonged to a young man in his late twenties or early thirties, Warren judged.

"And who might you be, sir?"

The question was unnecessary; the man was clearly his father's son. Although taller and slimmer, he had the same broad shoulders and strong jawbone, visible despite a thick goatee beard. His hair was a dark brown, cut short, in an unfussy but neat style. Unlike his father, he wore grey suit trousers and smart leather shoes, his jacket an expensive-looking Gore-Tex affair. A collar and red tie peeked out above the partially unzipped front.

"Michael Stockley. I own this farm." The man's accent was clearly the same as his father's, but his diction spoke of a better education and years spent in university and managerial workplaces, rather than low-paid menial jobs and prison.

So he still went by his mother's maiden name, Warren noted.

"We are inviting your father to attend a voluntary interview at Middlesbury police station."

Stockley curled his lip. "And you say that he hasn't been arrested?"

"Not unless he refuses to co-operate — in which case I'll serve the arrest warrant and contact his parole officer."

Acknowledging his father for the first time since arriving, Michael Stockley nodded in his direction. "You aren't under arrest, Dad. You don't have to answer any questions. In fact, say nothing until I've arranged a solicitor."

The older man nodded mutely, looking scared and bewildered. Stockley turned back to Warren.

"I didn't catch your name, Officer — nor have I seen any identification."

Warren locked eyes with the man for several long seconds, before fishing out his warrant card, which he held up in front of the man's face. Stockley nodded once.

"What's this about?"

"Just some questions relating to an ongoing enquiry." Warren had no intention of giving away any more information than he had to. He wanted to keep the man on the back foot for as long as possible.

"I believe that my father is entitled to have somebody with him during this questioning and that a solicitor may be present." He all but smirked.

Warren didn't like the way that this was going; he had to do something to shift the balance of power away from this smartly dressed amateur lawyer.

"Of course, assuming that Mr Cameron has something to hide, we can wait for a solicitor to arrive." Warren nodded back to the older man, who paled slightly.

"The exercising of his legal rights should not be inferred as any admission of wrongdoing on my father's part. And I believe that any attempt to deter him from seeking representation — or indeed questioning him before his solicitor arrives — would be contrary to the rules laid down in the Police and Criminal Evidence Act." This time he did smirk.

On the other side of the barn he could see Tony Sutton rolling his eyes in disgust. Warren agreed. *Spare us from barrack-room lawyers*, he thought.

Sensing a victory of sorts, Stockley pressed on. "I suggest you return to your cars, officers, whilst my father and I go into the house and call for his lawyer. I'll let you know when he arrives."

Warren shook his head slowly. "I don't think so, Mr Stockley. I was rather intending to do this at the police station. You can wait for your lawyer there."

Richard Cameron shook his head violently. "No, I've always said I'd rather die than set foot inside another prison cell and I mean it."

"My father is undergoing questioning voluntarily," Michael Stockley reminded them. "You cannot force him to attend the police station and you certainly can't put him in a prison cell whilst he awaits his lawyer."

Warren was getting impatient. "First, nobody has said anything about your father being placed in custody, let alone a cell. Second, I would remind you that I have a signed arrest warrant, so I certainly can compel him to attend the questioning. I'll let you decide how you want to do this."

The two men glared at each other. Finally, it was Richard Cameron who spoke up. "All right. Let's get this done with. But I ain't saying nothing until my brief arrives." With that, he slouched out of the door, heading for the parked cars. At a signal from Warren, one of the uniformed constables opened the rear door of his patrol car.

"Mind your head," he grunted, pushing down on the older man's unruly mane.

Stockley stepped towards the car.

"Hold on, Michael."

Now that he had them, Warren's instinct was to minimise contact between father and son as much as possible. He didn't like the way the younger man was calling all of the shots. Stockley blinked. "I'm accompanying my father to the police station."

"Not in there, you're not. Health and Safety," he lied, motioning towards the remaining patrol car, whose driver stood by the open rear door like a chauffeur.

"Health and Safety? Bollocks!" He made as if to protest further, but Warren merely waved the arrest warrant in the air. With a sound of disgust, the younger man turned on his heel and marched towards the waiting car.

With both men locked in separate cars, Warren addressed the remaining officers.

"DI Sutton will co-ordinate the securing of the property and then return to the station. I want a search team standing by and ready to go in case he gives us enough to raise a search warrant. We need to move fast before his lawyer starts putting up the roadblocks."

He turned to Sutton, who was smiling. "I liked the way you handled that, boss. His lawyer will be pissed, though."

Warren shrugged. The man was a convicted rapist out on licence. His complaints would fall on deaf ears.

"Tough. More to the point, though, if we can't get anything off Cameron in interview, we may have to let him go. And his lawyer will almost certainly challenge the grounds for any search warrant." As an afterthought, he fished out his own car keys. "Drive yourself back rather than wait for a lift. I want you in on any interviews. I'll keep Mr Cameron company on the way to the station."

Chapter 18

By the time Cameron, Stockley and Warren arrived back at Middlesbury police station, Stockley had already telephoned his father's solicitor. Although he wasn't under arrest, Cameron was still processed by the custody officer, who reminded him of his rights and directed him to a small room to await his lawyer. He ostentatiously left the door wide open so that he could listen in to anything the father and son might say, a mute reminder that their conversation would not be subject to the same privileges that a lawyer and client would be entitled to.

Thirty minutes later, Cameron's solicitor arrived. A portly, balding man in his late fifties, he'd not represented Cameron at his first trial — that solicitor had retired some years ago — but he had negotiated his release and the terms of his parole.

"What's he in for? I understand he's attended voluntarily for questioning, but you have an arrest warrant and have left a team in place should you be able to raise a search warrant."

Warren shrugged. "Just doing it by the book — complete chain of evidence and all that."

The solicitor grunted. "Not a lot of information for me to go on here, but I can read between the lines and I've heard the news. Can I see the arrest warrant?"

"No need, it hasn't been served." The arrest warrant contained details that Warren would only share if necessary.

The solicitor grunted again, letting it pass, although Warren was under no illusions that it would be forgotten about. Leading him towards the small room containing Cameron and Stockley, neither of whom had said a word yet, Warren let the door close behind him. Everything said inside that room would now be privileged.

Grabbing a coffee from the vending machine, Warren went to greet Sutton, who had just returned from the farm.

"The farmhouse is secure and a SOCO team are on standby."

"Good, but don't hold your breath. I've got a feeling that we aren't going to get much from Cameron. That bloody son of his is too smart by half and his brief is pretty experienced also, by the look of him."

"He is," confirmed Sutton, who'd been at Middlesbury for years. "He's pretty reasonable for a solicitor and knows when to fight his battles, but he does a thorough job and won't stand any bullshit."

"Well, then, let's see what Mr Cameron has to say for himself."

* * *

The opening volley of the interview came, unsurprisingly, from Cameron's lawyer. Warren had led Cameron and his lawyer into the small interview room. Unexpectedly, Michael had opted to remain outside, leaving his father in the hands of his solicitor. After ensuring that the voice recorder was set up and that Sutton had read the man his rights, Warren had sat back, arms folded, and waited patiently. Cameron's solicitor had started by complaining loudly and forcefully about his client's treatment thus far.

In a two-minute diatribe he accused Warren and his officers of being on a fishing trip — of bullying Cameron into attending an interview "voluntarily" by implying arrest if he didn't do so, then making up bogus Health and Safety regulations to isolate his client from his accompanying adult.

Warren could almost see the quotation marks hanging in the air around the word "voluntarily". When he'd finished he sat back in his chair.

Warren looked over at Sutton, who appeared to be in the process of picking his nose. A gesture that couldn't be heard on the tape, it nevertheless clearly stated the officer's contempt for the alleged trampling of the suspect's rights that had just been outlined. Warren fought back a smile. Sutton had a style all of his own.

Ignoring what the solicitor had just said, Warren leant forward in his chair.

"Mr Cameron, can you tell us where you were on the evening of Friday second December?"

Cameron glanced towards his lawyer, licked his lips and mumbled, "No comment."

Warren shook his head. "Come on, Mr Cameron. The sooner you answer our questions, the sooner you can go home."

The lawyer leant forward. "May I remind the detective chief inspector that my client is here voluntarily and that he is in fact free to leave at any time. Nor is he under any obligation to say anything that may incriminate him."

Warren nodded, as if conceding the point. "Absolutely right. Until — sorry — unless we arrest Mr Cameron, he is free to leave at any time. And of course, you are right — Mr Cameron has no need to say anything that might incriminate him."

He looked back at Cameron. "Can I assume that what you might have to say is incriminating?"

The lawyer's response was swift. "No, you may not, as you well know. Failure to answer a question may not be seen as an admission of guilt."

"Of course, you are absolutely right. However, it is quite possible that if Mr Cameron can account for his whereabouts on the night in question, he might just remove himself from any suspicion."

"That is a decision that Mr Cameron has the right to decide for himself and he should not be coerced."

There remained a silence for a few seconds, before Warren pulled open an envelope. He carefully laid out several A4 photographs, face down onto the table.

"Let's try something else. Are you familiar with the travel agents Far and Away?" Again Cameron glanced at his solicitor, before shaking his head. "No comment."

"Perhaps you are familiar with one of its sales advisors, Sally Evans." A flash of recognition appeared in the older man's eyes before being carefully suppressed. "No comment."

Warren turned over the first of the photographs, a smiling Sally Evans on holiday. "Perhaps this may jog your memory?"

This time the poker face remained in place. "No comment."

"Are you sure about that? We are turning over every inch of Ms Evans' life as we speak, investigating every person who ever set foot inside that shop. It won't look good if we find out that you have visited Far and Away."

"My client has declined to answer that question and I would like it stated for the record that there are very few travel agents in Middlesbury and so it is in no way incriminating should he be familiar with the business in question or its staff."

"I accept the point. What if I were to show you a picture of how you probably saw her last." Warren turned over a picture of Evans taken before her autopsy. Cameron glanced at it and looked away, his pallor suddenly matching that of the corpse.

"Chief Inspector!" The solicitor seemed genuinely angry to Warren. "You have just accused my client of murder. What do you base that assertion on?"

Not a lot, thought Warren ruefully.

"Ms Evans was assaulted prior to her death in a manner consistent with the methods used by Mr Cameron in the late 1990s, for which he was subsequently imprisoned, before being released on licence last year."

The lawyer's eyes narrowed. He was experienced enough to know when the police had nothing substantial to go on.

"That's it? That's all you've got? I think my client is right to make no comment and he should consider terminating this interview."

"It's enough for the time being," said Warren quietly. "Should I choose to arrest Mr Cameron, we will have at least another twenty-four hours to question him, whilst we search his house and cars for more evidence."

"Is that a threat, DCI Jones? Co-operate or we'll arrest you? You're treading a very fine line here. Rest assured I will fight any attempt to serve that arrest warrant or raise a search warrant."

"I never said or implied any such thing," Warren stated calmly for the benefit of the tape; he was confident that even if the lawyer did complain, there would be a very favourable interpretation of the recording. Cameron was a convicted serial rapist; he was unlikely to evoke much sympathy.

Cameron was looking increasingly uncomfortable; finally he

leant over and whispered something in his lawyer's ear. The lawyer nodded his assent.

"My client would like to request a short break to confer in private."

Warren and Sutton were careful to maintain neutral expressions as they turned off the recording device and left the room. Glancing back, Warren felt a surge of satisfaction. Nerves were clearly getting the better of Cameron — he'd just pulled a packet of nicotine-replacement gum from his pocket.

As was his habit, Warren first turned to Sutton. "Thoughts?"

Sutton was silent for a long moment. "He's scared."

Warren nodded, waiting for more. "The question is why? Is he scared we're onto him or is he simply terrified about going back to prison? He knows that if he can't persuade us of his innocence we might charge him and he'd spend months on remand until the case came to court. I think his parole officer might be right: the guy has a severe prison phobia."

Warren agreed. "I think he's going to stop the 'no commenting' and give us something. I'd like to see if he has any sort of alibi and if it can be verified."

At that moment, the door to the interview room opened. "My client would like to resume the interview. He is prepared to co-operate with the questioning on the condition that threats to arrest him are dropped."

Warren shrugged. "I'll have to make my mind up on that score depending on what he has to say for himself."

The lawyer nodded briefly, knowing that was the best he could do.

Resuming the interview, Warren decided to ask the questions in reverse order this time. Cameron's first admission was that the name of Sally Evans and her photograph were familiar, although he swore it was only from the TV news.

His next revelation was that he was familiar with Far and Away, having visited it some weeks previously with a view to booking a short holiday to Devon in the summer. He couldn't recall who he had spoken to, whether it was Sally Evans or another sales advisor. Warren made a note to have her client database checked for any reference to Cameron. Whenever he'd gone into a travel agency, he'd found that they required a huge amount of personal information, all of which was diligently entered into the computer. He doubted that they would have deleted the data before the Data Protection Act demanded.

Finally, they got onto the subject of Cameron's whereabouts on the Friday night.

"I was at home," he mumbled.

"Doing what?"

"I was tired and I went to bed for a lie-down in the late afternoon."

"What time would this have been?"

Cameron shrugged. "I dunno. I know I watched *Countdown*, but I can't remember much else."

"How long were you asleep for?"

Again Cameron shrugged. "It was quite late when I woke up. I was surprised how long I'd been out. I reckon it could have been eight o'clock."

"Can anyone confirm this?"

"Well, Michael was home, I think. I don't think he went out. He was banging around in the kitchen when I went to sleep. When I woke up he was on the sofa watching TV."

Sutton stirred. "Rather convenient, don't you think? Sally

Evans disappears late evening and you're all tucked up in bed, with no witnesses apart from your son."

Cameron snorted, showing the first glimpse of an emotion other than nervousness since they'd met him. "Hardly. I wish I could say that I was in the local pub, surrounded by the whole fucking village at the time that this young woman was murdered. But I can't. I don't go out in the evening. I watch telly and go to bed early, ready for the next day. My son Michael starts work at six, so he's in bed early also."

Was that a hint of self-pity? wondered Warren, feeling revulsion. He could feel a similar vibe from Sutton. He fought back an unprofessional comment, remembering that the tape was running.

It was time to let him sweat a bit more, decided Warren. Calling a pause to the interview, he stepped outside with Sutton.

"Having a snooze at the same time as Evans went missing — that's about as crap an alibi as you could get. And he all but admitted that he knew her." This time Sutton didn't even wait for the customary invitation to share his thoughts.

"It's flimsy all right, but if his son confirms it we need to let him go."

"Well, there's only one way to test that. I assume that he's still in the building?"

"Should be. I asked Steve behind the desk to let me know if he left."

The young man was still present and, to Warren's surprise, he agreed immediately to a voluntary interview, without a lawyer present.

After performing all of the necessary preliminaries, Warren got straight down to business. Like his father, Michael Stockley was familiar with Far and Away travel agency, having visited it with his father recently and on his own a few years previously. However, unlike his father he professed no knowledge of Sally Evans, claiming not to recognise her name or her photograph. He explained that he was aware that a body had been found earlier in the week, but hadn't caught any recent bulletins where she was named.

When it came to his father's alibi, he was more confident. "The old man went to bed early. He was knackered after a hard day."

"What time was this?" Warren questioned.

"Probably about four-ish, maybe a bit later. He didn't reappear until about eight-ish."

"And you are certain that he was in the house all of that time — you didn't leave at all?"

"No, I made myself something to eat, then I watched some TV and read a book."

This time it was Sutton that spoke up. "Four o'clock seems a bit early to knock off, even on a Friday. What do you do?"

"Actually, I finished work at about three. I start work at 6 a.m. I'm a business manager for a logistics firm."

"And there is no way that your father could have left the house without you knowing? It's a pretty big place, with lots of doors and windows."

"Well, I suppose that you could get out without passing me in the lounge, but I know that Dad didn't."

"How can you be so sure?" asked Warren.

"Because he snores like a bloody pig and I could hear him over the TV."

THURSDAY 8ᵀᴴ DECEMBER

Chapter 19

The following morning, Jones and Sutton sat in Jones' office, discussing their interviews with Cameron and his son. As feared, they'd had to let Cameron go when his son had confirmed his alibi and they'd had no grounds to raise a search warrant. At the moment, unless he did something silly like refusing to co-operate, Jones had little to justify an arrest and even then would probably not be able to get a search warrant signed. Nevertheless, he was unwilling to dismiss the convicted rapist just yet. Sutton agreed.

"Something's not right about those two," opined Sutton as he gulped down another mouthful of coffee. "That alibi is just too bloody convenient. Plus, I've never been a big believer in these prison conversions. I don't reckon a leopard changes his spots, especially not a deviant like Cameron."

Warren nodded a cautious agreement. "I tend to agree, although I think it could happen on occasion. I would say that Cameron appears sincere about his desire to stay out of prison."

Sutton shrugged. "Well, wouldn't you?"

"Undoubtedly. The question is, would that desire make me avoid that behaviour, or would it just make me more careful? And what if I couldn't help myself? What would I do if I was caught?"

"That's what worries me. Would he evade arrest or would he try and brazen it out in court?"

"Well, if he tried the latter, he would still have the terms of his licence revoked. If he was charged, he'd go straight back inside to await trial. There's no way he'd get bail."

"So that leaves a third possibility." Sutton didn't need to spell it out. Richard Cameron could very well attempt to kill himself — the question was, would he do it quietly, or would he try and take others with him? The man was a potential powder keg, Warren realised.

"We should keep an eye on him," Sutton declared, "and, God forbid, if any other bodies turn up, he should be top of the list."

Warren nodded. "Speaking of God, Pargeter mentioned that they were both involved in the local church. He implied that Cameron confided in his local priest. I wonder if he could give any insights."

Sutton shrugged again, wearily. "It can't hurt. With no warrants we have bugger all else to go on. His priest may at least give us some more insight into the man. Maybe we'll see if our gut feeling is correct."

The sudden urge to do something galvanised Warren into action. Standing up, he looked at his watch. "I doubt the good reverend is in church at the moment. Why don't I go and pay him a visit?"

* * *

Warren threaded his car down the narrow streets of the village of Stennfield. A few moments ago, he'd passed by the gate of the farm where Cameron and his son resided. Slowing down, he'd peered up the drive; the sky was dark and overcast and although he could just make out the shape of the roof through the trees, he couldn't tell if there were any lights on in the property.

Out of habit, he'd programmed the satnav to take him to the church, but he could see that it wasn't really necessary. The village was tiny, with only one main thoroughfare. Built before the age of the motor car, the winding street was barely wide enough for Warren's Mondeo. Navigation was made harder by the double-parked cars crowding the road. Small cottages without front gardens made widening the road impossible and large warning signs had been erected at the entrance of the village diverting lorries and other large vehicles to the more accessible northern end of the village.

The church was easily visible, its small spire overshadowing the one- and two-storey buildings that made up the high street. Driving slowly, Warren passed all of the essential ingredients of a small, rural English village. Two pubs faced each other uneasily across the road, both with wooden chalkboards advertising hot food and real ale, in a benign form of one-upmanship that neither seemed to win outright. The Fighting Cock had a quiz on a Tuesday night, Warren noticed, whilst The White Bull had bingo and curry on a Thursday. Never a dull moment in Stennfield, Warren noted wryly. It wouldn't have surprised him in the least if the landlords and staff of the respective pubs crossed the road for a quiet drink at their rival's bar on their nights off — it seemed that sort of village.

The road continued past yet more cottages, some with thatched roofs, then a small village shop, its otherwise quaint appearance blighted by garish Co-op signage. Empty hanging baskets hinted at the village's recent success in the local "Britain in Bloom" competition. A little further and the road widened, then forked. To the left, another narrow street with more picture-postcard cottages led towards the church. To the right, a wider road with signs pointing towards Cambridge.

At the centre of the junction a war memorial jostled for space with a bus shelter. Three teenagers sat listlessly smoking and drinking cider in the shelter, each plugged into their own world by a pair of white headphones. None of them so much as looked up as Warren drove past.

As he turned left he could just make out the dedication on the war memorial. For such a tiny village, the Great War of 1914-1918 had swallowed up a heartbreakingly long list of names. At the base of the memorial, weather-beaten poppy wreaths remained from the previous month's Remembrance Day. Warren found himself wondering who laid the wreaths. Did they have a ceremony? Surely there could be no one left in the village who remembered those days? Maybe the other side of the monument had a plaque from the Second World War? In this part of the country, with its proliferation of nearby army barracks, it was even possible that a newer, shinier plaque might mark the bravery and sacrifice of a whole new generation of village boys, killed on the distant streets of Helmand Province or Baghdad.

Another hundred metres and Warren was pulling into the small car park that served St Martin's Parish Church. A small, grey stone building, it resembled hundreds across England. A blue, wooden sign named the Reverend Thomas Harding as its vicar and listed the times of different services throughout the week. Next to the sign, a Perspex-fronted bulletin board spoke of a busy local community, with a dozen or so brightly coloured posters competing for space.

Parking next to the only other car in sight, an ageing but well-maintained Volvo estate, Warren got out and headed up a gravelled path, past the church to the modest house that served as the vicarage.

Warren rang the doorbell and waited, the warm light shining through the glass panels in the door a pleasant antidote to the miserable weather outside. After a few moments a shadow, its details blurred by the frosted glass, appeared and the door opened.

A short, slightly plump woman Jones guessed to be in her early sixties, wearing a flowery dress and a pink cardigan, greeted him with a smile.

"Hello, I'm Beverly Harding. My husband is on the phone at the moment. You must be Mr Jones."

After checking his warrant card, Mrs Harding led him over the threshold into the hallway. Straight ahead, Warren could see a dining room through a partly open set of wooden doors; to the left and the right, two more doors. The one on the right had a small wooden sign reading "Parish Meeting Room". As he followed the vicar's wife into the meeting room Warren glanced to his left and caught a brief glimpse of a modern-looking living room, with a large flat-screen TV and comfortable-looking leather sofas. In the middle of the room stood a tall, spare man, with a cordless phone pressed against his ear. Spotting Warren, he raised a hand in greeting, mouthing a silent apology.

The meeting room reminded Warren of the small space in the priest's house where he would sometimes help his grandparents count the church collection when it was their turn on the rota to do so. Stacked chairs, piles of prayer books and hymnals, even a dusty old desktop PC with a bulky-looking inkjet printer. That had been some years ago, he realised.

"Would you like a cup of tea, Detective?" asked Mrs Harding. Despite having put away several cups of coffee that morning already, the suggestion suddenly made Warren thirsty. A cup of refreshing tea might make a pleasant change, he decided.

As the vicar's wife left he noticed she was wearing slippers. She was probably relaxing in front of the TV when he turned up, but a vicar's wife was on call almost as much as her husband.

To be honest, he didn't know what to make of Mrs Harding. As a Catholic, Warren had never really met a vicar's wife and, although he disagreed with the church's demand that priests remain celibate, he also found it hard to imagine the priests of his childhood dating a woman or, God forbid, enjoying a sex life.

Deciding that the line of thought was inappropriate, he switched his attention to the bookcase. In amongst the various learned religious texts, volumes of prayers, suggestions for sermons and practical guides to dealing with the bereaved or marriage counselling, he was surprised to find a whole section on A level and GCSE physics, including what he recognised from Susan's bookcase as the latest version of a popular GCSE science textbook.

Did these belong to his children? Warren had noticed the framed pictures of two young people, a man and a woman, in different graduation gowns, smiling above the mantelpiece. But that didn't make sense. Both young people were beyond school age and would have no need for such an up-to-date secondary-school-level textbook. And unless the photos were a lot older than they appeared to be, neither subject appeared old enough to have a GCSE-age child at home.

"I'm sorry about that, Officer." Warren had been so engrossed that he hadn't heard the Reverend Harding enter the room.

Turning, Warren saw that the man still had the cordless phone in his hand. "One of my congregation is getting married on Saturday. A few last-minute nerves. I calmed her down though." He smiled, before cradling the phone and offering a hand. As Warren shook the proffered hand, the priest noticed what Warren had been looking at. "Remnants of my past life." He gestured at the bookcase. "I was an A level physics teacher for many years, before leaving and becoming a priest."

He chuckled at Warren's surprised look. "I get that reaction a lot."

"Not that long ago, it seems; if I'm not mistaken one of those revision guides is for the latest GCSE syllabus. My wife is a science teacher," Warren offered by way of an explanation.

"That's right. I still love physics and do a little teaching and tutoring for some of the local kids. Extra tuition for struggling students is largely the preserve of those with wealthy parents, I'm afraid, especially these days, so I do what I can to help those who can't afford it. I also mark A-level exam scripts for one of the exam boards. The money it pays helps fund a village school in Malawi that my old comprehensive used to have links with."

You really did meet all sorts in this job, thought Warren, not for the first time, as the vicar led him into the lounge.

Settling himself down on a leather couch, Warren waited whilst Mrs Harding served him from a teapot in a plain white china teacup. He looked around the room, marveling again at the ordinariness of it. Despite having accompanied his grandparents to his local priest's house many times, Warren had always been surprised by how normal priests really were. He remembered the first time he'd gone to the local Catholic club on a Saturday afternoon for a pint and seen two elderly priests, both with their dog collars concealed by Coventry City scarves, sipping Guinness and shouting at the match on the pub's big screen.

"Well, Detective, what can I help you with? You said on the phone that you wanted a chat about one of my parishioners."

Warren placed his teacup carefully on the saucer. "Yes. Richard Cameron and his son Michael."

The priest seemed unsurprised. "I suspected as much. The congregation is pretty small here and so when I read about that poor young woman in the newspaper, it didn't take much to work out who you wanted to talk about."

"So you are aware of Mr Cameron's past?"

"Yes, I'm afraid so. I joined the parish about twelve months before those terrible events. When Richard came out of prison last year, he rejoined the congregation."

"And how did you feel about that, Father? Sorry, Reverend."

"It's OK, you can call me Father if you prefer, I don't mind." He paused, clearly choosing his words carefully. "I would be a liar if I said I didn't have a few misgivings. What he did left deep scars on this community. Although none of the young women were particularly regular church-goers this is a small village and it affected my congregation greatly. They've all left the parish now. Two left within twelve months of their ordeal, the third stayed and tried to make a life, but left a few months before Richard was released.

"Victims of rape are afforded anonymity under the law, of course, but that's meaningless in a small community like this. Everybody knew who they were and what had happened. The two ladies that left both said they couldn't move on whilst living in a village where everybody looked at them with sympathy. The third young lady stayed with her family and managed to put back the pieces of her life — but she couldn't face the thought that she might bump into him one day.

"What that man did had repercussions far beyond the lives of his victims. Whole families were torn apart. The heart of the village was for ever changed." Warren could see in the man's eyes the pain and sorrow he was feeling. Evil had come to this tiny part of England and the aftermath had changed them all for ever.

"So how did you feel when Mr Cameron started attending your church again?"

The priest paused, blowing on his tea as if to cool it, although it had long since become comfortable to drink. "I would be lying if I said that I welcomed him with open arms at first. But Jesus preaches that we should forgive sins, especially if the sinner is truly remorseful."

"And is he remorseful, do you think?" Warren watched him carefully. The priest nodded firmly. "Yes. I believe that his regret is genuine. He knows that what he did can never be undone and he has never asked me for absolution. I think he knows that I would not be able to give it." The priest looked relieved.

"How did the village react?"

"Not well. For the first few months graffiti regularly appeared on his house walls and unmentionable material was posted through his letter box and smeared around his car door handles late at night. I don't think that he or his son have set foot in either of the village pubs since his release and Michael does most of their shopping. They attend the much quieter 9 a.m. Sunday service and sit at the back. Even so, numbers are a fraction what they used to be, with some switching to the later 11 a.m. and many simply stopping coming."

"We have talked to Mr Cameron's probation officer and he

suggested that you spoke to him and counselled him." The statement was an invitation.

"Ah, yes, Mr Pargeter. An interesting fellow, to be sure. You don't meet his sort very often. More's the pity."

Warren chose his words carefully. "We're trying to build up a picture of what Mr Cameron is like. I realise that anything that is said within the confessional booth is regarded as sacrosanct, but we would be interested in any insights that you may have into Mr Cameron's character and what he is like."

The priest waved a hand dismissively. "First of all, Detective, you need not concern yourself with notions of confidentiality. We do not as a rule offer the sacrament of penance as Catholics understand it. You are free to hear anything that Richard and I have discussed. In fact, I have had several conversations with Mr Cameron. I regard my role as helping him rebuild his life, helping him to slay or at least resist the demons that plague him. Both for him and the greater good."

"And does he have these demons still?"

The priest gave a cautious nod. "I would say so. As I said before, he is truly remorseful for his past actions — I would even go as far as to say he deeply regrets the harm that he has caused to those poor young women, this village and his own family. Nevertheless, those desires run deep in a man. I don't know if he will ever truly be free of them or if he will simply learn to live with them and not act upon them."

"In your opinion, do you think that Mr Cameron is in control of those demons?"

The priest thought carefully before answering. "In my opinion… yes. I think so, although I must hasten to add that he has fooled those who thought they knew him before. After his first attack, he reportedly sought advice from another local vicar, but was careful enough to make it sound as though he was merely troubled by dreams and fantasies. This priest advised him not to worry, that fantasies are normal as long as they are not acted upon, and advised him to pray for forgiveness and strength. In retrospect, he should have suggested professional counselling and perhaps even contacted the police. He retired shortly afterward, unable to forgive himself for not making the connection between Richard's admission and the rapes." The priest's face was a complex mixture of emotions.

"Does Cameron seem a changed man to you?"

The priest looked apologetic. "That I can't say, I'm afraid. Although his wife was a regular church-goer and she usually brought their son, he rarely attended other than feast days. He tended to spend Sunday in The Fighting Cock, before driving back to the farm. How he didn't kill anyone I'll never know. He was well known for having a nasty temper when he was drunk and, although I've never been told directly, there was a clear implication that he may have taken this out on his wife and perhaps their son."

"Speaking of their son, what do you know about him? He appears to be standing by his father, despite all that has happened."

The priest's demeanour brightened considerably. "Yes, Michael is a remarkable young man in that respect. When it emerged what his father had done, both he and his mother severed all contact with him. Angie divorced him and they both changed their names to Stockley, her maiden name. Richard didn't contest the divorce and signed over the deeds of the farm without protest.

"Michael was in year eleven at the time, barely sixteen years old. The villagers, I'm pleased to say, were surprisingly supportive of the two of them, but, of course, schoolchildren can be cruel and it was decided that it would be best if Michael left Middlesbury and went to Cambridge for his sixth-form studies. I wrote a letter to Long Road Sixth Form College on his behalf and they were kind enough to take him on, even though the stress had resulted in far weaker GCSE results than he was capable of."

"What happened then?"

"I only had intermittent contact with him for the next few years. Angie continued to come to church, but Michael — or Micky as he liked to be known then — moved away to university. It broke his mother's heart, but she understood his reasons. He needed to get away from his father's shadow."

"So how did he come to be living with his father again after he left prison?"

"Just before what would have been his final year at university, his mother was diagnosed with lung cancer. The illness was mercifully short, but it affected Michael greatly and I believe he had some counselling. He finally got himself back on track and completed his studies a year later. He now owned the farm, of course, but it was very run-down and wasn't worth very much, so, rather than sell it, he decided to move back here.

"I think it's fair to say that he has never really fitted fully into village life. He still feels tainted by his father's actions and the farm is a little distance away. However, he has a good job and he eventually started coming to church again. That's when we started to have our meetings."

Warren motioned for him to go on, suddenly interested. "What were they about, if I may ask?"

The priest looked a little uncomfortable and started fussing with the teapot, clearly deciding how much to say.

"He was understandably a rather troubled young man. He blamed his father for the death of his mother and had clearly never really forgiven him for making him leave first his school, then later Stennfield. He admitted to me that although the villagers were accommodating enough, he always felt he would be the 'rapist's son' first and Michael Stockley second. He even worried that his father might have passed down something in his genes. Ultimately, I realised that what he needed to do was to confront his fears and to visit his father in prison to clear the air, so to speak. The first time he went, I drove him there, although I didn't go in.

"Pretty soon the visits became quite regular and Micky became more forgiving of him. He was still in his early twenties then and I think that the death of his mother had made him realise that Richard was his only real family.

"Although he has never said as much, I think that his decision to help his father, rather than abandon him, was a way for him to help remove the stain on his family's honour."

Warren nodded thoughtfully as he sat back; the priest had left him with a lot to think about. One final question remained.

"In your opinion and in strictest confidence, do you think Richard Cameron is capable of having raped and murdered this young woman?"

The priest sat back in his chair slowly. This time he didn't fiddle with a teacup or otherwise try to bide time; he just sat there thinking. Finally, he said, "I don't think so. First of all, he never killed his other victims. What he did was terrible, but he never crossed that final line. Furthermore, he is terrified of prison. Even though he was on the sex-offenders wing of the prison, he was regularly abused by other prisoners and even, he claims, the guards. He attempted suicide several times. I genuinely don't think that he would chance prison again. I fear that he might even try to take his own life if he thought that he was in danger of returning."

The priest leant forward, his eyes imploring. "Please remember that, Detective. No matter what he has done in the past, don't leave him feeling under threat of prison as you conduct your investigation. He is a very fragile individual. If you find that he has committed this awful crime, then throw away the key — until then please treat him with care."

* * *

Warren sat in his car, thinking over what he'd just heard. Something wasn't right. On the face of it, Cameron seemed an unlikely suspect. He had two very strong character references and an alibi. Furthermore, he had seemed genuinely scared about prison.

But on the flip side, the MO fitted perfectly and it was a hell of a coincidence that Cameron should be released and free in the same area as these attacks that used his old method. And, of course, if it was Cameron, then it was probably a stranger killing and Warren still thought of those as the exception rather than the rule.

So where did that leave them? The two next likeliest suspects both had some history of offending and both could be seen as having a motive. Again, Warren felt himself drawn back to the statistic that most murders were committed by people known to the victim.

* * *

Back at the station, time seemed to have slowed down to a crawl. Now that the exciting, obvious leads had dried up, it was down to basics and good old-fashioned detective work. After a brainstorming meeting with the team, Warren divided the detectives into smaller groups and assigned each of them specific tasks.

Sally Evans' father, Bill Evans, was not yet out of the frame and so DC Willis and DS Johnson continued trying to track down his clandestine lover and verify his alibi. A small team from Traffic continued to study CCTV footage from around Far and Away. Now that a witness had confirmed that Blackheath's distinctive car was outside the couple's flat at the time of the murder, corroborating his story, he was no longer of interest to the team. However, Evans had disappeared during rush hour and the local surveillance and traffic cameras had picked up literally hundreds of different vehicles during the short window during which she was believed to have disappeared. With no direct coverage of the alleyway that Evans had been waiting in, the team was undertaking the tedious task of trying to piece together each vehicle's journey from the many different cameras in the surrounding area, working out which of them would be realistically capable of kidnapping Evans from outside the rear entrance to her workplace.

Following Warren's belief that stranger killings were the exception rather than the rule, most of the rest of the team were busy turning Sally Evans' life upside down. Friends, family, co-workers, ex-boyfriends, former neighbours, other students from her university days, all of them were scrutinised, sometimes even contacted.

In the meantime, Richard Cameron's world was also probed. Everything the police and CPS had on the man from his original convictions, as well as more recent information gathered by the probation service, was scrutinised. The team looked for a link, no matter how small, between Cameron and Sally Evans.

By early evening, Warren could feel the enthusiasm in the office starting to wane as the team hit more and more dead ends. A phone call to Welwyn confirmed that it would be the next day before a report detailing the first results from the numerous outstanding forensic investigations was available. Warren tried to put a positive spin on it, by telling the investigators that what they were doing at that moment was preparing the ground so that they could act upon the next day's evidence, but even to his ears it sounded like a meaningless platitude.

As he drove home that night, Warren felt low and dejected. Sally Evans had been killed almost a week ago and the investigation was already starting to lose momentum. The case needed an injection of something game-changing; it needed some sort of breakthrough, but at the moment Warren couldn't see where that was going to come from. He grimaced in distaste, knowing what Detective Superintendent Grayson would suggest: A press conference.

Chapter 20

As Warren settled down in front of the TV with a glass of beer and brooded, on the other side of town Carolyn Patterson decided to take advantage of the relatively mild weather and walk the mile home from her weekly boxercise class. It was the last session before Christmas and Carolyn was feeling a little guilty. With the festive season approaching, she'd vowed not to put on any weight, in preparation for her younger sister's forthcoming wedding. She knew of course that on the big day all eyes would be on the bride; nevertheless, the beautiful bridesmaid's dress hanging in her wardrobe was still a little too tight and she had no intention of appearing bloated in the wedding photos. She was maid of honour, newly single and determined that she was going to make an entrance that every single man in the room would remember.

She'd been doing really well, up until tonight when the pre-Christmas atmosphere had meant that her normal post-exercise glass of wine with the girls from class had somehow become three. This had then been followed by a slice of the fantastic chocolate cake on offer behind the sports centre's bar. She pouted at the memory. It was hardly fair, she thought, offering such eye-catching treats to people who'd just spent an hour exercising — it was like shooting fish in a barrel.

Not only did they make a huge amount of money from charging three pounds a slice, they also ensured a return visit to their facilities by guilt-ridden dieters desperate to atone for their moment of weakness. With that in mind, she decided that her New Year's resolution would be to bring a banana and a bottle of water with her to class and to steer clear of the centre's bar. At least until after the wedding.

Pulling her collar up to shield her face from the slight breeze and setting her iPod to shuffle, she set off towards her flat at a determined march. A fifteen-minute walk home, even at a brisk pace, wasn't nearly enough to compensate for three glasses of sweet white wine and a slab of double-chocolate cake, oozing with chocolate icing, but it was a start, she decided. Tomorrow was her day off and she was planning on doing some Christmas shopping; if she walked into town instead of catching the bus and went for a swim at lunchtime, then maybe tonight wouldn't be a complete disaster.

As she strode along the darkened side street connecting the main road housing Middlesbury Sports and Leisure Centre to the busy thoroughfare that led eventually to her housing estate, she was suddenly bathed in the bright white lights of a vehicle behind her. Glancing over her shoulder, she was a little surprised; it was unusual to see one at this time of night. Then she remembered that she was walking home at least an hour later than usual.

Mentally dismissing it, she turned her attention back to her music. Lady Gaga was describing how she was stuck in a bad romance. Carolyn smiled to herself; twelve months ago she could have related. All over now though, she thought. She'd finally seen sense and given that creep the boot. It would be the first Christmas she had celebrated on her own in four years. As daunting as that was, it would also be the first New Year's Eve and who knew what might happen as Big Ben rang out?

Turning the music up slightly, she fought the urge to sing along. Steady on, girl, she admonished herself. She didn't want to wake the neighbours up!

The song ended and she realised that the glowing lights behind her had stopped moving some time ago, yet in the silence before the next track started she could still hear the growl of the engine.

It was the sudden change in her pace as she turned instinctively that threw her attacker off balance. She caught a glimpse of the man as he stumbled past. He was dressed in a dark hoodie with the lower half of his face covered in a scarf; the rest of his face looked strangely rubbery in the gloomy glow of a distant streetlight.

Time seemed to slow for Carolyn, her senses taking in information from all directions. The rational part of her brain had no idea what was going on; the next song on her iPod had started, distracting her. Fight or flight? The question that would for ever seal her fate. Adrenaline surged around her body and her muscles tensed. Her attacker had recovered quickly and he turned on the spot. In his hand he held what seemed to be a white cloth. Carolyn's nostrils flared at the pungent, chemical smell.

Chocolate cake and Riesling notwithstanding, Carolyn was a fit woman in her twenties. She was wearing training shoes and still dressed in her loose, casual gym clothes. If she'd chosen flight, she might well have made it to the well-lit main road before her attacker. Would he have followed? Disguised as he was, he might have chosen to risk exposure by bringing her down and dragging her back into the murky shadows. More likely, he would have given up, slinking away, back into the darkness.

Neither of them would ever know.

After an hour spent hitting punchbags in the gym, Carolyn followed her instincts and struck out at her assailant. It was a good blow, her fist catching him squarely on the jaw, rocking him backward. He had yet to get his feet under him and for a moment his arms pin-wheeled as he stumbled backwards off the kerb.

Had she turned and run at this point, she might still have made it to safety. Unfortunately, there was one thing that they neglected to tell you in boxercise classes: hitting somebody hurt — and hitting somebody on the jaw really hard hurt even more. Carolyn felt as though she had shattered every bone in her hand. Not even alcohol and adrenaline could mask the pain. The shock was so unexpected, she just stood there.

And then he hit back. A short, vicious jab to the abdomen that drove the air from her lungs. Carolyn doubled up in pain, gasping as her diaphragm spasmed. With no air she couldn't make so much as a squeak, let alone scream for help. And she was powerless to resist as the white cloth was forced over her face. Whatever chemical the cloth had been soaked in smelt oddly sweet. She clawed wildly at the cloth as the portion of her mind still working rationally warned her not to breathe, to hold her breath, to avoid inhaling the toxic fumes. But it was useless; her lungs weren't listening. With a choking sob, she finally drew breath. Immediately, she started to feel light-headed and the rushing noise in her ears grew louder and louder. A wave of nausea passed over her for a brief second, before finally the world started fading away, even the pain in her fist becoming muted. Her last thought before everything finally disappeared was one of sadness. *I'm going to miss your wedding, little sis...*

FRIDAY 9TH AND SATURDAY 10TH DECEMBER

Chapter 21

The next two days passed slowly, filling Warren with a sense of mounting frustration. One by one potential leads petered out. His team made endless phone calls and arranged countless interviews with Sally Evans' acquaintances, both old and new. Each person contacted had an alibi and none of them could suggest a reason why the apparently popular young woman had been killed.

As he'd predicted, Detective Superintendent Grayson had recommended enlisting the help of the public and on Friday evening called another press conference to update the media with the progress so far, including an account of Sally Evans' last known movements and a detailed description of what she had been wearing that day. He also confirmed that she had been raped; an indisputable fact that needed to be part of the public record, but also one that might just engender enough revulsion in somebody protecting the perpetrator to step forward.

With the case now several days old, it had slipped down the news agenda somewhat and so the conference was more of a briefing and recorded footage of the event didn't make it any further than the local, late-night news. The next day's newspapers chose to use stock photos of Sally Evans and the spot where she had been found, rather than Superintendent Grayson in his dress uniform with Warren sitting uncomfortably beside him.

There was limited success to the appeal, the most promising call from a worker in the building next door to Far and Away, who claimed to have seen Sally being picked up by Darren Blackheath the evening she disappeared. Unfortunately, deeper questioning revealed that the well-meaning member of the public had got his dates confused and was describing the previous evening. At least it confirmed that Darren Blackheath did regularly pick her up.

There was also a full confession; however, Caller ID had identified the phone used as that of a local crank who over the years had confessed to everything from shoplifting to 9/11. His inability to describe Sally Evans' hair colour, despite her photo being splashed everywhere, ruled him out in seconds.

So far, the team was left with three possibilities: her father, Richard Cameron or a complete stranger.

Something wasn't quite right about Bill Evans, Warren felt. As yet, no evidence of the existence of his clandestine lover had been uncovered. The dating site, run by an overseas company, was reluctant to disclose any details to the team and so Welwyn's legal experts were busy drafting a case for court orders; unfortunately, the mobile phone number was an anonymous Pay As You Go.

Late on Friday, forensic analysis of Bill Evans' car came back. As expected, evidence existed of Sally Evans' presence in the vehicle — particularly the passenger seat, but nothing in the boot nor any traces of blood. The results were consistent with Bill Evans' story about meeting Sally the day before her disappearance. In addition, the team working the traffic cameras had placed Bill Evans' car near to Sally Evans' workplace at lunchtime the day before her disappearance. The lack of cameras immediately adjacent to the scene meant that they couldn't say with certainty that he'd met her there, but it was a reasonable explanation.

None of the evidence so far ruled out Bill Evans as a suspect — but then, as Warren had pointed out to his team on more than one occasion, it was up to the police to provide evidence in favour of his guilt; it wasn't up to him to provide evidence for his innocence.

Richard Cameron was proving difficult to rule out or in. The only leads that the police had to go on were the similarity of Sally Evans' attack to Cameron's attacks over a decade before, plus the huge coincidence that he had only recently been released from prison into the immediate area. The Crown Prosecution Service would laugh Warren out of the room if he tried to raise an arrest warrant and charge Cameron based on such flimsy evidence. They'd argue, quite rightly, that one couldn't really claim that a similar *lack* of forensic evidence in two cases was as strong a link between the crimes as finding similar positive evidence at both scenes.

Furthermore, the first argument about similar methods could equally well apply to the other two, unrelated, unsolved attacks in Reading and Bristol. He'd had long conference calls with both local forces about what was known and they had agreed to send their files over for him to examine.

It was looking increasingly likely to Warren that the murder was a random, stranger killing. The hardest kind to solve. Reasoning that Sally Evans almost certainly must have been removed from the scene in some sort of vehicle, it was decided to increase attention on the CCTV surrounding the alleyway. Assuming that she was taken within the fifteen-minute window between her leaving work and Darren Blackheath arriving to pick her up, a total of one hundred and fifty-four different vehicles had been identified as within the vicinity. This rather daunting number had been whittled down to a more manageable forty-eight, when each vehicle's possible routes and timings through the camera-free zones were calculated and the practicalities of them being involved in Sally Evans' kidnap determined.

Nevertheless, the number soon grew in size again when it was decided that if the killer knew Sally Evans' routine, he or she must have observed her on previous days. If he did so on foot, then Warren knew that the likelihood of identifying him amongst the tens of thousands of commuters caught on CCTV in that area was next to zero. Furthermore, as it was during the 6 p.m. rush hour, it was likely that many of the same faces would crop up time and time again on different days, making patterns difficult to spot. The same argument could be made about cars, Warren supposed, but he still instructed the team to go back over the previous fortnight's recordings to look for any suspicious vehicles. It would be a long, slow slog and Warren wasn't expecting results any time soon.

* * *

It was late Saturday afternoon when the investigation took an unexpected and unwanted twist. Warren and Tony Sutton were in Warren's office drinking coffee and rehashing what little facts they had for the umpteenth time. There was a knock at the door and Gary Hastings entered. The younger officer looked annoyed and embarrassed at the same time. Warren could feel the bad news hanging in the air. Sutton looked up expectantly. "Spill it, son, no point waiting."

"It's Blackheath, sir. He might not have been parked outside his house that night when he said he was."

"What do you mean?" asked Sutton in surprise. "We have an eyewitness. Bloke across the road. Let's face it, it's not the most subtle of cars. Surely, you'd know if the Twat-Mobile was parked opposite your house."

"Well, none of the other neighbours can remember if they saw it or not."

"So what's he done — changed his statement?"

Hastings looked embarrassed, although it surely wasn't his fault; he only processed the information.

"We've just had the witness' daughter on the phone. She visited her old man this morning to find him talking excitedly about the visit he'd had from the police. Turns out the old boy has Alzheimer's. He seems quite lucid when you first meet him, chats nineteen-to-the-dozen, but he's hopeless with dates and times."

"Shit!" Sutton threw his pen down in disgust.

"Can we verify what his daughter claims? Is his memory as bad as she says it is?" Warren was clutching at straws and he knew it.

Hastings nodded glumly. "That wife he was supposed to be picking up from bingo has been dead three years — and the venue became a Wetherspoon's pub eighteen months ago. The daughter had to come pick him up that evening after she got a call from one of the door staff who realised he was confused, not drunk, and did the decent thing. Neither of them were in a position to comment on whether Darren Blackheath was parked outside his flat at the time Sally Evans was being raped and killed."

Warren put his head in his hands with a loud groan. "You know what this means, don't you?"

"Yeah, we have to start all over again with Blackheath." The three men were silent for a few moments, contemplating the new twist.

"Do you think he could be guilty?" asked Hastings. "Up to now, you've seemed pretty certain he's innocent."

Warren exhaled loudly, before shaking his head. "At this point, Gary, I just don't know."

He glanced at his watch. "What I do know is that it's getting late and I've had enough. My brain has turned to sponge. I'm going home. I'll be back in tomorrow."

Chapter 22

The call came at 7 p.m. as Warren and Susan were just settling down in front of the TV with a takeaway curry and a DVD. After such a frustrating day, Warren needed to relax for a few hours with his wife. He knew from experience that he required at least a few hours' distraction and a good night's sleep to let his subconscious chew over events and come up with new strategies in the morning.

Susan had spent a rather more productive day, having decided that she wanted to shift as much of her marking pile as possible before the Christmas holidays — not least because she would be taking in a new pile of coursework next week for marking over the break — and she was now tired and hungry.

The couple looked at each other for a few long seconds, before Warren sighed and fished the phone off the arm of the settee. He glanced at the screen and all thoughts of a lazy evening evaporated. Reading his expression, Susan tried to look supportive as she placed the cardboard lid back on Warren's Chicken Jalfrezi and carried it out into the kitchen, giving him some privacy. By the time she'd replaced the cork in the unpoured wine, Warren was in the hallway, phone pressed to his ear as he wrestled his heavy-duty, insulated coat on.

Susan didn't need to hear both ends of the conversation to work out what was being said; the grim cast of Warren's face told her everything. Finally he hung up and turned to Susan.

"Go," she ordered before he could say anything. "It can't be helped. Your dinner will be in the fridge. If you return at a decent hour, we'll have a late-night snack together."

Warren leant over and kissed her on the lips. "I'm so sorry, sweetheart. I'll call as soon as I'm able and let you know what time I'll be back."

With that, he finished zipping up his coat, slipped his boots on and stepped out into the dark.

Susan stood at the window and watched as Warren pulled away from the kerb, his headlights illuminating a few lazy snowflakes. She looked over at the DVD sitting in its rental case, a comedy that they'd both wanted to see for a while. A few months previously, they'd got as far as the cinema queue when Warren's mobile had rung and they'd had to get back in the car.

For a brief moment she was tempted to sit down and watch the damn thing now and tell Warren the ending whenever he got back from wherever he'd been called to... But no, the film was something that both of them wanted to see and she was determined that they'd see it together, even if it meant watching it on catch-up TV in twelve months' time.

Flicking on the television, she skimmed the channels, seeing that at this time on a Saturday night the schedules were wall-to-wall rubbish, nothing but talent and game shows. With a sigh, she turned it off, walked back over to the dining-room table and picked up her red pen.

* * *

This time, the woods were on the opposite side of Middlesbury; nevertheless, Warren felt a strong sense of déjà vu as his car slowly bounced along the dirt track. As usual it seemed that Tony Sutton had been the senior on-call officer when the body had been found and he had been the one to phone Warren. One of these days, Warren vowed, it would be his turn to call Sutton out of his nice warm house to some godforsaken corner of Hertfordshire in sub-zero temperatures.

The scene as Warren parked up was depressingly familiar: to his left was Sutton's Audi, to his right a patrol car and a SOCO van. It had been barely five days since Warren had been through this exact same routine when Sally Evans' body had been found and already the connections were disturbing. Two bodies, less than a week apart. He shuddered; was it a coincidence or was there a predator operating around Middlesbury?

After showing his warrant card to the young female constable logging visitors, he pulled on his white paper suit, grabbed his torch and followed the directions to the site where the body had been found.

This time, the dumping spot was barely inside a thick, wooded area bordering a barren field, the portable field lights clearly visible. The poor weather had turned the soil into a boggy marshland and Warren found himself alternately slipping and sticking as he navigated the treacherous ground, carefully following the police tape to make sure that his footprints didn't obscure any left by the killer. It was good procedure, but Warren doubted there would be much to find. The rain had almost certainly obliterated any impressions; realistically their best hope lay in the area around the body, sheltered as it was by the trees.

Finally, he reached the forensics team and Sutton, who were

standing on plastic boards that allowed them to move around without disturbing the scene. They also reduced the likelihood of slipping over on the slimy mud, although the dark stain that covered the back of Sutton's white suit suggested that he'd taken at least one tumble.

As usual in this area of Hertfordshire, Andy Harrison was the Crime Scene Manager and he greeted Warren with a wave, before turning back to what Warren assumed was the body. Seeing the arrival of his boss, Tony Sutton carefully moved along the plastic walkway to greet him. This time, neither man joked about their appearance. Two bodies in less than a week hinted at something neither man wanted to contemplate. Even Andy Harrison appeared subdued as he busied himself with a digital camera.

"What have we got, Tony?"

"It's like I said on the phone. A lone body, female, probably in her late twenties. She's been here a couple of days at least, found by a group of teenagers doing a Duke of Edinburgh night hike."

"Where are they now?"

"Andy took their boots off them to examine for trace and we sent them back to the station to make a statement. Fortunately, as soon as they realised what they'd found, they freaked out and stayed well away, so the scene hasn't been compromised." He shook his head. "Poor kids, they were putting on a brave face, especially the lads, but you could tell they were pretty upset by the whole thing."

Warren nodded soberly. Finding a dead body was distressing for anybody. He could only imagine what effect it would have on a group of teenagers, out in the woods on their own. He suspected that at least a few of them would not be completing their training.

"Let's get it over with, then."

Sutton nodded, taking the lead again although it was hardly necessary, since they were barely thirty metres from the edge of the cordoned-off crime scene. The plastic boards shifted and creaked under the two men's weight, but held firm.

The woman was dressed in what appeared to be a sports jacket over a dark blue tracksuit. Her trousers and knickers were pulled down to her knees and her T-shirt had been roughly pulled over her head. Her sports bra had been pulled up, exposing her breasts. A scarf was tied tightly around her neck. Even in the artificial glare of the lighting rig Warren could see that she had once been an attractive young woman, with long, curly dark blonde hair and a pretty face. Her body was well toned and she had clearly been fit.

Looking away from the poor woman, he addressed Andy Harrison.

"What have we got, Andy?"

"On the surface, at least, it's similar to last time. A young woman, probably mid-to-late twenties. Possibly raped; almost certainly throttled with her own scarf."

"How long do you think?"

"A couple of days at least, but anything more accurate would be a guess at this stage."

"What about the scene — footprints? Tyre tracks? If it's anything like the last time, she was dumped here."

Harrison raised a calming hand; he could sense Jones' frustration. "All in good time, Chief. It's early days yet. You start trying to identify her back at the station — leave us to sweep the scene. If there's anything here we'll find it." He looked at his watch. "We'll get a preliminary report to you before midday tomorrow."

Warren took a few deep breaths; the man was correct. It was

early days and there was nothing to be gained by rushing the CSI team.

"You're right, of course, Andy. We'll get out of your hair and let you get on with your job."

As they trudged carefully back to their cars Sutton and Jones talked over the evening's find.

"I'm worried, guv. That killing's a little too like last week's for comfort."

Warren agreed. "They're close together as well. If Andy Harrison is right with the timing we're looking at less than a week. Either the killer has some sort of plan or timetable that they are following or they've developed a taste for it and aren't fully in control."

"Either of which suggests that we could be looking at more bodies and sooner rather than later."

SUNDAY 11TH DECEMBER

Chapter 23

Warren was awoken by a combination of the alarm on his mobile phone and a nagging feeling of indigestion. By the time he'd returned to the station, interviewed the teenagers who found the body and started the ball rolling on the murder investigation it had been well into the early hours of the morning.

He'd arrived home to find Susan had gone to bed some hours before. He'd been tempted to slip into bed beside her so he could at least awake beside her — Sunday mornings were often the only time the couple had anything approaching a lie-in together — but he'd decided it wasn't fair on her. He was planning to be in the office early and he'd been reluctant to disturb her unnecessarily.

After a hot shower to chase away the cobwebs and a careful and precise shave, Warren returned to the spare room, which conveniently doubled as the couple's wardrobe, and put on his most sombre suit and a black tie. No identification had yet been made of the young woman but, when it was, Warren was going to accompany the family liaison officers when they broke the news later that morning. It was a job that Warren absolutely hated; however, he wanted to see the reaction of the family for himself. As always, the odds were that the killer was a close acquaintance of the victim and Warren wanted to see the response of those acquaintances up close.

Walking downstairs, Warren was very pleasantly surprised to see Susan, yawning in her dressing gown and pouring coffee. A moment later the toaster popped up. Crossing the kitchen, he kissed her on the forehead. "You didn't have to get up so early. You deserve a lie-in."

"I know — that's why I'll be returning to bed with a good book as soon as you've gone. But I couldn't let you go to work on a Sunday with an empty stomach. Don't forget the canteen is closed — why don't you take that curry and reheat it?" Susan obviously hadn't opened the kitchen bin yet that morning. Seeing Warren's guilty expression, she looked around the kitchen, noting the lack of dirty dishes. Opening the refrigerator, she made a face.

"Well, unless you've taken to washing up in the early hours of the morning, you didn't place the curry on a plate, those tin-foil containers can't be microwaved and I doubt you heated the oven up at that time. From that I can only deduce, Detective Chief Inspector, that you ate the Chicken Jalfrezi cold. Am I right?"

Warren nodded, sheepishly.

"You are so gross. I hope you have indigestion."

* * *

CID was buzzing when Warren arrived at seven-thirty. The first order of the day was to confirm the identity of the victim. A photograph of the young woman was displayed on the far wall. He called the team into the briefing room.

"What have we got?" he asked a tired-looking DS Khan, who was due to go off shift.

"Nothing yet. We're going through the missing persons database as we speak. She certainly hasn't been reported missing locally or recently. We managed to get at least a couple of clear fingerprints off her body, but she isn't coming up on the computer, so she hasn't been convicted of anything."

"Any other ID?"

"No, she was travelling light. From the way she was dressed we think that she had probably been to the gym or an exercise class. She had no wallet on her, just a few pounds in her coat pocket and some house keys. She wasn't carrying a phone — or if she was it was taken by her attacker. Her iPod has no user information on it, not even an iTunes account. We found no bag with her. Unfortunately, her clothes are pretty much off the peg, nothing unusual."

"Sounds as if it's going to be dental records, then. When is the PM scheduled?"

"Mid-afternoon. We should have her ID by late tomorrow."

Warren sighed. "That's a long wait. The sooner we identify who she is, the sooner we can start investigating properly. Let's see what else we can use to identify her."

"If she'd been to the gym, she might have had a bag, you know, with a towel and that. We should see what's been handed in. We might get lucky and find her wallet."

"Good idea, Mo, but that assumes that she went to a sports centre. If she just went out for a jog, she might only have needed her house keys, iPod and perhaps a few quid for a drink afterwards." Warren paused thoughtfully. "I wonder if Forensics could tell us whether she had been running or exercising in a gym? They might be able to tell from the scuffs on her shoes. We should also ask the coroner to check if she had showered recently or not. That might tell us if we are looking for a bag."

"We could start showing her photograph around local gyms, see if anyone recognises her," suggested Gary Hastings helpfully. Tony Sutton, who had just appeared, still dressed in his thick overcoat, shook his head firmly.

"Let's not get too far ahead of ourselves. First of all, we don't know that she went to a gym, second, do you know how many gyms or similar venues there are in Middlesbury?"

Visibly chastened, Hastings shook his head.

"Me neither, but I'll bet it's a lot. And that assumes she was local. She could have been snatched off the street in Cambridge or Hertford, or anywhere in between." Looking at the young officer's crestfallen face, Sutton tried to repair the damage to his self-esteem. "It's a good idea though — we just need to whittle down the range of places first."

"Where does this leave the Sally Evans murder? Are they connected, do you think, sir?" asked Karen Hardwick.

Warren sucked his teeth; the reluctance to commit was clear on his face.

"It's too early to say. We can't overlook the similarities so far and the timing — it's too coincidental to ignore. On the other hand, we can't risk getting carried away with looking for a link where none exists. As much as I hate to admit it, sometimes coincidences do happen."

Clearly nobody was buying that theory.

"I think we'll treat them as two different murders for the next twenty-four hours or so, at least until the second victim is identified, then we'll revisit the issue. In the meantime, we should start looking for any potential overlap between the two victims. If they are linked, then there may be clues to the killer's identity."

With that, the team broke up. Karen Hardwick turned to

Gary Hastings. "It's scary to think that if they are linked there's somebody killing young women out there, perhaps for no reason. I never thought when I joined CID we'd be hunting a serial killer."

Before Hastings could respond Sutton, who'd overheard Karen's comment, interjected, "He's not a serial killer. Officially you need three separate murders to qualify as a serial killer." He paused. "It's our job to make sure he never gets that label."

Chapter 24

During the course of the day, progress was slow but steady. At Warren's request, the forensic team studying the unknown victim's clothing had focused on her shoes. An early report landed on Warren's desk by late morning, which he immediately shared with the rest of the team.

"Women's size six Nike. Mid-range, all-purpose, luckily for us, relatively new. They won't commit themselves either way, of course, but the scuffing pattern and absence of deeply embedded stones suggest that, although the trainers have been worn outside, the owner hadn't done significant outside running. The inside lining of the shoe is worn, so it's unlikely that the lack of scuffing is due to lack of use."

"Which suggests that she may have been returning from a gym session rather than a jog," interjected Sutton. Warren inclined his head in a cautious acknowledgement.

Just after midday, a phone call from Welwyn all but confirmed this theory and reduced the likelihood that they would find the young woman's bag discarded somewhere. The force's master locksmith had examined the keys on the victim's key ring. Two of the keys were obviously house keys — a standard Yale and a 5-lever mortice Chubb. Both of them were off-the-shelf generic locks and no records existed to link the keys to a specific property.

The third key was more illuminating, however. What Warren had at first assumed was a window or back-door key was in fact a locker key. There was no label or key ring to help identify the keys if stolen — or even the locker number. However, Warren knew that many people would remove any such identifier, reasoning that the last thing you wanted was for somebody who'd stolen your keys to know which house, or indeed locker, they unlocked…

For now, it was enough to start on and since Gary Hastings had all but suggested the idea, Warren assigned him to ring around the different sports centres in the area to find out which gyms offered locker facilities to paying members.

* * *

Shortly after lunch, Detective Superintendent Grayson made an appearance. Warren spent the next half an hour taking his superior through the case's progress so far.

"We need to issue a press release. Reporters are already sniffing around. We have to give them something before they start appealing for witnesses and muddying the waters with half-baked theories and questionable facts. Do you think we should use it to ask for the public's help in identifying the body?"

Warren had been thinking about this himself and recommended against it. "Give us another twenty-four hours to try and work out who she is otherwise we'll put the wind up every parent whose daughter's forgotten to charge her mobile phone. The public are on edge after Sally Evans as it is. I suspect the switchboard will receive dozens of calls regardless, but 'blonde, average build, late twenties' is too vague to keep the numbers down."

Grayson tapped his teeth with an expensive-looking pen as he mulled over Warren's proposal. "OK, Warren, we'll play it your way. We'll just release the barest of details for now in a written statement, no questions, but if you haven't identified her by tomorrow evening, we'll put a photo out and ask for help."

Warren repressed a sigh; he hadn't missed his boss' not so subtle use of phrases such as '*your* way' and if '*you* haven't identified her'. As usual, responsibility was being laid on Warren's shoulders in case of failure — no doubt any successes would be a team effort, with Grayson poised to reap any praise from his peers in Welwyn.

Pushing those thoughts to one side, Warren made his excuses and left.

* * *

By late afternoon, the autopsy was complete on the unidentified young woman and Professor Ryan Jordan offered to run the results over to Middlesbury. Warren was glad that the American was on duty and would have requested him if he weren't; if the two murders were linked then he hoped that by using the same pathologist any similarities, no matter how small, would be noticed.

This time, Warren invited Tony Sutton in for the consultation.

"First of all, let me stick my head on the chopping block and say that I am pretty sure it's the same killer."

Warren let out a breath that he didn't realise he'd been holding. His first emotion was one of relief — with only one killer to look for and two different crime scenes to process, he felt that the chances of finding this killer and bringing him to justice were much increased. Two crime scenes meant two opportunities for the killer to leave evidence — two opportunities to make that crucial mistake that Warren and his team could exploit.

Warren's second emotion was one of sudden, renewed pressure. It was as if a clock had started ticking in his head. Two murders, less than a week apart, spoke of a cold, calculating killer, not some slave to a crime of passion. Even more worrying was the thought that he might strike again. Had he acquired a taste for it now? Did he have a list of victims? Would he end when he reached some goal or was he going to keep on going until he was stopped?

The pathologist had opened his file and was reading from it, Warren and Tony following the narrative on colour photocopies.

"Victim is a white Caucasian female, mid to late twenties, with blonde, shoulder-length hair, no distinguishing scars or body decorations. She has a full set of adult teeth, plus two wisdom teeth which we've X-rayed for dental analysis. She was one hundred and sixty-four centimetres tall and about sixty-two kilogrammes. She is of a medium-slim build with slightly above average musculature suggesting that she works out regularly." He looked up at the two officers. "I know it's a bit premature to draw conclusions from just two cases, but, given that their physical differences in body type would be largely concealed by loose clothing, you could argue that both this victim and Sally Evans conformed to a 'type'. Perhaps an indication of the killer's sexual preferences or somebody that he is angry with?"

Warren nodded thoughtfully. He'd noticed the similarity himself, but it was good to have it confirmed by somebody else.

Having the same pathologist examine both bodies was the right call, he decided.

"Overall, the victim's health was good. Clean lungs, normal-sized heart and no apparent abnormalities in any other organs. Cause of death was likely strangulation. Ligature marks on her throat were consistent with her scarf being used. Petechiae — ruptured blood vessels — on the whites of her eyes from increased inter-ocular blood pressure confirm this. They also confirm that she was still alive when strangled. We'll have to wait for toxicology results to confirm, but I smelt a faint chemical smell suggesting that she may have been anaesthetised with solvent."

"Just like Sally Evans," muttered Sutton uncomfortably.

"When did she die?"

Jordan removed his glasses and sighed. "Difficult to say with any certainty. Her body had cooled close to ambient temperature, but in those conditions that means little. We performed an intra-ocular potassium measurement, and within the margins for error I would suggest a minimum of thirty-six hours. However limited decomposition had set in and she hadn't been very disturbed by local wildlife. If it helps, her stomach contents revealed chocolate cake and white wine, probably consumed within an hour of death. There were also some traces of pasta and sauce, probably eaten about four to six hours before death. She was also freshly showered and wearing clean underwear and a fresh T-shirt. It didn't look as if she had worked up a sweat whilst wearing them."

"That suggests she was killed two evenings ago," stated Sutton.

"Why not yesterday morning?" Warren suggested, for the most part playing devil's advocate. "Thirty-six hours would be early to mid-morning. Plenty of people go to the gym before work."

"Yeah, but they don't usually reward themselves with chocolate cake and white wine mid-morning and do their workout after a 5 a.m. breakfast of spag bol."

"You're probably right, but let's try and keep an open mind at this stage."

Jordan cleared his throat slightly. "Can I also suggest that late night in the dark would make it easier for the killer to take his victim than in broad daylight? Unless he picked her up somewhere very secluded or followed her home, we can probably assume that he wanted to subdue her with the minimum of fuss — hence the solvent. And she did put up a struggle."

"Oh, what else have you found out, Professor?" Warren's interest immediately piqued; perhaps the young woman had made a noise and alerted witnesses.

Rifling through the sheaf of photographs, Jordan picked out one of her right hand. The fist was visibly swollen, with reddened knuckles, even against the pallor of her skin.

"Whatever she hit, it was solid and she hit it damned hard — I X-rayed the fist and she's broken two of the small bones in the hand. If I had to speculate, assuming that she wasn't in the habit of punching walls, she gave her attacker a bloody good right-cross to the jaw."

"Good for you, girl," breathed Sutton. Everyone nodded respectfully.

"So our suspect may well have a bruised jaw? I suppose it's a bit much to hope for some trace evidence?"

The pathologist shook his head, apologetically. "Sorry. Nothing on her knuckles. She'd have been better off punching him on the nose — it makes his eyes water, doesn't break your fist and if you're lucky the bastard bleeds his DNA all over you."

"What about the rest of the autopsy — any other marks?"

"Her other fist was slightly reddened as if she had been hitting something with that also, but there was no damage. It's possible she was working out on the punchbag, wearing light mitts. She has pretty well-toned biceps and triceps, which would be consistent with someone who did bag work — and might explain her instinctive reaction to hit her attacker.

"More significant, though, is a bruise beneath her sternum. It's broadly fist-shaped and probably about as old as the broken hand. She was slim and toned, but she didn't have hard abdominals. I'll bet the punch left her completely breathless."

"So what are we suggesting here — they fought, then he subdued her with the chloroform or whatever the hell he used?"

"That would be my guess. I suspect he probably tried to subdue her with the solvent initially, but she wriggled away. I imagine that she hit him first and then he hit her back, doubling her over before smothering her with the solvent. Sally Evans didn't put up a fight, which suggests to me that his preferred method would be to subdue with the minimum of fuss, somehow catching them off guard. In this case, he made a mistake and she fought back.

"What's clear from the extent of the swelling is that he didn't kill her immediately. I estimate at least an hour passed before she died."

"Where did she die? Was it at the dumping spot or somewhere else?"

"Looking at the patterns of lividity I would say that she died on the spot where we found her."

"So what happened in that hour? Presumably, he had to transport her to the dumping spot. Did he kill her immediately, or not?" Sutton didn't want to say it.

"All I can say is that some time prior to her death she underwent vigorous sexual intercourse, probably penile, leading to bruising. Given the earlier signs of a struggle, I think we can say that she wasn't compliant, but there is limited evidence to suggest that she put up much of a fight during the sex, suggesting that she was either terrified into submission or sedated."

Given how hard the young woman had fought earlier, Warren was willing to bet that she was sedated. A sudden flash of anger surged through him. *I really hope that bastard's jaw is hurting*, he prayed.

"Any trace?"

Jordan shook his head in frustration. "It's just like the previous case. We found no traces of any semen, foreign pubic hairs or skin flakes. Just the same traces of lubricant, latex powder and adhesive. He pulled her clothes apart to expose her breasts, but we can't find any evidence that he touched them — no fingerprints, no saliva."

"Shit. So we have nothing, then?"

"Nothing from the PM, I'm afraid. There was some other trace found at the scene." He pulled another file out from his soft leather briefcase. "CSM Andy Harrison asked me to pass on this preliminary report from the scene. He says there's more to come over the next few days. Most noticeable is that brown dust, probably cardboard again, and some more fibres on her coat. He's going to run them against the database and compare them to the first scene."

"Anything else from the immediate area?"

"There are some partial boot prints immediately adjacent to the body and a mixture some distance away, probably from the kids that discovered her. They're mapping the crime scene as we speak; he'll have more for you tomorrow."

With nothing else to offer, the tall pathologist stood up, shaking both officers' hands.

"I really hope you catch this one. Call me any time day or night. I'll make sure my secretary puts your calls through regardless." He looked at them solemnly. "One murder is unpleasant enough, but it's part of the job. Two and it starts to feel personal."

* * *

By now it was well into Sunday evening, but CID still buzzed with activity. As soon as Professor Jordan left Warren's office, Gary Hastings took the opportunity to speak to the boss.

"I've been working my way alphabetically through all of the gyms in a thirty-mile radius of where the body was found. I've got as far as 'T', but it's gone seven and I'm starting to get answer phones from some of the smaller ones. From what I can tell, it is unusual for sports centres to let customers have a permanent locker. So far, only three places do and only for those on the most expensive membership plans."

He showed Warren a printed map of the surrounding area, with neatly drawn red crosses. Another small circle in blue lay just south of them.

"I reckon that rather than starting phoning around again tomorrow morning, I can visit all three of those places on my way into work and see if the key matches their lockers. If it does, we've saved some time. If it doesn't, I'll just carry on phoning around. I'll take a photograph with me, see if anyone recognises her."

"That's good work, Gary. I'm impressed with what you've done in such a short time. The sooner we get this poor young woman identified and speak to her family and friends, the sooner we can start tracking down this man."

Hastings smiled, before returning to his workstation. Warren himself had to stifle a smile; he knew for a fact that Hastings lived towards the north of the town. Either he was making a huge detour or coming in from the south, as the blue circle had indicated. It looked as though Karen Hardwick would be getting up early also...

MONDAY 12TH DECEMBER

MONDAY 12TH DECEMBER

Chapter 25

The ringing of her alarm clock woke Karen Hardwick from a fitful sleep. Groping blindly, she found the snooze button and depressed it, craving the extra ten minutes it would tease her with. Monday morning and she felt tired and unrested, the day ahead looming like a darkening shadow. Beside her, the reason for her sleeplessness grunted then sat up. Gary Hastings was one of those people for whom the day couldn't start early enough. For the briefest of moments, Karen hated him for it.

Prising her eyes open, she was rewarded with the full glare of the bedside table lamp. Cursing softly, she buried her head in the pillow as she waited for the sting of the light and the red and green spots it caused to fade. By the time she risked another peek at the world, Gary was already up, swallowing his morning painkillers with a glass of water. Leaning over, he kissed her lightly on the forehead.

"Morning. Did you sleep well?"

As he stood up Karen saw his bare chest, the left side puckered by an ugly six-inch scar. When the two young officers had first spent the night together, Gary had been self-conscious, refusing to take his T-shirt off. It had taken weeks of gentle persuasion from Karen for him to finally expose the wound that had so nearly killed him, just months before. Though she said nothing, the sight of it sent a chill down her spine and it was all she could do not to touch her own reminder, concealed beneath her fringe.

Outwardly, Hastings was almost mended. He had returned to light duties at work and had started to jog again, trying to regain his fitness. He now only took a couple of mild painkillers in the morning to ward off his aches and pains and had even taken to joking about how close to death he had come. Inwardly, though, Karen was worried. A keen swimmer, he had yet to return to the pool, reluctant to display his scar to the world. He had not resumed his beloved jiu-jitsu — he wouldn't discuss it and Karen wasn't sure if it was because his skills had proven to be so lacking in that final encounter or if he couldn't face the use of knives, even plastic replicas, in training.

Then there were the nightmares. At least every other time they slept together, Karen would be woken by his shouting and thrashing about. The words he yelled were incoherent but the way he finally subsided, sweating profusely and crying, cradling the left side of his chest, left Karen in no doubt as to what he was reliving. Despite the violence of the dreams, he never seemed to wake up, even as Karen soothed him with whispered words and gentle caresses. In the morning he claimed no memory of the episode. For Karen, though, the experience was shattering and left her wide awake and worrying for much of the rest of the night.

At the force's insistence, Gary attended weekly counselling sessions to cope with the trauma. However, he hated them and was counting the days until he was declared fit enough for full duty. Karen had contemplated contacting the counsellor herself to tell her about the dreams, but she could see no way in which the subject could be broached by the therapist without implicating her. She worried that Gary would see it as a betrayal.

Looking up at her lover, Karen forced a smile. "Like a baby, sweetheart. Like a baby."

* * *

After a hurried breakfast, the couple parted ways. This was the way it had been since the start: both of them would drive separately to work, neither of them ready to announce their relationship to their colleagues. Much good it had done them, thought Karen, thinking back to her awkward conversation with Tony Sutton a few days ago. She knew that she really should declare the relationship to her superiors. Relationships between co-workers weren't exactly banned — and the two officers were the same rank, so there could be no issues about favours or abuse of position. Nevertheless, guidelines stated that workers in an intimate relationship should inform their line managers, in confidence if desired, and it went without saying that whilst at work a professional attitude should be observed at all times. In fact, there were two married couples in uniform in Middlesbury and an openly gay couple worked Traffic down in Welwyn, so it wasn't exactly new territory.

However, she had yet to broach the subject with Gary. Why? Was she afraid that their relationship was too new? That they were still finding their feet? That it might not yet be strong enough to withstand the inevitable outside scrutiny from her colleagues?

And then if they were going to tell their co-workers, shouldn't they also tell friends and family? Karen's parents and her best friends had been dropping hints that it was time to move on from her last boyfriend, a topic she kept on avoiding. They meant well, of course, but Karen had taken an almost perverse pleasure in insisting that she was happy single — that she was doing just fine as an independent woman, thank you very much. Maybe she should just change her Facebook status, she thought ruefully, announce it to the world with one, computer-generated line of text and be done with it.

Finally, she pulled into the car park at work. As she swiped herself into the building she felt the slight frisson of excitement that she still got every day as she entered work. All thoughts of Gary evaporated; the first day of a new week — who knew what it would bring?

* * *

It was fair to say that no such angst was bothering Gary Hastings as he drove to the first of the three gyms on his list. On the passenger seat beside him, in a plastic evidence bag, was a copy of the locker key, which he could use to test different lockers with if appropriate; a colour photograph could be shown in lieu of the genuine piece of evidence.

The previous night had been extremely pleasant. For a few hours the young couple had left behind all of their worries and simply enjoyed each other's company. A grin tugged at his lips as he remembered how the evening had been concluded. Truth be told, he was still pinching himself as to how lucky he was. He'd fancied Karen Hardwick from the moment the trainee detective had joined Middlesbury CID in the early summer. Of course, he'd had no chance. She'd been newly single, and to all accounts not looking for a replacement, something that a couple of his peers had found out for themselves. Gary himself was a detective constable of several years, contemplating taking the sergeant's exam sometime in the future.

Of course, that was on the back burner for the time being. A break of a few months to recuperate had set things back a bit, but the note of commendation for bravery in his file more than made up for that. Unfortunately, a black mark gained for a serious mistake that seriously compromised an investigation, delaying the apprehension of the suspect, loomed large in his latest evaluation. The two events didn't quite cancel each other out unfortunately and a tactful, but serious rebuke had been delivered by DCI Jones, a man that Hastings was starting to admire greatly. It was the feeling that he had let Jones down, despite saving the man's life, that Gary felt worst about.

But then again, as the saying went, every cloud had a silver lining. As he'd lain in Intensive Care, then later in a regular ward recovering from his injuries and recuperating from several bouts of surgery, he'd been visited daily by Karen Hardwick. She'd taken time off to recover herself, from her less serious injuries. As their friendship had developed into something more, Gary had worried that it was just a reaction to the trauma they had both endured — that she somehow felt an empty infatuation born of his admittedly fool-hardy heroism. Gary still felt responsible in part for the danger that she had found herself in, although Karen insisted that he had done nothing wrong.

Eventually he'd decided to just take what was on offer and enjoy the ride. And if some of her feelings were a little misplaced, well, hero-worship certainly worked wonders in Hollywood movies. And who said that life couldn't imitate art?

The first gym on the list was actually part of an exclusive hotel on the outskirts of the town. "Platinum" guests staying in the business suites received complimentary access to the state-of-the-art gym, sauna and spa. For a frankly eye-watering monthly payment, outside users could also have unlimited access to the centre. There were only fifty places available and a waiting list of several dozen, the manager proudly told Hastings. Each of those customers had access to their own locker and complimentary fresh towels.

Towels aside, Hastings couldn't see what this gym offered that others a fraction of the price didn't, other than exclusivity and bragging potential. Either way, it didn't look as though their unknown victim was a member. The moment he showed the photograph, the manager shook his head. Even a cursory comparison with a spare key showed that the unidentified key would never fit one of their lockers.

Thanking the man for his time and politely declining an application form to join — either he was taking the mickey or the man hadn't the faintest idea how much a police constable earned — Gary crossed the gym off the list and headed back to his car.

The next gym was far less exclusive — lockers were available to rent for a monthly fee or as part of the "unlimited plus" package. Again, the key was very clearly a different make from that which fitted their lockers.

The final gym on Gary's list was part of a much larger sports complex. Gary crossed his fingers as he entered the lobby. If this one didn't pan out, it was back to the office to start ringing from the letter T onwards and re-calling those that had gone to voicemail when he'd phoned the previous night.

But what if none of them paid off? Would he have to increase the radius to fifty miles of the crime scene? What if it wasn't a gym locker? What if it was the key to her locker at work? He shuddered slightly; he could be on the phone for the next month if that was the case.

He needn't have worried. The deputy manager took one look at the photo and produced an almost identical key from a locked cabinet behind the till.

"If it's not one of ours, then it'll fit another gym that uses the same make of locker. You could always ring the manufacturer and ask for a list of who they've sold them to — save you some leg work." Hastings thanked her for the suggestion.

Next he produced the photograph of their unknown victim. The pathologist and Photoshop had worked their magic and the young woman, though pale, looked to be sleeping peacefully. The deputy manager stared at it for a long moment, before shaking her head sadly.

"She looks familiar, but I can't place her name. I usually work the early shift. I rarely do lates. She could come here seven evenings a week and I probably wouldn't know her."

"Is there any way we could find out who she is from your records? Do users have a photo-ID card perhaps? Maybe you have the photos on file?"

"No, I'm afraid not. If she's a member of the gym, she would have an ID card, but we ask them to bring in a passport photo and we just laminate it onto a piece of card and they have to show it — we're a bit low-tech I'm afraid. Most of the other users are attending classes or hiring courts or the artificial turf pitches. If they attend a class or are a member of a team that train here regularly then we insist that the instructor or coach records details of all participants and we keep a copy of the records for health and safety purposes, but if you walk in off the street and pay for a squash court, we just take your money."

"And can anybody hire a locker?"

"Yes, although we also have normal refundable ones for single use — most of the people that hire a locker train several times a week and don't want to carry their stuff to and from here. A lot of the martial arts guys keep their gear here."

"What sort of details do you take from them if they hire a locker?"

"They have to pay by direct debit or credit card, so we have their name, address and bank details."

Hastings paused for a moment, before sighing and asking the inevitable question.

"And how many lockers do you have?"

"Well, between you and me, they're quite a money-spinner. They pay for themselves within twelve months, then it's pure profit. We just installed a whole bank more when we refurbished both of the main changing rooms and put some more out the back opposite the canteen. We've pretty much rented the lot."

"I had a feeling you might say that," he said, trying not to sound too unenthusiastic. "Give us a ball-park figure?"

"Adding up the women's lockers plus the unisex ones outside the canteen — about three hundred."

* * *

DCI Jones had been profuse in his praise when Gary had called in to report his findings. A way of softening the blow, he supposed, as he knew just what he'd have to do next.

"Looks as though our unknown victim was probably a member

of the Middlesbury Sports and Leisure Centre," Warren informed the murder team. "Gary Hastings says the key matches the type used in their lockers. The manager on duty says the photo looks familiar but can't put a name to it for us. However, if we match the key to the locker, they will have her credit-card details on file."

"What's he going to do when it matches?" asked Sutton.

"I said I'd send you over with a SOCO to secure the locker and its contents, whilst we track down who owns the locker and see if we can trace her family."

"Sounds like a plan. How many lockers are there?"

"About three hundred."

"Ouch, bad luck, Gary." Sutton picked up his insulated coffee mug and headed towards the urn, before pausing to look at the surprised team. "What are you looking at me like that for? The sports centre's less than a five-minute drive away. Gary has the only key. Assuming it takes him ten seconds per locker, that's three thousand seconds — fifty minutes to test them all. He won't want me breathing down his neck all of that time. There's plenty of time for me to make a coffee before going over there." He registered Karen Hardwick's disapproving stare. "If it makes it any better, I'll take him one as well — pass me his mug, will you?"

"He isn't going to test all of them, is he? He'll stop as soon as he finds the one he's looking for. It could be the first one he tests."

Sutton shrugged. "Yeah, but what's the likelihood of that happening?"

* * *

The likelihood of that happening was actually quite good in this instance. Hastings had started with the oldest lockers first, reasoning that if the young woman had been coming to the gym for some time — and the autopsy suggested she was a regular gym user — then she would have got a locker some time ago and was thus less likely to have been in the newly installed block.

On top of that, the duty manager, although extremely helpful, had dropped some fairly big hints that it would be better for business if he could be in and out of the female changing room as quickly as possible and ideally whilst it was quiet. Gary decided it would be best not to mention, unless strictly necessary, that if the locker was in the women's changing room then Forensics might need to seal off the room and spend several hours going through her locker.

Unfortunately, the key did fit a locker in the female changing room — number thirty-four — and Gary found it within four minutes, completely undermining Tony Sutton's predictions. By the time Sutton arrived, followed shortly by a junior evidence officer, the women's changing room was locked and the poor manager, who Gary now knew to be called Rachel, was dealing with several irate customers as she awaited the arrival of the centre manager to take charge.

In the meantime, Gary had kept his head down in the office out the back as he worked his way through the files, learning what he could about the owner of the key and presumably the newly identified murder victim. As for the increasingly shrill middle-aged women who insisted that their whole day had been ruined by the inconsiderate actions of Hertfordshire Police — well, that sort of public relations was better suited to a more experienced detective inspector, Gary decided. He knew full well that it was only a five-minute drive from the station and that Sutton was probably trying to avoid the drudgery of checking three hundred lockers, one by one. Dealing with wealthy middle-aged women who didn't work for a living and felt their morning trip to the gym was more important than official police business was just up DI Sutton's alley, he decided with a grim smile.

As it happened, the DI didn't have the patience to deal with the public that morning. Sizing up the scene immediately, he put on his most ingratiating smile. "Of course, ladies, I fully understand that you are probably a bit smelly after this morning's session and need to shower and change, but it is technically a crime scene—" he gestured to the paper-suited junior crime-scene officer who was just about to enter the locker room "—so please ignore Jimmy here as he goes about his work. He's an experienced crime-scene officer and he deals with dead bodies all the time. There's nothing he hasn't seen."

The two women stood with their mouths open, trying to work out if they had just been insulted or not. Jimmy's cheerful smile and friendly, "Don't mind me, ladies, I'm a professional," further confused the issue. In the end, they decided to return in a few hours.

"What have we got, Gary?" Sutton was all business now as he placed the DC's coffee on the table. Hastings nodded, apology accepted.

"The key fitted locker number thirty-four in the women's changing rooms. No question about it, it slotted in and turned as smooth as butter. I wore gloves, obviously. I haven't disturbed the contents, but I could see when I opened the door that it contained at least one towel, some shampoo and shower gel and a hairbrush. A carrier bag looked as though it might be full of dirty washing. A pair of boxing gloves and training mitts were hanging from a hook inside."

"So she was a boxer? The autopsy suggested that it looked as though her knuckles had been bruised from bagwork and, of course, it looks as though she gave her attacker a hell of a punch in the jaw. Could the punch to her sternum have come from a sparring session rather than the attack?"

Hastings shook his head vigorously. "She wasn't a boxer. We've identified her as Carolyn Patterson, twenty-eight years old and, according to the records, in addition to a gym pass, she also did a weekly boxercise class. It's non-contact, no sparring. They hit bags but it's basically an aerobics class based around the cardio side of boxing training."

"OK, what else have we got?"

"Because she rented the locker and had a gym pass, they have her name, address et cetera on file. They also have a next of kin; her parents live over in Saffron Walden. According to the records, she did a boxercise class on Thursday night, seven until eight. We have the name of the instructor and a full class list, so we can talk to witnesses."

Sutton patted the younger man on the shoulder. "Good work, Gary. Let's leave Jimmy to his evidence collecting and get back over to CID." His face turned sombre. "I imagine that this afternoon at least one of the team will be putting on a black tie and going door-knocking."

Chapter 26

With a name, address and next of kin, plus a list of contacts who might have seen the victim shortly before her death, there was a renewed feeling of excitement in the CID briefing room. The Sally Evans case had started to feel that it was going nowhere as each lead had either fizzled out or seemed to be hanging in limbo. With the two murders almost certainly linked, a whole new avenue of potential leads had opened up.

One of the first things that Warren did was instruct the team to list all similarities and differences between the two cases — no matter how small — as the investigations proceeded. In the meantime, a small team would visit Carolyn Patterson's apartment, a short walk from the sports centre, and check that the other keys would fit.

Warren decided to include Tony Sutton and Karen Hardwick in his team and by 11 a.m. the three officers were pulling up outside the small flat.

"Police. Open up, please."

The apartment felt empty to the three officers standing on the doorstep of the ground-floor entrance. The curtains were closed and the free newspaper was sticking out of the letterbox. Both Karen and Tony verified Warren's recollection that it was delivered on a Friday, suggesting nobody had been home since at least then.

The flat next door had lace curtains and Warren noticed one of them twitch, a shadow behind them. Taking out a copy of the house keys, Warren fitted them into the locks, one by one. Perfect fit. Announcing his presence once more and receiving no response, he led the team inside.

The flat was a generous affair, certainly more spacious than her own meagre bedsit, Karen noted. It was tidy and, although it was clearly decorated in that functional but cheap method beloved of landlords across the country, Carolyn Patterson had obviously put some thought into making it her home. That it was her house left little doubt. Photographs of the young woman were all over the apartment; spanning almost a lifetime and showing a dozen different hairstyles and poses, they were all unquestionably of the person lying in a refrigerated cabinet in Hatfield.

All three officers were wearing gloves, but Warren was keen that they didn't disturb the flat any more than was necessary before the CSIs arrived.

"Name matches the bills, no other names listed." Tony Sutton was leafing through a pile of mail on the kitchen table. Karen Hardwick was looking at the photographs dotted around the apartment.

"Lots of pictures of her with different people, but, aside from obvious ones of her parents and a few of what looks like her best friend, I can't see any evidence of a boyfriend, husband or other special person."

"That's the feeling I'm getting. Karen, could you have a look in her bedroom and wardrobes and see if you can work out if she lives alone?" Warren gestured to the living room. "Tony, see if there's anything interesting in her living room. I'm going to look at the bathroom and the kitchen."

It took Warren less than five minutes to work his way through the two rooms and decide that there was enough food in the cupboards for one person and only one set of hygiene products in the bathroom. On the counter next to the kitchen stove was a saucepan half filled with pasta sauce. A dirty bowl, stained with what looked to be the same sauce, sat unwashed in the sink. If Warren had to reconstruct the scene, he would suggest that Carolyn Patterson had made herself a meal of pasta sauce — he remembered the pathologist's report — of which she had eaten half, then left the remainder on the side to cool, intending to chill it and clean up after returning from her boxercise class. Judging by the traces of mould appearing on the sauce, it had been a few days since the meal was prepared. Milk in the fridge was a day past its use-by date, although, thinking back to the times when he was a lone bachelor, he acknowledged that wasn't necessarily indicative of absence.

There was no washing machine in the kitchen, which might explain the bag of dirty clothes in the locker — she probably used the launderette that sat more or less equidistant from the sports centre and her flat.

Returning to the hallway, he met Karen Hardwick. "No traces of any men's clothing. If she has a live-in girlfriend, they are a very similar dress size and have the same taste in perfumes."

Tony Sutton concurred. "Living area has nothing but chick-lit novels and rom-com DVDs — definitely a female, no trace of a bloke."

Karen, whose taste in entertainment ran the whole spectrum from chick-lit to gory thrillers and from romantic comedies to science fiction and superhero movies, wondered what Tony Sutton would make of her own apartment.

"The other end of the room is a bit more interesting. It seems to be her office. Judging by the piles of sketches and magazines, I would say that she is some sort of graphic designer who works from home a lot."

"OK, good work, folks. Let's lock up and get Scenes of Crime in to process the place properly. In the meantime, we'll see what the neighbours have to say before we go and break the bad news to Carolyn Patterson's parents."

The shadow Warren had spotted through the lace curtains next door turned out to be Carolyn Patterson's eighty-year-old neighbour, Arthur Beddlington. A widower for ten years, he'd moved into his flat about five years previously.

"It wasn't the same without Polly" he said wistfully, explaining his decision to leave their marital home, "and it was too big for me on my own. These places are the perfect size for a young couple or someone single."

"Does Ms Patterson live alone?" asked Warren as he steered the conversation back around to the reason for their visit, careful to refer to the deceased young women in the present tense. The last thing he wanted was for Mr Beddlington to ring the unsuspecting woman's parents to pass on his condolences.

"Oh, yes, she moved in about nine months ago. She's had a few friends around now and then and I've often seen her parents, but I haven't seen any boyfriends." He paused for a moment, before continuing awkwardly, "I'm not a very modern man, but I don't think she has a girlfriend, if she was that way inclined."

"Do you know how she earns a living?" asked Tony Sutton.

"Yes, she's a graphic designer. She works from home a lot but she goes into town about twice a week. Wednesday and Thursday, I think. She dresses up smart then, I think she works for some company a couple of days then spends the rest of the time at home."

"When was the last time you saw her?"

The old man paused for a moment. "I heard her front door slam Thursday evening. I didn't see her, but she normally goes out about half-six, dressed in a tracksuit. I think she goes to that sports centre round the corner."

"And you didn't hear her return?"

He thought for a bit longer. "No, I didn't, as it happens."

"Would you expect to? Could she have returned without you knowing?"

"I don't think so. I watch TV in here and I can hear her front door quite clearly. Besides, there's a security light with a sensor — it didn't light up." The old man's eyes brightened slightly as another thought occurred. "Come to think of it, I don't think she put her bins out either. Bin men come Friday morning. I'm an early riser so I put mine out first thing then walk around the newsagent's to get me paper. Most folks round here put their bins out Thursday night. I don't 'cos it encourages the foxes. Her bin wasn't out." Warren remembered that the kitchen bin had been close to full when he'd looked that morning.

After a few more minutes, it was clear that the old man knew little else about his neighbour. Leaving behind his card and asking the old man to keep quiet about their visit until they had a chance to talk to her parents, Warren and the team left.

Checking his tie in the rear-view mirror one last time, Warren put the car into gear. Next stop, the Pattersons' and a job that nobody was looking forward to.

Chapter 27

The drive to Carolyn Patterson's parents in Saffron Walden took about half an hour. Strictly speaking, Walden was in Essex, but it was so close to the border with Hertfordshire that Warren met no resistance at all when he suggested that Hertfordshire's Family Liaison Officers took over after Warren and his team broke the bad news.

The family home was a fairly modern affair on the outskirts of the town. Attractive in its own way, it nevertheless lacked the charm of the listed buildings that populated the centre of the ancient town, some of which could be dated as far back as the medieval period.

Two cars were parked on the wide, open driveway, suggesting that both of her parents were home. Informing both parents at the same time meant they could offer each other support.

Pulling to a halt in the street outside the house, the three officers got out immediately, walking purposefully up the drive. In Warren's experience, it was best not to delay when delivering such news. Taking time to find gentle words was a waste of time and could be counterproductive, if it led to misunderstanding, confusion and false hope. There was no way to soften the blow ultimately — better to get on with it and stand ready to pick up the pieces.

Taking a deep breath, he rang the doorbell. Inside he heard the immediate yapping of a small dog, followed by a loud shushing noise. A moment later the door opened.

The woman on the threshold was unquestionably the victim's mother. Late middle-age, with ash-blonde hair, the woman had a slim figure that had clearly influenced her daughter's own physique. Her face spoke loudly of the power of genetics. Aside from a few extra wrinkles, the two women looked more like sisters than mother and daughter.

Warren was holding his warrant card aloft and had barely asked for confirmation of the woman's identity before she clapped her hand over her mouth and screamed for her husband, Carl.

Seconds later a similarly aged man in a thick cardigan appeared at her side. He took one look at Warren's identification and his serious expression before he too let out a moan. It was only the fast reflexes of Tony Sutton that stopped him from simply hitting the floor where he dropped.

* * *

After helping a wobbly, but otherwise healthy Carl Patterson to a seat, Warren introduced the three officers and confirmed the news that the couple had already guessed.

It seemed that the two parents had been worrying about the whereabouts of their daughter since the previous night when she had failed to make her regular Sunday evening phone call. When she hadn't phoned by 10 p.m., her mother had called both her landline and her mobile phone, leaving messages on both.

Carl Patterson was twisting a white handkerchief in distress. "Carol was worried — well, we both were — when she didn't phone. We saw what happened to that other young woman on the news and of course we'd heard about that body being found. She wanted to drive over or call the police, but I said, 'No, she's a grown woman with her own life. You can't call the police over a missed phone call.' Maybe she was out or had company…" His voice broke. "Now I wish I'd listened to her. Maybe she'd still be alive…"

Tony Sutton leant forward immediately, putting a reassuring hand on the man's shoulder. "I'm sorry, Mr Patterson, but there's nothing that you could have done by then. We found her on Saturday night. Unfortunately, she didn't have any identification on her so it took a little while for us to identify her, or we'd have been here sooner."

Warren saw the sudden flash of hope in her mother's eyes and knew exactly what was coming next.

"Could it be a mistake, then? Maybe it's some other poor girl?"

Warren knew it was a false hope; her mother's uncanny resemblance aside, a family picture of the couple standing proudly either side of their daughter at her university graduation stood above the fireplace. It was unquestionably the same young woman. Nevertheless, he took out the colour photograph of the victim from the morgue.

The wrenching sob from her mother and the stifled cry from her father was all the confirmation they needed. Karen Hardwick leant forward and gently touched Carol Patterson's hand. "Can I make the two of you a cup of tea or coffee?"

Carol Patterson looked up, blinking; her voice was distant. "Of course, where are my manners?" She started to rise, before Karen touched her hand again. "No, I'll make it. You just sit here. Is that the kitchen through there?"

Not for the first time Warren was impressed by the young officer's instincts. After taking orders, she disappeared into the kitchen; as she did so she discreetly signed to Warren the universal symbol for a telephone, mouthing the words "Family Liaison?" Warren nodded. He'd wanted confirmation that the body was that of Carolyn Patterson before arranging for the team to travel all the way over from Welwyn.

Carl Patterson touched the photograph tenderly. "She looks so peaceful..." he murmured. "How did she die? Did she suffer?"

"No, she didn't suffer. We believe that she was sedated with a chemical before she was strangled. She won't have felt a thing." Strictly speaking it was a bit of a white lie — they couldn't know if Carolyn Patterson had been semi-conscious or not during her ordeal and there was no telling how much pain she was in before she was sedated. Her broken hand could have been excruciating. However, it was a lie that Warren was comfortable with — there was no need at this stage for too many details. A glance from Tony Sutton showed his agreement.

Sutton looked at the graduation photo above the fireplace. Another picture next to it, taken on the same day, featured Carolyn Patterson next to a gangly, dark-haired girl of about fifteen or sixteen. Despite the acne and an impressive set of wire braces showing through her smile, the resemblance was unmistakeable. However, whereas Carolyn Patterson was clearly her mother's daughter, the teenager was obviously Daddy's girl.

"Is there anybody that you would like us to contact for you?"

Carol Patterson tore her gaze away from the photograph. "Oh, no, Caitlin. How can we tell her what's happened? She'll be devastated."

"We have another, younger daughter, Carolyn's sister. She's

at Durham University and just about to submit her master's dissertation. She's due to come back at the weekend to celebrate Christmas, then it's full steam ahead for the 'wedding of the century'." Carl Patterson gestured at the photo above the fireplace. "That's her. She's six years younger than Carolyn. She was so excited and proud when she graduated. Although she'd never have admitted it at the time, of course, she idolised her big sister." He smiled wistfully. "Carolyn's final year was also the year Caitlin took her GCSEs. She didn't know what she wanted to do and wasn't taking her studies at all seriously. She was hanging about with the wrong crowd at school and we were a bit worried about her, to be honest. Carolyn insisted that she stayed with her for a few days during the October half-term. She came back full of how much she wanted to go to university and really started working hard." He took his wife's hand affectionately and his face creased slightly at the memory. "Between you and me, I think Carolyn's housemates had the biggest influence on her — good-looking boys, all three of them."

"And the beer," his wife reminded him.

"Oh, yes, I think Carolyn got her into the Students' Union one night — not that we approved, of course — but she certainly came back with a newfound attitude."

Both Jones and Sutton smiled along with the Pattersons, sharing a brief moment of lightness on this darkest of days.

"We can arrange for Durham Constabulary to break the news to her and bring her home, if you'd like. Or you could phone her or go up there in person. We can assist you in any way necessary. You don't have to decide now," he added, noting the indecisive look on the couple's faces.

"What did Carolyn study?" asked Karen as she returned with a tray of coffees.

"Graphic design," answered her father, cupping his hands around the coffee as if he were standing outside in the cold, rather than a slightly stuffy, overheated living room. "She worked for a few years in London, then moved to Middlesbury about four years ago. Strictly speaking, she's freelance, but she has a long-term relationship with a small publishing house in town and pretty much works full-time for them now, doing the odd freelance job on the side to earn a bit of 'play money' as she calls it."

"Did she work from home a lot?" Warren was careful to keep on using the past tense to refer to Carolyn Patterson, whilst not correcting the couple's use of the present tense. Coming to terms with such a loss was a very individual thing and Warren knew that the couple would need space and time to deal with it in their own way.

"She did most of her work at home on the computer. She went into their main office about twice a week to drop off and pick up work and to meet with clients. She loved her work."

There was a lull in the conversation as the group sipped their coffee. Warren tried to decide how to broach the more delicate subject of suspects. However, Carl Patterson saved him the job.

"She was murdered, wasn't she? Was it the same person that killed that other poor girl?"

Warren nodded cautiously. "We are keeping an open mind, but, yes, she was and it looks as though the two may be linked."

Carl Patterson's voice shook. "We've been following the news and we saw the announcement earlier in the week about what happened to that other girl. Was Carolyn also... interfered with?"

Warren nodded again. "It looks as though that might have been the case, although we have no clear evidence either way. Her clothing had been disturbed."

Carol Patterson bit down on her fist as if to stifle a cry.

"I'm sorry, I have to ask, but do you know of any connection between your daughter and Sally Evans, the other victim? We're looking into any links between the two women, but it would help greatly if you could think of anything."

To help them, he produced a number of photographs of Sally Evans. Both parents shook their heads, recognising neither the name nor the pictures beyond what they'd seen on TV.

"When was the last time that either of you saw or spoke to Carolyn?"

"Last Sunday lunchtime, we met up in a pub near Duxford. We'd do that sometimes, split the distance between us."

"And how was she?"

"Very happy. She's really enjoying work and looking forward to Christmas. She's really excited about Caitlin's wedding. She's going to be maid of honour. She picked out the dress a couple of weeks ago and…" Suddenly she stopped talking as she realised what she was saying. Carl Patterson placed his arm around his wife and hugged her to his chest as the dam finally broke and the tears flooded free.

The three officers sat helplessly, knowing that there was nothing they could do. Had this been any other type of death, a road traffic accident or other tragedy, then this would have been the time to step back and let the professionals, Family Liaison, take over. But it wasn't, it was a murder investigation; the clock was ticking and Family Liaison weren't here yet.

After a few moments, Warren cleared his throat.

"I'm so sorry but I need to know — are you aware of anybody that might want to harm Carolyn? Any ex-partners or people that she had disagreements with?"

The couple looked at each other for a long moment before Carl Patterson let out a long breath. "Her ex-boyfriend, Alex Chalmers. They split up back in February. It didn't go well, but I can't see him being responsible."

"He hit her."

"What?" Carl Patterson turned to his wife in disbelief.

"She denied it, but a mother can tell."

Carolyn's father looked at his wife as if seeing her for the first time. "When? Why didn't you say something?"

Carol Patterson's voice shook. "It was about eighteen months ago. You were away a lot, during that frantic last six months before you retired. I popped in to see her one day unannounced. I woke her up before she had a chance to put on her make-up. She had a bruise under her eye. She insisted that it was from her boxercise class, made a joke about it. Said she ducked when she should have dived.

"I wasn't sure and I didn't want to worry you. I knew you wouldn't take it well."

Carl Patterson looked sick. "I can't believe it…"

"Was it just the once, do you think?" asked Warren, his interest piqued.

"I don't know. Thinking back on it, I think it must have happened more than once. There were little signs."

"Like what?"

"We knew that they were arguing a lot in the last few months. They had moved in together after only a couple of months of dating, but he seemed nice enough. A bit rough around the edges, but Carolyn was happy. She hadn't had much luck with boys before, so we were pleased for her."

"When did things change?"

"Back the summer before last they had a big row. I don't know what it was about but she phoned me up in tears. Said that he had been really abusive and called her some really horrible names." Carol Patterson's voice shook. "At the time I thought it was a lovers' tiff. I calmed her down and reassured her that he loved her and told her that it was probably nothing. Like I said, he's a bit rough around the edges, he had a tough upbringing, so I put the horrible language down to that. I should have told her to run away…"

"You weren't to know. But I wish you'd told me." Carl Patterson sounded hurt.

"She begged me not to; you know what a temper you have. She was worried you'd go around there and make things worse."

"And do you think he was hitting her then?" Warren prompted.

"Maybe. I wasn't sure. I've been retired a couple of years now and so sometimes we'd meet up for lunch during the week when she was working from home. Do a bit of shopping in Cambridge. A couple of times she cancelled at the last minute and we'd not see her for a week, then she'd turn up wearing far more make-up than normal. Once we met up on a hot July day, and she wouldn't take her cardigan off. We caught the Park and Ride into Cambridge, standing room only. Anyway, the bus swung around a corner really fast and I knocked into her arm. Not very hard, but she let out a real gasp of pain. Again, she blamed boxercise.

"Anyway, after they broke up, I looked up this boxercise thing on the Internet and it seems that they don't hit each other, so she couldn't have got her bruises from there. By now they'd split up, of course, so I didn't say anything; I couldn't see the point."

"When did it end?"

Now Carl Patterson took up the story. "February. It was

completely out of the blue. She just phoned up one evening and said, 'It's over. Here's my new address. Don't tell Alex.' She didn't want to talk about it, but she must have been planning it for some time. She moved into a new apartment in less than twenty-four hours.

"It seemed to take Alex by surprise as well. The following evening he phoned up demanding to know where she was, claimed he came home from a weekend with his brother to find all of her stuff gone and a note on the kitchen table. We refused to tell him and hung up.

"The next night he turned up on our doorstep, banging on the windows convinced she was staying here. He wouldn't leave until we threatened to call the police. A week later he turned up again, claiming that Carolyn owed him her share of the outstanding rent and bills as he'd had to give notice on the flat they shared. He was brandishing a piece of paper that he said was their contract and that they were co-signatories. Reckoned he'd take her to small claims court if she didn't cough up. In the end I wrote him a cheque for six hundred quid on the understanding that he never tried to contact her again. We never told Carolyn — she didn't need to know."

"And did he contact her again?"

"Not as far as I know. Carolyn never mentioned it. Although my wife may know differently — it seems there's a lot she doesn't share with me."

Warren almost winced at the barbed remark. At times like this, the couple in front of him needed each other more than ever; he truly hoped that this issue wouldn't become a wedge between them. To the side of him Tony Sutton also shifted uncomfortably, but said nothing. Doing his best to steer the conversation away from the topic, Warren asked about any other people that might wish Carolyn harm. After thinking hard, the couple said no.

Finally, the doorbell rang as two officers from the family liaison unit arrived. With the Pattersons in good hands, Warren and his team left. The drive back to Middlesbury was quiet, each officer deep in their own thoughts.

Chapter 28

Whilst Warren, Tony Sutton and Karen Hardwick had been with the Pattersons, Middlesbury CID had been busy piecing together Carolyn Patterson's last night. First Gary Hastings had tracked down the instructor who gave the boxercise class. An insurance broker by day, Mandy Albright also taught aerobic classes weekday evenings to keep fit and earn a bit of extra money. She'd been understandably shocked to hear of Carolyn Patterson's death.

She'd confirmed that it was normal for several members of the class to go for a quick drink in the sports centre bar after a session. Normally it was little more than a half-hour and one drink. However, Carolyn and three of the other women in the class had decided to stay for a bit longer, since Ms Albright's upcoming ski trip meant it was the last class before Christmas.

The part-time fitness instructor had been able to furnish Gary Hastings with the names and details of Carolyn's three friends from class and he'd spent the next couple of hours tracking the women down and getting a description of the night in question. All four of the women had agreed to attend the station in the next couple of days to undergo a full interview.

Whilst he did this, a small team of detectives had descended upon the Middlesbury Publishing Services Group — the closest thing that the freelance Carolyn Patterson had to an employer. A modestly sized business operating out of a converted farmhouse, MPSG specialised in performing various jobs for small, individual publishing houses.

"Some of these publishers are so small and specialised they only produce a handful of titles a year," the company's managing director had explained. "They can't afford to have a dedicated marketing department or to employ full-time artists. We act as a sort of one-stop shop, matching individual jobs to our pool of freelancers. Strictly speaking, all of our employees, except for myself, our accountant and our human resources manager are freelance. But for a skilled and reliable worker like Carolyn, we could all but guarantee full-time work for her. In fact, some of her clients even requested her personally and were willing to wait until she was available."

In a typical week Carolyn would visit the offices on a Wednesday and a Thursday; she didn't have her own desk as such, rather a large cubby-hole where her mail and any physical work would be stored. Her work was becoming increasingly computer-based these days, but clients often liked to meet her face-to-face and discuss their requirements and so the building had a plush meeting room for this purpose.

Carolyn had been in work on the day that she died and so brief statements were collected from everybody who had met her. Again, everybody was shocked and upset and willing to attend the station to give a more detailed statement in the future if necessary.

By the time the CID unit assembled for an after-lunch briefing, Gary Hastings had largely pieced together Carolyn Patterson's last known movements.

According to her work colleagues, Carolyn had been at MPSG between about 9 a.m. and 5 p.m. on Thursday, joining in their traditional weekly cake session. She had been described as happy and cheerful, looking forward to Christmas. One of her colleagues remembered her refusing a second slice of cake, since she still had a few pounds to lose before her sister's wedding. When another colleague suggested that she could eat the cake then go for a jog, she'd turned her nose up, saying it was too cold, she'd just work extra-hard at boxercise that night.

After she left work, there were no sightings of her until she arrived in time for her fitness class at about five to seven. She only lived about a mile away and preferred to walk rather than drive or catch the bus. As usual, she simply paid for her class with cash and signed in on the paper register. CCTV images showed her wearing the same outer layers that she had been found in. She went into the changing rooms but emerged about a minute later dressed in the same tracksuit bottoms and a yellow T-shirt, carrying her boxing equipment. After the class, she disappeared back into the changing room for about fifteen minutes, before emerging redressed with apparently damp hair.

A T-shirt similar to that seen on the CCTV was stuffed in a carrier bag in the locker along with several other dirty T-shirts and underwear. A second bag contained clean underwear and T-shirts and a towel in the locker appeared to have been used and allowed to dry several times. The best explanation was that Carolyn got changed into her gym kit at home, then walked the mile to the sports centre, discarding her overcoat in the changing room and picking up her boxing gloves from her locker.

After class, she would have a quick shower, swap her sweaty underwear and T-shirt for a fresh set, then join her friends for a drink in the bar. She didn't have a washing machine, but there was a launderette on the way home so she probably did a load of washing every few weeks.

On the night in question, she apparently followed her usual routine, except that she stayed about an hour longer in the bar than normal. It looked as though she'd had a meal of pasta and sauce before leaving the house, leaving half of it to reheat at a later date, consistent with the pathologist's report. Her blood alcohol levels were also what one would expect from somebody who'd drunk three glasses of white wine.

Her friends had described her as happy and full of fun; they'd all left at the same time a bit tipsy and giggly, but not drunk. One friend had offered her a lift home, but she'd declined, saying she needed to walk off the chocolate cake she'd eaten.

The CCTV put her time of leaving at 21:34h. It was being examined and an attempt made to identify every person leaving at about the same time.

The team was now eager to exploit the new leads and Warren lost no time assigning jobs. The most likely time for the abduction was at some point during her walk home from the sports centre. As a precaution, SOC were checking her apartment for signs of a struggle, but her next-door neighbour had seemed pretty confident that he'd have heard anything too violent. Superintendent Grayson had already arranged for the uniform division to loan him a few bodies and so Warren assigned a detective sergeant to organise door-knocking on the streets between Carolyn Patterson's flat and the sports centre. Realistically there was only one route that she could have taken and so he also arranged another team to close those roads and start a search for any evidence of foul play.

It had been nearly four days since Carolyn Patterson's disappearance and the streets were busy, residential areas. Warren wasn't overly optimistic that they'd find anything. Similarly, he wasn't expecting much in the way of CCTV evidence, beyond that from the sports centre itself.

"Remember, Carolyn Patterson broke her routine that night and stayed in the bar longer than normal. Assuming that her killer planned the abduction, he probably wasn't expecting that. He may have been loitering in the area for over an hour, waiting for her. Somebody might have seen something or someone."

By far the most promising lead so far was that of Carolyn's ex-boyfriend, Alex Chalmers. Using the information given to them by her parents, they didn't take long to track him down. Records from the Police National Computer were even more interesting.

"'Alexander Liam Chalmers, thirty-one years old,'" Warren read. "No convictions, however, the domestic violence team attended three incidents between 2002 and 2005. Arrested but released without charge on two of those occasions. Neighbours called the police each time, but his then girlfriend refused to press charges and there wasn't enough evidence to proceed.

"We know that he was with Carolyn Patterson from about 2007 until February of this year, but nothing is on the system for then. However, neighbours called the police again in August of this year after loud noises came from the flat he shares with his new girlfriend. Different flat, different neighbours, but the same outcome. She denied everything and the attending officers didn't have enough to make an arrest."

"So we have his address, should we pay him a visit?" Tony

Sutton's voice was grim, but Warren could see that he was keen to meet the man.

Warren glanced at his watch.

"The file says that he is a postman. I'm willing to bet he's finished for the day. I think we should go and pass on our regards."

Chapter 29

Warren's hunch proved right and Alex Chalmers was home, but he wasn't pleased to meet them.

After they rang the bell twice, the door was finally opened by a heavily pregnant young woman who looked to be in her early twenties. Stick-thin, aside from her protruding belly, she appeared nervous and edgy as she opened the door. Her eyes widened even more when she saw Warren's warrant card. Even in the dim light from the greying afternoon sky it was obvious how much make-up she was wearing. Nevertheless, a dark smudge across her jaw hinted at the sins concealed beneath.

"He's having a snooze upstairs; he did a long shift at work today. Could you come back later?" The young woman's voice was barely a whisper and she subconsciously glanced towards what Warren assumed was the bedroom. Her hands shook slightly.

"I'm very sorry, it can't wait, Ms…?"

"Oliver. Katie Oliver." The name matched that in the police report, although no mention had been made of her being pregnant. Assuming she was about eight months pregnant, she would have only been about four months or so back when the complaint was filed. Maybe she wasn't showing then. Either way, assuming it was his baby it seemed that Alex Chalmers hadn't wasted much time before getting back into the saddle, so to speak.

"I suppose you'd better come in. I'll go and see if Alex is awake." The poor woman looked terrified at the prospect.

Ultimately, there was no need. As Katie Oliver led the three officers into the living room heavy footsteps sounded on the stairs.

"Can't a man get some fucking rest in his own fucking home? Who the fuck are you?" Alex Chalmers glared at a nearly tearful Katie Oliver, even as he addressed the three police officers.

Warren resisted the urge to reply with, "We're the fucking police", answering instead with, "Detective Chief Inspector Warren Jones, Middlesbury CID, and these are my colleagues, DI Sutton and DC Hardwick. You must be Mr Chalmers? I'm very sorry to disturb you, but I'm afraid I have some bad news, sir." He gestured towards the sofa. "Would you care to take a seat?"

Warren's approach took the man completely by surprise and he sat down without another word. Taking the armchair opposite, Warren took a moment to scrutinise the man before him. He didn't like what he was seeing. A hair's breadth under six foot, with a shaven head and several days' worth of dark stubble on his face, the man was dressed in a dirty grey vest, and a grubby pair of boxer shorts. He was sitting with his legs open and the slit in the shorts revealed more than Warren was comfortable with. The man either didn't notice or didn't care. His meaty upper arms and flabby beer belly spoke of a man who did a hard physical job, but also had a taste for beer and lots of it. Both biceps were encircled by those oddly pointless tattoos that seemed to be all the rage. They symbolised nothing as far as Warren could tell. He could at least understand tattooing the name of a loved one or similar, but why on earth would somebody want barbed wire around their arm?

Chalmers reached out his right arm, and ensnared Katie Oliver, pulling her down onto the threadbare sofa beside him. The gesture seemed more proprietary than affectionate. Then, without so much as a glance at his heavily pregnant girlfriend, he fished a cigarette out of a half-empty pack of Marlboros on the coffee table and lit it left-handed with a Bic lighter. Katie Oliver's nose wrinkled, but she said nothing.

Not for the first time, Warren wondered what someone as attractive and intelligent as Carolyn Patterson had seen in such a person — he saw no hint of any unappreciated hidden depths. And why did women put up with such a man when he turned violent? Even more perplexingly, how could these men continue moving from one woman to the next, never changing their ways?

"Go on, then, out with it."

"I'm very sorry, but your former girlfriend, Carolyn Patterson, has been killed."

Chalmers said nothing, just took an extra-deep drag on his cigarette. After a few seconds he exhaled, before taking care to tap his ash into an already full ashtray.

"When?"

"Thursday night, we believe."

Chalmers shrugged. "We was in watching TV that night." He looked at his girlfriend. "Weren't we, babes?"

Katie Oliver paused a moment before nodding. She never once raised her gaze from the floor.

Chalmers reached out again, patting Oliver's bump. "That's how we spend most of our nights — getting ready for the big day. Not long now, eh, babes?"

Again, Katie Oliver kept her gaze on the carpet as she nodded. Chalmers patted her bump again. Warren maintained a poker face. Chalmers patted his girlfriend's belly like a farmer patting the rump of a bull he was particularly pleased with — the man gave no indication that his future son or daughter was gestating peacefully within. God help the poor mite.

Up until this point, Tony Sutton had been quiet. Now he leant forward. "Strange, I don't remember DCI Jones asking where you were. Why would you need to tell us that?"

For the first time since they had arrived, Chalmers' arrogance faltered. Regaining his composure, he shrugged casually. "Well, I figured that would be your next question. I ain't stupid. I watch *CSI* and *Law and Order*. First thing you coppers always do in a murder is go for the boyfriend, or her ex if she ain't been able to find a new one yet. Figured I'd save you the time."

"How do you know she was murdered? Again, DCI Jones just said she was killed. You seem to know an awful lot about this, Alex. Interesting that you had an alibi prepared."

This time it took even longer for Chalmers to respond.

"Well, I just assumed, didn't I? We saw the news about that other bird and then you said you'd found a body at the weekend. Stands to reason, doesn't it?" He sat back, obviously pleased with his answer.

"Why do you think police in those shows target the victim's ex-partners?"

"I dunno. Lazy scriptwriters, I suppose." He grinned, proud of his wit, turning to his girlfriend for appreciation. With effort she returned the barest of smiles. He turned back to the three detectives, none of whom were smiling.

"They do it because often they are the only people with a motive," replied Warren quietly. "Carolyn Patterson was a sweet girl that nobody had a bad word to say about. She didn't hang around with scum and low lifes; she wasn't the sort of girl who'd end up dead because of the people she associated with…" He paused. "At least not these days. That's why we look to the past for clues."

It took Chalmers a few seconds to realise how deeply he'd been insulted.

"Yeah, well, she wasn't all sweetness and light, you know. Bitch walked out on me, remember. Took everything and just left me a note." He paused before having a flash of inspiration. "Besides, she pissed off without paying what she owed me for rent and all that. I was saying just the other day how I needed to go to the court to get that back." He smiled triumphantly. "Can't do that if she's dead, can I?"

"Strange, I heard her father paid you six hundred pounds to cover that debt."

Chalmers faltered. "There were some other things that cropped up," he said weakly.

The silence stretched between them, before Karen Hardwick spoke up. "I'm sorry, I know it's rude but we've been on the road all day — I couldn't use your bathroom, could I?"

Katie Oliver stirred. "I'll take you there." Heaving herself to her feet, she led Karen up the stairs.

Now it was just the three men in the room, Tony Sutton took over again.

"OK, let's cut the crap. You know why we're here. We've read your file and we know you like to make your women do as they're told. What did Carolyn Patterson do that meant you had to go around and sort her out after all this time?"

Chalmers snorted derisively. "If you'd really read my file, you'd know it was all bullshit. They dropped all the charges. My neighbour was a twat — he used to hear us having a disagreement, then he'd call the police and make up shit. You can ask her anyway — she'll back me up."

A thought suddenly occurred to him. "Anyway, Carolyn never reported nothing to the police. You haven't got anything on me. I never laid a finger on her and nobody claims I did." He sat back, smugly.

Warren stared him directly in the eye, his voice low. "You're right, she never made a report. But people know. The black eye eighteen months ago, the bruises on her arms that she tried to cover with her cardigan in the middle of July. Of course, she claimed it was the boxercise, but people aren't stupid — they know that boxercise is non-contact." He leant closer and spoke directly into the man's ear. "We know. Other people know." He gestured upstairs with his head. "She's how many months pregnant? Make-up only hides so much.

"Well, we hear things. We're the police. It's our job. Sometimes things can't be dealt with in a courtroom, but justice still needs to be done." He sat back. "You're on my watch list, Chalmers."

The air was still tense when a few seconds later the toilet flushed and Karen Hardwick reappeared with Katie Oliver in tow.

She looked at the three men, all sitting silently.

"Are we done?"

* * *

"She's covering for him," was the first thing that Tony Sutton said when they pulled away from the house.

"No question about that. The question is, how much and is it important?" Warren tried not to let the questions distract him as he negotiated a particularly badly thought-out roundabout.

"I can't decide whether he was expecting us or not. All that stuff about assuming it was a murder because of the body being found at the weekend — it's not an unreasonable guess. Besides, like he said, he watches TV. He must know that you don't have three detectives turn up on your doorstep to tell you that your ex got knocked over crossing the road."

Warren agreed. "And I suspect that a man like that would look for an alibi regardless. He just wouldn't want a run-in with the police. Even if he was doing nothing more than having a quiet pint down his local, he'd go for the easy option and get the missus to claim he was in all night. Either way, I'd like to break that alibi if we can. We should also find out what he was doing the night Sally Evans disappeared.

"On a different note, did either of you notice if he had a bruise on his chin?"

Both officers said no. "He had too much stubble. He might not have the option of wearing make-up like his girlfriend, but I have to say that his five-o'clock shadow is pretty effective," elaborated Tony Sutton.

"Speaking of his girlfriend, Karen, did you get anything from her?" Warren glanced in the rear-view mirror at the detective constable.

"Nothing concrete, sir. She's clearly terrified of him, but she wouldn't say anything. Domestic Violence have been around in the past but she wouldn't admit anything to them. I gave her my card and said that she could phone any time if she ever wanted to talk." She paused thoughtfully. "We might get lucky — she probably can't see any way out at the moment. If she reports him for domestic abuse, it'll be months until the court case and if it gets dropped she'll be petrified he'll want revenge. Even if he gets convicted, unless he's done something really outrageous to her and gets a GBH conviction, he'll be out pretty soon.

"On the other hand, if she breaks his alibi and he goes down for murder, he's never coming back to harm her and her child."

"Not to mention the fact that she thinks she might be living with a murderer — that's got to make her worry. Nicely done, Karen." In the mirror, Warren saw the flush of colour in her cheeks.

"Thank God women always go to the toilet in pairs, eh?" joked Sutton.

"Speaking of which," Karen Hardwick spoke up from the back, "you couldn't put your foot down a bit, could you, sir? Like I said, it has been a very long day."

In response to the two men's surprised glances, she sighed. "I was busy interrogating a witness. I only flushed the toilet for cover." She paused. "Besides which, you saw the state of their living room — you don't want to know about the bathroom."

Chapter 30

Back at the station the remainder of the crime-scene forensics were waiting. Analysis of the various footprints around Carolyn Patterson's body yielded little in the way of helpful information. The only clear footprints in the periphery of the dumping area belonged to the unfortunate teenagers who had stumbled across her body. Closer to the corpse, imprints had been made of only a couple of partial footprints. Comparing these patterns to those found near Sally Evans' body confirmed another connection between the two murders.

Unfortunately, piecing together the fragments from both sites still produced at most 40 per cent of the right shoe and 30 per cent of the left. It was enough to identify the boots as size ten, male work boots, but little more. Very little in the way of distinguishing marks were found, meaning a detailed comparison would have to be conducted with any suspects' boots to make a connection. No matching hits were found on the HOLMES database.

Even less helpful were the foreign fibres found on both victims' clothes. Microscopic analysis revealed them to be the same — dark blue nylon threads. Unfortunately, that proved little. Included in the briefing pack on Warren's desk was a printout of a clothing catalogue. The Chinese writing on the front was translated underneath into English and revealed it to be the product listing for a Chinese clothes manufacturer that exported most of its product to Europe, including the UK.

The fibres were identified as being part of a standard cloth, used in many of the company's different clothing lines. As he leafed through the book Warren saw that somebody had circled the different garments currently available using that cloth. By Warren's estimate, at least a quarter of the company's range of clothing could be made using that fabric if a client so desired. Everything from men's tracksuit bottoms to women's fleeces, even some children's school jumpers. Furthermore, they supplied own-brand clothing to pretty much all of the supermarkets and down-market chain stores.

Tony Sutton threw down the catalogue in disgust. "Shit. I've probably got at least a couple of these garments in my own wardrobe."

Gary Hastings nodded in agreement. "I think I recognised one of those tracksuits."

"So it looks as though we're going to get little from forensics. This bugger's really careful," Warren summarised.

"Well, we know at least one person who is pretty good at avoiding leaving any clues behind. I think it's time for another visit to the farm, don't you, DCI Jones?"

* * *

"I'll bet he's got an alibi, probably from that sleazy son of his," opined Sutton as they headed out to Richard Cameron and Michael Stockley's farm.

"I suspect you're probably correct, but we still need to ask him," Warren agreed.

"What do you think the chances are that he's the perpetrator?" asked Sutton.

Warren paused, thinking. "I honestly don't know. All we've really got is that the person committing these crimes is using a method to avoid leaving trace that was a signature of Richard Cameron a dozen years ago, and the fact that he was released back into this area last year.

"Taking a step back, it looks weak, even on paper. Remember, we're basing this similarity on how there is a lack of evidence — the world has moved on since Richard Cameron came up with his flash of sick genius. TV scriptwriters, authors and film-makers are constantly coming up with new and inventive ways to try and fool forensic investigators and the police. It's not impossible that somebody else hit upon a similar idea to Richard Cameron to avoid leaving trace evidence behind. Hell, I wouldn't be surprised if the exact details of how he did it aren't sitting on some crime blogger's website, just waiting for some deviant to stumble across them with a Google search. Most of it will have come out at trial and be part of the public record.

"Plus, it's hard to believe that he'd be foolish enough to kill Carolyn Patterson twenty-four hours after we questioned him over Sally Evans' death. Taking the two murders separately and ignoring Cameron for the moment, there are definitely valid alternative suspects in both of these cases."

"So you think it might be worth discounting Cameron for the time being?" Sutton sounded sceptical. "Don't forget, we pretty much know that these two murders were committed by the same person and the method leads us right back to Cameron."

Warren raised a hand. "Bear with me for a moment; if we discount Cameron that leaves us with two murders committed by the same person. I suggest that if we can find what links these two cases together, then it will lead us to the killer. Or killers."

"Killers? You think there could be more than one person involved?"

Warren shrugged. "I suggest we keep all possibilities open at the moment. We mustn't run the risk of becoming closed to other ideas — translating what we see through a filter based on our preferred theories." He didn't need to remind Sutton of the problems that could lead to — the past summer's events were fresh in both men's minds. "Besides, if Richard Cameron is responsible, then finding a link between these two victims will strengthen our case against him."

Sutton grunted, clearly not entirely convinced yet. "It's a good theory. But what if there is no link between these girls? What if he really is just a sick pervert who selects his victims based on nothing more than their appearance and vulnerability? What if these truly are 'stranger' killings?"

To that, Warren had no answer.

* * *

Richard Cameron was not happy to see Warren and Tony Sutton appear at his front door, accompanied by another marked police car. Nevertheless, he knew that he had no choice and so assented to being driven to the station. Again, Richard Cameron's lawyer met them there.

As before, it was his lawyer that opened proceedings.

"Chief Inspector, you are bordering on harassment here. You've had my client in for questioning before over the death of that unfortunate young woman and been supplied with an alibi for that time. As I recall, you had no evidence whatsoever of my client's involvement. I suspect that if you had any evidence now, you would have arrested him immediately."

Warren ignored him; he was just doing his job.

"Mr Cameron, what were you doing on the night of Thursday eighth December, from about 9 p.m. onwards?"

Both men looked surprised at this. Grayson's press conference had been pretty low-key and it was possible that the lawyer had missed the announcement that a second body had been found. Warren kept his gaze resolutely on Cameron. The surprise appeared genuine enough, but the man in front of him was a convicted rapist so who knew how his mind worked?

"Can I ask what this is about, Officer?" interjected Cameron's lawyer immediately.

Warren ignored him. "Please just answer the question, Mr Cameron."

"No comment."

Warren sighed, exasperated.

"We've been down this road before, Mr Cameron. Now you are just wasting our time." He turned to Cameron's lawyer. "Can you advise your client that if he has nothing to hide, then this 'no comment' business is just a waste of everybody's time. If he can't produce an alibi, fine, just say so and we'll eliminate him from our inquiries by other means."

"I most certainly will not. Mr Cameron is not under arrest and has a perfect legal right to refuse to answer a question, particularly when he is kept in the dark about why he is being asked such a question." The response was exactly what Warren expected. The lawyer could also have berated him for addressing him instead of his client, but he let the breach of etiquette slide.

"I'd like a private conversation with my lawyer, please."

Nodding, Warren turned off the tape and left the room.

He walked down the corridor to Sergeant Harry Kumar, the custody sergeant for the shift, who informed Warren that Tony Sutton was still trying to track down Michael Stockley, Cameron's son.

A few moments later, Richard Cameron's lawyer poked his head out of the interview suite to inform Warren that the client conference was over and they were ready to continue.

Despite his protestations to the contrary, Cameron's lawyer clearly had suggested that there was probably little to be gained by stalling with "no comment".

"On Thursday night, I felt tired. I went to bed early, about seven o'clock. I didn't wake up until about five the next morning."

Warren let his scepticism show. "Another early night? You must really need your beauty sleep."

"Yeah, well, I'm not as young as I used to be. Besides, I do a proper hard job. I don't spend all day sitting behind a desk," snapped Cameron.

Warren let that last comment ride, before standing up abruptly and pausing the tape recording. "You'll have to excuse me for a moment." He left the room immediately.

The rapid exit was necessary. Cameron was under no obligation to remain and if he felt that the interview was over, he might make noises about leaving. Warren didn't want him going anywhere until he had spoken to Tony Sutton about verifying Cameron's alibi with his son.

Sutton was standing in the corridor waiting. The two men ducked into an empty room for privacy. "What have you got?" asked Warren.

"No joy. Stockley is out of the office at a meeting up in Liverpool. His mobile's off and he isn't expected to be back before tomorrow."

Warren cursed quietly.

"We can't keep Cameron locked up until then and we can't risk them colluding over his alibi."

"Can we get Merseyside to bring him down here for questioning?"

Warren thought for a moment. "Tricky. We've not got any grounds to arrest him and I can't see him voluntarily coming all the way down here, abandoning work. Plus, it'll be pretty expensive. I can't see Grayson signing off on the expense willingly."

"Day trip?" Sutton didn't look enthusiastic. With no direct train routes from Middlesbury to Liverpool, they were looking at multiple connections and a seven- or eight-hour round trip at least or a similar length journey by car. Warren felt the same.

Warren pinched his lip thoughtfully. "I have an idea."

* * *

"Pretty much matches what Cameron told me himself. Lights out about seven. Either he's telling the truth or the two of them co-ordinate their stories."

"You'd think if they were making something up, they'd try a bit harder though?"

Cameron and his lawyer had been extremely unhappy about the four-hour suspension of his interview and continued custody, but it had taken that long to arrange for Merseyside Police to persuade Michael Stockley to attend a local station for questioning on behalf of Middlesbury CID. The subsequent digital recording of the interview had been emailed to Warren and Sutton, who had listened to it in Warren's office.

Warren shrugged. "My gut tells me there's something fishy going on there, but I don't know what it is." He sighed. "There's nothing we can do though. Cut him loose. But let's keep on digging."

TUESDAY 13TH DECEMBER

Chapter 31

Warren was sitting at a large table. In front of him was a box of jigsaw pieces. He poured them out and started to turn them over, one by one; each piece had a picture of a person. Sally Evans, Carolyn Patterson, Darren Blackheath, Bill Evans, Alex Chalmers, Tony Sutton, Karen Hardwick… There were dozens of them. As he turned more and more pieces over he saw that there were also pictures of clues: footprints, a muddy crime-scene tent, the ligature used to strangle Sally Evans. He tried to fit the pieces together, but it was no use. None of them seemed to want to slot together. Looking at the edge of the box, he saw it was a thousand-piece puzzle; looking back at the pile, he estimated that there couldn't be more than a few hundred — where were the rest? How the hell was he supposed to solve it with only half the clues? He felt a surge of frustration, his breathing becoming more rapid. He knew his blood pressure was rising — maybe that was the ringing in his ears.

He closed his eyes, tried to calm himself down. To look at the problem from a different perspective. Maybe he didn't need to solve the puzzle piece by piece? He was just looking for the big picture — maybe he could work backwards. If he knew the picture then he could find the clues he needed individually. He turned the box over — nothing. The front of the box where the final picture was normally displayed was just a blank piece of white cardboard. With a scream of frustration, he hurled the box across the room. The ringing in his ears intensified and he heard himself sob. Weeks of working and he was no closer to finding the answer to his questions. Waves of exhaustion and a sense of failure washed over him like the sea crashing against the beach.

He felt the gentle caress of a pair of hands on his shoulders and the whispering of his name.

Susan.

All of his cares melted away. He leant back into her embrace as she continued to whisper his name… "Warren, Warren…"

"WARREN!"

Susan's voice jerked him awake like a slap. The ringing in his ears became the ringing of his mobile phone. The light was on and Susan was lying across him, trying to reach the flashing phone on his nightstand. The splash of cold water as she accidentally knocked the glass off the stand and over him chased away the last remnants of the dream.

Grabbing the phone, he glanced at the screen before he swiped the answer icon. 02:14.

* * *

Warren arrived at the accident and emergency ward at Addenbrooke's hospital in Cambridge just before 3 a.m. He'd phoned Tony Sutton, dressed quickly and raced out of the house. It had been quiet that night and he'd made very good time up the A10.

His "Police Business" card in the windscreen and the early hour meant he'd had no need to circle the sprawling hospital campus looking for a parking space. He'd pulled in between a North Herts police patrol car and Sutton's Audi right outside the main doors to A and E. The DI lived to the north of Middlesbury and had probably arrived a few minutes before Jones. Even if he didn't live closer, he drove fast and would still have beaten his boss in.

Entering through the double doors, Warren spotted Sutton immediately, talking to a couple of uniformed officers and a paramedic next to the reception desk. The rest of the waiting area was quiet, the number of bruised and troublesome drunks lower than it would have been at the weekend.

"Obviously, we wouldn't normally have been called, guv, but the call centre have been advised that we should be given first dibs on any murders, particularly of young women. It sounds as if somebody in the centre used their initiative and decided that a blatant attempted murder was good enough to fit the bill." Sutton looked as tired as Warren felt.

"Take it from the top, please."

The paramedic, a middle-aged black woman wrapped up as if she were doing a tour of the Arctic, spoke up. Her tone was confident and efficient; she knew exactly what the officers wanted and was clearly eager to get back out on duty as soon as possible.

"We received a call shortly after midnight that a young woman's body had been found in an alleyway off the back of Truman Street in Middlesbury." Warren nodded knowingly. Although not his area of specialty, he was well acquainted with Truman Street. It and the surrounding areas were about as close to a red-light district as Middlesbury got. At any one time a half-dozen or so sex workers could be found plying their trade around its dingy back alleys. The police worked closely with the council and the sex workers themselves to manage the area. Prostitution was certainly not tolerated — too many *Daily Mail* readers lived in

Middesbury for that to ever happen — however, it was controlled and the girls and their clients followed certain informal rules. In return, social and health workers, with the aid of the police, supported the girls, keeping them as healthy and safe as possible.

"When we arrived, the caller had vanished — not unusual around there — but we found her behind some large wheelie bins at the back of a greasy spoon café. At first glance, we thought she was dead too." At this the woman's professional façade cracked just a little. "In twenty-two years, I've never seen a beating like it. Whoever did it took a cricket bat or something similar to her head, repeatedly. If it wasn't for the way she was dressed, I'd have struggled to decide if she was male or female.

"Anyway, I checked for a pulse as a matter of routine and was amazed when I found one. She was barely breathing, so we intubated her and radioed ahead to warn that there was a serious head trauma coming in. There's nowhere to land an air ambulance, so we stabilised her in the back of the van. Lister is dealing with a multiple car accident south of Stevenage, so we were directed to Addenbrooke's. We got here at about half past midnight. She's been in surgery ever since."

"So you think it might be attempted murder?"

The paramedic shrugged. "Not really my place to say, but, like I say, in twenty-two years I've never seen anything like it. Whoever took that bat or whatever it was to her head was playing for keeps. And to be honest, she probably should be dead. I wouldn't get your hopes up too much. I don't rate her chances of surviving."

After thanking the paramedic for her time, Warren joined Sutton at the coffee machine. Wearily saluting him with the plastic cup, he broke the silence.

"What do you think, Tony?"

Sutton looked thoughtful. "I don't know, guv. On the one hand it sounds as if it was definitely attempted murder, the call-centre worker was right to flag it. On the other hand, it doesn't really fit the pattern. Firstly, the previous two victims were chosen as they walked home from work or the gym — if we assume that she was a sex worker, then his choice of target has changed. Second, the last two girls were dumped somewhere remote — presumably to buy him some time before we started investigating. Even if she hadn't been found by chance tonight, it sounds as if whoever put the bins out from the café the next day would have had a nasty surprise."

Warren nodded his agreement. "On top of that the previous two attacks have been meticulously planned. He took great lengths to avoid any contamination of the scene. And he subdued his victim with solvent beforehand. Without wanting to second-guess Forensics, I'm going to suggest that he went in swinging this time with little care — why?"

Sutton shrugged. "Like you said, let's not second-guess Forensics." His expression darkened more. "If things are as bad as that paramedic suggested, we may even get results from an autopsy."

* * *

It was 6 a.m. before Sutton and Warren arrived back at Middlesbury. At 5 a.m., the lead trauma surgeon, Mr Hira-Singh, had met the officers to discuss the young woman's prognosis.

"It's a miracle she survived. Remarkably I think we can probably thank her poor health overall and the freezing conditions, although I don't think she would have lasted much longer if she hadn't been found when she was."

Prompted by their surprised looks, he explained, "The human body is a remarkable thing and the human brain even more so. In recent years, we've found that much of the damage caused by traumatic brain injury or strokes actually occurs in the days or weeks after the initial insult. Cells surrounding the original injury site can be damaged or destroyed as a side effect of the body trying to repair the original injury or at least limit its effects. We're only just starting to understand what is actually happening at a cellular level, but in recent years it's been found that inducing a state of controlled hypothermia in patients can slow down cellular metabolism enough to buy us time to work on repairing the damage without the body's own mechanisms getting in the way." He removed his spectacles and rubbed his eyes.

Close up, the man had a neatly trimmed beard and still wore an elastic cap over his head; perhaps he would replace it with a full turban at the end of his shift.

"Well, the young woman in there — and she is young, no more than twenty, I'd say — was probably halfway to hypothermia before her attack even started. I didn't get much of a chance to perform an examination, obviously, and it's outside my expertise even if I did, but from what I saw she was very underweight for her height. If it wasn't for the obvious signs of drug abuse I'd say she was anorexic. She may still be. Either way, she has no body fat to speak of and she was dressed in skimpy clothes in a temperature of minus five at least. Her metabolism was probably so low, the very worst effects of the trauma may have been avoided. One thing's for certain — she won't have put up much of a fight." For the first time a note of anger crept into the man's voice. It was clear that after hours of battling to save this young stranger's life, he'd grown attached to her.

"What's her prognosis, doctor?" asked Warren quietly.

He sighed. "She'll almost certainly live. The next forty-eight hours are critical and she'll be in ICU for at least a week, but barring any unforeseen complications she should survive." He paused. "But what she'll be like when she comes around — if she comes around — is anybody's guess. We'll be doing regular scans to monitor any swelling or bleeding, but it'll be a few days until we can tell what level of permanent brain damage she's sustained. She'll need more surgery in the coming weeks to repair her skull. It's been fractured like a jigsaw puzzle."

Warren shuddered, the phrase bringing back memories of his earlier nightmare.

"I'm sorry, but I have to ask. Do you think she was raped?"

The surgeon shrugged. "I imagine that they'll do a proper rape kit when they get her up on the ward, but her knickers and stockings were intact. As was her top, for that matter, but I can't be any more precise than that."

With that, the surgeon stood up and shook hands with the two police officers. Both men could hear the sincerity in his voice as he wished them luck in finding her attacker.

* * *

Arriving back at the station, Jones and Sutton drank more coffee and planned out how to approach this latest turn of events. With neither man sure if the attack was linked to the killings, Warren decided to make that their priority.

At 7 a.m., the two men made their way to the scene of the attack. The sun was just starting to reappear and the cold, damp air held a light, gloomy fog that the poorly maintained streetlights did little to dispel. The area was well chosen. Warren could see how it would be relatively easy to stage an attack on a vulnerable young woman, especially late at night. The area was run-down and in desperate need of regeneration. Few people on legitimate business would be out and about after dark, making it the perfect area for sex workers and their clients to conduct their seedy transactions.

Once upon a time a main thoroughfare, Truman Street sported two terraced-rows of mixed-usage buildings. Most had a large glass store front, with a wide door for customer access on one side and another, more modest, wooden door on the other, leading to the upstairs floor of the building, which was either a flat or the back office for the business downstairs.

Today, at least half of the store fronts were boarded up, with "For Sale" signs in the windows or "To Let" signs advertising the upstairs flat. What businesses remained had graffiti-covered steel shutters padlocked to the concrete windowsill. Often it was unclear if they were closed for the night or closed for good. Rain-damaged flyers and posters advertised gigs from three years ago. It was bad news when even the fly-posters stopped visiting, thought Warren.

The alleyway where the attack occurred was marked off with blue and white crime-scene tape. A white tent protected the scene from the elements and the public.

As news of their arrival spread the familiar white-suited form of Andy Harrison emerged from behind the tent.

"Morning, DCI Jones, Tony." He nodded, not offering a hand. "We must stop meeting like this." As usual the Yorkshireman's sense of humour was inappropriate, but neither man commented. When you saw what he saw on a daily basis, you could be forgiven if your jokes were a little off-colour.

"Morning, Andy. What have you got for us?"

"Pretty straightforward, I'd say." He pulled back the awning of the tent, so the two detectives could see inside. "The alleyway is pretty narrow and dingy, not easily visible from the road, unless you are standing directly opposite and there's no reason to at that time of night."

Both men turned and saw that he was right. Directly opposite the entrance to the alley was a shuttered shop front. The peeling sign above the covered window read "Middlesbury Electronics Components" in faded yellow letters with a local number printed above it. The flat above had uncurtained windows with a "To Let" sign. Even assuming the shop was still in business, it wouldn't be open at midnight and it didn't look as though the flat above was occupied. The greasy spoon café on the left of the alleyway was open eight to five and the florist's on the right-hand-side appeared to have been closed for some time judging by the state of the "For Sale" sign in the window. Later in the morning, a team would go door-knocking in an appeal for witnesses, but Warren felt it unlikely that they'd find much.

"The paramedics found the young woman behind those bins there." He gestured at the battered-looking large metal containers. Warren was a little surprised to see them; he remembered them from his schooldays — huge things on wheels, about five feet tall, that needed to be lifted by a special attachment on the back of the lorry. He guessed that colour-coded, plastic recycle bins hadn't yet made it to this part of town. He wondered how many times a week these bins were emptied. According to the large, colour-coded calendar on the back of his kitchen door, he and Susan put out their four different bins up to twice a week, depending on the colour of their lid and their contents. Unless it was a bank holiday — then, of course, all bets were off.

Regardless, these bins would do a very good job of hiding the woman's body from passers-by.

"We've found a large pool of blood here, mixed in with blonde hair and bits of flesh. We've also found small splinters of wood, presumably from the weapon—" he waved his hand in a large arc "—and blood-spatter traces all over the bins, the walls and the floor. That may give us some ideas about the attacker. We're looking for traces leading to or from the alleyway." He pointed down the far end. "As you can see, the alleyway is open both ends. The far end leads onto a back access road. If we can find which way he entered or left that might narrow down the search for witnesses."

Warren nodded his approval. "Good thinking. Any idea about the weapon?"

Harrison smiled. "I can do better than that." He turned to one of his assistants. "Sam, could you show the detectives what you found in the bin?"

Another paper-suited form turned around. Truth be told, Warren had no idea until she spoke whether "Sam" was male or female. It made him feel slightly uncomfortable. Why? Surely it didn't matter what Sam's sex was, just as it didn't matter what ethnicity or sexual orientation she was. Nevertheless, Warren had always found the shapeless, unisex suits to be a little discomforting.

Pulling out a clear evidence bag about the size of a carrier bag — it reminded Warren of the duty-free bags you now had to put your liquids in at the airport — the forensic technician showed him a length of wooden two by two about eighteen inches long. The last six inches of one end were chipped and frayed and stained with blood. A few hairs had caught amongst the splinters.

"There's a pile of this in the back of one of the nearby gardens — we'll have to check and see if it matches, but it's clearly been sitting outside exposed to the elements for some time." Warren took her word for it; it wasn't clear at all to his eyes. "Which unfortunately means that unless we can get prints or other trace evidence off the wood, it's probably not going to lead us to the killer."

"Damn it. Good find though — anything else? The paramedics didn't find her handbag and her pockets were empty. Sex workers usually carry all sorts with them."

Sam shook her head. "Nothing so far, but we haven't started a fingertip search yet. I just happened to spot the wood by accident, poking out of the bin."

"Do me a favour, then, could you? Keep an eye out for it. If you find it, it could give us some clues to her identity and maybe even the motive. Call me as soon as it turns up."

With nothing else to see, Jones and Sutton decided to leave the crime scene team to it and return to the station. On the way there, Warren picked Sutton's brains.

"On the face of it, it looks unrelated to the murders. The MO doesn't match and her handbag is missing. I would say either a disgruntled client or a mugging."

Warren nodded slowly. "I can see your point of view, Tony, but when does a mugger bash the victim's brains out like that? Or a pissed-off client, for that matter?"

The two men rode in silence for a few minutes.

"You know, I don't know what worries me more," started Warren. "That our murderer has changed his tactics, or that there are two different killers in Middlesbury."

Chapter 32

By the time morning briefing ended at 9 a.m., Warren was starting to flag. A team of officers were door-knocking around Truman Street to see if they could find any witnesses, but he didn't have much hope. More promisingly he was due to meet one of the liaison officers who worked with the sex-worker support team. Assuming last night's victim was local, Warren was hopeful that they could identify her and perhaps shed some light on what had occurred. For that, they would probably need to send a team of specially trained officers out after dark to canvass other sex workers in the area. He knew from briefings that the support workers laboured hard to gain the trust of the girls and that they co-operated to keep them safe. Maybe a witness had seen somebody acting strangely in the area? Warren felt a wave of hopelessness washing over him.

Two murders and an attempted murder and his team seemed to be hitting dead ends at every turn. And everyone was looking at him for inspiration. For the first time since taking his new post in the summer, Warren found himself wishing he could turn back the clock, to the days when he was just one of a team of detective inspectors working in the comfort of the huge West Midlands Police Service — free to get on with his job, safely insulated from the politics and the pressures by a layer of DCIs and Detective Superintendents above him.

Snap out of it, he commanded himself, feeling revulsion at his self-pity. *You wanted this promotion and now, after a few late nights, you want to give up?* He stood up abruptly, hoping the sudden movement would translate itself into a surge of renewed energy. Although he knew he probably shouldn't, he made his way out to the communal coffee urn. This was, what, his fifth — sixth? — cup of coffee this morning? His stomach growled as he filled his mug. His fifty-pence piece chinked against the handful of others in the honesty jar — all of them his. He wondered briefly how long he would keep up his one-man crusade to get his colleagues to pay for their coffee. The first sip of the coffee scalded his mouth and left an acid feeling in his stomach. Was he developing an ulcer?

Susan had once explained that stomach ulcers were normally caused by a bacterium that ate away at the protective lining of the stomach and that too much stress, or coffee or spicy foods couldn't cause them. She'd even shown him some colourful posters drawn by her year eight pupils, gleefully recounting how some Australian researchers had proven this theory and won a Nobel prize by drinking a beaker of the bacteria and making themselves sick with ulcers. Nevertheless, Warren did worry that his irregular and questionable diet and prodigious coffee intake might be rotting him from the inside out.

Returning to the main office, he heard his office phone ringing. Breaking into a trot, he nearly spilt his coffee as he dived for the handset, snatching it up just before the call was diverted somewhere into the bowels of the police station's voicemail system.

"It's Harrison," the crime scene manager stated unnecessarily.

"We've found the victim's handbag and purse. Chucked over a fence and covered in what is almost certainly her blood."

"Brilliant news. What have you found out?"

"We'll have to do a full look-see back at Welwyn, but it could be robbery. The handbag is full of what you'd expect: lots of condoms, some lube, tissues, ciggies and a lighter, plus what looks like a crack-pipe and a couple of rocks. There's also a mobile phone, a rape alarm and a can of what looks like pepper spray. Her purse was unclasped and has a bank card, but no money. I'm no expert, but prostitution's usually a cash business. Unless she had a very slow night, you'd expect her to have at least a few quid in there."

"That's great, Andy. What's the name on the cards?"

"A Miss Melanie Clearwater. She has a basic Lloyds-TSB debit card and not a lot else. I'm guessing that either the attacker took the rest, or more likely she didn't carry any valuables in case she got mugged."

Warren made a note of the name. "You say the rape alarm and the pepper spray were in the handbag?"

"Yeah, towards the bottom. It doesn't look as if she used them."

"Suggesting either she was taken completely unawares or she knew her attacker and felt safe."

A rustling down the line suggested a man in a paper suit shrugging. "Above my pay-grade, Chief, but you could be right. Anyway, I think we're done for now. It's up to the lab folks down at Welwyn. I'm going to knock off and get some sleep. I'll have a report with photos for you tomorrow lunchtime."

After thanking him and hanging up, Warren leant back in his chair to mull over the latest findings. Harrison's mention of sleep had reminded Warren just how tired he felt. He glanced at his clock; he probably had twenty minutes until the support worker was due to arrive. His office door was closed and nobody could see in…

The ringing of his desk phone jerked him back to full wakefulness. Shaking his head to clear the cobwebs, he grabbed it.

"Constable Yvonne Fairweather from Welwyn to see you." It was the main reception desk. He looked at the clock; she was fifteen minutes early. For the briefest of moments, he felt an irrational anger — couldn't a man get just a few minutes' shut-eye around here? Was that too much to ask? He felt a sudden urge to tell the receptionist he was in a meeting and that he'd see her at ten as agreed.

"Send her up," he ordered, with as much authority as he could muster. Picking up his coffee, he saw that it was cold. He swallowed it anyway, grimacing slightly. He didn't know how Susan did it. She was discouraged from taking her coffee cup into her teaching laboratory with her, so as often as not would scald her mouth as she tried to drink as much of her coffee as possible in the five minutes she'd snatch at break-time after tidying her lab and talking to students, before leaving the cup to cool for the next hour, then downing the rest in the five-minute gap between successive lessons.

Her prized possession was a massive coffee mug bought as a leaving present by her mentor when she finished her teacher training — a deliberate wind-up since she never had the time to finish a normal mug of coffee, let alone the pint or more that this monster held. It was therefore rather strange that neither Susan nor Warren could stomach iced coffee.

A few moments later, the liaison officer arrived at his office. A tall, willowy woman of about thirty, she was dressed in jeans and ankle-length black boots, with a blue woollen jumper underneath her thick padded coat.

"Sorry for the attire, sir, but we try not to dress like police officers. It scares off clients and makes us unpopular with the girls."

Warren waved his hand dismissively. "No need to apologise. I quite understand."

"I've been to the hospital and seen the victim." Warren noticed the young woman's mouth twitched slightly as she fought for control. "She's one of my regulars, sir. Goes by the name Mel on the street."

Warren nodded. "We found what we assume is her purse. It had no money but had a bank card in the name of Miss Melanie Clearwater."

"That would be right. What was it, a robbery? I'd expect her to have a couple of hundred pounds in her purse at least by midnight."

Warren shrugged. "We're keeping an open mind at the moment. We also found what we think is some crack cocaine in the handbag — could she have just paid her dealer?"

Constable Fairweather shook her head. "I doubt it. She wasn't a particularly heavy user and even if she had just paid off her dealer she'd probably still have had some cash left over. What we do know is that she doesn't appear to have been raped. Her clothing and underwear were intact and an investigation shows no sign of significant bruising. It's always difficult with prostitutes obviously, but they found no traces of any semen, suggesting that she hasn't had either vaginal or anal sex last night. They've taken swabs, of course, but if it was a normal night she'd probably already had a handful of clients — the DNA will be a mess."

"I must admit I don't really know much about this side of policing and I'm new to the town. It might help if you fill me in on what it is you do and how the sex trade works in this area."

The constable paused, weighing up her thoughts, before leaning forward and steepling her fingers. "Well, basically, the local sex trade for Middlesbury and the surrounding villages is mostly centred around Truman Street and its offshoots. With the council, we operate a sort of containment operation. I assume that you've been down there?"

Warren nodded his assent.

"Well, as you can see, it's almost entirely non-residential, so that keeps the antisocial behaviour to a minimum. These days, the sex trade is very different. The girls get a lot of their business online. They probably only walk the streets a couple of nights a week. The clients come from all over and each girl probably does a half-dozen or so a night. It's mostly kerb-crawling. The girls operate an informal network and look out for one another. They make a note of the licence plates of any weirdos. Regulars who can be trusted get serviced quickly; clients that the girls don't like are ignored. They are encouraged to report any assaults et cetera to the police. It works fairly well. It's always going to be a dangerous business, but serious assaults are a fraction of what they were ten years ago."

"So if we went out tonight asking for witnesses, would the girls be likely to co-operate?"

Fairweather smiled tightly.

"Not for you, but they would for my team. But bear in mind, these girls only work a couple of nights a week, usually on an irregular schedule. We'd probably need to go out a few nights in a row to pick up everyone that was working last night."

Warren conceded the point. He'd leave the questioning to the experts — besides which, his team were busy enough as it was; he didn't really want them up half the night as well.

"By the way, I notice that you haven't mentioned pimps yet — do the girls have them?"

Fairweather shook her head. "Not in the way I'm imagining you are thinking. The days of flashily dressed thugs standing on street corners, watching over the girls and taking their earnings and dealing out beatings are largely gone. That being said, many of the girls, Mel included, work for so-called 'Escort Agencies' that source clients online for them. They then take a cut of the girl's earnings."

"Do you know anything about Mel's… agent? I ask because it's possible that she knew her attacker. We found a can of pepper spray and a rape alarm buried in the bottom of her handbag. They don't appear to have been readily available to her, suggesting that she wasn't feeling threatened."

"I wouldn't read too much into the pepper spray. It used to be that the girls would carry flick knives. We managed to discourage that, but have agreed to turn a blind eye to pepper spray or mace. The problem is, the girls can't conceal a can of pepper spray the way they could a flick knife, so they get left at the bottom of their handbag."

"And what about her agent?"

For the first time, since meeting, the PC looked uncomfortable.

"I think it's unlikely that he's responsible. He's no knight in shining armour, but he is a sensible businessman and he looks after the girls on his books. We have an… understanding with him."

Warren looked at her sternly.

"Be that as it may, Constable, one of his workers was beaten to within an inch of her life last night and might never regain consciousness. There is good reason to suspect that she knew her attacker and so I intend to interview this so-called agent and see if it generates any leads, relationship or no relationship."

* * *

Constable Fairweather had a BlackBerry smartphone with a list of the contact details for most of the local "escort agencies". Mel had worked for a local agency called the Discreet Companions Agency. It had a glossy website that advertised well-turned-out ladies of all ages, suitable for private dinner dates, business meetings and companionship. Prices were negotiable with the escort and subject to a booking and administration fee. No mention was made of any "extra services".

"The agency is run by a Daryl Hedgecox as an apparently legitimate business. He supplies women on demand for social functions or dates. He charges a hefty upfront administration fee, then the girl negotiates her own terms with the client and pays about 25 per cent to him to remain on his books. The girls are freelancers and he refuses to engage in any discussions regarding 'extra services' that the girls may supply. That way he is insulated from any suggestions that he is living off immoral earnings. He pays his taxes and apparently encourages the girls to do likewise. He skirts pretty close to the wind, but on the face of it he's a legitimate businessman."

"And nobody has tried to close him down? There must be something you can get him on?"

Fairweather looked irritated. "Look, I realise that it seems as if we are giving him a free pass — and perhaps we are — but people like Daryl Hedgecox are far better than the alternative. He's an intelligent man; he knows that if he treats his girls OK, doesn't rip off his clients and pays his taxes, we'd rather he ran things than some of the other scumbags out there. He also helps the girls report any dodgy clients and keeps his own records of who can be trusted. He doesn't deal in drugs and he doesn't threaten the girls with violence. Like I said before, he's no knight in shining armour, but he's better than a lot of the alternatives."

Warren nodded.

"I understand your argument and I'll try not to step too hard on your toes, but we need to work out exactly what happened to Mel last night and he could well provide clues. Do you have any idea where he might be?"

Fairweather still didn't look entirely satisfied, but she clearly knew when to fight her battles.

"He's probably still in bed at this time of the morning. He tends to keep the same hours as his girls. He lives just south of Cambridge. If we go now, we'll probably still catch him before he gets up."

"Always the best time," Warren agreed. "I find folks aren't at their sharpest when you've just woken them up."

Chapter 33

After picking up Tony Sutton and filling him in on the way, the three police officers pulled into the large, semi-circular, gravel drive in front of Daryl Hedgecox's palatial home.

"Christ, guv, we're in the wrong business," opined Tony Sutton as he craned his neck to get a good look at the mansion in front of them. Warren parked between a brand-new Range Rover and a classic Mercedes soft-top.

"He can't have made all of his money in the escort business, surely?"

Fairweather shook her head. "Unlikely. Rumour has it, he bought a whole load of cheap houses when the market was just right and rented them to students. A few years ago he offloaded some of them at a huge profit. Where he got the initial capital from, we don't know."

Warren grunted. "I wonder if his neighbours know what he does for a living."

"I doubt it very much. Apparently, Mr Hedgecox has wormed his way into the local community since moving here. He sits on all the local committees. He even applied for an Enhanced Criminal Records Check to become a member of the governing body at his daughter's primary school. Seems he'd forgotten about an early conviction for selling hardcore pornography under the counter in his father's video shop in his late teens. That put the kibosh on that ambition." Fairweather smiled briefly.

Warren was relieved she still remembered that he was ultimately not the sort of person you wanted associated with local schools.

After walking up a short garden path, the officers found themselves standing on a covered porch between two carved sandstone lions flanking the door. Money couldn't buy good taste, mused Warren.

Taking a deep breath, Warren pressed the doorbell. Deep inside the house a sonorous chime echoed. A few moments later, Warren depressed the button again. Finally, they heard a shuffling behind the door.

"Yeah? What is it? What do you want?"

The voice was rough-edged with sleep and irritation.

"Mr Hedgecox, it's the police. Can we come in and ask you a few questions?"

Warren held his warrant card up to the door's spyhole.

"No. Speak to my lawyer. I have nothing to say."

"Well, you don't even know what we're here for, Mr Hedgecox, so how can you be so sure?"

"I'm a legitimate businessman. Speak to my lawyers if you wish to ask anything."

Warren paused. "Are you quite sure about that, Mr Hedgecox? All we need to do is ask you a few questions as part of a routine enquiry. It's your choice. Either you invite us in, we do this all civilised and we'll be on our way in a few minutes with nobody any the wiser, or we can return with an arrest warrant and blue flashing lights and those really annoying, deafening sirens that tell all of your neighbours for miles around that the respectable Mr Hedgecox has just had a visit from the Old Bill. Like I said, it's your choice, Mr Hedgecox."

For the next few seconds, all that the three officers could hear was muffled swearing. Eventually that subsided and was followed by the sound of heavy locks and chains being undone.

It was clear that they had woken him up, thought Warren with some satisfaction. The man in front of them had a dark, swarthy complexion, with heavy stubble. About six feet two inches and medium build, he wore a grey-and-black-striped felt dressing gown, with tufts of black chest hair visible, just below his neck. His shaved scalp made it impossible to place the age of the man; he could have been anything between thirty-five and fifty-five.

"I suppose you'd better come in, then," grunted Hedgecox after introductions, leading the three officers into a large living room whose décor suggested a man with more money than taste. There was no question in Warren's mind that had they been having this meeting thirty years ago, the wall above the fireplace would have been home to three china ducks positioned as if they were flying home.

Sitting down on an uncomfortable, rather firm leather sofa, Warren began, "I believe that you employ a young girl named Mel — short for Melanie."

Hedgecox immediately raised a finger in correction. "I don't employ anybody, Officer. I am merely involved in introducing girls that I know to clients who wish to spend time with those girls."

"For which you charge a handsome fee," Sutton pointed out.

Hedgecox shrugged. "I'm a legitimate businessman. I pay my taxes and do nothing illegal. The girls negotiate their own terms with a client." He turned to Yvonne Fairweather. "Haven't we been through this before, Officer? Don't I do my best to co-operate with the police to keep the girls safe and ensure that rules are followed?"

Interrupting before Fairweather had a chance to speak, Warren interjected, "Your understanding with the authorities is none of my concern. What I want to know is what you know about this attack, which took place last night." He showed the pimp the screen of his phone on which he had taken a photograph of Melanie Clearwater as she lay in the hospital bed.

The sudden intake of breath and the draining of blood from his face couldn't be faked, decided Warren as he carefully observed the startled escort agent.

"Jesus… is that little Mel? What the hell happened?" The man's voice shook. The photograph had left little to the imagination.

"All we know is that she was attacked last night with a piece of wood and left to die. Her handbag and emptied purse were found a few metres away over a fence. We want to know why."

"Is she dead?"

Warren realised that the photograph was rather ambiguous on that score. The bandages and swelling and her grey pallor could easily have suggested a post-mortem photograph. Still, Warren saw no reason to lie. "Not quite."

"Will she be OK?"

Credit to him for asking, decided Warren grudgingly.

"We don't know. The next forty-eight hours are crucial. As for the long-term…" He shrugged.

Hedgecox shook his head slowly in disbelief. "Poor kid. Do you think it was a robbery? Seems a bit violent."

Warren shrugged again. "We're keeping an open mind, but you are right, it is violent. Most muggings are quick affairs. People get stabbed or injured all of the time, but as soon as the mugger has what they want it ends. But this was multiple blows to the head. We're treating it as an attempted murder."

"Where were you last night, Mr Hedgecox?" Tony Sutton had said little so far and now he leant forward. From what Yvonne Fairweather had told them and Hedgecox's reaction to the photograph, none of the officers really suspected Hedgecox of being directly involved; nevertheless, the perception that co-operation was in his best interest might help loosen his tongue even more.

As expected Hedgecox recoiled in surprise. "Woah, you don't think I had anything to do with this, do you?" He turned to Fairweather. "Tell them. I'm just a businessman. As long as the girls turn up for meetings and don't try and rip me off, we're cool. I only arrange meetings with clients who contact me through the agency. I don't have anything to do with what they do down on Truman Street — that's their own business."

"So where were you last night, between about ten and midnight?"

"Where I always am — down my brother's club having a drink, waiting for phone calls from the girls. I can get you the address. I'm sure I'm on the security cameras." He was clearly eager to please now and Warren decided to press home the advantage.

"Had Mel worked for you recently?"

Hedgecox's brow furrowed as he thought hard.

"Not for a couple of weeks, no. She's not the most popular of our girls, to be honest."

"Can you be a little more precise? I'm told you pay your taxes, so presumably you must keep a record of each job."

Hedgecox scowled briefly, before sighing and getting up.

"Yes, I keep detailed records on my laptop for my accountant."

As he walked over to a laptop sitting on the coffee table Warren asked him what he meant by Mel not being so popular.

"To be honest, she was a bit too skinny and young-looking — sure, some guys like that sort of thing, but the majority of my business these days comes from lonely, middle-aged businessmen looking for a date or an escort to a business function. They want an attractive but respectable-looking woman in her thirties or forties. The sort of woman that if they are seen with in public will get them admiring glances, not suspicious stares. They don't want a skinny young waif — too many questions."

As he told them this he booted up the laptop and opened an Excel spreadsheet. Warren couldn't help trying to look at the screen, but Hedgecox twisted the laptop away from him. "Not without a warrant, Chief Inspector," he said with a smirk. "I'll help you track down whoever hurt Mel, but you aren't sniffing through my files."

Warren shrugged non-committally. Hedgecox manipulated the track pad before clearing his throat. "Just as I thought. I last placed Mel with a client three weeks ago." He smiled slightly. "The guy's a regular. Never had any bother with him before." He clicked the track pad again. "Feedback is clear. No complaints from him, feedback from Mel and other girls who've met him note nothing unusual — just your usual lonely, middle-aged man looking for a bit of company."

"And that's it?"

"Well, it depends how far you want to go back. She had a bit more work over the summer, with the tourists and, to be honest, before she lost so much weight. You've seen her, no doubt — stick-thin. She used to have a bit more meat on her bones." He looked at Fairweather. "You remember, I'm sure. Bloody drugs,

I'm guessing. At least she has the sense not to use them in front of the clients."

The constable nodded her agreement. "If anything good can come of this, we may be able to wean her off them now she's in hospital."

"I'd like the name of that client, if you don't mind, Mr Hedgecox."

"No way." He shook his head violently. "Not without a warrant. If word got out that I gave my clients' details away to anyone who asked, I'd be out of business. We're called 'Discreet Companions' for a reason. Besides which, this was three weeks ago. I doubt very much that he's responsible." He folded his arms resolutely.

Warren eyed him for several long seconds before turning to Sutton.

"DI Sutton, could you pop back to the station and get a warrant drafted? Constable Fairweather and I will stay here and keep Mr Hedgecox company."

Sutton stood up. "Certainly, guv. Should I take your car or organise a lift?"

"I think the tax-payer can afford the petrol. Why don't you phone the station and ask for a patrol car and a driver? Tell them to use the lights and the siren — we don't want them to get stuck in traffic and waste any more of Mr Hedgecox's time."

Hedgecox slumped back on his chair with a look of disgust. It was clear that he was weighing up the potential damage to his business from naming a client and the very real damage to his personal reputation from having a police car with lights and sirens parked on his front driveway. In the end personal reputation won over any slight risk to his business and he grudgingly wrote down the mobile phone number and contact details of the client.

"It's likely that this gentleman will have nothing to do with this and have an alibi, but I assume that we can rely on your discretion to keep this between us, Mr Hedgecox?" Warren and his two colleagues were on their way out of the front door, having got what they came for.

Hedgecox snorted. "He won't hear anything from me." His expression turned uncomfortable, before he addressed Constable Fairweather. "I'd like to send Mel some flowers. Maybe pop in and see the poor kid. She's had a hard life — she didn't deserve this shit. Where is she?"

He seemed sincere, but Warren was relieved when Fairweather shook her head. "I'm sorry, Daryl. She's a vulnerable young woman. It wouldn't be appropriate for me to divulge that sort of information."

He looked a little nonplussed, before nodding his head. "I understand — in that case, could you hold on a moment?" Before they could reply he darted back inside again, before emerging a few seconds later with a bulging leather wallet. Without pausing he opened it and peeled off a pile of ten-pound notes, pressing them into the startled Yvonne Fairweather's hand.

"Buy her some flowers, will you, and use the rest to get her anything she needs? Judging by the photos, she may be in some time. No need to tell her who it's from."

And that's why police work would never get dull, thought Warren. You really did see every facet of human life.

Chapter 34

Three hours later, Jones and Sutton pulled up outside the bungalow of Mr David Woods, Melanie Clearwater's last client through
Daryl Hedgecox's Discreet Companions Agency. A search of the
Police National Computer had revealed no records and they'd
relied on the mobile phone company to provide them with an
address. With no evidence that the man had done anything
wrong, the officers had no justification for pulling him in and so
had decided an informal interview was the best approach.

Parking outside the house, the two officers started up the
driveway.

"Something's not quite right, guv," muttered Sutton quietly.

"I feel it, too. I'm sure we're missing something." He looked
around at the neatly manicured garden. It seemed as though Mr
Woods was home; his car sat on the drive. But something didn't
quite seem right.

The two officers looked at each other. With nothing more to
go on than a vague feeling of uneasiness, Warren couldn't justify
calling in reinforcements. Nevertheless, he took a deep breath,
exchanged glances with Tony Sutton and counted down from
three before ringing the doorbell.

After what seemed like an age, the door opened. Neither man could have been prepared for what they saw.

* * *

"That bastard Hedgecox must have known," ranted Sutton in the car on the way back to the station. "I'll bet he's laughing all over that stupid, smug face of his."

"You're probably right." Warren stole a glance at his colleague, whose foul temper was as much to do with a lack of sleep as a genuine grievance.

"You've got to admit, it was pretty funny, though."

Sutton scowled, before slowly shaking his head and eventually breaking into a grin. "We must be knackered. I can't believe we missed all of the clues. The car, the driveway… It was all there in front of us."

"Well, at least we know he wasn't responsible for last night's attack — he'd never have got down that narrow alleyway."

Both men burst out laughing.

"I'll remember the look on your face as long as I live." Sutton chuckled. "The way you were staring at eye height as the door opened, before slowly looking down until you saw him. Then the way you asked, all hopeful, 'Is Mr Woods in?' and he replied, 'I am Mr Woods.'"

Warren shook his head, enjoying the brief moment of levity. The suspect had been a surprise to both of them. A hugely obese, older man, he had appeared at the door to his especially adapted bungalow on his mobility scooter.

"Still, can't be too careful, boss, and I think it was quite right that you didn't make any assumptions and asked if he could account for his whereabouts last night."

"Yeah, I thought he was a bit rude, to tell the truth. Probably a good job I didn't ask him about the last time he had an escort around the house."

Chapter 35

Back at the station, Warren was definitely feeling the effects of his early wake-up call. He chugged yet more coffee as he sat back at his desk, reading reports. It seemed that some progress had at least been made with the mysterious woman that Sally Evans' father claimed to have been with the night that she was killed. DC Willis and DS Johnson had been working with the IT department, the financial crimes section and local magistrates to put pressure on the dating site to reveal details about Bill Evans' lover, "Boadicea".

They finally traced her payment details, linking it to a credit card belonging to the rather less flamboyantly named "Mary Samson", who lived in the small village of Cottenham just north of Cambridge. Aware of the need for a degree of sensitivity, Warren decided to take only DC Annabel Willis along with him to interview her.

They arrived unannounced at a smart-looking cottage on the outskirts of the village, close to the local secondary school. After they rang the bell, the door was answered by an older man in his late fifties or early sixties, wearing a clerical collar. Two small, identical faces peeked around his legs. His heart sank. The possibility of red faces all around had just increased exponentially. He'd have to be tactful here.

"Er, hello, my name is Detective Chief Inspector Warren Jones and this is Detective Constable Annabel Willis. We're looking for Mrs Mary Samson. Is she home?"

"Reverend Christopher Samson. I'm afraid that she has just popped out to take some cakes over to the school disco. You're welcome to wait for her. She's due back any moment — although she's chairing a council meeting in an hour or so. Is there anything I can help you with?"

Oh, dear God, this just got worse, thought Warren. Vicar's wife and mother, local councillor, heavily involved in the local school... He would be treading lightly to say the least.

"I'm afraid that we need to speak to Mrs Samson directly; just a couple of questions to help us in a routine enquiry. Your wife isn't in any trouble, I assure you."

The vicar laughed heartily.

"I never thought for one second that she was. She's as honest as the day is long, my beautiful Mary. Please, come in. The kettle has just boiled."

Entering the house — the vicarage, Warren now realised — they made for the living room. As the priest headed for the kitchen Warren turned to DC Willis.

"I know what you're going to say, sir, and I'm quite happy to let you do the talking," she interrupted, grinning puckishly.

"Probably for the best. This one has the potential for embarrassment all around." Warren sighed.

The two officers sat awkwardly for the next ten minutes, sipping tea. The Reverend Samson was a genial host and, whilst he was clearly very curious about the reason for their visit, he managed to avoid asking any questions.

Finally, the front door opened and a short, skinny, dark-haired woman Warren guessed to be in her early forties bustled through the door, carrying an armful of empty Tupperware cake boxes. A young teenage lad followed behind, similarly laden.

"The cakes went down well, sweetheart," she called out as she entered the room. Seeing the two officers, she stopped.

"Oh, I'm sorry, I didn't realise you had company." She didn't seem at all surprised; unexpected visitors were clearly not unusual in the vicarage.

"Actually, my dear, they are here to see you." The Reverend Samson stood up.

Mary Samson looked surprised, but her open face was guileless.

Warren introduced himself and Annabel, before reassuring her that she wasn't in any trouble, they just needed her assistance in a routine enquiry. The Reverend Samson was either very tactful or it genuinely was time for the twins to get ready for bed, so Warren was spared the awkwardness of having to ask for a private word.

When he had gone, Warren gestured for her to sit down. Looking at her, he could see that she was even younger than he had first thought; he wondered if she had even had her fortieth birthday yet.

"What is this about, Officer?" she inquired. She still looked bemused, with no traces of guilt. The woman obviously had a clear conscience, at least as far as the law went.

"Can you tell me if you know a Mr Bill Evans?" started Warren.

The woman in front of him thought for a moment, before shaking her head.

"No, I don't believe so. We have a large parish and I can't claim to know the names of everyone, but the name isn't familiar."

Warren resigned himself to the fact that she wasn't going to make it easy for him.

"You may know him by another name, Arthur, and he would know you by the name Boadicea."

It was as if he'd slapped her across the face. The flush of redness was almost alarming and she nearly dropped her cup of tea.

"How…? Who…? How did you know about that?"

"That's not important, right now. Could you tell us how you know Mr Evans?"

The woman stared at the floor, before continuing in a shaky voice.

"I don't really know him at all. He's just an… acquaintance. I don't see what I could possibly help you with."

Warren leant forward. "Mrs Samson, we're not here to cause you any trouble…" He glanced meaningfully at the door that her husband had left through. "I appreciate that this could be a very delicate situation. I assure you that once we have found out what we need to know, you are unlikely to hear from us again."

Mary Samson took a handkerchief out of her sleeve and wiped her eyes with it. Taking a deep, shaky breath, she started talking.

"I've known Arthur… er, Bill, for about a year. We met on the Internet on a special website catering for people who wanted, well, you know…" Warren nodded sympathetically, motioning for her to continue.

"It's not that I don't love my husband. Really, I do, and we have three beautiful children. It's just that he's a lot older than me — twenty-two years, can you believe? When we first met, he wasn't a priest, he was just a deacon. I'd finished a very stressful relationship and he was so kind to me… Anyway, one thing led to another and we ended up getting married. My friends all said it wouldn't work, of course — he was nearing fifty and I was barely twenty-five — but it did and I haven't regretted a single moment."

She paused for breath and Warren felt obliged to interrupt her.

"You don't have to justify your actions to us, Mrs Samson. We're just here for information."

Mary Samson shook her head. "No. You are the only people apart from my best friend that I've told about this. The guilt has been eating me up inside. In fact, my New Year resolution was going to be to break it off."

"So how did your arrangement work?"

"Well, at first it works pretty much like any dating site. You put in your preferences and what you are looking for and they send you a series of matches. If you find someone that you like the look of, you can chat to them through their site. However, unlike normal sites, if you decide you want a bit more privacy and to move away from the site, they will — for a small fee — send you an unregistered Pay As You Go SIM card for your mobile phone and arrange anonymous email addresses so that you can continue getting to know each other.

"Eventually, we decided to meet up for coffee. We decided from the start not to use our real names. I think he's married as well. Well, we hit it off and one thing led to another... Anyway, we agreed early on that it was just sex. We had no desire to start a relationship beyond that, so we decided to just keep it as a regular appointment. A few days before the first weekend of the month, I'd log onto my email account and send him an email and we'd arrange when I could call. Then I'd put my SIM card in at the appropriate time and call him and we'd arrange when to meet up."

So far, the story matched Bill Evans' version, but Warren wanted a few more details before he accepted his story and verified his alibi.

"Can you tell us where this... liaison... takes place?"

"There's a Travelodge just north of Cambridge. As far as

Christopher, my husband, is concerned, I go out to the movies with my best friend each Friday and stay with her overnight in Huntingdon. Christopher has no interest in the cinema and so he's quite happy for me to go with Michelle."

"Can you tell us when the last time that you met up with Bill was?" asked Warren.

"The first Friday of this month, our usual time — I guess the second."

"And at about what time did you meet?"

"We don't like to be seen around, so we meet at a country pub out in the sticks somewhere, have a meal, then go straight back to the hotel. We met up at about 6 p.m. in The Queen and Corgi near Peterborough last time."

A pub meal followed by a dirty rendevous in a Travelodge — how romantic, thought Warren wryly, concentrating on keeping a straight face. They'd need to verify what they'd been told, but it seemed that Bill Evans' alibi was true and that he was the better part of fifty miles away when Sally Evans was kidnapped.

After a few more procedural questions, the two officers stood to leave.

"You won't need to mention my name in whatever it is you are investigating, will you?" The dark-haired woman chewed her lip nervously.

"I can assure you that it is very unlikely that we will need to name you publicly," stated Warren, before taking his leave of the red-faced woman.

Climbing into the car, Annabel Willis finally spoke up.

"A vicar's wife living in a tiny little rural village, having sordid sexual encounters in the local Travelodge. You couldn't make it up, sir."

"You definitely see all sorts in this job," agreed Warren.

"I've also won a fiver as well, sir."

"Really? How so?"

"Sergeant Johnson was convinced that with a username like Boadicea, she had to be tall, blonde and Nordic-looking with a huge cleavage. He'll be ever so disappointed."

* * *

It was approaching 7 p.m. when Warren and Annabel pulled into the station car park. Waves of tiredness were starting to roll over Warren as he trudged wearily up the stairs. Just a quick word with the troops and one last check of his email for anything urgent and it was time to leave, Warren decided. He desperately needed a good night's sleep.

After a few minutes spent briefing a similarly exhausted Tony Sutton and the rest of the team, Warren found himself slumped in front of his office computer. Realising that he hadn't been processing anything that he'd read for the past few minutes, Warren decided to right-click his most recent emails, re-categorise them as 'unread' and return to them in the morning.

The sudden drill-like vibration of his phone, resting next to his elbow on his wooden desk, startled him into wakefulness.

"I hope you haven't forgotten that you were supposed to be picking me up and driving us to the party at seven," was Susan's opening line when he picked up.

Warren glanced at the clock — ten-past, "No, of course not. I just got out of a meeting," he fibbed. "I'm just about to leave. I'll pick you up on the way."

He couldn't tell from Susan's tone if she'd bought the lie or not.

"Don't forget we're also picking up Rachel and her husband Paulo on the way."

"Yes, of course. Ring them and let them know I'm on my way."

Hanging up, Warren allowed himself a brief ten seconds with his eyes closed. He groaned quietly. He had been looking forward to an early night; the last thing he wanted to do was attend Susan's staff Christmas party. However, he'd promised to drive her and her colleague, Rachel. The party was being held midweek in a local hotel — a venue large enough would have been prohibitively expensive on a weekend this close to Christmas.

Apparently the Christmas party a few years ago had been a riotous affair, leaving such a legacy of gossip and ill feeling that the head teacher had stipulated that in future staff should be encouraged to bring their spouses or partners, in the hope that this would curb the worst excesses. Regardless, Susan had admitted that the following day the kids were likely to be treated to a selection of DVDs and rather less challenging lessons, and woe betide anyone who misbehaved before the staff had their morning coffee break...

Fortunately, the unpredictable nature of his work meant that Warren kept a few different changes of clothes in a locker downstairs and he hastily changed into a pair of smart black jeans and a plain, short-sleeved shirt. With no time for a shower he made do with a quick puff of deodorant and a squirt of cologne.

Running a comb through his hair in front of a mirror, he realised that he had nearly two days of stubble and hadn't brushed his teeth in almost twenty-four hours. There was nothing that he could do about the beard — maybe he could pass it off as a fashion statement — but he could at least give his teeth a quick scrub to get rid of the worst of the coffee breath.

By now, Warren's stomach was rumbling. He'd skipped breakfast and only managed a cheese sandwich and a banana for lunch. Would there be food at the party? He hadn't thought to ask. At least he was driving — the way he was feeling, the last thing he needed was alcohol on an empty stomach. That really would be asking for trouble.

Snatching up his coat, he headed for the car park. At some point in the last twenty minutes it had started to rain heavily and he found himself playing a rather ungainly game of hopscotch as he tried to avoid the rapidly growing puddles.

Susan's first comment as she clambered into the car outside the house was a discouraging, "Is that what you're wearing?"

Susan was dressed, Warren noted, in a pair of sheer tights and a very nice red figure-hugging dress. He couldn't recall ever seeing it before, suggesting that she perhaps hadn't been entirely forthcoming when she told Warren the party was "just casual".

Warren's apologies for being late fell on deaf ears and they drove the short distance to Rachel and Paulo's house in silence. Fortunately, the mood lightened considerably when Rachel joined them. A buxom blonde Geordie, she was dressed in a dark green dress and wrapped all over in shiny red tinsel. From the amount of giggling it was clear that she'd already started partying at home. Her husband Paulo was an on-call IT trouble-shooter and had been called out at the last minute to fix a client's computer. Consequently, Warren's tardiness was suddenly a lot less of an issue.

The party was well under way when they arrived and was pretty much what Warren had expected. A large multi-purpose function room decked with Christmas decorations — all safely out of the reach of drunken revellers, removing the need to redecorate after each party. A bored-looking twenty-something sat behind an Apple Macbook and a rack of portable disco lights, playing some sort of game on his mobile phone.

To Warren's disappointment, there was no sign of any food. He'd play it safe and wait until Susan was well oiled before he slipped out to find a chippy, he decided.

Rachel insisted on getting the first round of drinks in as a thank you for driving her. By the time she had fought her way back from the bar, Warren had been introduced to everyone within arm's reach and his head was swimming with names and faces. It didn't help that some of the people he was introduced to didn't work in Susan's department, so their names hadn't cropped up in previous conversations.

Unfortunately, everyone seemed to know exactly who he was — the detective in charge of a double murder enquiry, he was something of a minor celebrity at Susan's school. Despite his discomfort, Warren felt a slight warm glow. It was clear that Susan spoke of him at work. When she next came within arm's reach he took the opportunity to give her a peck on the cheek and a gentle squeeze.

By half past eight, Warren found that he was actually rather enjoying himself. The DJ, for all of his flaws, was attentive to the audience's mood, successfully identifying and then predicting the sort of music that would go down well, rather than trying to impose his own taste. After a couple of stress-filled weeks, this rare opportunity to unwind was welcome and he even found himself on the dance floor bopping to those Seventies and Eighties disco classics that any party DJ worth his salt had a hard drive full of.

By 10 p.m., Warren had found a quietish corner and was enjoying a debate with the head of physics about the comedy show *The Big Bang Theory* and whether it was doing the reputation of physicists good or reinforcing negative stereotypes about them. By way of comparison Warren held that the many police parodies over the years had softened the public's perception of the service.

By now, there were more than a few merry souls lurching around the dance floor and Warren was struck by the similarities between this and a typical police party. In the far corner a group of young NQTs — Newly Qualified Teachers — were guzzling shots, eying up their colleagues and bouncing around their part of the dance floor like things possessed — the teaching profession's equivalent of probationary constables, Warren decided. Standing around chatting or dancing in small groups were older, more experienced teachers, ranging in age from about twenty-five to fifty. These would be the equivalent of the middle ranks; they made up the bulk of the workforce and did the lion's share of the work.

Standing back from the action and talking earnestly over pints were the people Warren had mentally classified as inspectors through to chief superintendents: middle- and senior-management types. These would be heads of year or subject leaders, maybe even the odd assistant head. Warren noted that the chief constable and his deputies — the head and deputy head teachers — had already left. They'd been there at the beginning of the evening, awkwardly wishing colleagues season's greetings, before leaving the troops to enjoy themselves and behave in a manner that they wouldn't normally dream of doing with the boss in the room.

Finally, sitting in their own small groups chatting amongst themselves were a mixed bunch of mostly women ranging in age from barely twenty to mid-sixties — admin staff and the site team, Warren judged. A bit like the civilian support workers that were essential to the police running smoothly from day to day; if they disappeared overnight, things would grind to a halt within twenty-four hours.

Feeling rather pleased with his insight, Warren shared his thoughts with Susan and Rachel the next time they decided to take a break from the dance floor.

"You forgot the LSAs," Susan shouted over the music, her words slightly slurred.

"The what?"

"Learning Support Assistants." Rachel pointed towards a mixed group of revellers propping up the bar. "You can't do anything without them. They're like an extra pair of hands, one-to-one tutor, translator, shoulder to cry on and bouncer rolled into one. They deal with more challenging individuals and let you get on with teaching the class."

Warren thought for a moment. "PCSOs. Community Support Officers. They deal with a lot of the low-level crap and the public so you can focus on your job."

Susan nodded her agreement. "A pretty good summing up, DCI Jones, but you got one thing wrong."

"Oh, what's that?"

Susan pointed to a huge woman with massive shoulders and an even bigger scowl dancing as if she were shadow-boxing Muhammed Ali. Warren noted that, despite the crowded floor, there was nobody within arm's reach of her.

"That's Caroline. She runs the school. Everyone's terrified of her."

Warren blinked in surprise; he'd met the head teacher at a welcome evening for new staff a few weeks ago. He was a man and about half the size of this gorilla. None of the deputy head teachers or other senior staff bore any resemblance to this flesh mountain.

"Head of the governing body? Chair of the PTA?" Warren tried.

"Nope, far more powerful. She's Head of Reprographics. Piss her off and you don't get any of your photocopying done for a week." Susan shuddered.

Remarkable, thought Warren. The civilian support worker in charge of Middlesbury police station's reprographics was similarly feared. Was it something to do with the toner fumes?

WEDNESDAY 14TH DECEMBER

Chapter 36

Six-thirty a.m. The lie-in was in deference to the previous night's revelry, but the extra half-hour was not nearly enough. The DJ had finished his set at midnight with the obligatory "New York, New York"; however, the hotel had been in no particular rush to force the partygoers to drink up and leave. By now, despite several pints of full-sugar Coke, Warren was dead on his feet. Finally, he managed to pull Susan and Rachel away from workmates that they were hugging in a manner that belied the fact that they were going to be seeing them again in less than eight hours.

By the time they got in it was a lot closer to 2 a.m. than 1 a.m. and Warren was so tired that he was convinced that without the drunken giggling from his passengers he might have fallen asleep at the wheel. Nevertheless, a sharp ache in his stomach demanded it be filled and he forced a couple of cheese sandwiches down his neck in record time, before collapsing, socks and T-shirt still on, into bed.

Walking into the CID office, Warren was not happy to see a jovial Tony Sutton busy joking with Gary Hastings and Annabel Willis. They all looked as if they had slept for a week, with bright eyes and a palpable sense of energy. Grunting good morning, he headed into his office to check his email and finish a second cup of coffee whilst he prepared for briefing.

An insistent warning buzz from his mobile phone reminded him that he had forgotten to plug it in to charge overnight and that the power-hungry device was down to its last few percentage of battery-life. He'd have to ask around the office after briefing to see if anybody had a compatible charger.

The morning briefing was a complex affair, with three cases now under investigation simultaneously. The Sally Evans and Carolyn Patterson murders were obviously the most advanced, being attacked on multiple fronts by several teams following leads and looking for links between the two crimes.

The jury was still out on whether the attempted murder of Melanie Clearwater was linked to the other two killings, so it had been decided to also keep the case in-house at Middlesbury CID, rather than handing it over to a team from Welwyn. Later today a number of additional detectives from HQ would be relocating to Middlesbury to increase their available manpower. Warren was glad — his small team was getting stretched and, with the holiday season approaching, it would only get worse. That being said, he wasn't sure where they were going to house all of the new people. It looked as though at least one of the briefing rooms was going to be filled with tables, chairs and laptops, but it would be a squeeze.

In the meantime, it was all hands on deck chasing down potential leads. Warren decided he would continue to follow up on Alex Chalmers and track down his ex-girlfriend — the one who he had reportedly assaulted on three occasions between 2002 and 2005. He doubted that she would have much insight into whether he was responsible for Carolyn Patterson's murder, but he was interested in a further glimpse into the man's life.

Pulling the appropriate file from the archive, Warren read the scant details available before setting about tracking down the whereabouts of his alleged victim, Josephine Bogg. The electoral register listed a Josephine McCaulley (nee Bogg), with the same date of birth, as living with a Lewis McCaulley on the opposite side of town to where she'd lived with Alex Chalmers until they split in 2005.

With the team so stretched, Warren felt it was hard to justify taking a second officer to accompany him on such a tangential part of the investigation. He probably should have assigned a junior officer to the task, but he needed to get out of the office. The warm stuffiness of the central heating was doing nothing to help him fight his fatigue.

Outside it was raining and the air had a decided bite to it; despite this, Warren drove with the window partly open, enjoying the freshness. By the time his satnav informed him that he had reached his destination, he was more invigorated.

The house was a small affair, designed with a couple or new parents in mind. The doorbell was answered immediately with the muffled instruction to wait for a moment. The better part of a minute passed before the door was opened by a slightly dishevelled woman of about thirty, carrying a contented-looking baby with a slightly crooked nappy.

"I'm sorry if I caught you at a bad time," Warren apologised as he held up his warrant card.

"Don't worry, there's rarely a good time when they are this age. Isn't that right, you mucky devil?" She directed this last part of the comment at the squirming baby, who had suddenly become fascinated with his mother's ear and was trying to cram it into his mouth.

"Mrs McCaulley, I presume? I wonder if you would be willing

to give me a few moments of your time to help with an ongoing enquiry."

"Of course." The woman suddenly seemed interested. A bored housewife, Warren decided. Stuck at home with the baby all day and craving a bit of adult conversation, she'd jump at the chance to help the police. It was probably the most exciting thing that had happened all month. He felt a little guilty that he was about to burst the bubble by dredging up unpleasant memories.

The living room was plainly decorated, but filled with brightly coloured plastic toys and baby equipment. Clearing a space on a couch covered in freshly laundered ironing, the harried young mother gestured for him to sit down. As he did so, Warren felt a vibration from his pocket. Apologising, he retrieved his mobile phone from his pocket. Expecting a text message, he was annoyed to see a flashing warning about his fading battery life, before the screen went dark. Cursing himself for forgetting to charge the phone before he left, he returned the useless handset to his pocket and turned his attention back to the young mother in front of him.

Sitting opposite, she balanced the young baby on her lap. Warren's inexperienced eye suggested that the baby was still some months shy of his first birthday, but old enough to sit up comfortably. Nine months?

"How old is this young man, then?" asked Warren awkwardly as he cast about for a way to bring up what was likely to be a painful subject.

"Alfie here is nine and a half months," she answered proudly.

"I see. And, er, what about Mr McCaulley? Is he out?" Warren asked carefully, trying to work out the family dynamics before he got into the questioning.

"He's at work today. He manages a small bookstore in town."

"I see. Before we start, were you previously known as Josephine Bogg?"

"Yes, I married Lewis two years ago and took his name."

"Mrs McCaulley, what I am about to ask you may be uncomfortable or even upsetting and for that I apologise. However, the information that you have may be significant in a serious investigation currently under way."

The woman opposite him started to look worried.

"Did you have a relationship with an Alex Chalmers between 2002 and 2005?"

The woman took a sharp intake of breath.

"I never thought I'd hear that man's name again," she murmured, her hands starting to shake. Sitting on her lap, Alfie squirmed slightly, as if picking up on his mother's discomfort.

"I'm very sorry to bring up painful memories for you. According to our reports, neighbours called the police on three separate occasions between 2002 and 2005, concerned for your safety."

Josephine squeezed her eyes shut. "I'd rather not talk about it." She gestured with her head to the room and her son. "I've moved on in my life and I've no intention of revisiting old wounds."

"I fully understand, Mrs McCaulley. I'm not here to discuss pressing charges or anything like that — although if you wished to do so, I could put you in touch with one of our specialist domestic violence officers — rather I am trying to build a picture of what sort of a man Alex Chalmers is, to help us with an ongoing investigation."

She took a shaky breath, before fixing Jones with her gaze. "I've seen you before, haven't I? You were on TV. That young woman who was murdered. And wasn't another dead body found at the weekend? Is Alex a suspect?"

"I can't really go into any details, I'm afraid. I'm just making routine enquiries."

She eyed him in silence for a long moment, before sighing deeply.

"I met Alex in the middle of 2001. I was working in a bar in town, a student, earning some extra cash. He was a lot of fun at the time. He had a good job at the post office and had a bit of a reputation as a ladies' man. He was also pretty hot." She blushed slightly. "Lifting all those parcels, he had a really big upper body.

"Anyway, we started dating and by the middle of 2002, when I finished my course, we decided to move in together." She looked wistful. "I was naïve, I admit that. It was my first serious relationship and I didn't know what to expect.

"I probably could have been a bit more understanding but I had a large group of friends from college and still wanted to party like things hadn't changed. Alex, of course, is a postman. He gets up at 4 a.m. for some shifts. I was working in a clothes shop — I didn't have to get into work until nine. I didn't go out in the week very often, but I would often go out on the weekend until all hours.

"On the other hand, Alex finished work some days at 1 p.m. He'd go out drinking with his mates after work and by the time I arrived home at six, he'd be really pissed. It was that which started the arguing.

"Looking back on it, we should have split up ages ago. We just weren't compatible, not on a practical level at least. But we were such a good couple and he was always so apologetic after we argued. I was terrified that if I left him I'd never find anyone like him."

"So when did he start hitting you?"

"It was just before Christmas 2002. I'd gone out for a drink with colleagues after work, nothing much, just a couple of glasses of wine. I got home about eight-ish, to find Alex really drunk. He'd been in the pub since one, before getting home at six expecting to find me there. Instead of phoning to see where I was, he'd decided to keep on drinking, and by the time I got back he was practically incoherent. He accused me of having an affair and called me a slut. We ended up screaming at each other. Finally, he threw a punch at me. He was so drunk he missed me completely and smashed a vase. It was then that the police arrived.

"I look back on it now and I realise that if they hadn't he would have just kept on going and could have really hurt me. At the time, with no physical evidence of an assault the police couldn't do anything without my say-so and I refused to press charges. I don't know why — I guess I was in shock. We'd rowed before and it had never got physical. I guess I just wanted to believe it would be a one-off. Anyway, after the police left, he was all apologetic and crying and we ended up having the most amazing sex.

"After that we had a number of rows. Each time we'd make up and it'd be like the old days, before the arguments. Since then I've read a lot of books about the subject and I realise that I was a classic case; I just kept on going back because part of me felt guilty. As if I had brought it upon myself. That I had driven him to those lengths. I actually felt as though it was my fault that he was violent and when I saw how upset he was after each episode, I felt responsible for his torment."

"So how did you end it?"

She laughed bitterly. "Daytime TV, would you believe? I had the morning off, since I was working the late-night shopping shift, and I was watching some breakfast show. The presenter was interviewing the sister of a woman who had been murdered by her partner. She'd kept a diary and the sister read out extracts of it. I suddenly realised that she was reading out my life. That all of the feelings that I had were the same as that of this murdered young woman and that if I didn't get out of this relationship, I would end up the same way.

"At the end of the programme they put up a telephone number for more help and advice. I phoned it and, at the end of the week, took a day off work, packed everything I needed and left before he was home. He probably still has some of my old clothes and books. I never went back. The shop that I worked for were fantastic. He turned up to try and talk to me and the store security guards wouldn't let him in. When I left in the evening, my colleagues took it in turns to drive me to my new apartment. After about a month, he stopped calling me and I haven't seen him since."

She smiled and kissed Alfie on the forehead.

"A year later I met Lewis and realised what real love was all about. If this was a fairy tale, I guess you could say that 'they all lived happily ever after'."

Warren smiled.

"I'm glad to hear it and I'm sorry to have brought up such painful memories."

Josephine shrugged.

"He's a dangerous man, Mr Jones. I know you can't say anything but I think he is capable of seriously hurting someone."

She paused and Warren waited; it was clear that she had more that she wanted to say, but was uncomfortable.

"I don't know if this is at all relevant, but when we had sex, he did have some unusual tastes."

Warren said nothing, knowing she'd fill the gap.

"Sometimes he'd tie me up and then pretend to strangle me with my dressing-gown cord. Normally it was just a bit of harmless fun, but once he was drunk and went too far. I almost passed out. When I came to my senses, rather than being alarmed he was the most excited I'd ever seen."

Chapter 37

It was still raining when Warren left Josephine McCaulley and returned to his car. As he waited for the air-blowers to reach temperature, he plugged his flat mobile phone into the car's charger. With a muted beep, the phone started up. Within seconds of the phone gaining a signal, it started buzzing repeatedly as missed call after missed call came flooding in. Cursing his forgetfulness when going to bed the previous night, Warren opened the call list. A vague sense of unease passed through him. The calls had started an hour previously, with a call from his mother-in-law, Bernice, of all people. This was followed about fifteen minutes later by a missed call from Susan. A second missed call from her followed less than a minute later, presumably as she redialled in the hope that he'd just missed the first attempt. This time she left a voicemail. A few minutes later a missed call came from Tony Sutton and one from the station's main switchboard. A flashing envelope icon alerted Warren to the presence of two text messages.

Top of the list, sent two minutes after his missed call, was one from Tony Sutton.

Phone the missus guv. Urgent. Tony

The next down was from Susan, sent just after her missed call, and was similarly urgent.

Call me as soon as you can. Susan x

That Susan had apparently been able to call him then send a text relieved Warren of one whole set of worries, but he could only think of a few reasons why Susan would have called him repeatedly, then tried Tony Sutton and the main station switchboard. And why was the first call from Bernice?

Deciding that he'd wasted enough time as it was, Warren ignored the voicemails and rang Susan directly. She picked up on the second ring.

"Warren, you need to come home immediately. It's your grandmother."

And with that, the worst of Warren's nightmares came true.

* * *

The journey back to Coventry had been a terse, silent affair. After speaking to Susan, Warren had immediately driven back to his house. A call to the station on the way revealed that Tony Sutton had already spoken at length to Susan and that he'd tipped off Superintendent Grayson that Warren would probably need a leave of absence. Upon arriving home, he'd found Susan waiting with packed overnight bags for both of them.

Under normal circumstances, Warren would have resented the way that he seemed to have suddenly become a passenger in his own life. He'd have been annoyed that his subordinate, Tony Sutton, knew about his family problems before he did and had arranged to cover for him. And if there was one thing he really disliked, it was Susan packing his clothes. But today, he felt nothing, just relief that he didn't need to think of such things when his mind was reeling from shock.

Warren had insisted on driving and he'd pushed the car as fast as he'd dared westwards along the A14. A colleague in Traffic had once hinted at just what the trigger threshold was on the average speed cameras that lined the dual carriageway and Warren used that insider knowledge to get them to the junction with the M6 as quickly as possible without risking his licence; at least not for speeding.

An extended period travelling at fifty-six miles per hour whilst two arrogant lorry drivers drove at precisely the same speed, blocking both lanes of the carriageway, nearly caused Warren to undertake using the hard shoulder. Only Susan's calming presence restrained him. Instead, he took a perverse pleasure in phoning in the details and suggesting that colleagues with nothing better to do might want to do a spot-check to make sure that the lorries were roadworthy and the drivers' paperwork was in order.

Eventually Susan and Warren arrived back in Coventry, Warren's childhood hometown. Pulling up outside the row of grey terraced houses, he turned off the engine and reached for the door handle.

Susan stopped him. "We're here, Warren. No need to rush now — two more minutes won't make a difference. Get yourself together. You're no good to anybody racing in like this."

For a few more seconds, Warren was silent. To those that didn't know him, Detective Chief Inspector Jones was fully in control. His jaw was set like rock, his eyes as hard as stone. But Susan could feel the tautness of the muscles in his arms; his hands were shaking, she noticed, and she could see the faint glimmer of pain and fear in his eyes. Warren Jones the man was far from in control.

Finally, Warren slumped back into his seat. "You're right. Another couple of minutes won't hurt." His voice shook slightly.

Susan watched him with concern as he took deep breaths, before looking out of the window at the darkening street beyond. He stared at the houses that lined the cul-de-sac, but she doubted he was seeing what she saw. To her eyes, the street seemed sad, run-down. Most of the houses still had remnants of the pebble-dashing that had seemed such a good idea back in the Sixties. A couple of homeowners had decided to throw good money after bad and have it replenished. Another couple had cut their losses, stripped it off and replastered. Warren's grandparents had followed the rest of the pack and left it to nature to decide. It reminded Susan of a dog with mange.

Pebble-dashing aside, the houses in the street were a mixed bunch. Some, like Warren's grandparents', were clearly well maintained. Their house had a small garden with a postage-stamp-sized lawn, surrounded by carefully weeded flowerbeds that Susan knew would be a riot of colour in the spring. The front windows were uPVC, but the sills had been painted a cheerful red to match the front door and the garden gate. This splash of scarlet was one of the only colours visible in the miserable December gloom; all the houses in the immediate vicinity had retained the black-on-white colour scheme that they'd been built with.

The only other hint of colour visible was the rusty brown of the abandoned Ford Escort that littered the garden opposite. The owner, a shaven-headed lout with a half-dozen tattoos and even more kids, would periodically pop open the bonnet and fiddle around underneath it, thus keeping an uninterested council off his back and avoiding scrappage charges.

Finally, Warren was ready. Giving Susan's hand one last squeeze, he clambered into the driving rain and headed towards the gate.

Entering the house, Warren was greeted with an awkward hug from his second cousin Jane, juggling her eighteen-month-old daughter with one arm and her uncharacteristically shy three-year-old son in the other. Next in line, to his surprise, was his mother-in-law, Bernice.

Warren and Bernice had never had the closest of relationships. Bernice had done little to hide the fact that she thought that Warren, whilst a perfectly nice man, was beneath her daughter. That he was a detective chief inspector and a church-going Catholic were points in his favour, but he was never going to measure up to the investment banker husband of Felicity, Susan's younger and more fertile sister. Although, that being said, with the way the economy was going things might change, Warren thought. The last he'd checked, nobody was holding the police accountable for the credit crunch or the Eurozone crisis...

"How is she?" Warren managed.

"The doctor says that she's comfortable, but she's not really with us." This was from Dennis, Susan's father. A stern glance from Bernice reminded him who the official spokesperson was for the marriage and he promptly shut up.

The dynamics of Bernice and Dennis' marriage never ceased to fascinate Warren. Dennis was, by all accounts, a successful and highly respected businessman. Although officially retired, he still held a substantial interest in the company that he'd help set up and he was an active and vocal member of the board.

Bernice, on the other hand, was — to use an old-fashioned term — a kept woman. She'd raised Susan and Felicity in the family's large, expensive house in the leafiest part of Warwickshire, but, after the children had grown up, had settled into a life of church committees, charity fundraising and socialising.

To outsiders they seemed like that old stereotype of the powerful, bread-winning husband and the mousy housewife, whose role in life was to support her husband's career. To those that knew them, the opposite was true. It was immediately obvious that Bernice wore the trousers and Dennis was well and truly under the thumb. Regardless, Warren still wasn't sure why they were here and why Bernice had been the one to call him that morning.

"Why don't you tell us what happened, Mum?" suggested Susan.

"Jack phoned Dennis and me this morning about nine o'clock and said that something was wrong with Betty. She seemed very sleepy and her voice was slurred. He wanted to take her down to the doctor's, but he didn't think she could walk. He wondered if Dennis would mind giving them a lift."

Warren blinked. "Why on earth did he call you and Dennis?"

"Well, Jane had left to take the kids to nursery and we'd mentioned on Sunday when we took them to church that we weren't doing very much this week. He didn't want to make a fuss."

Warren's head spun. He'd actually been asking why his grandfather hadn't just called for an ambulance, but Bernice had, in her own unique way, answered something completely different and opened up another avenue of questioning. When had his wife's parents started driving his grandparents to church on a Sunday, and how did he not know about it?

Warren decided to deal with that question later.

"Why didn't Granddad call an ambulance? Especially after last time. He must have known it was a stroke!" Warren's voice had started to rise, and Susan laid a comforting hand on him.

Bernice leant forward, taking Warren's hand in her own; it was the most affectionate gesture she had ever made towards him since he had started dating her daughter.

"Warren, they had an agreement. Betty and Jack told us about it a few months ago. Last year, after Betty had her mini-stroke, she hated being in hospital. It was only a few nights, but she made it clear that she never wanted to go back in again. When Jack tried to wake her this morning, he knew what had happened but couldn't decide what to do. Dennis and I came straight over and persuaded him to call a paramedic, just to check her out. They confirmed that she has had a bigger stroke and that the rhythm of her heart is very irregular."

Warren could barely keep his voice steady. "So what happens now?"

"Dr Gupta, Betty's GP, came around an hour ago. Betty and Jack have both signed living wills outlining their wishes and he has agreed to respect them." She leant forward again, squeezing his hand tightly. "Warren, we think Betty had another stroke while Dr Gupta was here. She is probably going to have another stroke or a heart attack soon. They have given her medicine to keep her comfortable, but she's not expected to recover. I'm sorry, Warren."

Warren sat back, stunned. It had all happened so fast. In the space of just a few hours, his entire world had turned upside down. A world without Nana Betty seemed inconceivable. Of course, he'd known this day would come; both his grandparents were in their late eighties. Nana Betty's mini-stroke the previous spring had been a warning shot, but she'd seemed to recover from it, at least physically. Warren thought back to the previous Christmas, a few months after her stroke. She'd been quieter than usual, claiming that the pills she was on made her tired. Over the following year she'd lost weight, he realised. And she'd seemed less vibrant somehow.

And what was this about being given a lift to church? As long as they had been together, Betty and Jack had walked the three quarters of a mile to and from the small church where they had been married, come rain or shine. They'd claimed that the fresh air did them good and worked up an appetite for Sunday lunch. When had they become so tired that they had started getting a lift?

Warren realised that the woman who meant more to him than anyone else in the world, save Susan, had been slipping away from him without him even realising. *Or did I realise, and just convinced myself otherwise?* he asked himself.

"Can I see her?" he asked finally.

"Of course, dear — she's in the bedroom."

Warren rose to his feet and, taking Susan's hand, walked to the stairs that led up to the house's three small bedrooms. Each step brought back memories. The carpet, a faded green had been there as long as Warren could recall. He remembered clearly as a young child being told not to climb the stairs in case he fell down; a few years later he was scolded for chipping the paint on the skirting board at the bottom by making his toy cars fly off the top step; another memory was that of a rare smacked bottom after he'd tried out his brand-new sledge on the nearest thing to a slope in the vicinity. He smiled at the memory. The weatherman had promised snow that year and he didn't know who was more disappointed when it failed to arrive, he or Granddad Jack.

Finally, Warren arrived at the door of his grandparents' bedroom. Out of habit, he knocked quietly.

"Come in." It was recognisable as Granddad Jack's voice but weaker.

After a deep breath, Warren entered the room.

The room was much as he remembered it from the rare occasions that he'd entered it in the past. The radiators were on full blast; nevertheless, his grandfather was dressed in a woollen jumper and a checked shirt. His hands felt cold to Warren when he hugged him. Warren could feel his bones through the layers of clothing. As Jack turned to embrace Susan, Warren realised with a start that he'd shrunk. Suddenly, there was a mismatch between the Granddad Jack of Warren's memory — a short but robust man with powerful hands who could pluck a squealing six-year old Warren off the floor with one arm, sling him over his shoulder and carry him up to bed — and the frail eighty-seven-year-old standing in front of him.

As he glanced over at the bed the mismatch was even more pronounced. Warren felt a weakness in his knees. When did she become so thin? he asked himself. Steeling himself, he walked around to his grandmother's side of the bed. A dining-room chair had been carried upstairs and Warren sat down on it. Despite the warmth, the old lady was completely covered in multiple blankets. Only her head and her hands were visible, peeking above the bedspread. Her eyes were closed and Warren could hear the rasp of her breathing. Reaching out, he took her hand. It was cool to the touch, the skin paper-thin. Beneath the soft, pale flesh, Warren could feel the fluttering of her pulse, weak and erratic. He could tell that things were very wrong.

Leaning over, he kissed her softly on the forehead. "Hello, Nana, it's Warren," he whispered quietly into her ear. To his amazement, he felt the slightest of squeezes from her hand as a faint smile creased her face.

"She knows you're here, son," said Granddad Jack quietly. Raising his voice slightly, he addressed his dozing wife. "Warren and Susan are here, Betty."

She squeezed his hand again, but made no more response.

Without letting go of her hand, Warren pulled over the chair. "I'm sorry about this, son."

Warren looked up in surprise, "Sorry for what?"

Granddad Jack looked uncomfortable. "For not telling you what me and your nana decided. And we told Bernie and Dennis not to say anything either. We didn't know how to tell you, especially after your dad an' all."

Warren nodded numbly. "I'm just surprised. I didn't think you and Nana were the type to, you know…" He struggled to find the word.

"Give up?" suggested Jack, immediately waving away Warren's half-hearted protestations to the contrary. "Betty and I both believe that God puts you upon this earth to do what he wants you to do to the best of your ability and when that's done you get your reward."

The old man shuffled his chair around so he could take hold of both Warren's hand and his wife's.

"We brought up your dad to the best of our abilities and then when he… passed away… we tried to help your mum with you boys. Now our work's done and maybe it's time for our reward."

Warren couldn't say anything; behind him he could feel the warmth of Susan's body as she hugged him silently.

"Your nana and I are both eighty-seven years old this year. My parents died in their sixties and your nan's were even younger. Two of my brothers, Freddie and Tommy, died before they were twenty during the war. We've been blessed with such long lives. Did you know that we nearly had two more babies after your dad?"

Warren started. "No," he managed.

"Two little girls. Neither quite made it. Then we were told that we couldn't have any more. Nearly tore your poor nan apart." The moist glint in his eye betrayed his own feelings on the matter.

"Well, pretty soon, Betty here will meet our little girls for the first time and be reunited with your dad and your mum. So many have gone before us, she ain't going to be lonely up there." He squeezed his wife's hand affectionately and kissed her sleeping head. This time Warren could see no flicker of response.

* * *

Late afternoon stretched into evening, time marked by the ticking of the bedside clock and endless cups of tea. At seven o'clock Jane left to put her children to bed, Susan accompanying her with her laptop. She'd already phoned her school to tell them that she wouldn't be in for the remainder of the week, but like all teachers she was still expected to plan and set detailed cover lessons to be taught in her absence. Warren had been horrified one morning when he'd been woken before 6 a.m. by a nauseous Susan logging on to her laptop to write, then email cover work in to school. It was no wonder so many teachers struggled into work when others would stay at home; Susan's friends maintained that setting cover from home was harder than dragging yourself in, especially when you were teaching chemistry and the cover teachers weren't allowed to do practical experiments with the pupils.

At eight o'clock, Father McGavin stopped by. Warren did a double take when he saw him. Old and stooped, he was no longer the robust, stern, Irish disciplinarian that Warren remembered from his childhood, who could stop fidgeting in the pews with little more than a glare. He must be even older than Nana and Granddad, Warren realised.

As Warren helped him out of his coat, the elderly priest explained that he had been retired some years now, but that the new priest would still call him when any of the older parishioners were in need of support.

"I've known Betty and Jack for over sixty years. I married them and baptised you and your father. I also laid him and your mum to rest. Seems right that I be here with Betty for her final journey."

The last-rites ceremony was simple and touching. Composed of three sacraments, first came the forgiveness of sins; although Betty was unable to make a confession, absolution was given on the assumption of her contrition. Next came the "anointing of the sick" with oil of chrism, in this case olive oil blessed by the local bishop the previous Maundy Thursday. Finally came the administration of the Holy Eucharist, referred to on this last occasion as "Viaticum" — literally the *provision for the journey*. With Betty unable to take solids, this was administered in the form of Eucharistic wine, representing the blood of Christ rather than the bread that represented the body.

After the administration of the sacraments, Father McGavin stayed for a cup of tea, before accepting Dennis' offer to drive him back to the small home he shared with other retired clergy.

To Warren's astonishment, Granddad Jack then disappeared into the bathroom for a few minutes, before emerging dressed in grey, stripy pyjamas and clambering into bed alongside his wife. Warren got up to go, but Jack bid him to stay.

"In sixty-two years of marriage, your nana and I only spent five nights apart. One each for the birth of our children and two nights last year after her stroke…" His voice caught as he stroked Betty's hair. "I'm certainly not abandoning her now."

Automatically, Warren's eyes flicked to the wedding photo on the bed-stand, a black-and-white portrait of the two of them: Jack in his Army uniform, Betty resplendent in a traditional white dress. Warren recognised the front of the church that had played such a part in his family history. They looked so young, he thought sadly.

Looking back, Warren realised that he and Susan had spent more nights apart in their first year than Betty and Jack had in their entire marriage. A long weekend apiece for their closest friends' stag and hen do easily added up to five nights, and then there were the nights that Warren had spent in the spare bedroom to avoid waking Susan after completing a night shift. Settling back down, Warren took hold of Betty's hand again.

Over the next few hours, the old house emptied, Warren insisting that Susan return to Stratford-upon-Avon with her parents to get some sleep. As the hours ticked by the house became quieter, the room only disturbed by the quiet rasp of Betty's breathing. Warren was starting to nod off himself, when he was started awake by the sound of Jack's voice.

"I wish your father could see you today. He'd be so proud of you."

"What do you mean?"

Jack sat up slightly, talking quietly so as not to disturb his wife, although they both knew that was no longer possible.

"Your old man was a bloody good man. I don't care what they say about him. He was a copper through and through — it's all he ever wanted." In the dim of the bedside table lamp, Warren saw that Jack's eyes were misty. "I remember that for his fifth birthday I got him a policeman's helmet and a toy truncheon." The old man chuckled at the memory. "I think he must have arrested every person in the street at least twice that week. When he got his first bicycle that Christmas, I painted blue stripes down the side and stencilled 'Police' on it. Then the neighbours had to put up with him racing up and down the pavement making an awful wailing noise like a police siren." Jack smiled. "I'll have to dig the photo out for you."

His tone turned sombre. "I know they say that what your father did was wrong, but we never heard his side of the story."

"No, we didn't." Warren's voice was cold. "He didn't stick around long enough to tell us."

"Warren, I know that you feel betrayed by what your dad did, but I've always believed there was more to it than we ever knew."

"Well, it's all in the past now and maybe that's where it should stay." Warren could see that Jack wanted to say more, but he didn't think that now was the time or the place. The old man nodded finally and changed the topic.

"She was so proud of you. We both were." He motioned towards Betty's still form. "When you were promoted to Detective Inspector, she'd watch *Midlands Today* religiously in case you or any of your colleagues were mentioned. She has an envelope full of newspaper stories about you and your team. When you moved to Middlesbury and were promoted to DCI she was heartbroken until Mr Cartwright three doors down showed us how to reprogramme the Sky box so that we could pick up other BBC TV regions. We heard all about that nasty business at the university over the summer." He laughed quietly. "I haven't watched *Midlands Today* since August. I've no idea what the weather will be like in Birmingham tomorrow, but I know they've forecast more rain for Cambridge with a short sunny spell for North Essex."

Despite himself, Warren found himself smiling. He squeezed his grandmother's hand. "What are you like, Nana?" he whispered into her ear.

"We both knew that you'd go into the police. Even as you did your exams downstairs and then went to university, we knew that you'd end up serving. It's in your blood."

Warren thought back. He could picture himself at the dining table downstairs with his books out. After his father's death, the atmosphere at home had been tense and fractious. A young Warren had taken to turning up unexpectedly at his grandparents' house after school. Wordlessly, his grandmother would open the door and he'd come in and sit down at the big wooden table in the dining room and do his homework. Nothing was ever said; it was just accepted. Granddad Jack wouldn't even blink an eye as he returned home from work, he'd just ruffle Warren's hair and ask if he needed any help. After eating his tea, he'd do a bit more homework or watch a bit of TV, before walking the mile back home.

At the time, Warren never really understood how his mother knew that he was safe around his grandparents' but he realised now that they had phoned his mother the moment he arrived and let her know when he left.

This ad hoc arrangement continued throughout Warren's GCSEs and A levels, and when he went to university he'd spend at least some of the holidays at his grandparents'. Now with his mother also gone, he realised that for much of his life Nana Betty and Granddad Jack had been his de facto parents.

The two men quietly settled back into their own thoughts. Outside, a dog barked. An hour later a babble of voices advertised the closing of the local pub. As the clock ticked past midnight, the road outside quietened, with only the occasional shushing of a car on the wet road. Soon, the only noise was the relentless tick of the clock and Betty's increasingly laboured breathing.

At a quarter past one, even that stopped.

THURSDAY 15TH DECEMBER

Chapter 38

Much to Warren's surprise, he'd actually dozed off in the early hours of the morning, sleeping until gone eight when the winter sun finally poked its way through a gap in the curtains. His back was stiff from sleeping in the chair and he struggled to the bathroom without making any noise.

When he returned, Granddad Jack was awake, looking at the peaceful, still form of his wife.

"I suppose we need to make some phone calls," he said sadly, his voice cracking with emotion.

Warren nodded and squeezed the old man's shoulder. "I'll do it."

The next few hours passed in an unreal daze for Warren. After phoning Susan at Bernice and Dennis' house, he called the family GP, who arrived at almost the same time. After formally pronouncing Nana Betty deceased, he left everyone to say their final goodbyes before the undertaker came to take her away.

For once, Warren didn't mind Bernice's fussing as she insisted on making him and Granddad Jack breakfast. Whilst they ate, Dennis and Susan started phoning around. Warren was in a daze, the cumulative lack of sleep from the past few days numbing his grief. He still couldn't believe what had happened.

By midday and after several cups of coffee, he felt composed enough to phone work. Detective Superintendent Grayson was very sympathetic; Susan had explained the special relationship that Warren had with his grandparents and he had generously recorded it as the equivalent of the death of a parent, allowing Warren the maximum amount of time off available.

After thanking his boss for his understanding, Warren redialled the station and was put through to Tony Sutton. His colleague and friend was similarly sympathetic, reassuring Warren that everything was under control and grudgingly promising to keep him informed of any developments on the outstanding cases.

After thanking him, Warren stood up and carried the phone out into the backyard for a little extra privacy.

"I need a favour. Discreet and off the books."

"Sure thing, guv, whatever you need."

"I need you to track somebody down for me. James MacNamara, born Coventry, June twenty-sixth 1969. He might be using the surname Jones. He may be living in Surrey, but that isn't confirmed. He left Coventry in about 1989, if that's any use."

Granddad Jack had shown Warren Christmas cards from the last few years that Nana Betty had kept. She'd also kept the envelopes that they'd come in and Warren had been able to identify the smudged postmarks.

"What would you like me to do? Do you want me to arrange for someone to visit him?"

"No, I'd rather do that myself."

If Sutton had guessed why Warren wanted to track this man down, he had the discretion not to say anything.

Ending the call, Warren returned to the living room to greet Father McGavin and the current parish priest, Father Sutton, a broad-shouldered, middle-aged man with an equally broad Brummie accent. After a few minutes praying for the soul of Nana Betty, they pencilled in a date for the funeral, deciding on the forthcoming Monday, with her reception into church the night before.

With the arrangements in place, Warren set about the sad task of phoning relatives and family friends to inform them of the news. Bernice, Dennis and Susan had all volunteered to help, but Warren felt it was his responsibility. In the end, he allowed the others to organise the social club for after the funeral and to put the death notice in the local papers. Bernice sat with Granddad Jack and between them they chose the order of service for the funeral mass.

All of these jobs could have been safely put off for twenty-four hours, but Warren was filled with the need to do something, to keep busy. He'd been running on adrenaline and caffeine with too little sleep for the past fortnight and he was scared that if he took his foot off the accelerator pedal he'd grind to a halt and give in to the desire to crawl into bed and never come out. The fact that his workmates had been so understanding perversely made matters worse, increasing the temptation to hide away until after the funeral and hope it all magically went away.

By early evening Warren had called everybody that needed calling and done everything that could be done. The atmosphere in the house had become oppressive and, by mutual agreement, it was decided that it was time to retire to the pub and celebrate the life of Nana Betty with a few drinks.

As everyone put their coats on, Warren's mobile rang. Checking the caller ID, he saw that it was Tony Sutton. Motioning for the others to carry on, he walked through to the kitchen for some privacy.

"I'm sorry, guv. We haven't been able to track down an address for James MacNamara. We pulled his National Insurance number up and traced it to a rented house in Surrey. Unfortunately, he left about nine months ago and didn't leave a forwarding address. According to HMRC he hasn't paid tax or NI since that time and the DVLA have no records of any motor vehicles or car insurance in his name either. I managed to pull a few strings with a mate at the border agency who confirmed that he has a valid passport, good for the next five years, but he couldn't tell me if he'd left the country without a warrant."

"OK, thanks for trying, Tony."

Warren hung up, his emotions in turmoil. He felt slightly guilty at the relief he felt. He hadn't seen James since their mother's funeral and even then the two men had little to say to each other. Monday's funeral promised to be a difficult enough affair without the added strain of his estranged brother. It seemed that his older sibling had kept in touch with his grandparents — or at least sent a Christmas card each year — but he hadn't left a forwarding address. He clearly didn't want to be contacted. Warren wondered how long it would take for news of Nana Betty's death to reach him. At least Warren's conscience was clear — he had tried his best to get hold of him.

Putting his coat on, he left the house to join the rest of his family. Dennis was driving and Warren intended to get good and drunk.

SATURDAY 17TH DECEMBER

Chapter 39

The man in the mask crouched silently behind the stinking wheelie bins. Dressed entirely in black, with the hood of his coat cinched tight and the lower half of his face covered by a dark woollen scarf, he was entirely invisible to any passers-by. The wheelie bins, although still malodorous, were long since emptied after the restaurant that they belonged to had closed down two months before. It was the third time he'd staked out the mini-supermarket at closing time in the past fortnight and he knew the routines of its small group of workers by heart. A brisk walk past a few hours earlier had allowed him a glimpse into the shop, where he could see his target restocking the shelves. He'd been dressed entirely differently, of course. He had resisted the urge to enter the shop, to see the object of his desire close up — he knew that the police would immediately impound any video surveillance footage from the shop as soon as the young woman went missing and he didn't want to appear on any recordings, even if he was disguised.

Nevertheless, the glimpse of her slim, attractive form, the pale, smooth flesh of her arms below her green work T-shirt and the curve of her neck had been enough to make him rush home to the privacy of the bathroom, to satisfy his urges. The urges that, once unleashed a few weeks before, were becoming stronger every day.

It was as if by finally giving in, after weeks, months, even years of planning and discipline, he was now on a pre-programmed course. Call it destiny, fate, genetic pre-programming, whatever, his path was now set and he would follow it to the end.

Once upon a time, of course, he'd thought that his desires were wrong, evil. Even as he lay, night after night, sweating and panting in the sticky aftermath of his fantasies, he'd recognised that what he wanted, what he dreamt about, wasn't in accordance with society's norms. Keeping it bottled up inside, he'd eventually hit a low point and indulged himself. Even as he'd revelled in the fact that he'd successfully got away with it, he'd been sickened by his actions. Society's brainwashing affected even one such as he, he realised.

Finally, he'd sought help. His deliberate vagueness and lack of detail had convinced those in whom he confided that his fantasies were just that. Never did he let on that he had acted upon them; put thought into deed.

The counsellors had been sympathetic and understanding and naively sought to soothe his troubled soul.

"Fantasies are normal," they'd reassured him. "Everyone has them. Society is full of rules and regulations and our imaginations rebel against them. As long as you never act upon them, they are harmless. Learn to accept yourself.

"It's not your fault," they soothed him. "It's inevitable that you feel confused or guilty, but you shouldn't.

"It's not your fault."

It took a long time for him to finally accept the truth of what they were saying. Years in which his desires were repressed, his demons locked firmly away.

It wasn't his fault. Of that he was now certain. He'd been made this way. His return to the church had helped and his faith was becoming stronger every day but he was conflicted. Surely his desires contradicted the teachings of the gospel? Eventually he had come to a realisation that he was just like anybody else. God has a plan for us all, he decided, and His reasoning might not be clear. But in the end, as long as he maintained his faith and asked for forgiveness for his actions, then Jesus would grant him eternal reward. He would follow his desires, he decided, and let God choose his fate.

One day he would be caught — if life had taught him nothing else it was that eventually something would go wrong. Some small detail would be overlooked; some random stroke of bad luck would curse him and the law would catch up with him. But until then, he would live out his desires and await his fate.

Of one thing he was certain though: that fate would not include prison. The memories of those concrete walls, the metal doors with keys held by another, the routines decided by others, they haunted his dreams. No, that wouldn't happen. He wouldn't let it happen. He fingered the small glass bottle that he'd taken to carrying with him. According to the instructions from the Internet, just a teaspoon would be enough. The bottle contained a mouthful. One gulp and it would be over in seconds.

This fatalism, this acceptance of destiny didn't mean he was in any way careless, of course. He had planned for years, waiting for the opportunity and the right circumstances. Each attack was meticulously worked out; the victim was researched, dry runs were performed and the getaway prepared with precision. He felt sure that any observer who had seen him on his reconnaissance missions, as he liked to think of them, would fail to recognise him — dressed, as he was, differently each time.

His current target was called Gemma, or at least that was what her name badge said. He didn't know her surname and he didn't really care. Maybe in her early twenties, she worked mostly evening shifts. What she did during the day, he had no idea. Perhaps she was a student earning money over the Christmas break? Perhaps she was under-employed, struggling to make ends meet as she fired off endless applications for a better job. He wasn't really interested.

What he did know was that she lived alone in a small bedsit about a mile or so from the shop where she worked. There were no direct bus routes. If she had a boyfriend or her parents lived nearby they didn't pick her up after work. By last thing at night, she was the only member of staff working so nobody offered to drive her home. The elderly Sikh man who owned the shop lived above it and pulled the shutters down after her, before retiring upstairs for the night.

Gemma was a fan of dance music — he had heard it blaring out of her headphones at deafening volume as he'd stalked her on her route home twice the previous fortnight. Even at the safe distance he'd maintained, he could make out every drumbeat. He was confident that she'd had no idea that he was following her. You'd think that with all the publicity about his previous victims, young women would be less likely to walk home in the dark, and that they'd switch off their music and pay more attention. But Gemma was young. She was invincible. She was careless.

The man in the mask had hit upon a winning formula, but still he constantly refined his technique. The first victim had been reported missing too early, he realised. Although it had little impact that time — she was merely listed as missing until her body turned up days later — the police and the general public were now on full alert. Any young woman going missing would be promptly reported and an exhaustive search mounted.

Therefore his second victim had been chosen more carefully. He'd found out that she lived alone, did an exercise class at the sports centre each week and, more importantly, had the following day off work. That had bought him over twenty-four hours to cover his tracks before anyone figured out that she was missing.

Of course it hadn't all been plain sailing. She'd been unusually late leaving the gym and he'd ended up spending an hour waiting for her to emerge. He remained confident that nobody had noticed him, but it was a risk he didn't want to take again.

So this time, he had parked around the corner, halfway down the road that the young woman always walked. Again, he was confident that nobody would think it strange to see the vehicle, even at that time of night. Instead of waiting inside, though, he was skulking around the wheelie bins, waiting for his victim to emerge. The plan was to slip out under the cover of her deafening headphones, follow her down the secluded street until she was within a few paces of the back of the vehicle, before pouncing and subduing her, then dragging her into its rear.

Finally, he heard the metal bang of the steel shutters being pulled down. Not long now, he realised.

"See you Monday, Hardeep," the young woman called out, before setting her face against the wind and crossing the road. She fiddled in her pocket and seconds later he could hear the tinny beat of some dance track he didn't recognise. He squatted, absolutely still. He'd read an article once that claimed that the human eye was tuned to pick up on movement, even in the dark, so he waited without moving a muscle until she walked by the mouth of the alleyway. She didn't so much as glance in his direction.

She passed within a few metres of him and he held his breath. Even over the stench of the empty rubbish bins he imagined he could smell her scent. A faint, citrusy perfume, faded after hours of working. She passed out of sight. It was all he could do to count to five slowly before carefully standing up. The piece of blue plastic sheeting that he'd knelt on rustled in the faint breeze that made its way down the alleyway. To his keyed-up senses it sounded deafening, but he knew that there was no way she could possibly hear it. Moving carefully to the edge of the shadows, he checked both ways. The road was empty. The only vehicle in sight was his. The only person, his target.

He carefully unscrewed the lid of the jam jar that held the chloroform-soaked rag. The smell immediately wafted out, suffusing the air around him with a sickly sweet odour. Fortunately, the young woman was upwind of him and so couldn't smell the anaesthetic solvent. The first time he'd tried this, he'd put the rag into a carrier bag and then watched in surprise as the volatile solvent dissolved the plastic bag. He'd learnt his lesson from that episode and now kept the piece of cloth in a glass container.

Emerging from the shadows, he saw that his timing had been perfect. The young woman was just a few paces from the rear of his transport. Her head bobbed in time to the music; she was oblivious to any danger. Walking briskly, he closed the distance between them.

It was probably his shadow cast by the streetlamp behind them that alerted Gemma. The one thing he hadn't thought to check. Glancing over her shoulder, she opened her mouth in a silent scream of terror. With the element of surprise now gone, he pounced at her, bringing the rag into position, wrapping his powerful arms around her.

To his surprise, instead of screaming and putting up a fight, she immediately went limp. Had she fainted? There was no way the chloroform had acted that fast. Even as he struggled to cope with the sudden dead-weight in his arms, she suddenly snapped her head backwards, catching him full in the face.

As he staggered back, the young woman twisted, a feral snarl on her lips. A sharp pain erupted in his ankle as she stamped hard on his instep. Stumbling in surprise, he dropped the jam jar with a clatter "Bitch!" he gasped as he struggled to regain his composure. This wasn't the way it was supposed to be.

With one last wriggle, the young woman squirmed out of his grip. A blast of cold air on his face told him that the scarf and his mask had been pulled away, revealing his features in the streetlight. They locked eyes, before she took off.

It was the loss of his disguise that spurred him on. Ordinarily, the pain in his ankle and across his nose would have been enough to make him call off the attack. To slink away into the night, leaving the young woman shaken but wiser. Plenty more fish in the sea, as they said. But now that was no longer an option — she'd seen his face. Only a glimpse, to be sure, but what if she recognised him? Her description might not be detailed but it could be enough. Would she describe him well enough for that police officer to recognise him? The one who'd sat staring at him in the police station? He couldn't take that chance. Gritting his teeth against the pain in his ankle, he took off after her.

She was fast. Her coat tails flapping in the wind as she raced down the street. The end of the road was barely a hundred metres away. The thoroughfare that it intersected wasn't especially busy, but there was a pub a few doors down from the junction. The smoking ban meant that, even on a wet and dismal evening in the middle of December, there was a good chance that there might be a nicotine addict standing in the doorway, enjoying their fix.

The gap was opening up between them. Even as he pushed himself on, lungs and heart straining, he could see that she was going to reach the main road before him.

What should I do? he asked himself. What was the safest course of action? If he somehow caught up with her on the main road, he ran the risk of being seen by other, more reliable witnesses. There might even be CCTV cameras on the front of the pub. On the other hand, what had she seen when she pulled away the scarf? The streetlight had been behind him, casting his face into shadow. He had no distinguishing marks. He doubted she could even guess his age.

Reluctantly, he started to slow down. *You're a lucky girl, Gemma*, he thought silently. He felt a twinge of regret as he remembered the way her uniform had risen up her back as she bent over some boxes, revealing a small tattoo above the base of her spine. He'd fantasised about that tattoo for a fortnight.

It had been that which had first marked her out as his next target, as he'd entered the shop to buy a newspaper. A spotty youth in his late teens had served him, but it had taken all of his willpower not to turn around and drink in the young woman with his eyes as she wrestled with a plastic box-cutter. As he'd left the shop he'd realised with a start that the lad behind the till could have given him a pound's worth of change for a fifty-pound note and he would never have noticed.

* * *

334

Up ahead, images of the two murdered local women filled Gemma's vision. The story had dominated the local newspapers for the past few weeks, their photographs staring at her from the news stand across from the till. In quiet moments at work, she'd read the stories, discussing them with her co-workers and regular customers. They'd shaken their heads in sadness, commenting on what the world was coming to when even a town like Middlesbury could witness such crimes. Of course, it had never occurred to her that she could be the killer's next victim.

The end of the road seemed to be a thousand miles away. Behind her she imagined that she could hear the pounding of her pursuer's feet. She turned around, desperate to see how close he was. Could she make it to the main road before he did? And if she did, what then? Her chest was heaving; did she have enough breath to scream for help? What if the road was deserted? She thought that there might be a pub on the main road, but which way? Left or right? Could she make it to the pub before he caught up with her? What if she chose the wrong direction?

He was slowing, she realised, and limping. She must have caught him better than she thought. The skills learnt in self-defence classes from her schooldays had come back when they were needed most. He was giving up. A tide of relief rushed through her. All she had to do was get to the junction and cross the road. He wouldn't come into the light, she realised. He couldn't catch her before the end of the street, so he was breaking off his attack. Suddenly, it was as if a weight had been lifted. Was it her imagination, or did her speed actually increase?

Behind her, the man in the mask wheezed and gasped, trying to catch his breath as he planned his escape route. Should he return to his vehicle, or should he ignore it as if it had nothing to do with him? Safer to ignore it, he decided. He might be able to retrieve it later; failing that, he could cover his tracks if he needed to.

* * *

Ahead of him, approaching the junction, the young woman turned. A look of relief crossed her features as she saw that he had broken off his pursuit.

And then she tripped. Just like that. Whether it was a broken paving slab, or a thoughtlessly neglected dog turd, he had no idea. But one moment she was upright, arms and legs pumping, the next she was crashing down, face first onto the pavement, her momentum propelling her into an ungainly and painful heap, too surprised to even cry out.

All thoughts of quitting vanished; ignoring his heaving chest and throbbing ankle, he redoubled his speed. And suddenly, he was upon her. Ten metres from safety for her — still in the secluded darkness that spelt safety for him — he pounced. He'd dropped the chloroform-soaked cloth a hundred metres back when he'd started the mad dash, but it didn't matter. He was in no mood for finesse. He grabbed a handful of her long blonde hair and pulled her head back. Her face was bloody, her nose probably broken, teeth missing. A soft moan escaped her lacerated lips. Her eyes were rolling in their sockets as she fought to remain conscious.

With a loud crack he slammed her head on the pavement, putting her out of her misery.

MONDAY 19TH DECEMBER

Chapter 40

At 6 a.m. Gordon Hathaway awoke, as he had done almost every day for the past sixty-eight years, without the aid of an alarm clock. Flicking on the dimmed bedside lamp, he turned to his wife, Allie, sleeping beside him. Her long hair, now more grey than brown, was tightly secured in the pink rollers she'd worn to bed every night for the forty-seven years they'd been married. She shifted slightly in her sleep, her breathing quiet and steady. Careful not to wake her, he leant over and kissed her on the forehead. Once upon a time she'd have got up with him, but these days she needed an extra couple of hours in bed. Hell, she'd earned it — they both had.

As he stood he stifled a quiet groan. The constant ache in his joints was at its worst first thing in the morning; he knew from experience that after a couple of hours of hard, physical work it would recede to a background nag.

Padding softly to the bathroom, he closed the door before switching on the light. As he shaved and brushed his teeth he stared at his face in the mirror. Craggy. That was the word that best described him these days, he decided, although Allie still insisted he was as handsome as the day she'd first seen him at the Young Farmers' Club Christmas party.

Although summer was long gone, he still retained the remnants of a faint tan — on his face and his arms. Nothing below the neck, of course; his wiry body was as pale as a glass of milk. His tan was that of a man who worked outdoors for a living; it had been over twenty years since he'd last lain on a beach with his top off. A week in Majorca, a present from their sons for their twenty-fifth wedding anniversary. He smiled at the memory. Good lads, both of them, they'd made sure the farm ran smoothly in their parents' absence. That meant Eddie their youngest, had booked several days off work himself to help his older brother, Rory, who'd followed his old man into the farming business and still worked alongside him to this day.

After getting dressed, he went downstairs. First order of the day was to let their elderly collie, Shep, outside. With relief, he saw that the old girl hadn't made a mess in the night. It wasn't so much the cleaning up — Lord knew, he was a farmer, he was used to that and worse — it was more what it portended. At seventeen years old, the black and white former sheepdog had enjoyed a damn good innings, but that was over a hundred in dog years and time was catching up with her. As a farmer he wasn't supposed to be sentimental about his animals — but he knew he'd have a tear in his eye when he had to dig that hole.

Flicking on the stove, he poured skimmed milk into a saucepan, opened a packet of Quaker Oats porridge and popped two slices of wholemeal bread in the toaster, flicking the on switch for the kettle as he did so.

The reappearance of Shep coincided perfectly with the milk boiling, the toast popping up and the kettle boiling. Like clockwork — he smiled.

Waiting for his porridge to cool, he spread some Benecol

margarine onto his toast. As he did so he gazed wistfully at the frying pan hanging, spotlessly clean, on the wall. For forty-six of his forty-seven years of marriage, Allie had woken with him and the couple had started a hard day's work with a good, healthy fry-up. Well, perhaps not so healthy as it turned out.

The heart attack had been small — a warning shot, the cardiologist had termed it. Nevertheless, he would never forget the terror he'd felt when he'd returned home for lunch to find his beloved Allie slumped over, clutching her arm, her face a grey, sweating mask of pain. Ignoring her protestations — she never did like to make a fuss — he'd bundled her into the Land Rover and driven at breakneck speed to Addenbrooke's hospital in Cambridge, the nearest hospital with a casualty department.

Two clogged arteries and a third narrowed more than was healthy and so a triple by-pass had been scheduled and carried out the very same day. After the initial shock had worn off, and Allie was pronounced stable, with a good chance of a complete recovery, her cardiologist had turned to him. A thorough check-up — the only extended amount of time he'd spent in the care of the medical profession since a boyhood broken leg — revealed a healthy heart, the product of a lifetime of hard physical labour, but a dangerously high cholesterol level and blood pressure bordering on hypertensive.

Twelve months on and a combination of statins, healthy eating, margarines containing plant sterols and blood-pressure pills had reduced his cholesterol to a more acceptable four point eight and his blood pressure to one hundred and thirty over ninety. Allie had shown a similar improvement, but her days of getting up at 6 a.m. were behind her.

They were getting old, damn it. They shouldn't still be working at this age — that hadn't been the plan. They should have retired at sixty, sixty-five at the latest, and Rory should have inherited the farm that he had worked so hard on since leaving school. As it was, with the economy in its current mess and the downward pressure on prices from his buyers, they wouldn't be able to sit back until their mid-seventies. Rory had looked into getting a loan to buy out his father — he'd get the money back in the estate one day anyway — but the banks just weren't lending.

The crunch of gravel on the drive signalled the arrival of his eldest. At 7 a.m. on the dot as usual. By the time Rory had let himself in, the dishes were in the sink soaking and Gordon was pulling on his work boots. Taking a final mouthful of his full-strength, full-flavour coffee — any coffee he consumed for the rest of the day would be decaf — he stood to greet his son.

"Right, the forecast is cold but clear, so what say we go down to that back field and have a look at that fence that came down last week? See what needs doing."

"Sounds like a plan, Dad." Rory looked out of the window at the darkness outside. "Let's see what we find."

* * *

Ninety miles away, DCI Warren Jones was also up early. He'd lain awake all night, his mind a turmoil. Even the three fingers of Scotch he'd drunk with Granddad Jack hadn't been enough to lull him to sleep. Eventually, as the faint chimes of the antique clock in the living room had struck six, he'd given up and slipped quietly downstairs.

The reception of Nana Betty's body into church the night before had been a quiet, sombre affair. The hearse had glided silently up to the doors of the church, the driver effortlessly navigating the narrow entrance to the car park. Immediately all of the awkward conversation from the assembled mourners quietened. Unlike the funeral, which was due to be held the following morning, the reception into church was a short and simple affair. Many of those who would be travelling over to attend the funeral in the morning were unable to attend the reception, so it was a small congregation that watched as Warren and Jack and Dennis — assisted by three carefully height-matched pall-bearers — had shouldered her simple casket and marched it slowly into church, where it would rest overnight before the funeral service in the morning.

If anybody asked him, Warren couldn't tell them what had taken place during the reception. It was as if his memory had blanked it out. Nevertheless, he'd joined Bernice and Dennis as they thanked the various parishioners — mostly elderly women — who had attended the service.

Warren inhaled deeply, before taking a large swig of the black coffee and swallowing two paracetamol. The whisky might not have sent him to sleep, but it had combined quite nicely with the sleeplessness and general stress of the past few weeks to give him a rumbling headache. Something he didn't need this morning.

Warren felt as if he'd been in a time warp since Nana Betty had died, as if he'd been transported back to his childhood. The living room had played host to a never-ending stream of visitors, many of whom he hadn't seen since his mother's funeral years before, whilst he'd sat drinking endless cups of tea reminiscing about half-forgotten events and reliving old memories.

It had been a relief to drive back down to Middlesbury on Saturday evening to retrieve his smart black mourner's suit and spend the night with Susan in their own bed. He'd known that

Susan was feeling similarly stifled and she'd been happy to spend a few hours visiting her friends whilst Warren showed his face at the office.

After a leisurely Sunday morning lie-in, they'd felt recharged enough to return to Granddad Jack's by midday ready for Sunday lunch and the reception. Already, he had started mentally referring to the house as "Granddad Jack's", he realised, not "Nana Betty's and Granddad Jack's" — despite all of the memories, it was as if her spirit had departed the house along with her body.

Sitting down at the dining-room table, he switched on Susan's laptop before remembering that his grandparents didn't have wireless Internet. In fact, they didn't have any type of Internet connection. Digital TV had been the last big technological revolution to hit the elderly couple and only then because the government was switching off the analogue television signal whether they wanted them to or not.

Apparently, Warren could "tether" Susan's laptop to his mobile phone and access the Internet that way — however, this was neither the time nor the place to try and figure that process out, so he resigned himself to the tiny screen on his smartphone.

His work email box had continued to accumulate messages whilst he'd been away but none of them were urgent. Most were the routine, housekeeping emails beloved of any big organisation, plus a handful of reports and replies to questions or requests that he'd asked. Nothing of any great insight or importance. Tony Sutton had thoughtfully emailed him a set of minutes from the team briefings that he'd missed, but he'd summarised them in the first sentence with "No significant progress".

Warren read all of the emails fully, replying where appropriate. After that, he caught up with the news on the BBC website and scanned Facebook to see if anything interesting was happening in his friends' lives.

Finally, he could put it off no longer and he turned back to Susan's laptop. Waking it up from its pre-programmed sleep, he opened the Word document that he'd been agonising over for the past three days.

It had never occurred to Warren that anyone other than he would deliver the eulogy at the funeral. Who else was there? Who else would be able to say all the things that needed to be said about her? Granddad Jack would be far too upset and he couldn't see any of her friends from the church, lovely as they were, rising to the occasion. As for his various cousins and aunts and uncles, none of them knew her well enough. He couldn't bear the thought that it might be left up to Father McGavin, who might have known Betty for over sixty years, but hadn't grown up with her, had his scraped knees bandaged by her or loved her as Warren had.

Not that that made it any easier to write. Over the past few days he'd phoned friends and relatives of his grandmother, spoken at length to Granddad Jack and trawled his own memories for his fondest recollections. Everyone had been clear: it should be a happy speech. One that celebrated a life well lived and a person well loved. That, to his surprise, had been the easy part. There were so many memories to include that he struggled to whittle them down. His final paragraph would be an apology for those not mentioned.

However, as it stood, the document was just a list of memories, of anecdotes, many amusing, but it lacked structure and an opening. He glanced at the clock. *Come on, Warren, not long now. You need to get this around to Jane's for printing — you can hardly haul a laptop up to the lectern.*

It reminded him of his A levels and GCSEs all those years ago, sitting at this very table, struggling for inspiration. Nana Betty would appear at just the right moment with a cup of tea and a plate of custard creams; it was as if she knew...

Suddenly Warren started typing, his fingers stumbling over the keyboard as he tried to get down the words that suddenly fitted.

"I didn't know how to start this speech. I couldn't think what to say. I sat at the oak dining table in Nana and Granddad's dining room and struggled for inspiration. It was as if I'd gone back in time twenty years to when I sat at that same table and did my schoolwork. Often then I would struggle, as I did today, and just when I thought I'd never get it Nana would appear, cup of tea in hand and a plate of custard creams. The break was just what I needed. This morning, it was as if she was with me again, cup of tea and biscuits at the ready — helping me out of another tight spot..."

* * *

By the time Gordon and Rory had loaded up the old Toyota pickup truck with tools and trundled over to the far field, the sun was starting to appear. It was still too faint to chase away the night chill; nevertheless, the extent of the day's work was clear to them in its weak rays.

A particularly gusty weekend had finally brought down an old tree. It in turn had uprooted the better part of thirty yards of wooden fencing separating his field from the bridle path that encircled his neighbour's field.

Annoyingly, he'd marked that tree out for attention only a few weeks ago, but at the time he'd been busy sowing his winter crop. Now that he had a bit of time to deal with it, it was too late.

"Looks as though we're going to have disentangle the fence wire from the tree and pull the tree out. We can probably use an axe to chop the roots off and then loop a chain around the back of the truck." A couple of hours' work at least.

Rory was walking along the line of downed fence. "At least there's some good news, Dad. Most of these fence posts are intact — they've just been pulled out of the ground. No need to waste money on new ones."

"Well, that's something, I suppose." The old man reached into the back of the truck and pulled out an ancient, but well-maintained woodman's axe. "Right. I'll start chopping this old tree up and you start pulling out the broken fence posts."

Without another word, the two men started their tasks. Another day on the farm, mused Gordon. His grandson had a rather rude T-shirt that summed it up pretty well — "Same shit, different day".

* * *

The funeral service was beautiful, as was his speech. That was what everyone said as they shook his hand or kissed him on the cheek. Warren was just glad it was all over. The empty beer glass in front of him neatly summed up how he was feeling — drained. Or perhaps the paper plate in front of him, stained with the remnants of some of his grandmother's home-made chutney, worked better — empty. There was a certain irony to them eating his grandmother's chutney at her funeral, he thought.

OK, enough. He shook himself mentally, his wandering thoughts a sign that he'd had enough to drink, he decided.

The service had been standing room only and the large

congregation had all joined in with the hymns, most of which had been selected by Nana Betty herself. The order of service was a work of art. Put together by his second cousin Jane's husband, a graphic designer, everything from the choice of photographs to the powder-blue titles, carefully matched to his grandmother's favourite colour, was just right. Warren couldn't thank him enough.

Warren's eulogy had gone down well, with his choice of anecdotes well received. At the end of it the congregation were both crying and smiling — pretty much what he'd hoped for. And if his voice had wavered once or twice — well, no one was saying anything.

The weather had behaved itself and the skies had remained clear, as Warren had stood with his back to his parents' grave and lowered the coffin on canvas straps into the freshly dug hole next to them. A few prayers had been said and then it was back to the local Catholic club for the wake.

The next few hours had passed in a blur of yet more handshakes, kisses and half-remembered faces from years gone by. As the drinks had flowed, though, the mood had changed. Funerals were a funny contradiction, he thought to himself. On the one hand, they were by their nature a sad time and no one wanted to go to one — on the flip side, they were like weddings. A time when scattered members of the family came together, perhaps for the first time in years. And that was no bad thing. Inevitably, when celebrating the life of someone who'd had a long and fulfilling existence such as Nana Betty, the good memories outnumbered the sad ones. It wasn't long before the quiet, respectful muttering had become a vibrant babble with laughter ringing out from all corners of the room. Even Granddad Jack, sitting with friends from the couple's over-sixties social club was chuckling as they recounted memories.

Finally, the room started to empty out. More handshakes, more kisses and promises to keep in touch. As the last few mourners headed home Warren found himself sitting in a corner with Susan, Jack, Bernice and Dennis.

To his surprise, Warren felt oddly happy. Perhaps it was the alcohol, combined with the relief of stress, but it seemed that for the time being the feeling of emptiness had been banished.

"You know the worst thing about today, son." Granddad Jack's voice was slightly slurred but his eyes were bright. "Your nan loved a good party — she'd be gutted she missed this one."

* * *

By lunchtime, the old tree had been uprooted, chopped into manageable chunks and loaded onto the back of the pickup Rory had retrieved most of the broken fence posts and reckoned they needed no more than six replacements — a few less than he'd feared. He offered to nip down to the building supplies merchant and pick them up. With the shortest day of the year pretty much upon them, both men would be eating their lunch on the go, trying to squeeze as much out of the daylight as possible.

By 2 p.m., the two farmers were back by the fence line, Rory on the far end wrestling with the last overturned post. It was still partly embedded in the ground and was proving especially difficult. Pausing to catch his breath, he contemplated how much easier backing the pickup and wrapping the chain around it would be. Unfortunately, he couldn't see any easy way to secure the chain

349

and, even if he found a way, the last thing he wanted to risk was splitting the wood and having to fork out for another post.

As he leant on his stubborn adversary, he spotted a flash of something pale partly buried in a small clump of blackberry bushes further along the bridleway. His curiosity piqued, he walked the fifteen yards or so along the fence line. Moving closer, he saw that whatever had caught his attention was partly obscured by discarded carrier bags blown in the wind and now hanging off the bare branches of the bushes like cheap and nasty Christmas decorations.

He leant closer, trying to see what was hidden in the bush.

Gordon Hathaway would never forget the shout of horror as his forty-five-year-old son fell backwards, scrabbling in the mud, before throwing up his lunch.

* * *

The mourners had returned to Granddad Jack's and were now sitting in the living room, working their way through a bottle of wine. Was it the second bottle or were they still on the first? Warren wasn't entirely sure.

Now that the wake was over, the empty feeling had returned. What now? Carry on as normal? After all, the world kept turning. The whole point of today was to put a lid on events, to help people move on. Warren looked over at Granddad Jack, snoozing in his favourite armchair. How was he going to move on? Even now his left hand was draped over the armrest of the seat next to him — Nana Betty's chair. How many nights had they sat here watching TV or chatting, Granddad Jack gently caressing the arm of the woman he loved? Warren was sure he could see a slight smile on the old man's lips. Happy dreams, Granddad, thought Warren, sadly.

The silent vibration of his phone in his pocket jerked him from his reverie. Getting up, he walked quietly into the kitchen, closing the door behind him. It took three attempts to get the damned slide thing on the touchscreen to work and Warren was worried it would divert to voicemail before he could answer it.

Finally, he answered it in a more or less coherent fashion. "Jones."

It took a moment for him to recognise Tony Sutton on the other end of the line. "Guv, it's me." An awkward silence. "How did it go today?"

"Fine. It went fine. Thanks to everyone in the office for the card and the donation — it was much appreciated." There was a silence on the line again. Warren waited. Tony Sutton hadn't rung him up to ask how his grandmother's funeral had gone.

"I'm sorry to ring you, guv, but I know you'd want to be told. We've found another body."

TUESDAY 20TH DECEMBER

Chapter 41

Leaving at six meant that Warren beat the rush-hour traffic and he arrived in Middlesbury at 7.30 a.m. As it was now the school holidays, Susan had stayed with Granddad Jack. They had originally planned to stay until Tuesday night before returning home. Warren would need to return to work and she wanted to finish some marking — or at least that was her excuse. Susan could see the writing on the wall and knew that Warren was dangerously close to cancelling his holiday leave and working Christmas. If he did that and Susan was still in the Midlands it would be very difficult for her to extricate herself from her well-meaning parents and return to be by his side.

Because that was where she intended to spend her Christmas. Even if Warren spent his Christmas Day in the CID office, she would be waiting at home for him. This year he needed her more than ever.

She would have to come back down to Middlesbury at some point before Christmas, if only to get some fresh clothes for the holiday. They'd figure the logistics out for that at a later date. There was a regular train service between Middlesbury and Cambridge and equally frequent trains from Coventry to Cambridge.

The atmosphere was leaden in the CID office as Warren

entered. He knew that at least some of that was due to his own personal circumstances — that was human nature.

"Before we start, I'd just like to thank you all for your thoughtfulness. The card and the contribution to Nana Betty's favourite charity was very much appreciated."

There was a collective sigh of relief. Clearly the boss wasn't going to collapse in a heap on the floor and they wouldn't need to tiptoe around him.

"Tony, can you bring us all up to speed on this latest murder?"

"We have a positive ID: Gemma Allen aged twenty-three. As you can see, blonde hair and pretty — just like the other two. The missing persons report actually came in as we were attending the scene; it seems that she was due to start a shift in her local Costcutter first thing yesterday morning. When she didn't appear, her manager Mr Hardeep Singh tried to contact her, ringing her parents and her mobile. Eventually, he closed up and drove around to see her in her flat. When the neighbours said they hadn't seen her since Saturday morning — when she left to go to work — Mr Singh hit the panic button and rang the police. I suppose that's at least one positive effect of all this publicity — people don't hesitate to contact us.

"Once we were confident of her identity, myself and DC Hastings travelled to Stevenage to meet her mother. She took it very hard and we had to call a doctor to sedate her. Family Liaison stayed whilst her sister came over." He looked apologetic. "Sorry, she was in no fit state to be interviewed. We'll try again this morning."

Apparently, the body had been discovered at about 2 p.m., partly concealed in a blackberry patch off a bridle path between two farms. It had been gone 10 p.m. before Sutton had phoned him. At first Warren had been annoyed — he was the senior investigating officer and he needed to know these things as soon as possible. But as usual, Susan had spoken sense to him. Two o'clock was in the middle of the wake; no way would Sutton be crass enough to phone him then.

If he'd phoned earlier in the evening, then what could Warren have done? He wasn't in a fit state to drive to Middlesbury and so he'd have just spent all evening worrying about it and harassing them by phone. As it was, by the time Sutton had called him, pretty much everything Warren suggested had already been done, the team moving swiftly and smoothly. At Warren's insistence, Sutton had sent photographs of the crime scene and the victim but, with no wireless connection or obvious means to transfer the photos to Susan's laptop, he'd been reduced to looking at them on the phone's tiny three-inch screen.

Sutton, with the blessing of Detective Superintendent Grayson had moved quickly. A preliminary search of Gemma Allen's apartment had revealed no signs of a struggle. It also suggested she had lived alone — something that her mother had yet to confirm. Photographs suggested that she might have a boyfriend; however, Mr Singh, the shop owner, wasn't entirely sure.

With the time of death as yet unconfirmed — but probably at least twenty-four hours previously and the autopsy scheduled for first thing Tuesday — Sutton had decided that it would be prudent to assume that Gemma Allen had been abducted on her way home from work on Saturday night. He'd blocked off the streets on her route home and organised parties of police officers to go door-knocking. Starting first light today, teams of officers would scour the roads, looking for evidence.

In this case, everyone was hopeful that the streets might yield something useful. A small pool of dried blood had already been identified close to a junction and samples taken for typing. At first glance, pictures of Gemma Allen's battered face indicated that she had ended up face first with considerable force on a surface consistent with pavement at least once. The area immediately adjacent to the blood spot would serve as one of the focal points for the search.

Meanwhile, a list of Gemma Allen's workmates and friends was being drawn up. The list was short so far as her mother was too shocked to speak still and Mr Singh knew precious little about his employee. One thing was for sure, however: at seventy-nine years old with an artificial hip and a cataract in his left eye, the old man wasn't very high on the suspect list.

Because of the injuries to her face, the team was so far cautious about linking this latest murder to that of Sally Evans and Carolyn Patterson. Her age, build and long blonde hair weren't really sufficient to do so. The autopsy might reveal a closer link.

Whether the attack was linked to Melanie Clearwater, the battered prostitute lying unconscious in hospital, was a different matter. Both women had serious facial injuries with a possible attempt to batter them to death; however, Clearwater hadn't been raped so far as they could tell. Had Gemma Allen supplemented her wages at the Costcutter with work as a prostitute? It was a line of inquiry worth pursuing, decided Warren.

Tony Sutton had suggested roles for the team and Warren signed off on them. With the meeting concluded, the team leapt to their feet, a sense of urgency in the air. Three murders plus an attempted in two and a half weeks. The signs were ominous. If this was the work of just one man, he was now officially a serial killer and everybody was worried that it wasn't going to end until he was stopped.

Chapter 42

By 10 a.m. it was time for yet another visit to grieving relatives. The routine was becoming depressingly familiar and part of Warren had wanted to take up Tony Sutton's kind offer to perform the duty on his behalf. However, Warren was too involved now. He couldn't imagine not being there.

Checking his tie in the mirror one last time, he met Tony Sutton and Karen Hardwick in the car park. The young detective constable had shown a finely judged mixture of compassion and insight in her previous dealings with the victims' loved ones and Warren was keen for her to take part in this latest interview.

The three police officers were silent during the half-hour drive to Gemma Allen's mother's house in Stevenage. Warren had the car radio tuned to the local BBC radio station, listening to the news. The body's discovery was reported in detailed fashion and, despite the lack of information released by the police, speculation was rife that the murder was linked to the previous two cases. Detective Superintendent Grayson was expecting to give another press conference later that afternoon. Warren resigned himself to the fact that he would be spending yet more time in front of the cameras.

Gemma Allen's mother lived in a shabby-looking two-up,

two-down in one of the housing estates a mile or so from the leisure complex. Blocky grey high-rise flats cast their shadows over the untidy street. A police car sat outside the house, a uniformed constable deterring reporters and the curious. Although Gemma Allen had yet to be named, word had spread fast through the community and already bunches of flowers and soft toys had been left either side of the front gate.

Parking his car under the watchful gaze of the PC, Warren led the team up the cracked front path. Before he got a chance to ring the doorbell, the door swung open, a family liaison officer greeting them.

According to the details given to the team before they arrived, Gemma Allen's mother, Lucy Allen, was a fifty-year-old cleaner-cum-dinner-lady at the local primary school. Gemma was her only child. Gemma's father had left when she was three years old, leaving her upbringing to her mother, assisted by her grandparents and her mother's older sister.

The woman sitting on the couch could have been in her sixties, Warren decided, the stress of the previous twenty-four hours adding years to a face already aged by a lifetime of poverty and hard work. Traces of her daughter's pretty features could clearly be seen, beneath the lines and creases, but she looked more like Gemma's grandmother than her mother. Sitting next to her, holding her shoulders, was another woman, probably her sister.

Paramedics had sedated the poor woman the night before; her shaking hands and unfocused eyes, along with the smell of whisky, suggested that she had also been self-medicating. Nevertheless, her voice was clear without slurring and she insisted that she was ready to talk.

After accepting a cup of tea and expressing the team's condolences, Warren started with a bit of general background. Gemma was twenty-three years old and had lived in Middlesbury for the past year and a half. By her mother's own admission, the two had had a difficult relationship since the girl's late teens. Gemma had been "a bit of a handful"; skipping school, smoking, drinking and dabbling in drugs. Warren had already read the police reports, noting a couple of cautions for shoplifting in her late teens. She'd moved out of the family home to stay with some friends at seventeen and had drifted in and out of casual jobs for the past few years.

However, about eighteen months ago, she'd finally realised that her life was going nowhere and decided to get back on track, renewing her relationship with her mother and restarting her education.

"It was that Facebook thing that did it. I don't understand computers myself, but apparently you can get in contact with people you went to school with and that. She said that she was reading about some of the girls she remembered from class. Some were married with kids, others had been to university or were settled down in good jobs. She said she realised that if they could have a nice life like that, so could she.

"She also had a bit of a scare after a one-night stand at a party. It turned out to be a false alarm, but she realised that she didn't want to be a single mum on benefits in some shitty housing estate like this." Lucy Allen smiled through her tears and laughed hollowly. "At least she learnt something from her old mum.

"Anyway, she decided she needed a clean break. She moved to Middlesbury and managed to wangle a job at a corner shop, then went to the local college. She passed her GCSEs in English and

Maths last summer." Lucy Allen's voice broke. "I was so proud of her."

Her sister handed her another tissue and whispered comfortingly in her ear.

"Anyway, she'd just finished a six-month hair and beauty course at the college and enrolled on a new, more advanced one. She was going to start in January. She was going to come and spend Christmas with me for the first time in years."

This last pronouncement resulted in yet more tears from the distraught woman and Warren and the team waited patiently whilst her sister comforted her.

"I'm very sorry, Ms Allen, but we are going to need to ask some more questions." The woman nodded and Warren continued, "Can you think of anyone who might want to hurt your daughter? Perhaps somebody she knew before she moved to Middlesbury that she didn't get on with?"

Her mother shook her head. "She had the odd falling out with people, but nothing recently. She was generally pretty popular."

"Did she have a boyfriend, anyone she was seeing?"

Again a shake of the head. "She was too busy. She was working as many hours as the social would let her without losing her benefits and she was getting ready for college." Her mother paused again, before deciding to continue. "She was also doing a bit of cleaning on the side, to make a little extra money. I don't think she had the time."

Given the previously poor relationship between the mother and daughter, Warren was uncertain that she would have necessarily known about Gemma's social life — especially since she lived in a different town. He was deciding how best to phrase the question, when Karen Hardwick spoke up.

"You said that she made a clean break of it when she went to

Middlesbury. Do you know if she had any special friends that she kept in contact with after she left Stevenage?"

Her mother thought for a moment. "She kept in touch with her friend Chantelle. I don't have her phone number, but her mum lives across the road at number forty-five. I know that she used to catch the train to Middlesbury occasionally to spend the weekend with her."

Mrs Allen was clearly becoming distraught again and so the three officers agreed to take a break for a few minutes. In the meantime, Tony Sutton suggested that they had a look at Gemma's old room.

The moment he entered the room, Warren figured it was probably a waste of time. The room was pretty much empty, the only remaining furniture a single bed with a plain pink duvet set, a wooden wardrobe and a bedside table with a cheap reading lamp. Faded rectangles and scraps of Blu Tack on the wallpaper suggested the removal of long-standing posters. Faint indentations in the carpet hinted that bookcases and a desk might have once sat there; Warren was willing to bet that furniture matching the dimensions of the marks would probably be found in Gemma Allen's Middlesbury flat.

The wardrobe was almost empty, save for a few empty clothes hangers. The bottom two drawers of a three-drawer unit inside the wardrobe yielded only dust-bunnies. The top drawer had a couple of pairs of plain knickers and bras, some faded T-shirts and a small wash bag with a used toothbrush and toothpaste. The toothbrush was dry. Probably in case she visited and decided to stay overnight unexpectedly, Warren decided.

With the help of Tony Sutton, Warren lifted up the single bed, looking for anything that might have slipped down the back or underneath. Karen Hardwick meanwhile removed the drawers from the wardrobe and the bedside cabinet, checking for anything concealed within.

It took little more than five minutes before the team had exhausted all of the possibilities in the small room. It was clear that when Gemma Allen had moved out, she'd taken everything with her. Her flat in Middlesbury was now her home; her childhood bedroom was just the guest room where she stayed when visiting.

Returning to the living room, Warren was taken to one side by the young woman serving as Family Liaison Officer. "If you want to ask Lucy any more questions, I'd suggest that you do so sooner rather than later," she whispered quietly, nodding discreetly towards the grief-stricken woman. "She had another large glass of whisky whilst you were upstairs. I don't think she'll be much use to you if you delay any longer." She bit her lip, clearly not sure what to do. "I think she has a drinking problem. What should I do?"

"There's not a lot you can do, Constable. It's not our place to intrude at the moment. Just keep an eye on her and maybe put her to bed if needs be. See if you can get her sister to help out."

Walking back into the room, Warren could see that Lucy Allen was increasingly under the influence. After a couple more questions, it was plain that she was fading fast, her words slurred and her eyelids drooping. She'd probably fall asleep soon.

Getting up, he promised to keep her informed and once again passed on his condolences. As he headed towards the door Lucy Allen suddenly lurched to her feet, grabbing his hand.

"Please promise me that you'll catch this animal. Please," she slurred through the tears. "I wish we lived in America, where they have the death penalty. Prison's too good for him, after what he's done to my little girl and those other poor women." She pulled Warren closer. "Please promise me that if you catch him, you won't let him go. He has to pay for what he's done."

"I promise you, I won't let him go. He'll be locked up for a very long time."

"It's not enough," she sobbed. "My little girl is dead and he gets to live. He shouldn't get to live. Not after what he's done. How is that right?"

Warren couldn't answer that question.

* * *

Arriving back at the station, Warren was pleased to see that there was a message from the pathologist waiting for him on his voicemail, asking him to call.

Professor Jordan picked up immediately. "I have just finished the PM on Gemma Allen, the latest victim. Results of tests are still pending, of course, but I thought you'd want to know what I've got so far."

"That's great, Professor, and thanks for doing it so quick."

"Like I said before, it's getting personal now. I want this bastard put away as much as you do.

"First up, I'd say it's almost certainly the same attacker, but his method has changed. I think this attack may have gone wrong. We found the same traces of latex and adhesive around the genital areas — he prepared himself for the rape in the same way. What I didn't find was any evidence of sedation by chloroform. However, he wouldn't have needed it. You saw the scrapes to her face? Traces of gravel embedded in the wound suggest that she fell face first onto the pavement — probably where that puddle of blood was found. The impact loosened some teeth and broke her nose, probably enough to make her woozy, maybe enough to briefly lose consciousness.

"However, he then turned her over and slammed the back of her head into the concrete, at least once. Reddening of the scalp and the loss of a small clump of hair suggests he grabbed a fistful of her fringe and used that to do it. The result was a fractured skull with serious bleeding on the brain. If it's a comfort to the family she would have certainly been unconscious from then onwards."

"What next?"

"It followed the usual pattern, minus the chloroform. He took her to the dumping spot and probably raped her there. He then strangled her, although this time she didn't have a scarf so he used the belt of her coat. That was probably unnecessary; the amount of internal bleeding in her skull would have killed the poor woman pretty soon anyway."

"So we basically have more of the same. Have you spoken to the crime scene manager recently?"

"Yes, they are still doing a fingertip search of her route. They've taken samples of the blood patch and are waiting for a positive match to the victim. Apparently, they've also found some glass fragments with a strong solvent smell about ninety metres from the patch of blood. We've sent it off for analysis. It could be the chemical that he uses to sedate his victims."

"If he dropped the glass bottle or whatever he keeps his solvent in, that might explain why he had to bash her bloody brains out on the pavement."

"Quite possibly. It's also possible that she put up a bit of a fight. I've found traces of what looks like rubber under her fingernails — I'm sure you've read the original reports of those girls that were raped in the Nineties. The attacker wore a rubber mask when he attacked them. I've sent the samples off for analysis."

Warren felt his heart skip a beat. "It was the use of a distinctive rubber mask that led to Richard Cameron's arrest back then. Could history be repeating itself here?"

"I wouldn't necessarily get your hopes up based on that, Chief. They were lucky in the Nineties that the mask was so unusual. You might not be so fortunate this time. However, that's probably just the icing on the cake. If it was Richard Cameron up to his old tricks again, we'll know soon enough."

"What do you mean?"

"It seems like he was a little careless. If I had to guess, I'd say the condom split. We found a semen sample. If you're willing to sign off on a priority request, we can have a DNA profile by tomorrow morning."

WEDNESDAY 21ST DECEMBER

Chapter 43

Warren had left clear instructions that he be told immediately when the DNA test results came in from the semen sample retrieved from Gemma Allen. This caused a slight conflict for the young administrative assistant who took the call, given that Detective Superintendent Grayson, with whom Warren was meeting that morning, had stipulated that he *wasn't* to be disturbed. In the end common sense won out and he knocked tentatively on the senior officer's door. It was the right decision, with Grayson ordering the call be rerouted directly to his office phone, which he placed on speaker.

The technician on the end of the phone had no idea what the results were that he was reporting on — it was simply a rush job that he had been asked to process asap, with the results passed on immediately. Slightly fazed by the fact that he had been placed on speaker phone to at least two senior officers and goodness knew how many other, unannounced listeners, the poor lad stammered a bit at first, before rallying and reading directly from the printout in his hand.

"A complete copy of these results are available on the server and a direct link has been emailed to you, DCI Jones, but, in summary, sample no 2011/12/NH116-A12 — sample of semen retrieved from victim Gemma Allen — positively matches an historic DNA sample on the DNA database 1998/01/NH002-C34 — a mouth swab taken from a suspect, Richard Cameron."

"Gotcha", said Warren quietly.

* * *

The briefing room was a babble of competing voices as pretty much the entire CID team gave their opinion on the shock results.

Warren and Tony Sutton had been making numerous, hasty calls for the last fifteen minutes; Superintendent Grayson was locked in his office, starting the ball rolling on the next part of the operation. Finally, Warren had time to address the team.

"OK, everyone, quieten down. As I'm sure you have all heard, a positive match has been found between the semen left at the scene of Gemma Allen's murder and the previously convicted serial rapist Richard Cameron.

"As we speak, Superintendent Grayson is organising an arrest and search warrant, which we will be executing as soon as possible. The last thing we want is for him to slip through the net and go on the run."

DS Hutchinson raised his hand. "What about Sally Evans and Carolyn Patterson? What happens to those investigations?"

"They proceed as before — the DNA profile only links Cameron to Gemma Allen so far. We need far stronger evidence than we have to link him to those other two killings. It'd be nice if he put his hand up to those as well, but, as you all know, even a confession can be overturned these days with a smart enough lawyer."

DS Richardson this time. "What about other avenues aside from Cameron? Should we continue pursuing those?"

Warren nodded. "Yes. We can't be certain that Cameron was working alone or even that he committed all three murders. We need to keep on tugging at those other leads, see what happens."

It had been almost three weeks since this nightmare started. Warren exchanged a tight smile, with a similarly tense Tony Sutton. Time to bring this to an end.

* * *

The atmosphere in Jones and Sutton's unmarked patrol car was tense. Tony Sutton was driving, whilst Warren rode shotgun, juggling his radio and his mobile phone. By now, it was pitch black, clouds obscuring the stars and moon on the shortest day of the year.

A preliminary scout team had reported that lights were on in the Cameron farmhouse with movement spotted behind the curtains. Michael Stockley's Jaguar was parked in the driveway. The elderly Land Rover with its canvas roof was nowhere to be seen; however, the large barn, easily big enough for both vehicles, was closed for the night.

The relative isolation of the farmhouse made securing the area a lot easier than a residential street, but the arrest team still had an eight-member armed-response unit as well as a forced entry team, complete with battering ram and a large team of uniformed officers. Approximately five miles away, a surveillance helicopter from Chiltern Air Support was hovering, awaiting a call if Cameron escaped.

Everyone wore ballistic protection gear; not only was Richard Cameron a suspected serial killer, but an exhaustive computer check had turned up an expired shotgun certificate in the name of his son. It was entirely possible that Michael Stockley had disposed of his shotgun some years ago, hence him not applying for a renewal of his licence — but nobody was taking any chances. Richard Cameron plus shotgun was a potentially lethal situation. His oft-repeated vow that he would never set foot in a prison again made him a danger to himself, if nobody else.

The officer in charge of the firearms unit was Sergeant Bill Crossing, and he was also an expert in forced entry. Despite being Senior Investigating Officer and the person ultimately in charge, Warren deferred to the older man's experience.

"This will be the third time that Richard Cameron has been questioned by the police in connection with these ongoing murders. In the previous two cases, he has been compliant and non-violent. The aim here is for DCI Jones and DI Sutton to attempt to repeat this and for the arrest to be peaceful.

"Complications include: one, he is aware of the mistake that he made and is expecting to be arrested and charged. Worst-case scenario, he puts up a fight, possibly using an unlicensed shotgun. The armed response unit will follow their standard rules of engagement for these situations. Alternately, he may refuse us entry or try to escape through the rear of the property — in which case we have both forced entry teams plus officers ready to apprehend him. With force if necessary.

"He has given indications that he may try to take his own life. All teams will be standing by and ready to stop that as per training.

"A big unknown variable is the presence of his son, Michael Stockley. We don't know what his response might be. He has demonstrated some verbal aggression during a previous encounter, but for the most part he has been reluctantly compliant.

A possible, though unlikely scenario could be that Cameron uses his son as a human shield. In that case, we will switch to standard anti-hostage procedures and the hostage response team on standby in Welwyn will be called in."

After a few operational questions, it was time for everyone to get into position. When everyone signalled they were ready, Sergeant Crossing nodded to Warren and Tony Sutton.

"Good luck, sirs."

* * *

The unmarked police car crunched slowly over the gravel; with its headlamps on, but no flashing lights, the hope was that they wouldn't spook Richard Cameron into doing something rash.

Pulling to a halt and dousing the car's lights, the two officers looked at each other, before taking a deep breath and climbing out of the car. The night air was bitterly cold, but Warren was glad. It gave the two men an excuse to wear big, heavy winter coats, easily concealing the bulky bulletproof vests that they wore underneath. It was just a shame they couldn't cover everywhere else as well, thought Warren. Bulletproof vests weren't much use if you were shot in the head.

Walking steadily towards the front door, Warren kept his gaze forwards, studiously avoiding looking at the black-clad forced-entry team hidden either side of the door. He took comfort in knowing that similarly well concealed were several trained police snipers, their night-vision optics lighting up the scene as bright as daylight.

The sturdy wooden door had a trio of small windows arranged in an arch at head-height, through which light spilled from the hallway behind. Unfortunately, the glass was heavily frosted, making it impossible to see any detail. Through the door came the muffled sounds of a TV set.

After pausing for a few seconds, to make certain that everyone was ready, Warren depressed the doorbell. Deep inside the house a chime echoed. A few seconds later, an increase in the TV's volume and a brightening of the light escaping through the door's windows signalled that the living-room door had been opened. A scratching and scraping noise indicated the removal of the door chain and the two officers tensed themselves. Finally, the door creaked open.

Michael Stockley was red-eyed and dishevelled, his shirt collar unbuttoned, his tie loosened. A few days' worth of stubble darkened his cheeks.

Recognising the two officers, he simply shook his head. "I've been expecting you. I haven't seen Dad since Saturday."

Chapter 44

Michael Stockley had been sitting in the interview suite with his lawyer for the past hour. Outside the room, Warren and Tony Sutton were discussing what to do about the missing rapist's son. Michael Stockley had clearly been resigned to his fate and had simply stepped to one side and let the armed response team search the house and grounds for his father. No trace was found, and the wanted man's photograph as well as the licence number and details of the missing Land Rover were being circulated to national and international police forces. A press briefing was being prepared for first thing in the morning. When confronted, Stockley admitted that his father had taken his son's shotgun and ammunition and so Cameron was described as armed and dangerous.

"Let's see what he has to say for himself first, before we start threatening him with perverting the course of justice. His full co-operation in finding his old man is probably more valuable than us getting him some jail time."

Tony Sutton reluctantly agreed. "You're probably right, guv. But if that bastard in there hadn't lied about his father's whereabouts the first time we picked him up, then he could have prevented at least two murders and we wouldn't be organising a bloody manhunt and hoping to God he doesn't strike again. When this is all over, he needs to stand in the dock for something."

"I agree, but we'll cross that bridge when we come to it. Maybe we'll use it as leverage."

Pushing open the door, Warren led the way into the interview suite, Tony Sutton following. After checking that the PACE recorder was working and that Stockley was aware that he was not as yet under arrest, the two officers started.

Immediately, Stockley's solicitor interrupted the two officers. "My client informs me that he wishes to be fully compliant with the police investigation and to render whatever assistance he can." The solicitor glanced at Stockley, clearly not entirely happy with what he was about to say next. "He would also like it to be noted that he was not entirely forthcoming in the two previous interviews that he gave. That was from a sincere, but misguided attempt to protect his father from the charges of which he is accused; charges which my client still believes his father is innocent of."

Warren and Sutton exchanged surprised glances, before Warren answered with a non-committal, "I see."

The unexpected frankness of Stockley gave Warren pause for thought, but after a couple of seconds' thought he decided to run with it and see where it got them.

"Then perhaps that should be where we start from. In what way were your previous statements inaccurate?"

"On the previous two occasions, you and the team in Liverpool asked me where my father was when Sally Evans and Carolyn Patterson were believed to have been abducted. I stated that my father had gone to bed early on both nights and that I could hear him asleep upstairs."

Stockley licked his lips and looked at his solicitor. The lawyer's face was a mask.

"I lied both times."

"So, where was your father?"

"I don't know. He was out on both nights and I didn't hear him come back. I went to bed about 10 p.m. — I have to get up early in the morning."

"Why did you lie to us?" Tony Sutton asked.

Stockley sighed. "Because I knew how it looked. The police are always going to go for the most obvious target — and that's my old man. The first thing you want is an alibi. Dad didn't have one." He looked at the two officers pleadingly. "But so what? If I asked you to randomly account for your whereabouts at any time, could you?" He answered his own question. "Of course not. People spend hours every day on their own, with nobody to vouch for their whereabouts. My old man more than most, probably."

"And you didn't think it at all significant that your dad was out late at night on both those evenings?"

Stockley shook his head. "No. It wasn't out of character." He sighed again.

"Ever since Dad got out of prison, he's really valued his freedom. But he's also a bit of a loner. He likes to take long walks or go out shooting rabbits. With the nights pulling in, he likes to drive to some country pub in the middle of nowhere, where nobody recognises him, and just enjoy a pint in the corner and read the newspaper for a few hours. He doesn't like crowds. He's been doing this a couple or three nights a week for months. When you pulled him in, I panicked. I knew he didn't have an alibi so I lied."

"What makes you so sure he's innocent?" asked Sutton.

"He's a changed man; prison changed him." He ignored Sutton's sceptical look. "He hated being in there. He nearly didn't survive it. I know he still has nightmares about being locked up. He removed the lock on his bedroom door and he sleeps with it open, because it reminds him too much of his cell. He was definitely abused in there; certainly by other prisoners and maybe even the guards. He won't really talk about it.

"The thing is, I can't see him ever doing anything to land himself back in there. He's still on licence and he's paranoid about getting into trouble. He drives everywhere five miles below the speed limit and when he goes out of an evening he has one pint then stays for an extra couple of hours drinking Coke just to make sure there is no alcohol in his system, in case he's pulled over."

Sutton did nothing to hide his disbelief. "Perhaps that just means he'll be more careful about getting caught. You know what they say about a leopard and his spots…"

"No way. Dad would rather die than go to prison again. He wouldn't risk it." Stockley's tone was firm.

"So what's made you change your mind this time and co-operate?" asked Warren.

"I haven't seen Dad since Saturday. I watched the news and saw about that new girl being found. I've called his phone but it's turned off. I'm really worried about him."

"Why? What are you worried about?"

"I think he's scared that he will be blamed again. You've already brought him in for questioning twice. Both times he was really upset for the next two or three days. I don't think he could stand another interrogation."

"And you don't think it could be that he's guilty; that he's done a runner because he's about to get caught?" Sutton scowled at the man in front of him.

"No. He's heard about the murder on the news and he's disappeared. He's just hoping you'll find the real killer and it'll all blow over."

"And why would you think that? You've said that he's taken your shotgun and that he'd rather die than go to prison. Couldn't he have gone into the woods somewhere and finished himself off?"

Stockley shook his head. "No, I don't think so. Dad was getting his life back together. He'd not just give in. Sure, if he thought he was going to get stitched up he'd kill himself rather than go back to prison, but I don't think he's suicidal. It hasn't reached that yet."

"You sound very confident of that, Michael." Warren stared at him long and hard in the eyes. "Why is that? What aren't you telling us?"

Stockley sighed. "Before he went, he emptied out our joint bank account."

"How much are we talking here?" Sutton asked.

"Twenty-three thousand pounds. It was the business account that we used for the farm. That money represented the farm's operating costs for next year: all of our seeds, fertiliser, diesel costs — you name it."

Warren and Sutton exchanged glances. Twenty-three thousand pounds was a lot of money. He could lie low on that sort of money for a long time, assuming that he was careful.

"So you reckon that your old man is completely innocent? That he's just keeping out of sight until we find the real killer and that he's taken that money to help hide himself."

Stockley nodded vigorously.

"And what if your father were to be found guilty? What if he did commit those crimes? Where does that leave you then, Michael? You've been helping a convicted rapist pick up where he left off."

Stockley stared at the tabletop for a long time. Finally, he raised his gaze and looked Warren in the eye. His voice shook.

"Then I will never forgive myself. And my father can rot in hell."

There was a long pause, before Warren spoke softly. "I'm sorry, Michael, but you've backed the wrong horse here. First of all, you say your father disappeared Saturday — we didn't announce Gemma Allen's death until Tuesday."

Stockley's mouth dropped open in horror. "No, there must be some mistake. Maybe I've got the dates wrong…"

Warren continued, "And we just received confirmation that DNA samples retrieved from the scene match your father."

Stockley's face crumpled and he covered it with his hands. Behind them, he could be heard mumbling, "No, no, no," again and again.

"Michael, listen to me." Warren's voice was gentle now. "You can help us make things right. Help us find your dad before he kills anyone else. Help us put him away, to bring a little peace to those poor families." It was shameless exploitation, he knew, but he didn't care. "Next week is Christmas. Think about those poor mothers and fathers sitting around their Christmas trees without their daughters. Hell, they probably won't celebrate Christmas this year. And it'll never be the same for them again. Think about that. At least give them the comfort of knowing that Richard Cameron is no longer out there. Do it for them. And save your father from himself."

Warren could just about make out the nodding of the man's head.

* * *

Outside the interview suite, Sutton was thoughtful.

"You know, if Stockley can't vouch for the whereabouts of his old man, his own alibi is suspect also?"

Warren nodded. "My thoughts exactly. Make sure that nice Jag of his is also impounded and searched. Traffic haven't spotted it on CCTV yet, but let's be certain."

"That goatee of his hides his chin quite effectively, don't you think? Almost as well as his old man's beard."

Warren grunted. "I hear you, Tony, but it's been almost two weeks since Carolyn Patterson. I doubt there'd be much of a bruise left from her punch even if the pathologist's speculation is correct and she caught him with a right hook."

"Agreed. Still, I'm going to ring Merseyside and see if they noticed anything when they interviewed him."

Chapter 45

The farmhouse fairly swarmed with scenes of crime officers. They'd entered as soon as the armed officers had ensured that Richard Cameron wasn't waiting for them with his son's shotgun.

A preliminary search of the house revealed nothing of immediate relevance beyond a number of items of clothing in each man's wardrobe that looked as though they might match the fibres found on all three victims, although their forensic worth would be of questionable use, given the ubiquity of the cloth.

In the back office sat a PC. This was bagged and sent immediately to Welwyn for analysis by the computer crime division. It was possible that there were details on the computer about Cameron's recent attacks and maybe even any future attacks. Warren authorised the extra cost for it to be put through as a priority.

Down in the garage, one of the team had found a set of perfect muddy footprints by the back door. It looked as though a pair of dirty work boots had sat there until recently. There was no sign of any matching boots in the rest of the house and Warren made a note to ask Stockley if they belonged to his father. The investigator took high-resolution photographs to allow comparison with the partial prints that had been found at the murder scenes.

For the rest of the night, the team searched the house for clues to Cameron's whereabouts as well as evidence linking him to the current attacks. Of particular interest was what Tony Sutton had dubbed his "rape kit". Based on what the pathologist had found from the autopsies, they expected him to have access to pairs of latex gloves, condoms and adhesive tape to help him avoid leaving trace evidence during the rape. He also used some sort of solvent, probably chloroform, to sedate his victims.

By the early hours of the morning the team reported that no sign of this kit had been found. An inventory had been taken of each of the chemicals in the kitchen, bathroom, garage and barn, but an expert chemist had ruled out any of them as being suitable for use as a sedative.

Richard Cameron, it seemed, had disappeared into the wind. Even more alarmingly, he'd gone prepared to kill again.

THURSDAY 22ND DECEMBER

Chapter 46

With the DNA profile confirming Richard Cameron as the rapist, the pressure was now on to find him before he struck again or disappeared for ever. His likeness was released to the media with the obligatory warnings not to approach him and a description of his Land Rover was circulated.

Michael Stockley was understandably upset by the realisation that his father had returned to his old ways and that his own lies clearly raised suspicions. Nevertheless, with preliminary forensics on his Jaguar car showing no traces from any of the victims and Merseyside police unable to confirm or deny any obvious visible bruising from when they'd interviewed him, the team had no reason to detain him.

Despite his name change, it was all but inevitable that he would be linked to his father by the press. The Reverend Thomas Harding generously stepped in and offered him a discreet place to stay, saving Hertfordshire Police the expense of protective custody. The son of the man the papers were calling the "Middlesbury Monster" was unlikely to be safe from vigilantes, although, considering that his lies had helped prolong his father's killing spree, few in the CID unit were losing sleep worrying about his safety.

Stockley had furnished the police with a list of relatives and old friends that his father might contact, although he admitted that the two of them had been pariahs since Cameron's release. So it was a surprise to nobody that the afternoon Gary Hastings spent contacting these people bore little fruit beyond a fervent promise from Cameron's second cousin that should he come into contact with his wayward relative he'd "personally deliver the bastard to the police trussed up like a Christmas turkey". The general consensus of Richard Cameron's former friends and family was that "hanging was too good for hi" and that they were ashamed to be related to him.

"He has to be staying somewhere. The problem is that twenty-three thousand pounds in cash can hide a man pretty well. We don't even know he is still in the area," groused Warren as he and Tony Sutton drank coffee in his office.

"At least we know he is probably still in the country," pointed out Sutton, gesturing towards a report from the UK passport office that confirmed that the expired passport the search team had found in his office drawer was his only one and that it hadn't been renewed. Still, the UK border patrol remained on the lookout for him, along with every other law enforcement agency in the country. Unfortunately, with so much money at his disposal, he had no need to use credit cards or cashpoints and his mobile phone was either switched off or destroyed.

Mid-afternoon on the first day of the search, things took a rather macabre turn. A team scanning the farm's immediate grounds found a patch of freshly disturbed earth and the specialist sniffer dog trained to detect cadavers had become extremely excited.

Fearing the worst, the team had carefully dug up the area, taking care not to disturb any evidence or damage whatever was buried. Eventually they had revealed a shallow pit, containing the partially decomposed corpses of half a dozen wild rabbits. A quick and dirty autopsy in a tent at the scene was unable to identify the cause of death for the small creatures, but did reveal the telltale marks of a snare on their front legs.

As Warren stared at the mound of grey fur he felt a chill rundown his spine. He had no idea why the rabbits were significant. But he was convinced that they were.

* * *

The most useful thing retrieved from the farmhouse was the computer. An off-the-shelf PC, it turned out to be a treasure trove of useful information. Pete Robertson, a computer expert from Welwyn, took Warren and Tony Sutton through what he had found.

Most people meeting Pete Robertson for the first time couldn't help a double take. The man looked as if a person of normal proportions had been stretched vertically. Everything from his legs to his arms and even his head seemed to be about 25 per cent longer than it should be. At the moment, Robertson was folded under a regular-sized desk. Despite the remarkable length of his digits, he typed with the grace of somebody who had spent eight hours or more every day of his adult life in front of a computer keyboard.

"The computer is a pretty simple set-up. Bog-standard, PC World, a few years old, with a Windows operating system. It's been configured so that two people can use it independently. A standard log-in screen with a username and password to access each person's private files. It's the basic home edition, so that caused no problem.

"Each person has a private user area to save files, plus separate settings for their desktop environment. As you would probably expect, Michael Stockley, who has worked with computers most of his life, has heavily personalised his environment, with a custom colour scheme and his own choice of background wallpaper. His father uses the Windows defaults.

"Most interesting, though, is the Internet history. Michael Stockley watches quite a bit of TV on the BBC iPlayer, is a big *Star Trek* fan and does a lot of online shopping through Amazon."

"OK." Warren bit his lip; Pete Robertson liked to milk the moment a bit and he fought the urge to hurry him along.

"Richard Cameron deletes his Internet browsing history each time he logs off…" the look on Robertson's face suggested that it hadn't posed much of an obstacle "…and his favourite webpages include extremely hard-core bondage sites, Google Earth images of the places he dumped his victims' bodies and, rather alarmingly, a number of websites giving instructions on how to make cyanide from fruits such as apricots."

Tony Sutton swallowed, his face pale. "Well, I think we can guess how those poor rabbits died."

Chapter 47

"So why does he kill these women with their scarves, rather than cyanide?"

Warren and the team were having the day's latest briefing.

"Maybe the cyanide wasn't ready for use?" suggested Karen Hardwick. Tony Sutton shook his head. "They reckon those rabbits have been dead for weeks. He clearly had a working batch a while ago."

"Maybe he's run out? I imagine it would take significantly more poison to kill a grown human being than a small animal like a rabbit. Perhaps by the time he'd made his batch, he used the whole lot on those rabbits," Gary Hastings proposed.

Warren nodded. "You're right that it does take a lot more poison to kill a human being. However, assuming he followed the instructions properly and he used all of the stones from the ten kilogrammes of apricots he bought online, then he will have made many times that needed to kill a healthy adult."

A collective shudder ran around the table; somebody like Richard Cameron in possession of that amount of deadly poison was a chilling thought.

"Maybe the cyanide is a back-up? Judging by the nature of some of those bondage and porn sites, it looks like the sick pervert gets off on women being strangled. Maybe throttling her is part of the way he gets his rocks off. The cyanide is there just in case he gets disturbed and can't finish her off," Tony Sutton suggested.

Warren shrugged. "It's as good a reason as any, Tony."

He picked up another report. "We have some more news from the house. The muddy footprints in the garage, which Michael Stockley has confirmed probably come from the missing work boots his father normally kept in that spot, are a positive match for the partial impressions pieced together from the different crime scenes. They are also doing an analysis of some of the mud and looking to see if they can match it to the crime scenes. It looks as though we have at least some evidence connecting Cameron with the other murders."

"It's a start, but it feels a bit flimsy," stated Sutton. "We need something a bit more substantial if we want to charge him with all three murders."

"Forensics are working on that. Andy Harrison reckons that the strange cardboard powder probably came from the vehicle that the victims were transported in. If we can find Cameron's Land Rover, we may find traces of the powder. It's pretty unusual and he's unsure where it originally came from, but that will make it a more significant clue. We're also trawling through CCTV footage to see if the vehicle turns up where it shouldn't. Nothing so far, but we've got them pretty busy at the moment."

"Speaking of the Land Rover, where is it? It can't just have disappeared. And how is he transporting the victims otherwise?"

"A good question. We've got some tyre tracks from the driveway and we're comparing to partials found near the murder scenes, but the weather we've had lately hasn't helped preserve them; ideally, we need the Land Rover to compare to directly.

However, it seems to have completely vanished. Nothing on the ANPR system or from patrols. He's either hidden it or switched plates with a legitimate vehicle."

"Wouldn't the owners report the plates missing on their vehicle?"

"Possibly, but it might be that he has sourced new plates from somewhere and just swapped his own. As long as he doesn't get caught on speed cameras or stopped by the police and sent a court summons, then the registered owners would never be any the wiser."

"I thought the sale of licence plates was restricted to stop just this sort of thing happening?" asked Gary Hastings.

Warren gave an open-handed gesture of uncertainty. "You can get pretty much whatever you want these days on the Internet and with twenty-three thousand in cash he can pay for it."

"Sounds pretty sophisticated for a man just out of prison with no computer skills to speak of. But we should still mention it to IT, get them to look at the PC again and see if Cameron communicated with anyone we already know about or visited sites that could put him in contact with such people," Tony Sutton suggested. "On a related note, have IT found any pointers towards his next attacks?"

"Nothing useful. The Google Earth images all relate to past dumping spots and were accessed days in advance. We have no new surveillance images that can't be accounted for. Either he's given up," Warren said, "or he's found another way to choose his spots and victims. Maybe just a good old map book."

"What about the rubber traces under Gemma Allen's fingernails? Does it tell us anything useful?" asked Karen Hardwick.

Warren shook his head. "It's a cheap latex mix found in millions of different products made in China. Halloween masks mainly but some celebrity and other novelties. Unfortunately, they are sold everywhere from the pound shop to Sainsbury's so we aren't going to get lucky the way they did back in the Nineties."

The morale in the group was dipping again, Warren could feel. Three days before Christmas and again the direction of the investigation seemed to be dictated by what others, mainly Richard Cameron, did or didn't do. They needed to take charge of the investigation again. But how?

Christmas

He awoke sweating and out of breath. Lying still, he reached out with his mind, grasping the slowly evaporating memories of the dream, piecing them together, trying to resurrect the intense eroticism of the subconscious fantasy.

The lingering physical effects of the dream were slowly fading and so he reached down, trying to conjure up those feelings again. Finally he lay there, panting, tingling, looking forward to the day ahead. A contented smile spread across his face as a thrill of antici-pation ran through his body.

Today was the day, another conquest, perhaps the best so far. He'd been planning this one for weeks, ever since he'd first seen her. He'd learnt lessons from every attack so far; none of them had been perfect. The last one had been fraught with problems, but he'd overcome them. This time he'd thought of everything. This time there would be no mistakes.

That thought brought renewed energy. No rush, he decided, no need to get up just yet. He reached down again.

Chapter 48

Warren and Susan pulled into the wide gravelled drive of her family home in Stratford-upon-Avon. The guilt that Warren felt over taking holiday during such an intense investigation had gradually lifted as Middlesbury receded behind them, like the slow emptying of a heavy rucksack. Earlier that week, Warren had reluctantly cancelled his Christmas vacation. Susan had been upset, but understanding, and Warren had felt awful. If anyone needed a break, it was her and she had been looking forward to a few days' celebration for weeks.

With all the pressures of his job, Warren often forgot the strain that Susan was also under. Since Easter, when confirmation of Warren's promotion had come through and she had been forced to hand in her own resignation, Susan had worked flat out. Her old school had squeezed as much out of her as possible during that last term, setting her the task of completely rewriting the Biology GCSE schemes of work in preparation for the new syllabus being introduced from September.

Come the summer, whilst Warren had prepared for his new posting in Middlesbury, Susan had taken the lead in organising the couple's move south whilst at the same time preparing for her own new position as Head of Biology and lead teacher in charge of improving the school's poor science GCSE grades. As if this weren't enough, no mention had been made at interview that the school was expecting an OFSTED inspection sometime in the next year and was likely to be placed in "special measures" — the category reserved for schools considered to be "failing". It further transpired that Susan's predecessor had left behind a legacy of badly written schemes of work and limited procedures for increasing pupil achievement whilst the head of science was taking early retirement. Susan would effectively be the acting head of science, with an expectation that she would become the new head at the end of the year.

Then the murder at the university had occurred — Warren's first big case as a DCI and lead investigator. Suddenly Warren had been working around the clock solving the crime, then dealing with the bureaucratic aftermath, and Susan had been left in charge of the house as well as her new responsibilities. It had all been too much to bear and in the end it was only her parents staying and helping her decorate the house that had kept her together, emotionally.

The couple had finally arranged a long weekend at half-term, spending a few days in Paris sightseeing and simply relaxing, but Susan had still spent the remainder of the holiday working, updating teaching schemes, devising methods to monitor and raise pupil achievement and catching up on her marking.

Finally, the end of the longest term in the school calendar was here. Susan knew she would spend the few days before Christmas marking and planning for the upcoming term, but now she felt she was getting a handle on her new job. She had a clear plan of action for the department and at last felt she was getting to properly know her new colleagues and, most importantly, the one hundred and eighty new pupils that she had gained this year.

It had been intervention from two unexpected sources that had finally convinced Warren to at least take a couple of days off over Christmas and join his wife in the Midlands. The first had been from Dennis, Susan's ordinarily mute father. He'd phoned Warren at his desk during Friday lunchtime. Susan had broken the news the night before that they would be unlikely to make it back for the festive period. It was the longest conversation that Warren had ever had with the man. He'd been quietly persuasive, describing how not only Susan needed a break, so did Warren.

"You've been through the wringer, both at work and at home these past few months. When I was your age, I missed Christmas twice because of work. You and Susan don't have kids yet, so you probably think it doesn't matter. And I know your job means that some years you won't have any choice — but if you can, you should make the effort. It's Jack's first Christmas without Betty — he really needs you."

There had been a heavy, smothering silence, before Dennis started again, his voice even quieter. "The second of those Christmases that I missed was my mother's last. She died in the February. I still wish I'd been home that year and celebrated one last time with her. Jack isn't well — he's taken Betty's loss really hard. Don't miss these special moments. You don't want to end up regretting not being there."

The line had gone quiet again. "I can't pretend to know how busy you are and whether it is possible for you to come home, but it's the twenty-first century. You have a mobile phone. I'm sure you can check your email on it and you can be back in Middlesbury in less than two hours if they need you. Please think about it."

Warren had hung up, feeling the guilt tearing at him from both sides. He was the DCI in a major multiple murder investigation;

he needed to be in charge. Policing didn't stop for the festive period and since joining the service he'd worked his fair share of Christmas Day shifts and expected to work plenty more. Plus, it wasn't exactly a dilemma unique to the police. Thousands of miles away hundreds of soldiers would be out on foot patrol in Afghanistan under constant threat of death or life-changing injury from an enemy that not only didn't celebrate Christmas, but would probably revel in the symbolism of a major offensive during such an important festival in the West. Back at home, the ambulance and fire services would be looking after a celebrating public, nurses and doctors would be caring for their patients. Even farmers would be out in the cold, tending their livestock.

But on the other hand, he had booked annual leave. Staffing for the festive period had been decided well in advance with a full complement of experienced senior officers supported by more junior ranks. On paper at least, Christmas would be no different from any other weekend. And Dennis was right: he could stick to soft drinks and leave his phone switched on.

A couple of days would help recharge his batteries and make the world of difference to Susan. The couple hadn't even put a tree up in their house yet and full Christmas dinner with all of the trimmings didn't seem worth it just for the two of them. And how could he leave Granddad Jack?

The dilemma had gnawed at Warren all day, until a second, even more surprising event had made his mind up for him.

"Warren, you look knackered."

That was how Superintendent Grayson had concluded their twice-daily briefing. Warren had drunk two cups of coffee as the two men had pored over the latest reports from the various investigations.

The older officer had leant back in his chair and eyed his subordinate. "Rumour has it that you've cancelled your leave over Christmas."

Warren had shrugged helplessly. "Can't be helped, sir. Three murders, plus an attempted and a serial killer on the loose who may well strike again — I need to be here."

Grayson stared at him for a few long moments. "The first of these murders was, when, the second of this month? The latest was the seventeenth. We've got Richard Cameron square in the picture with a nationwide manhunt under way. You've done the hard part, Warren. The DNA evidence is compelling, we have him bang to rights for Gemma Allen's murder, we just need to link him to the others. Hell, he might even confess to them if we catch the bugger alive.

"You've worked around the clock for three weeks solid and, in that time, you've also suffered a significant bereavement. There is a lot more that needs to be done on this case. It'll drag on well into the new year and I need you operating at peak efficiency.

"DI Sutton is the senior on-call officer over the period and I'll be on hand for anything serious. Welwyn can always spare a few bodies if we need them. I promise that if anything significant turns up, you'll be the first to know. Leave your phone switched on, keep a full petrol tank and don't get too pissed. I don't want to see you from lunchtime Christmas Eve until first thing on the twenty-seventh."

So that had been it. Susan's delight when he told her had made Warren feel even more guilty about the way he'd treated her, but that was in the past. A record-breaking sprint around the shops that night had put a fair dent in his credit card, but the car boot full of inexpertly wrapped presents and festive fare was worth it.

The phone call at midday as Warren had finished tidying his desk had nearly made him cancel the trip, even at this late hour. Saskia Walker, a twenty-six-year-old sales assistant, hadn't turned up at her work's Christmas party the night before. Ordinarily, the last thing her co-workers would do on the busiest shopping day of the year was run around chasing after an absent colleague, but the recent spate of murders had the residents of Middlesbury on edge and Saskia was a hard-working, ambitious member of staff and such behaviour was out of character.

After several unanswered voicemails, an increasingly worried store manager had finally contacted Saskia's best friend, who had keys to her flat. She reported that the apartment was untidy with an opened pint of milk beginning to smell on the kitchen counter and a washing machine full of damp clothes; the full litter tray, empty food bowls and two very grumpy cats suggested that she had been absent a couple of days, but hadn't planned it. Her friend noticed that her running shoes were not by the door in their usual place, nor was her lightweight fleece hanging on the coat rack.

Normally, such a disappearance would be logged by the police, investigations would be made to rule out foul play, and the case passed onto the missing persons unit. But these weren't normal times. The call had been flagged immediately for the attention of Warren's CID team and a meeting hastily convened.

This time it had been Tony Sutton who stopped his boss from cancelling his plans.

"Look, guv, this isn't a murder, not yet. It's just another missing person. You know the figures: more than two hundred thousand people go missing each year, with Saskia Walker's age group the most likely to disappear, especially at this time of year. According to her friends, she had a bad break-up with her long-term boyfriend last winter and had been suffering from depression. She also had a bit of an ill-judged fling with a co-worker back in October and has been avoiding him ever since — that may have been why she skipped the party last night, as he was there."

"But why hasn't she contacted her family? She was supposed to be spending Christmas with them. Wouldn't she have said something if her plans had changed?"

"Well, depression can do funny things to a person's judgement. Besides which, her best friend reckons her parents have a poor relationship and she doesn't care for her sister's husband very much — maybe she couldn't face spending it with them? She wouldn't be the first person to decide they'd rather spend Christmas on their own, instead of making merry and pretending to be full of festive cheer with the folks."

Warren had nodded. "I accept that, but it looks as though she went missing a couple of days ago. No one has seen her since Wednesday and the flat looks as if it hasn't been lived in since then. Surely if she was going away for a couple of days she'd have put out more food for the cats? And what about her missing running shoes?"

Sutton had shrugged. "I know, boss, I have a bad feeling also, but it isn't our concern yet. She's officially a missing person with no evidence of foul play. It's only because she's a young, attractive woman of the type that Richard Cameron favours that we've been given a heads-up. Hell, he may not even be in the area anymore."

Eventually, Warren had conceded the point and, after assurances that he'd be kept in the loop, had finally left the office. But the look on Sutton's face had broadcast feelings that exactly mirrored his own. Richard Cameron had struck again and pretty soon the defiled body of another young woman would be turning up.

Bernice's welcome was positively effusive. A faint smell of cooking sherry hinted at the reason for her uncharacteristic cheerfulness. Dennis made no mention of their phone call, merely grunting welcome and shaking Warren's hand, although he did give Susan a warm, welcoming hug. His slightly forlorn expression was probably caused by the truly hideous hand-knitted sweater he was wearing, Warren decided. He couldn't imagine it being Dennis' idea to don the brown woollen monstrosity with its slightly wonky reindeer pattern.

It was clear that Bernice was determined to make the festive period as cheerful as possible. Practically every surface was covered in tinsel and Christmas knick-knacks. Even Susan seemed taken aback by the decorations.

"You've been busy," she managed, diplomatically.

The gaudiness of the house made Granddad Jack's appearance all the more shocking. Dressed in a thick woollen jumper and a cardigan — despite the roaring fire in the living room — he was dozing in front of the TV, an unopened newspaper on his lap.

Warren paused at the door, taking in his gaunt appearance.

"Granddad," he called softly, not wanting to give the old man a fright. No reply. He tried again a little louder, still nothing. Finally, he leant down and took the old man's hand. As he did so he saw that he wasn't wearing his hearing aids. Warren couldn't ever remember seeing him without them.

The old man started in surprise. "It's just me, Granddad." Warren spoke loudly. Jack nodded his head, the puzzled look clearing from his eyes. A sad smile plucked at his mouth.

"Come here, son," he mumbled, and Warren leant down to hug

him, noticing the faint rasp of his stubble on his cheeks. Warren's heart fell, even as he forced a smile.

The old man seemed to have had the life drained from him. He'd clearly lost even more weight in the short time since the funeral and his skin was cold and papery. Even more worryingly, Jack had always been a proud man and for him to have taken his hearing aids out and not shaved when he was a guest in someone's house spoke volumes about his state of mind. At least he'd kept his teeth in.

Squinting over Warren's shoulder, his face brightened. "Susan, sweetheart, you're here."

Moving aside, Warren felt a small measure of relief as Jack reached out to hug his grandson's wife.

"Hello, Granddad, how are you?"

Jack's smile widened even more; he'd always wanted a little girl and when Susan had taken to calling him Granddad after their wedding it had brought tears to his eyes. Looking at the two of them, Warren felt the heaviness in his chest lift slightly. He glanced over at Dennis and Bernice standing quietly in the doorway. Dennis nodded once and Warren returned the gesture. Whatever happened in the future, Jack would be looked after.

* * *

Christmas Eve had always involved midnight mass. This year would be no different. Bernice insisted that they attend Jack and Betty's local church, rather than their normal service, and so they had all piled into Warren's car for the drive. Had she known what she was letting herself in for, Bernice would probably have been less insistent, Warren was sure. For the first time since they had arrived, Warren had spotted a mischievous glint in Jack's eyes as he thanked Bernice for her thoughtfulness.

"Does Mr Potter still play the organ at midnight mass?" whispered Warren to his grandfather, when he had a moment.

"I think so. The regular choir are down to play the morning services and they don't usually play both. Especially after that incident a few years ago." The smile took ten years off his grandfather's face.

The service was due to start at 11.30 p.m. with a short carol service, before the full mass started at midnight. The family arrived a few minutes early and Warren was touched by how many parishioners came over to wish them a happy Christmas and pass on their condolences if they hadn't already done so. Nevertheless, the church was surprisingly empty, something that Bernice commented on a little louder than Warren would have liked. She'd soon see why.

Finally, the quiet ringing of bells signified the start of the carol service and all became quiet. "O Little Town of Bethlehem" was the opening carol and Mr Potter, hidden behind the organ, started in with his usual gusto. The first couple of bars went well, with everyone joining in the familiar tune — then the problems started. First, Mr Potter hit a slightly off note. His immediate response was to backtrack slightly and hit the correct note. This caused those less experienced with Mr Potter's idiosyncratic style of playing to pause also, disturbing the rhythm. For those who had attended midnight mass at the small church regularly over the years, they knew that the correct response was to soldier on regardless of the discordant notes coming from the organ; experience had shown that Mr Potter would generally follow the choir and more or less catch up, rather than the other way around.

By the time the bell rang again to signify the start of the mass, Mr Potter had helped butcher a further seven carols, including "O Come All Ye Faithful", "Hark the Herald Angels Sing" and "Silent Night". Without the faintest trace of irony, the priest thanked Mr Potter for helping make the evening so memorable and launched into the service.

It was Bernice who broke the silence in the car on the way home.

"Well, after the lovely music at Betty's funeral, that was unexpected."

"The choir that sang then only do the daylight services on Christmas Day," Jack explained. "They haven't done midnight mass ever since one of Mrs McCaffrey's former pupils remembered who she was and insisted on giving her a sloppy kiss before telling the entire church, repeatedly, that she was the 'best teacher he ever had and had made him the man he was today'."

Warren chuckled. "I remember that! The man he was today was a drunk with three kids by different women and an electronic tag. I heard they arrested him Christmas morning because attending midnight mass — not to mention the pub — was a breach of his curfew."

"Seems a bit unfair to blame that on Mrs McCaffrey — she only taught him in Reception!" replied Jack.

As the rest of the car joined in with the laughter, Warren felt the tension in his chest easing even more. When they quietened down, Jack spoke up again. His voice was sober, but not sad. "You know, every time we went, I threatened to take my hearing aids out before the service, but I couldn't bring myself to do it." In the rear-view mirror, Warren could make out a wistful smile on the old man's face. "Betty used to tell me off for laughing about poor

Mr Potter. He only does it because nobody else will volunteer. But still, he has all year to practise — we sing the same bloody songs each year!"

* * *

After arriving home, Warren felt comfortable enough to finally relax. It was almost 1 a.m.; even if he received a phone call now, nobody would expect to see him before the next morning. With that in mind, he gratefully accepted Dennis' offer of a large whiskey and joined his grandfather and father-in-law in a depressing discussion about the likelihood of Coventry City avoiding relegation again this season. Not even a second glass of whiskey made that conversation any more cheerful.

By 2 a.m., everyone was yawning and they retired to bed. Warren's last thought as he turned out the bedside lamp was one of incredulity that he had ever contemplated missing Christmas.

Chapter 49

Warren awoke slowly, the unfamiliar bed adding to his disorientation as he hung for a moment between reality and the dream world. Then reality crashed in, with the childlike feeling of excitement that he still felt on Christmas Day tempered by a pang of sadness that Nana Betty wouldn't be here to celebrate with them. A glance at his phone showed it was seven-thirty and that he had received no text messages, emails or missed calls.

Beside him, Susan stirred. Leaning over, he kissed her on the nose and wished her a merry Christmas.

She sighed contentedly, before mumbling her own response.

"Is it too early to open our stockings?" Warren was referring to the bulging, garish sports socks hanging off the end of the bed. Susan might be a married woman in her thirties, but Bernice had made it clear that she was still her little girl and she was going to enjoy having her children home for Christmas. Now even Warren got one.

"I think it's a bit early for that," said Susan, a glint in her eye.

"Well, I don't think we can go downstairs and watch TV. It'll wake the grown-ups. What can we do for the next hour or so?"

Susan giggled and lifted her arms above her head. "Well, you could always unwrap one present, I suppose. Just something to play with until we have breakfast."

Breakfast was an elaborate affair, at least by the standards of Warren, who usually made do with a slice of toast or a banana on the rare occasions that he bothered. Three types of toast, rashers of crispy bacon and bulging sausages jostled for space with fried and scrambled eggs and a pan of baked beans. It was the odour of freshly brewed coffee that had finally tempted Warren and Susan downstairs.

"You know, if we eat all of this, then Christmas dinner, and all those chocolates in the lounge, we'll never fit in the en-suite shower tomorrow for a repeat of what we just did."

Susan's response was a blush and a slap. Fortunately, Bernice was playing a CD of Christmas carols and didn't hear him. Warren wished his in-laws a merry Christmas and thanked them for the gifts in the stocking. So far he'd used some of the shower gel, a squirt of the aftershave and was wearing a pair of black socks with a huge yellow smiley face on each ankle.

Bernice was dressed in a bright red jumper with "Santa's Little Helper" emblazoned on the front and black trousers. Flashing earrings and reindeer antlers completed the ensemble. Dennis was dressed even worse than the previous day, with a chunky hand-knitted sweater featuring Santa's face covering his stomach. The red hat with flashing lights did little to offset his morose expression.

Although he knew from previous Christmases that offers to help would be rebuffed, Warren felt obliged at least to ask. As usual it was Bernice who turned down Warren's assistance, even though Christmas lunch was strictly the purview of Dennis. To be fair, in previous years, Susan's father had managed to effortlessly juggle the many different dishes with the skill and timing of a West End chef and he certainly seemed happiest when clattering around the kitchen.

Knowing that the day ahead was likely to be an eating marathon, Warren paced himself at breakfast, managing to limit the amount of food that Bernice insisted on piling on his plate — even then, his frugality paled next to that of Granddad Jack. When the older man finally emerged, it was clear that he had barely slept the night before. He was clean-shaven and had both of his hearing aids in, but the lightness that had been present the night before had retreated once again. It was only Bernice's well-meaning pressure that persuaded him to take a slice of toast with his tea. After eating, he retired to the living room and was soon dozing in front of the fire again.

By common agreement, the family had decided to postpone present opening until the arrival of Susan's sister and family. Over Bernice' protestations, Warren and Susan had insisted on clearing up after breakfast. As they did so Warren voiced his concerns about Jack. He had clearly taken the death of Betty even harder than anyone had imagined and Warren was worried that the old man was in a downward spiral. Susan couldn't think of anything to say, other than to suggest they wait until after the Christmas period and see if he perked up. If not, she would see if they could get him to talk to someone.

Finally, Susan's sister Felicity, her husband Jeff and their three children, Jimmy aged three, Sammy just under two and six-month old Annie turned up. Their arrival reminded Warren of footage he'd seen of American forces entering Afghanistan. He watched with fascination as the red Citroën people carrier swept up the drive like a Black Hawk helicopter coming in to land, before disgorging two adults, three small children each with accompanying accessory bags easily large enough for their owner to fit in, and enough brightly coloured plastic toys to fill a branch of Toys R Us. And then came the presents, piles of garishly wrapped parcels, which Felicity added to the pile beneath the tree. At last, the invasion was complete, although Warren couldn't see how they hoped to get everything back in the car again.

Warren always felt slightly awkward at these gatherings. Felicity and Jeff were lovely people, but they seemed completely alien to him. Felicity was as different from Susan as it was possible to be. Barely five feet tall, Felicity was a giggly blonde whirlwind. Where Susan had studied biology at university, gaining a master's degree before starting teacher training, Felicity had travelled the world for two years, before doing a series of art courses, ending up working for some sort of hippy collective in London making and selling home-made jewellery.

Jeff, on the other hand, was an investment banker, working for a large credit company that Warren had never heard of. Within twelve months of their chance meeting, the free-spirited Felicity was living in a two-million-pound home in the leafiest part of the commuter-belt, engaged and pregnant — although that was diplomatically ignored by Bernice, who couldn't believe how well her wayward daughter had done for herself. By all accounts, it was a marriage made in heaven and Warren saw no evidence to the contrary.

Finally, it was time to open the presents. Warren had been looking forward to seeing Susan's reaction to the matching earrings and necklace that he had bought her and he was delighted with the Kindle e-reader that she had bought him, but to his surprise he found the most enjoyable part of the morning was watching the children open their presents. At just over three years old, Jimmy was old enough to understand Christmas and was suitably excited. Sammy wasn't overly thrilled by the presents but had a fantastic time climbing inside the boxes and playing with the wrapping paper.

"Jimmy was the exactly the same last year," confided Jeff. "I suggested to Felicity that we could save a fortune by just buying some wrapping paper and asking the supermarket for any old boxes, but she wouldn't have it."

However, star of the show was baby Annie. Dressed in a mini Santa outfit, she dissolved into fits of giggles every time Granddad Jack tickled her tummy.

Finally, Dennis announced that dinner was ready. With Susan's help, Felicity put Annie down in her Moses basket, whilst Warren and Jeff wrestled Sammy into his high chair. Jimmy would be allowed to sit in a "big boy's chair" between Granddad Jack and Uncle Warren as long as he behaved himself.

Warren checked his phone discreetly — no calls, emails or text messages, so he decided to have a glass of red wine with his lunch.

Dennis had done himself proud again. A huge turkey with all of the trimmings was surrounded by roast potatoes and parsnips. Three types of stuffing, steamed carrots, peas, broccoli and the obligatory Brussels sprouts, plus creamed potatoes and, finally, pigs in blankets. Thick gravy and cranberry jelly completed the feast.

Warren didn't like turkey or any other meat off the bone and was perfectly content to load up with vegetables and sausages; however, Felicity was a vegetarian and Dennis had made her a big enough bean and nut roast for everyone to have some.

Lunch was a boisterous affair with laughter all round and even

Jack and Dennis joining in. The Christmas crackers disgorged their usual cheap plastic toys — promptly moved out of the reach of the children — gaudy paper crowns and awful jokes. By the time the Christmas pudding was lit, Warren felt as though he might burst. He'd decided to chance a second, small glass of wine and was now glowing slightly.

Ignoring Bernice's protests for a second time that day — normally a pretty reckless thing to do — Susan and Warren cleared away the lunch whilst everyone else retired to the lounge. When they finally joined them, the whole room was almost silent, with the Queen's speech on mute and only Granddad Jack and Jimmy awake. As he watched his grandfather quietly reading a story to the small boy, Warren felt something stirring inside him. As if sensing his thoughts, Susan sat down next to him, slipping her hand into his and resting her head on his shoulder. At that moment, all thoughts of dead bodies and rapists were a million miles away.

* * *

All too soon the day was over. By 8 p.m., it was well past the children's bedtime and so the invasion went into reverse. Somehow everything that had come out of the people carrier went back in, along with several dozen more toys plus a number of large Tupperware boxes of uneaten vegetables and half a Christmas cake.

With the children gone, the house suddenly seemed empty. Granddad Jack excused himself and went to bed. Warren anxiously watched him as he climbed the stairs, but the old man's pace seemed tired rather than weary and he had kissed both Bernice and Susan goodnight.

The remaining foursome enjoyed a spirited game of Scrabble, which Bernice — president of the local book club —won by a large margin.

A little later, lying in the dark, Warren snuggled up close to Susan.

"I was watching Granddad with the kids. It got me thinking…"

Susan sighed. "Me too. But we decided to give it at least a year in our new jobs before we started a family."

In the darkness, she felt Warren nod. "I know and I agree. But let's not leave it too long. Who knows? By this time next year you could be eating for two and by the following year it could be our little baby dressed in a Santa suit."

Beside him, Warren could feel the bed start to shake. "What?" he demanded.

Between her giggles, Susan managed to speak. "Oh, you old romantic."

Not sure how to respond, Warren felt slightly defensive.

"Well, we have to make plans. You're a biology teacher — you know how complicated these things are. There are books to read, DVDs to watch, courses to do…"

Susan fully dissolved. "It's really not that difficult. Trust me, human beings have been having babies for millions of years."

"You know what I mean."

"Well, if you are that worried then maybe we should practise a bit before we start properly in the summer."

That didn't really require an answer, Warren decided.

* * *

It was almost 9 a.m., the longest lie-in Warren and Susan had had in months, when the phone went. Warren didn't need to look at the caller ID to know what it was about.

"Sorry to phone, guv. We've found Saskia Walker."

MONDAY 26TH DECEMBER

Chapter 50

It was barely noon on Boxing Day — less than twenty-four hours since he'd been tucking into Dennis' fantastic Christmas lunch and celebrating with his loved ones. As Warren stared at the pictures of the partially clad body it felt as though those events had been a lifetime ago.

"How was she found?"

"Sheer bloody fluke, by the sound of it." There was an undercurrent of excitement in Tony Sutton's voice. "I reckon Cameron wasn't expecting her to be found nearly so soon. He probably expected to have a couple more days' lead at least."

"What happened?" prompted Warren.

"She was found by a Polish lorry driver in a layby on the A505. Apparently, he broke down on Christmas Eve up in Scotland and by the time he got back on the road it was Christmas Day.

"By last night he was over his hours, so he pulled over to sleep. This morning, he got up to stretch his legs and decided to give the chemical toilet a miss and use a bush. Very nearly pissed on the poor girl. He reckons he was probably the only driver on the road Christmas night and figures the likelihood of anybody stumbling across her body before Tuesday or Wednesday was pretty slim."

Sutton was right to feel excited. Although Saskia Walker had been missing for several days, giving her attacker plenty of time to cover his tracks, he clearly hadn't expected her body to be found so quickly. Who knew what details Richard Cameron might not have dealt with yet?

"What do we have forensically?"

"Her body is still at the scene. Professor Jordan is coming in especially to do the PM." Sutton smiled grimly. "Everyone wants this bastard, sir. First time I've ever called a coroner out over the holiday period and not had to put up with them grumbling about it. I swear he was putting his coat on as we spoke on the phone."

Warren suspected he was right. Four murders and an attempted murder in the space of a month. For Warren, it had been personal since the moment he first caught sight of Sally Evans' body. For others, it had taken time to work its way from routine murder to serial killer, but now everybody was feeling it. Quite aside from the tragedy, it was an affront to the local community that they had all sworn to protect and to their professional pride.

The eagerness of Prof Jordan notwithstanding, arranging a full post-mortem on Boxing Day was always going to be a slow affair and Warren was warned that he couldn't expect to see any results until late evening at the earliest.

In the meantime, the team had plenty to do to keep them occupied. Although the smart money was on Richard Cameron being responsible, until they had positive proof of his involvement from the coroner or scenes of crime team they were obliged to keep at least some semblance of an open mind.

By one-thirty, Warren and Tony Sutton found themselves heading out, yet again, to interview bereaved loved ones. The drive to Cambridge took about forty minutes, a light drizzle turning into a heavy downpour. The atmosphere in the car was also leaden, all traces of Christmas cheer long since chased away.

After an abortive attempt at small talk — apparently both men had enjoyed Christmas and it had been good to get away — they lapsed back into silence. Eventually Sutton started leafing through the stack of CDs in the glove box. Warren winced. He had a horrible feeling that his credibility was going to take a beating.

"ABBA Gold? Tell me this is Susan's. What about this? The soundtrack to *Mamma Mia*?" Warren said nothing, hoping Sutton would get bored and give up. No such luck — he was like a dog with a bone.

"What else…? U2 Greatest Hits, Rod Stewart Greatest Hits, Elton John Greatest Hits… I'm spotting a theme here, guv. Do you own any actual albums or is it all compilations?"

"What can I say? I follow the masses," said Warren weakly, hoping Sutton had seen enough.

"Ultimate Eighties album, Seventies Party Hits, Disco Hits Volumes 1 *and* 2. Trying to recapture your youth, sir?"

"Speak for yourself, Tony. I'm too young to remember it first time around, unlike you; I discovered that lot at Friday Freak-out at uni."

"Count yourself lucky, guv. Most of this stuff was crap. I can't work out why it was so popular with students in the Nineties."

"Well, have you heard what new music we had to listen to in the Nineties?"

"Fair comment. Even Sister Sledge sounds good next to that car-alarm rubbish that blared out of every speaker back then. If I'd had my way, we'd have been nicking students for possession of an offensive CD."

Warren chuckled; the banter had achieved its desired effect and lifted his mood somewhat.

"Hello, what's this? Looks like a homemade compilation CD. 'Guilty Pleasures' — you don't appear to have filled in the inlay card. I have no idea what music is on here."

And you never will, vowed Warren. Thanks to the alphabetical track-listing on his computer, Guns 'n' Roses "Sweet Child O' Mine" followed the Beatles' "Strawberry Fields Forever" and "Sgt Pepper's Lonely Hearts Club Band". Thank goodness for shuffle. He snatched the CD out of Sutton's grasp lest it find itself being played on the station's CD player.

"Next time, you drive, DI Sutton, and we'll peruse your music collection, shall we?" suggested Warren, waspishly.

Sutton shrugged. "I stand behind my music collection. A song for every mood and nothing to be ashamed of. Perhaps when we've got a little extra time I'll help educate your ear, sir."

Before Warren could reply, the satnav sang out, announcing that they had arrived at their destination. Both men immediately quietened.

"Once more unto the breach?"

Sutton nodded. "Let's get it over with, then."

* * *

If it weren't for the unlit Christmas tree and the cards adorning the mantelpiece, nobody would have known it was the day after Christmas. The kitchen in which they sat was cold and uncomfortable. It was clear from the smell, or rather lack of it, that nobody had cooked a Christmas roast in here for loved ones or stuffed themselves with cake. The air contained no lingering traces of over-cooked vegetables or gravy. The smell of booze pervaded the room, but it was from the alcohol of sadness, of desperation, not the rich aroma of carefully chosen wines or freshly mixed party drinks.

The contrast with Bernice and Dennis' house couldn't be more pronounced and Warren desperately wished he had been able to heed his mother-in-law's pleading and stay just a bit longer. Unfortunately duty was duty and Bernice had eventually accepted that fact with ill grace. Granddad Jack had been understanding and Susan, of course, had been his rock.

Despite Bernice's misgivings, Warren had been unable to leave his in-laws and wife without an armful of Tupperware boxes containing leftover turkey and vegetables. Assuming that he got home at a decent hour tonight he'd be frying up the vegetables in what he'd always called the second meal of Christmas — a gravy-smothered plate of bubble and squeak. Then, he'd use the meat to make the third meal of Christmas — turkey curry.

The tension between Saskia Walker's parents was palpable and Warren thought it ironic and deeply sad that the only thing keeping them together was the death of their child. He doubted much time would pass after the funeral before they finally went their separate ways. He just hoped it wasn't too traumatic; this poor couple had suffered far more than anyone deserved.

"You understand that until we get the post-mortem results we can only speculate on who she was killed by and that we therefore must keep an open mind and pursue all lines of enquiry." The couple nodded wearily. This had all been explained to them by the family liaison officer before Warren and Sutton had arrived.

"With that in mind, we need to ask some questions that you may find uncomfortable. I apologise in advance if we upset you."

The couple nodded numbly and Warren proceeded. He'd reread the reports from her friends gathered at the time she went missing, as well as other interviews conducted by the missing persons team. First he established that, as far as her parents were concerned, she had not had a regular boyfriend since splitting up with a steady, long-term partner earlier in the year. They knew nothing of any flings with her co-workers, although that was hardly surprising. They were aware that she had been treated for depression recently.

So far, their stories tallied with what her friends and co-workers had reported on Christmas Eve. Both the ex-boyfriend and her one-night stand had been thoroughly checked out by missing persons and found to be clear of any involvement. The former partner was still in France where he had returned to rekindle his romance with a childhood sweetheart he had reconnected with through Facebook; as for the workplace fling, he had been at work all of the twenty-third before getting changed at work and going straight out to the works party that Saskia never attended. He'd then crashed on a workmate's couch and crawled into work much the worse-for-wear early the next morning. Enough people had seen him at various points over the twenty-four hours between Saskia Walker last being seen and then being reported missing that he was easily cleared of any direct involvement.

Saskia's sister and her husband, Tristan, had returned home to change clothes and freshen up after forty-eight hours sitting vigil with Saskia's parents. The family liaison officer had said that they had been nothing but a comfort to her parents throughout the ordeal. She suspected that they were exhausted and needed a bit of time to themselves to process their own feelings. They were probably also feeling slight guilt as both had clearly looked a little relieved when their expectations were finally confirmed and the body was found. It was insights like this that made family liaison officers more than just a convenient shoulder for the bereaved to cry on whilst he tried to get on with his job, Warren felt.

With the sister and her husband absent, Warren was able to broach the subject of tension between Saskia and her sister's husband, Tristan.

The brief expression of distaste on Saskia's mother's face spoke volumes. "I suppose you could say that we are a bit beneath him. His name is Tristan, so draw your own conclusions. Private education, wealthy upbringing, Cambridge University, then a highly paid job doing something to do with the Internet — everything you'd expect. He met our Flo when she was working at a small bakery around the corner from his workplace and apparently it was love at first sight.

"It was clear from the get-go that his family weren't impressed; they thought he'd found a bit of rough and he'd come to his senses soon." Her face softened slightly. "Bless him, he tries to be polite, but he really struggles. We have nothing in common. I left school at sixteen to work in a newsagent; he's got master's degrees and all sorts. When he visits, it sounds like he's talking to young children or people a bit mentally deficient. Saskia couldn't stand it and they had a number of rows."

Warren jotted the information down. It seemed unlikely that this Tristan character was involved and he was still banking on Richard Cameron being identified in the immediate future. Nevertheless, he felt obliged to have somebody check out his whereabouts at the time of the murder.

With little else to be gained from the grieving couple, Warren and Sutton stood to leave. As they did so Angela Walker stood also.

"My daughter never hurt anyone. She worked hard, ran in

those charity half-marathons and would help anybody. At work she won awards for her customer service." She choked back a sob. "Whoever has done this to our daughter is a sick man. He should be put down like a dog."

With that, she ran from the room, the fragile dam she had obviously constructed to keep her functioning finally giving way. After a moment's hesitation, her husband turned and scurried after her.

Sutton turned to Jones, muttering quietly, "It's hard to argue with sentiments like that. Perhaps the likes of Richard Cameron should be put down. No punishment will ever be enough and why should he live out his days in some cushy cell, paid for by the taxes of his victims' loved ones?"

Warren said nothing. There was nothing he could say, because, truth be told, he wasn't sure he disagreed.

Chapter 51

By the time Warren and Sutton finished speaking to Saskia Walker's parents it was late afternoon. With limited daylight remaining, Warren decided to drive them both to the layby where she had been found. Scenes of Crime had been processing the site since she was discovered early that morning and he was keen to take a look.

The stretch of layby where she had been dumped was set back off the dual carriageway. A thin line of concrete blocks separated any pulled-over lorry drivers from the traffic speeding past at sixty miles per hour. Warren wondered just how effective they were. Maybe he'd ask someone in Traffic one day.

The dumping site was protected from the wind, rain and any prying eyes by a large white tent, criss-crossed with police tape. The lorry driver had been thoroughly questioned and both he and his vehicle released, but the roadside was still filled with vehicles and investigators, some in white paper suits.

Warren looked around and saw the familiar sight of CSM Andy Harrison, who immediately waved and started to walk over.

"Still racking up the overtime, Andy?" asked Sutton by way of greeting.

The slightly portly forensic investigator shrugged. "What can

I say? I have three wives — two ex, one current — so I have to take whatever is on offer."

Warren knew that was a lie. The man lived locally and was regularly assigned to scenes in the area; more importantly though, he took his job as personally as Professor Jordan. He'd probably seen the job sheet and offered to work overtime, relieving some other poor CSI who'd rather be at home with the family than traipsing around a murder scene in the rain.

To the left of the scene an ambulance was parked, lights off. Through the windscreen Warren could make out two forms, clad in fluorescent jackets, drinking coffee and reading newspapers. His heart sank. If the ambulance was still here, then the body must also still be here, not yet removed from the shrubbery where it was found by an unfortunate lorry driver doing nothing more than answering the call of nature.

"Sorry, DCI Jones, she's still in situ. We had a heavy rain-burst a few hours ago and had to stop work to shore up the tent. She'll be on her way in about half an hour."

"Nothing was compromised by the rain, I hope?" asked Warren.

The CSI shrugged. "Hard to say definitively, but I doubt it. There's been rain several times over the past few days. If it were going to bugger anything up, it did so long before we arrived."

Warren nodded his acceptance, there was no point grumbling about it. It seemed unlikely that he would hear anything back from the PM until the following morning at the earliest.

Conscious of the fading light, Harrison decided to lead the two detectives on a whistle-stop tour of the scene himself. The first thing he confirmed was Warren and Sutton's feeling that the body had been hidden well enough to give Cameron time to escape and cover his tracks, yet not so well that it would lie undiscovered for weeks.

This was something common to all three previous murders and had been the source of some speculation back at the station. Ideas for why this was so ranged from simple carelessness, which seemed unlikely given that he went to such lengths to cover his tracks in other ways, to the killer needing to experience gratification from the police not being able to find any evidence. It was even pointed out that Cameron was, by all accounts, very religious and might be troubled that his victims wouldn't receive a proper and timely Christian burial if he concealed them too well.

The body was hidden from the road but would have been visible from the cab of any parked-up lorry. The Polish driver had only failed to spot her sooner because he had pulled over after dark and then had stumbled over to the bush for a pee the following morning, bleary-eyed and sleepy at the crack of dawn.

Regardless, Cameron probably expected at least another day or so head start. The fact that Saskia Walker was so local suggested that he was still in the immediate vicinity. Warren made a note to share that with the search teams scouring the country for the missing rapist.

Next, the two officers were taken to see the body. A large double tent had been erected over the scene. Before entering the inner tent where Saskia Walker still lay, the two officers donned paper suits and booties to minimise any contamination. Despite the cold weather, the air in the tent was starting to ripen.

The body lay on its back, its face clearly visible and unmistakably that of the missing sales assistant. Dressed in tracksuit bottoms and trainers, she was almost completely topless. A lightweight fleece jacket lay in a crumpled heap a pace away. Her bra had been ripped open and hung from one shoulder, leaving both breasts exposed. A red T-shirt was tied in a loose knot around her throat.

"Strangled with her own T-shirt?"

"It looks that way. The PM will tell us for sure. The other victims had scarves or belts. I guess this was the best he could do."

"I suppose that using her own clothes as a ligature means he doesn't have to bring his own — it's one less potential clue for us," mused Sutton.

"It looks as though she's been out jogging. We should see if any of her friends know her regular route. Somebody may have seen something," Warren commented to Sutton.

"Any other evidence?"

Harrison shook his head. "Very little. The rain did a good job. Indentations either side of her suggest he knelt astride her, but I'm not sure they'll tell us anything. There's a partial footprint, badly damaged by the rain. There might be enough to link it to Cameron's boot print from the farmhouse. We've done a fingertip search of the layby and recovered a ton of litter and rubbish, but there is too much to do anything with at the moment. If we can't link Cameron to the scene in any other way we could look for prints or other trace, but it'll be a big job."

He meant expensive, thought Warren ruefully.

"We've got a few tyre tracks, but most have been washed away and the layby is quite popular. We'll run them through the database and see if any match Cameron's Land Rover."

Warren noted that the CSM, a cautious individual, was freely assuming Cameron was the culprit.

"What's your gut feeling, Andy?"

"Cameron again," he replied without hesitation. "It's too similar to the last scenes for it to be a coincidence. If Professor Jordan suggests otherwise, I'll eat my booties."

"How long until you can move her?"

"Not long. We'll need to set up a clear path to the ambulance. With all of this rain washing everything, I'm especially keen not to disturb the ground protected underneath her. You never know what we might find."

The smell in the tent was becoming more cloying and Warren was keen to move on. The look on Sutton's face suggested he felt the same.

It had stopped raining, so both men removed their paper suits outside, breathing the fresh cold air deeply.

"So, almost certainly Cameron again. But it doesn't do us much good, does it?"

Warren nodded; he knew what Sutton meant. Cameron had gone to ground; finding him was now more of a manhunt than an investigation. Warren felt helpless. He knew it was irrational — police work was a team effort. His CID team had identified the suspect and their job was to now build a watertight case to lay against the man if — no, when — he was finally caught. But he knew that the case had moved into a new phase now. Cameron's likeness was being distributed around the country, his face staring out of TV sets and off the front pages of newspapers up and down the country.

The most likely scenario, assuming he didn't kill himself, was that an observant member of the public or a lucky police officer would spot him somewhere and narrow his location enough for them to swoop in and arrest him.

Middlesbury CID's role was far from over, but Warren knew it was unlikely that he or a member of his team would have the satisfaction of snapping a pair of cuffs on the man and reading him his rights. It almost seemed unfair.

TUESDAY 27TH DECEMBER

Chapter 52

Warren arrived in work the following morning ready for the challenges ahead of him. He and Sutton had stopped off for a quick Boxing Day pint before returning home the previous evening; however, neither man had felt like celebrating. Besides which, Tony's family were having a late supper. He'd invited Warren to join him, his wife, his ex-wife, his son and both his sets of in-laws but Warren had sensed it was more out of politeness than anything else. The two men had become friends since the summer and Warren liked both Josh and Marie, Sutton's son and wife, but he wanted his subordinate to switch off from work completely tonight, so that he would be refreshed the next day. Having the boss over would make that difficult.

Besides which, Warren wasn't sure he had the mental energy to deal with Sutton's complex and unique family set-up. Celebrating Christmas together this year was a huge leap forward that had put a spring in the older man's step, but the relationships were still fragile and Warren was reluctant to enter the minefield.

So instead, he'd gone home, had a long hot shower, made some bubble and squeak and enjoyed a leisurely phone call to Susan. By 10 p.m. he was flagging and decided to catch the rest of the evening's festive TV at a later date on the Internet. By the time the clock struck eleven, he was sound asleep, his new Kindle rising and falling slowly on his chest.

His early-morning drive had been quiet — too quiet, he realised. Despite it being two days after Christmas, when the guilt from over-indulging started to bite, he hadn't seen a single jogger. Perhaps that would change later in the day when the sun came up; nevertheless, he felt a surge of anger towards Cameron and his sick compulsions. As a police officer he was supposed to protect the public so that they could feel safe going about their daily business and he couldn't help but feel that, so far, he wasn't doing that. People, especially young women, he suspected, were too nervous to go out jogging where they might be snatched by the rapist and murderer.

At least the number of joggers being mugged or knocked over by cars would go down, he supposed, although he had no doubt that when Cameron was found people would soon forget about the dangers of running alone in the dark and things would return to normal. The thought both depressed him and energised him in equal measure.

First order of business, whilst they awaited the results of the autopsy, was to speak to Saskia Walker's friends to see if she had a regular jogging route. From there they would go door-knocking to see if anyone had seen or heard anything. Warren had a meeting first thing with Grayson to see if it was worth mounting a fingertip search of the route for clues. He hoped that the young woman's route wasn't too long. The cost to the force of this operation had long since surpassed a million pounds and he knew that they were starting to feel the squeeze. They had already brought in additional officers from Welwyn and other parts of the county to conduct the door-to-door enquiries and assist with the searches.

In addition to the regular costs associated with such redeployment, they were going to have to fork out some hefty overtime pay given that it was the festive season and many officers were off duty.

It was clear from the moment that Warren entered his office that Grayson was excited about something. He was almost dismissive of Warren's request for extra manpower, signing the appropriate requisitions with barely a glance. The reason for his excitement soon became apparent.

"We've got a slot on BBC *Crimewatch* tomorrow night. They're going to film around the areas that all four women were snatched and include a detailed description of Richard Cameron and that Land Rover of his. They want me to travel to Cardiff to make a direct appeal and help man the phones."

"Well, that could be a big help, especially if Cameron has left the area. We should make sure that the programme is advertised on the local news and in the local press. We did that in the West Midlands Police whenever we used *Crimewatch*. That way we ensured a spike in the number of local viewers who can't resist tuning in to see their local area on TV."

Grayson's enthusiasm dimmed slightly as he realised that Warren probably had more experience of the iconic BBC TV show than he had, given his years of experience in the WMP before moving to the comparatively quiet Middlesbury CID.

Truth be told, Warren had only ever been involved in the show once and thankfully not on camera. He'd worked with a couple of the show's researchers for a reconstruction of a serious armed raid on a jewellery store in Birmingham city centre. But he couldn't resist the urge to ask his boss to "Say 'Hi' to Kirsty and the team if you bump into her," referring to the show's attractive Scottish presenter.

Leaving Grayson to dream about his future TV career, Warren returned to his own office. Just as he crossed the threshold his desk phone started ringing, an external number from the ringtone.

"DCI Jones." He tried not to sound too eager.

"Ryan Jordan here. I've finished the PM on Saskia Walker. I'm heading home, but I can swing by now if you have the time."

"That's fantastic news, Professor. I'll assemble the team."

"Great, I'll be there in about twenty." The man yawned. "Make sure you have decent coffee and some of those custard cream cookies — that's about all that's keeping me upright at the moment."

* * *

Professor Jordan was dressed in "civvies" when he arrived and Warren thanked him again for this hard work.

"Just catch the bastard, that's all I ask." He yawned.

The briefing room was filled with Warren's team and the air was redolent with freshly brewed coffee. A couple of plates of biscuits — including custard creams — sat in the middle of the large table. A half-dozen colour copies of the report were evenly spaced around the table's edge.

"First things first: I'm willing to place good money on it being Cameron. The method is just too similar for it not to be." He looked down at his notes, reading them formally as if in court.

"The victim was a Caucasian female in her mid to late twenties, fitting the description of the missing person Saskia Walker. One hundred and fifty-nine centimetres tall and fifty-four kilograms, slim build with below average body fat. Naturally blonde—" He broke off for a moment. "I'd say she fits the type that this animal goes for." A series of quiet murmurs of assent prompted him to continue.

"All of her major organs were healthy and aside from a missing appendix — removed several years ago, consistent with her medical records — she was in good health and apparently reasonable fitness." He turned a page and the team mimicked him with their own copies of the report.

"Cause of death was strangulation with a ligature. Almost certainly using the red T-shirt, which we are assuming is hers. As in the previous cases, it looks as though she was subdued by an anaesthetic agent, probably administered by a cloth to the face. We've sent off for toxicology as usual, but we are still waiting to hear back from the first case — the backlog is weeks with all of the cutbacks over there.

"Externally, I can see little trauma. A fresh scrape on her left knee might have been caused during the attack, but it could equally have come from any other minor collision. No blood unfortunately. Her fingernails reveal no trace evidence. However, her coat has some of that powdery cardboard residue and some of those blue nylon fibres that we've seen previously.

"Her clothing was disturbed in the attack, as you can see, exposing both her breasts and her pubic region, but again we can find no fingerprints or traces of bodily fluid externally. However, it looks as though he's been either careless or unlucky again. An internal examination again reveals evidence of rough sexual intercourse and, as with Gemma Allen, traces of semen. We've put a rush on the DNA typing and we'll know by tomorrow if it's Cameron again."

"Thanks, Professor, that's very helpful."

Tony Sutton had been frowning for the last few moments.

"It seems a bit weird, don't you think? Cameron has been meticulous about not leaving behind any trace evidence that links directly to him, such as DNA or fingerprints. For the first two murders we still only have circumstantial evidence linking him. Yet with Gemma Allen, he leaves behind a semen sample. OK, maybe the condom split or whatever. Yet exactly the same thing has happened with this next victim. Two mistakes one after another?"

It was a fair point and it divided the room.

"Maybe he doesn't care anymore," suggested Karen Hardwick. "After the first slip he must have known that we'd pin it on him. And even without that evidence his face is all over the news and we are describing him as our number one suspect."

A few people nodded at her logic.

Hastings shook his head. "He still seems to be taking some precautions, though. There still isn't much evidence at the scenes and the trace evidence suggests that he's still pulling his trick with two condoms. I've been doing some reading about serial killers and I wonder if he's starting to break down. I think they call it 'decompensating'."

All eyes in the room turned to Professor Jordan. "The psychology of serial killers is above my pay-grade, I'm afraid, but what I do know, especially from cases I worked back in the States, is that Cameron is displaying signs of a loss of control. His attacks are very close together, barely a week apart. Serial killers often wait months or years between attacks.

"He is also making mistakes; it looks as though Carolyn Patterson managed to land a blow on him before succumbing to the anaesthesia and evidence from the crime scene where Gemma Allen was snatched, plus her facial injuries, suggests that she too put up a fight and may have nearly escaped. We'd expect him to be getting better over time, but it doesn't look as though he is."

"What might this mean for the future?" asked Warren.

Jordan puffed out his lips. "Now we're really straying from my remit. I think it is safe to say that he will probably strike again, and sooner rather than later. As to whether he makes a fatal mistake that leads to his capture — I can't possibly say."

Warren nodded soberly. "That's pretty much what I feared."

* * *

The remainder of the day was frustratingly slow. The team were busy following leads on all of the different murders but so far the only information that truly mattered — the whereabouts of Richard Cameron — remained stubbornly elusive. After the meeting with Jordan had broken up, the pathologist had remained for a few minutes to finish his coffee.

"I'll suppose there's at least one glimmer of hope in this whole sordid affair," he'd mused tiredly. "Cameron won't be fathering any more offspring. It looks as though the genetic legacy stops with him and his son."

Warren had expressed surprise at the apparent non sequitur.

"The technician that identified Cameron's semen sample from Gemma Allen commented that, even allowing for the time elapsed between her rape and us finding the sample, Cameron had a very low viable sperm count. The sample from Saskia Walker was even lower. The old boy's pretty much shooting blanks."

"Is there any significance, do you think?" asked Warren.

"Probably not, it's just an observation. However, some

medications are known to reduce the numbers of viable sperm. It did occur to me that Cameron might be suffering from a serious illness. Chemotherapy for cancer is known to affect sperm counts."

"Could Cameron be suffering from cancer? He appeared pretty robust when we interviewed him."

Jordan shrugged. "Hard to say without access to his medical records."

"If Cameron is terminally ill that might explain his behaviour — he hears the ticking of the clock and decides it's time for one last hurrah. That might account for why he has switched from adamantly claiming to be a changed man to going back to his old ways."

"It could also explain the short time between attacks — he doesn't feel he has time to waste," concurred Jordan.

Warren shuddered. If Cameron really was terminally ill with death beckoning, then what fear could the future hold for him beyond his own demise? With nothing to lose and nothing to fear, Cameron might be capable of anything.

WEDNESDAY 28TH DECEMBER

Chapter 53

Despite the lack of progress in recent days, Warren felt optimistic as he greeted the team from the BBC's *Crimewatch* programme the following morning. When a case such as this progressed to the manhunt stage, then leads from the general public became essential.

With a suspect clearly in the frame — and a phone call first thing from Forensics had confirmed Cameron's culpability for the Saskia Walker murder as well as Gemma Allen — the programme would focus on finding Cameron by direct appeal, using images of the convicted rapist and his Land Rover as well as shots of the four kidnapping spots and dumping grounds.

Although Detective Superintendent Grayson would be appearing in the Cardiff studios live that night, much to Warren's dismay he was expected to help narrate the crime scenes and do additional pieces to camera. How much of his discomfort would be evident on screen he would have to wait and see.

Filming was an impressively slick operation with several teams working simultaneously. Different members of Warren's team escorted each camera crew to the different scenes as they gathered background footage. Warren was then ferried from scene to scene to deliver short pieces to camera. Considering that they had less than eight hours of daylight, the camera crew shot an impressive amount of film, uploading it directly to the BBC studios in Cardiff, ready for transmission later that night.

By the end of the day, Warren was surprised to find himself looking forward to seeing the finished product. Just one viable lead was all he wanted. Just one lead...

It was a sentiment echoed by the whole of the team as they gathered for their end-of-day briefing at six o'clock that evening.

* * *

Warren arrived home at six-thirty. The *Crimewatch* episode was due to air at nine with a fifteen-minute update on any progress after the ten o'clock news. Warren wanted a shower, something to eat and a quick snooze before settling down to watch the show. Specialist call-takers would be manning the telephone hotline all night, passing on any information deemed useful to Warren's team, so he planned on returning to the station at eleven to deal with anything that came in. A few members of the team were planning on watching the show live in the briefing room, but Warren decided that he'd rather die of embarrassment in the privacy of his own home than in front of his colleagues.

Unlocking the front door, he was met by the smell of spices, and the glow of the kitchen light.

"Surprise!"

Susan greeted him at the threshold with a big hug and a kiss.

"I caught the train down this afternoon — I figured if you didn't arrive back home by the time the turkey curry was ready, I'd put it in a tub and drive over to the station."

Holding her tightly, Warren was lost for words. Immediately, the strain of the last thirty-six hours melted away; he hadn't realised how much he'd missed his wife.

Her mother had been a bit disappointed that Susan would rather spend time in an empty house whilst Warren worked than stay with her parents, but her father and Granddad Jack had both encouraged her to go, knowing that Warren could do with her support. Once again, Warren was reminded of how lucky he was.

The curry was almost ready, so Warren raced upstairs for a quick shower, all thoughts of a leisurely hot bath and a snooze vanquished. By the time he came back downstairs the aroma of spices filled the house and the table was set with fresh naan and poppadums. It would be a couple of hours before Warren was due back into the office so he enjoyed a small glass of red wine.

By the time the show was due to air, Warren was feeling relaxed and sleepy, curled up on the sofa with Susan, until the militaristic opening bars of the *Crimewatch* theme music roused him fully and the nerves came back.

The murders were given a generous portion of the show, almost half its running time. To Warren's amusement, Grayson, resplendent in full dress uniform, appeared stiff and uncomfortable in the ninety seconds or so that he appeared on screen. Warren, on the other hand, appeared surprisingly relaxed during the several minutes he spent describing the four murder sites and dumping spots.

"You're a natural," Susan whispered to him after a short segment showing Warren describing how Carolyn Patterson had put up a fight against her attacker. The producers showed several high-quality photographs of Richard Cameron and pictures of a near-identical Land Rover to the one he owned. In a recent development, the firm that Bill Evans worked for had generously underwritten a reward for information leading to his daughter's killer. If anyone was harbouring the man, then perhaps that might be the tipping point. Time would tell.

All in all, not too bad a performance, he decided. He suspected that John Grayson would be less satisfied. Warren couldn't help a slight grin at that thought.

* * *

The BBC ten o'clock news had featured a short segment about the murders followed by several minutes on the local *Look East* bulletin. During that time Warren had fielded calls from Bernice and Dennis and Granddad Jack, all congratulating him on his appearance and wishing him good luck. As an aside, Granddad Jack had said that Nana Betty would have loved it and that he was certain she was watching it "from upstairs". The short follow-up programme claimed that there had been several promising phone calls from the public and so Warren drove back to the station, his excitement overcoming his reluctance to leave Susan.

The first thing he noticed upon his arrival was that some wag had used gold tinsel from the Christmas tree to make a star around his office door nameplate. After enduring a bit of good-natured teasing about his performance, he entered the office to find that the jokers had gone one further and unscrewed a mirror from the bathroom, attached it to the wall and arranged fairy lights around it in a pastiche of a Hollywood dressing room.

"I'm glad you lot have kept yourselves busy," he yelled through the door to the sound of cackling laughter.

The practical joke had lifted the spirits in the office somewhat and so Warren was reluctant to get down to work, but they had a lot to do. The specialist call-takers had received several phone calls about possible sightings of Cameron and the team attacked the list with gusto. Nevertheless, by midnight, the team had nothing new to go on. Most of the leads were unreliable — a polite euphemism for hoax and crank calls — or could be easily eliminated by further questioning about specific details.

However, the producer of the show had remained optimistic. In a phone call to Warren he'd admitted that the nutters all called within the first half-hour of the show airing. More serious callers often second-guessed themselves and discussed it with partners before phoning the next day. The *Crimewatch* phone lines would remain open until the following midnight, whilst the charity Crimestoppers and the police's normal incident line would be open twenty-four-seven.

Consequently, Warren left the office in the hands of the night shift at 1 a.m., leaving strict instructions to call him if anything significant came in.

Susan was asleep on the sofa when he got in, shaking the light dusting of snow off his coat. She knew without asking that they had no new leads and so led him to bed without a word.

THURSDAY 29TH DECEMBER

Chapter 54

The following day started promisingly with two suspected sight-ings. One in a guest house in Leeds, another in a Travelodge near Bristol airport. Unfortunately, it took only a few hours for both leads to be dismissed by local officers. The first turned out to be a retired architect staying at the guest house since the daughter he was visiting for Christmas had no spare room. Officers reported that he bore a superficial similarity to Cameron but was clearly not him.

The second suspect was even less likely; a look at the hotel records revealed that the long-since-departed guest had checked in with his wife and two small children after a long-haul flight from Florida. An attached copy of the suspect's passport photo-graph had dismissed him completely.

As the day wore on, numerous calls claimed sightings of the young women shortly before their disappearances, firming up the police's reconstruction of events those nights. For Saskia Walker in particular, this helped narrow down the window during which she was snatched to only a couple of hours.

It was late afternoon when it was reported that Richard Cameron's Land Rover had been located.

"Two old boys on an early morning fishing trip spotted it

partially covered in a clearing about a week ago as they hiked down to the river. They noticed it had no plates and thought it a bit dodgy but after a few hours standing in icy water up to their bollocks forgot all about it."

Tony Sutton was reading from his scribbled notes.

"One of them saw the report in the newspaper and drove back out there this morning to find it was still there. Someone from Motor Vehicles has been out there and confirmed the vehicle's identity off the VIN plate. They're processing the scene now before taking it back to the garage for Forensics to look at."

The day's dead ends had made Warren twitchy and impatient and he needed to stretch his legs.

"Fancy a day out in the country, Tony?"

"I'll fetch the picnic blanket from the car."

* * *

A mass of black thundercloud was making it even darker than normal for this time of day and by the time Warren and Tony Sutton arrived at the small clearing in the trees they both had their Maglites out.

Even without licence plates, the Land Rover was clearly the one that the officers had seen parked up outside Cameron's house. A line of police tape marked a "No Go" zone around the off-roader and a police photographer was just finishing taking pictures of the foliage around the vehicle's wheels.

Warren could make out the form of an older man with a beard sitting in a police-issue Range Rover, dressed in a thick, dark green windcheater and wearing a cloth cap, sipping a plastic cup of coffee. Jonathon Fitzgerald, the man who'd called the vehicle in.

Warren and Sutton clambered into the Range Rover and thanked the man for his time. It was pretty much what Sutton had already stated. Mr Fitzgerald and his brother-in-law, both retired carpenters, had gone out for a spot of quiet fishing on the Friday before Christmas.

"I've always said I'd rather spend four hours standing in three feet of icy water and catch nothing than spend four hours queuing in bloody Marks and Spencer to catch a half-price jumper." He grinned, showing tar-stained teeth. "The missus says I'm a miserable bugger when I'm shopping anyway so she let me go fishing with Derek, her brother."

Warren smiled in sympathy and urged him to go on.

"Well, we parked up at that layby about a mile down the road and walked up here through the edge of the woods. There's a slope down to the riverbank there. We've been a half-dozen times over the past couple of years. Anyhow, as we cut deeper into the woods to get to the slope, I spotted the Land Rover parked up. I was a bit miffed at first. There isn't much space on the bank and we'd just hauled our kit a mile for nothing. Plus, you ain't supposed to drive into the woods — it damages the ground. But I figured, one rule for us, one rule for them. When I got closer I noticed he didn't have any licence plates, which I thought was a bit weird." He looked a little embarrassed.

"I'm sorry to say, but by the time we'd finished and gone to the pub to get something warm down us, both of us had forgotten all about it."

Warren dismissed his concerns with a wave of his hand.

"Did the Land Rover look as if it had been recently abandoned?"

The man looked thoughtful. "Truth be told, it looked as if it had been there a few days. It was pretty dirty and covered in

457

pine needles. I couldn't put a date on it, but I reckon it had been there some time."

"When was the last time you and your brother-in-law came through here?"

"Months ago. It definitely wasn't here then."

After a few more routine questions, the two men thanked Fitzgerald again and stepped back out of the car. A light drizzle had started.

The crime scene manager — not Andy Harrison for once, noted Warren with surprise — strode over to them.

"We're almost ready to lift it onto the truck. Do you want a quick look at the scene, first?"

"Wouldn't hurt," said Warren, although he had a sinking feeling in his stomach. If the vehicle had been abandoned as long as the witness claimed, then it was unlikely to be much use in tracking Cameron's current whereabouts.

"How long do you reckon it's been here?" asked Sutton, the expression on his face clearly showing his feelings mirrored Warren's.

The CSM bent down to point at the vehicle's wheels, which had sunk slightly into the mud.

"Its tracks have been entirely obscured by rainfall and weather, but it has sunk into the soil significantly, so we can make a few estimates based on that." He pointed to the piles of dead pine needles and other leaf-litter that covered the surface of the vehicle.

"There is plenty of detritus here. Based on what that gentleman said the car was already looking pretty covered when he saw it last week. It's purely speculation, of course, but I'm thinking at least ten days. If it was springtime we'd be able to measure plant growth around the wheels et cetera, but there's not much happening this time of year. Certainly not enough to give you an estimate with a precision in days or weeks, which I guess you guys want."

Warren sighed and thanked the CSM. The tow truck had now arrived and the car would soon be on its way down to Welwyn. The forensic team would stay for a while longer, looking over the newly exposed ground under the vehicle and performing a fingertip search for anything of interest, but there was nothing for Warren and Sutton to do here.

Walking back to the road, Warren mused aloud.

"If he was going to dump the vehicle, he must have had a way of getting back to civilisation."

"Either he had somebody give him a lift, he hitchhiked or he walked," stated Sutton.

"If somebody gave him a lift, then that implies somebody working in partnership with him. What about his son? He's already admitted to covering for his old man's absences — could he have got a call one night asking to be picked up in the middle of nowhere?" Warren chewed his lip thoughtfully.

"It depends on when the car was abandoned," Sutton agreed. "That old boy claimed to have seen the car Friday. Assuming that he didn't come and fetch it again, that pre-dates Saskia Walker. If he was correct about it already being covered in leaf-litter and the CSIs are correct in their guesstimates, then that suggests it was abandoned before Monday; Gemma Allen was taken on the previous Saturday."

"The same day Michael Stockley claimed his old man disappeared."

"So was this how he planned it? Or was he responding to events?"

By now the two men had reached their car and Warren started up the hot-air blowers.

"It could be that he was just responding to events. How's this for a scenario? Cameron snatches Gemma Allen. As we know, it wasn't clean. Maybe there was some blood. More worrying though, for him, the condom splits when he rapes her. He realises that the game is up as when we find her body we'll surely do a DNA test and link him to the attack. So he decides to do a runner. He hides the Land Rover up here — he knows that it's a liability now as we'll be trying to trace it. He has money and so he decides it's time to go on the run."

"The idea's got merit," conceded Sutton, "but there are still a few holes. If he was going to abandon the Land Rover, why bother hiding it so well? He couldn't have predicted that those two daft old coots would come down here in sub-zero temperatures to avoid the Christmas shopping. He went to a lot of trouble — he definitely didn't want it found."

"Maybe it has Gemma Allen's blood in the back. Anyone who watches TV knows we only need a pinprick's worth these days. Her face was pretty messed up — she must have bled a fair bit."

"I could buy that if he thought he could still get away with it, but didn't we already decide that he knew the game was up anyway after the condom split? In fact, if he was worried about ensuring there was no link between Gemma Allen and him, his best bet would have been to have disposed of her body fully and the Land Rover."

"Well, so far he's shown no interest in disposing of the bodies. He just leaves them in remote enough places that he gets a few days' head start. Realistically, how long could he have expected Gemma Allen to have been undiscovered? A week or so? He dumped her on the border of two working farms, in the middle of a public right of way. By the very latest you'd have expected some

460

ramblers to stumble across her body as they burnt the calories off on Boxing Day."

Warren shook his head. "I don't think he was prepared to dispose of her body. How would he do it anyway? This isn't Hollywood. No matter where he dumped her, she would be discovered eventually. And the ground's rock hard. He'd have half killed himself trying to dig a decent grave with a shovel somewhere and even then he probably knows that we can spot newly turned earth this time of year using thermal imaging cameras on helicopters."

Sutton shrugged, unsure about that idea. "So you think he decided to go on the run when the Gemma Allen killing went wrong? I suppose if he is being reactive rather than proactive, then our chances of catching him are better."

Warren sighed. "Maybe, but I can't help feel that he just activated a previously worked-out Plan B. His son said that he cleared out their joint account — when did he do that?"

Sutton flicked through his notebook. "The day before. He did it over the counter in branch."

"Wouldn't it take both signatures to close out a joint account?"

Sutton shook his head. "Ordinarily yes, but he didn't quite empty the account. He left a thousand pounds and wrote a cheque to cash for the rest — twenty-three thousand, five hundred and sixty-nine pounds. Writing cheques that large only requires one signature."

"He clearly planned this in advance to some degree. Still, the question remains — how did he get from here back home or wherever he went after dumping the Land Rover?"

Sutton pulled out the local map he'd noticed stuffed in the passenger door pocket. After a few moments' work he quickly identified their location and a nearby village about two and a half miles away as the crow flew. Perhaps an hour's walk.

A little over five minutes later Tony Sutton and Warren were standing in the centre of the village at the local bus station.

"Shit," breathed Sutton. "Who'd have thought a tiny little place like this would be so well connected?"

He was right. The village of Tootingbourne was little more than a hamlet, but the confluence of three major roads and the convenience of a large market square without a war memorial in the centre had prompted the local council to build a large bus terminal. From here, one could catch connections heading into each of the adjoining counties, Essex, Cambridgeshire, Bedfordshire and Buckinghamshire, whilst National Express Coaches serviced the four London airports and the north of England. Cameron couldn't have chosen a better spot to disappear.

* * *

Back at the station, Warren called an evening briefing. Nursing a cup of hot coffee, he felt the chill leaving his body. The leads from the *Crimewatch* reconstruction had dried up in the last few hours and morale was sinking again. News that Cameron had ditched his Land Rover did nothing to improve the mood.

"He could be driving anything now. With twenty grand in his back pocket, he could have bought any old clunker and paid enough for there to be no questions asked. It could be weeks before the previous owner realises Cameron hasn't informed the DVLA of the change of ownership." Warren turned to Gary Hastings.

"What's the news on CCTV from the bus shelter in Tootingbourne?"

Hastings shook his head. "Nothing there, I'm afraid. They

recycle the tapes after a week. It's just there to catch out vandals and the like. We've got hold of the records from the ticket machines for the past two weeks, but it's unlikely that he used his credit card. We're circulating Cameron's pictures around the different bus companies in case any of the drivers remember him and we'll have posters up in all of the bus stops but it's a long shot."

"Well keep at it and make sure that everything is logged. I've let Traffic know that we're no longer looking for his Land Rover, but I've decided to keep that from the public at the moment. We'll let Cameron think we're still looking for it — maybe he'll make a mistake. At least it'll free them up to look for more leads."

With nothing else to be said, Warren stood up. The team looked dejected.

"Keep your chins up, people. It's disappointing that we're now in a manhunt stage, waiting for information from others, but don't forget we have an important role to play here. The DNA evidence is good for Gemma Allen and Saskia Walker but we're still pretty circumstantial as far as Sally Evans and Carolyn Patterson are concerned. We still need good evidence linking Cameron to their murders. And let's not forget we still haven't ruled out an accomplice. Cameron is a sixty-year-old man who's spent much of the past fourteen years in prison. These crimes are pretty sophisticated for such a person.

"Regardless, it'll be our legwork that secures this bastard's conviction when we finally catch him. Let's make sure we can pin all four killings on him, not just two."

FRIDAY 30TH DECEMBER

Chapter 55

Friday morning greeted Warren with a light dusting of snow and icy patches. Warren and Susan's street was off any major thoroughfare and so the gritters left them to their own devices. Once he'd made it onto the main road, he was able to drive a little easier, but the wreck of a Vauxhall Nova wrapped around a lamp post was a salutary reminder to take care.

A check with the night shift revealed no new leads and so Warren found himself in his office eyeing the pile of routine paperwork that he'd been putting off for the past three weeks. Unfortunately the fact that Warren's team were involved in a major murder investigation was of no consequence to the regular criminals that were CID's bread and butter and he was still expected to keep up with the reports and remain on top of what was happening on his patch.

With an apparent lull in the murders, he knew he should take the opportunity to shift some of the backlog. After the summer's big case, Warren had been exhausted and the last thing he'd needed was to wade through the two-inch pile of paperwork and the hundreds of emails that he'd shoved to one side as he'd pursued the killer at the university. He'd vowed not to make that mistake again.

He'd kept up with his emails reasonably well, but the dream of a paperless office was as far away today as it ever was and he'd studiously ignored the growing pile threatening to spill out of his "non-urgent" in-tray.

With a weary sigh, Warren took a long swig of his coffee and settled down. After a few seconds' thought he got up and made sure his office door was partly open — the last thing he wanted was for one of his team to assume the boss was busy and decide not to interrupt him. *Please interrupt me*, he pleaded silently...

By lunchtime he had received no interruptions and his phone had remained stubbornly silent. On the plus side, he had worked his way through about three quarters of his backlog. Pleasingly, muggings and assaults were down, perhaps due to fewer people walking the streets. Similarly, the increased numbers of people staying in had no doubt contributed to a drop in burglaries — although at least some of that was probably due to a recent high-profile anti-burglary drive by the Communities team. Balancing out the positives was a significant increase in the number of thefts from vehicles. Christmas always saw a spike in such crimes as careless shoppers left enticing packages in plain view or the proud owners of new in-car gadgets installed them then forgot to put them in the glove box when they left the car unattended. However, some bright spark from Welwyn had noticed a possible pattern in such thefts, suggesting an organised gang. Warren signed off on the extra funding requested to allow them to pursue the lead. If they could make some arrests and pin some of these extra thefts on the miscreants, then it would make a nice dent in Warren's crime figures. And if the courts played their part and locked the little toerags up for a few months, they might even enjoy a dip in recorded crime next year.

Conscious of the amount of food he'd eaten over the past few days, Warren had opted for cheese sandwiches, yoghurt and an apple for lunch. Joining the rest of the team in the briefing room, he saw that most of them were being similarly frugal.

All except for Gary Hastings, who was cheerfully tucking into a bulging turkey sandwich with what appeared to be a pork pie and a wedge of Stilton waiting for him in his Tupperware box. A large slab of heavily iced Christmas cake wrapped in tin foil completed the mini-feast. Karen Hardwick sat to his left eating a tomato and lettuce sandwich, a look of barely concealed resentment on her face.

Oh, to be young again, thought Warren with a twinge of jealousy, although he was pretty sure he'd never enjoyed a metabolism quite like the young DC's. Still, it could be worse, he thought, glancing over at Tony Sutton grimly doing his best to enjoy some Ryvita crackers and extra-light Philadelphia cream cheese.

Warren believed strongly that a lunch break was an important time for the team to unwind and let their subconscious work on problems and for that reason he tried to discourage shop talk. So he was glad when Tony Sutton started an animated debate about which was the best Bond movie shown over the Christmas period. By the time Warren received the message that Forensics were on the line, the table was firmly split into two camps — those favouring the early Sean Connery movies and those taken by the latest Daniel Craig outings. Roger Moore didn't get much of a look-in, noted Warren as he left to take the call; a pity — *A View to a Kill* had been the first Bond movie he'd seen at the cinema.

* * *

"Cameron didn't use his Land Rover to transport any of the murder victims," Warren announced to a stunned team.

"What? Are they sure?" asked Gary Hastings.

"About as sure as they can be. They've ripped the thing apart. No signs of any blood, hair or other trace anywhere inside the vehicle. They also can't find any signs of that strange cardboard residue that the victims must have picked up in the vehicle. Furthermore, they've analysed mud and soil residue from all four tyres and under the wheel arches and found no match to the dumping sites. Apparently, the presence of pollen grains suggest that the car hasn't been cleaned since at least the spring, so they'd have expected to have found something."

"Damn," muttered Tony Sutton. "It explains a lot though. The amount of footage Traffic have analysed, it was getting beyond reasonable that we hadn't spotted the Land Rover near any of the crime scenes."

"The question remains, then: what was he driving?" Karen Hardwick asked. "He must have had something to transport them."

"It also raises the spectre of an accomplice again," suggested Gary Hastings.

"But who? And why?" Warren tried to hide his frustration.

"We need to find the link between these four women. I'm sure that's the key. How could Richard Cameron have come across them? None of them seem to be in his social circle, such as it is. But the attacks are too well-planned for him to have just randomly snatched women off the street. He knew their routines and we know from his computer that he researched the dumping spots in advance. If there is an accomplice involved, then maybe that person or even persons are the link. If we can find them, then maybe we can find Cameron."

***

Back in his office, Warren couldn't face returning to the paperwork pile. What was he missing? Somewhere there was a link between these clues. Unbidden, the dream from a few nights ago returned. It was like a jigsaw puzzle with lots of pieces, none of which seemed to fit together. He closed his eyes. There were clues out there, he was certain. But where?

The ringing of his telephone jerked him back to reality.

"DCI Jones."

"It's Yvonne Fairweather." Warren took a moment to place the name — the PC working vice.

"Yes, Constable, go ahead."

"Melanie Clearwater came round a few hours ago and she wants to talk."

Chapter 56

The call from the hospital had taken Warren by surprise. Melanie Clearwater had not only regained consciousness, she apparently had some hazy memories from the night of her attack. Realising that she might be able to shed some light on who had beaten her so badly, Warren lost no time driving over to Cambridge.

Warren felt a little guilty. With all of the focus on the four murders, the attack on Melanie Clearwater had been put on the back burner. It wasn't that she had been forgotten about — far from it, teams of specialist officers had been questioning the working girls down on Truman Street night after night and Warren had read their reports daily — but a random assault on a prostitute had definitely been a lower priority. However, progress in her case could lead to an arrest and the removal of another dangerous predator from the streets of Middlesbury.

Introducing himself to the doctor in charge of the intensive care unit, Warren was told that the young woman was very agitated and that the only reason he was being allowed to speak to her was because they felt it might calm her down if she knew that the police were taking her seriously.

Entering the room, Warren was shocked again at the appearance of the young woman. Small-framed and very underweight, she was swallowed up by the large bed. The mismatch made her seem even more childlike. Because of that, the huge swellings, visible even under the bandages, seemed all the more horrific.

Sitting down at her bedside, Warren introduced himself. PC Yvonne Fairweather had just left and so she knew who Warren was and why he was there. Clearwater's speech was slurred, a combination of her badly swollen mouth — she had lost several teeth — her pain medication and whatever damage had happened to her brain during the beating. Nevertheless, she appeared lucid and the gaze through her puffed-up eyes seemed steady.

"You say that you remember the attack and the events that led up to it?"

Clearwater nodded slowly, her voice raspy but coherent. "Remember it all. Have seen man before. Was why I went down alley with him."

Warren's heart skipped a beat.

"You know the man? Do you have a name?"

"Yes." She shook her head at the same time. Warren interpreted this as yes, she knew him, but no, she didn't have a name.

"How do you know him?"

"Went with him a few days ago." Melanie had been in Intensive Care for two and a half weeks and probably had little idea of how much time had passed, so Warren interpreted this as some days before the attack. About three weeks ago, he estimated.

"He was a former client?"

She shook her head. "Hired me. Somebody else client." Her voice shook slightly and Warren could plainly see that she was fighting sleep. He frantically tried to work out what she meant. "Do you mean that he hired you — but on behalf of somebody else?"

She nodded her head slowly; already her eyes were closing. "Birthday."

"Melanie? Are you still awake, Melanie?" There was no response.

"You will have to come back tomorrow." The nurse in charge of the unit had appeared silently beside the bed.

"Can't you wake her up, just for a moment?"

The nurse's tone was firm. "Absolutely not. You saw how exhausting just that short conversation was for the poor girl."

A wave of frustration swept over Warren as he stood up. "You don't understand. She was about to tell us who attacked her."

The nurse's voice became harder. "I know, Detective, I was listening. We all want to know what animal did this to her, but you can't rush her. It's an absolute miracle that she's awake, let alone speaking and remembering the incident."

Warren glared at the nurse for a few seconds, before letting out the breath he'd been holding. "You're absolutely right, of course. I'm sorry."

The nurse smiled at him reassuringly. "I fully understand. I'll contact you as soon as she is ready to speak again. And if she says anything, I'll make a note of it."

Warren nodded his thanks, recognising that the busy nurse was trying to be as helpful as possible. Picking up his coat, he cast one last glance at the battered young woman. Even when asleep, she looked stressed and tired. He got the impression that she had looked like that before the attack. *I hope you get the help you need*, he whispered silently as he left the ward.

For the first time since the young woman's attack, he actually felt the first stirrings of hope that he might actually solve this crime. Now if only they could get a lead on the other murders, then he would be able to rest a bit more easily himself.

SATURDAY 31ST DECEMBER

Chapter 57

December the thirty-first. The last day of the year and Warren couldn't help a bit of introspection. The past twelve months had been a roller coaster to say the least. This time last year, he and Susan had been living in a rented flat in Birmingham. He'd been a detective inspector with West Midlands Police and Susan had been enjoying her job as a teacher in a Birmingham comprehensive. They'd celebrated Christmas with Bernice and Dennis and Felicity was just starting to show the early signs of her third pregnancy. They'd spent a night at Granddad Jack's and Nana Betty's and were preparing to attend a New Year's Eve fancy dress party with some friends of Susan.

Fast forward twelve months and Nana Betty was gone and the couple were in their own house a hundred miles away. Warren was now a DCI in charge of catching a serial killer and Susan was busy trying to turn around the science department of a failing school. At this precise moment, Warren couldn't decide if the pluses of the last twelve months outweighed the negatives. At least they had a party to go to that night, he thought.

Warren's first job when he got in that morning was to ring the hospital to see how Melanie Clearwater was doing. The news wasn't good.

"She's been up all night vomiting and has a fever. We're doing tests but it looks as though the winter vomiting bug has struck the ward."

"How long do you think it'll be until she's well enough to talk again?"

The pause was ominous.

"She's a very poorly young woman. It really is touch and go at the moment. Besides which, even if she does pull through, we're about to initiate a lock-down of the ward to stop it spreading any further. No visitors for forty-eight hours at least whilst we do a deep clean and get the patients stabilised."

Forty-eight hours. Warren fought a surge of frustration. He managed to keep his voice calm as he thanked the nurse. It wasn't her fault and the stress in her voice suggested that she was having at least as bad a day as he was.

The rest of the day passed in an equally frustrating manner. Although New Year's Eve wasn't technically a bank holiday, this year it fell on a weekend and so the CID team's phone calls were as often as not redirected to voicemail. By six o'clock it became clear to Warren that he was just wasting time in the office. He'd all but cleared his paperwork backlog, which was something at least. The thought of coming back to that on January the third was too depressing. Strictly speaking he was off-shift until after the bank holiday, but his team knew that he would be immediately contactable and he insisted on being copied in on each day's briefing notes, no matter how threadbare.

Arriving home, he tried his best to put work out of his mind. They were going to a party thrown by one of Susan's colleagues and when he arrived, Susan was just about to get changed. The last few days had been stressful and the couple had spent little quality time together, so it didn't take much persuasion on Warren's part for her to relent and invite him into the shower with her.

Warren decided that the likelihood of any major breaking leads that night was pretty slim and so decided to splash out on a taxi to the party. He certainly wasn't going to get drunk, but he doubted he'd be in a fit state to drive, especially in the icy conditions.

Warren had expected a small intimate gathering with people crammed into a living room and kitchen, whilst somebody with a musical bent commandeered the stereo system. He was not expecting a humongous country pile sitting on its own acre of land. It was at least twice the size of Bernice and Dennis' not insubstantial residence.

"My God," he breathed, "all this on a teacher's salary?" He pecked Susan on the cheek. "I married better than I thought."

"Don't get your hopes up, Chief Inspector. It was Clare that married well in this case. Her husband, Mark, founded a profitable pharmaceutical firm in Cambridge. He employed her as a researcher. When they got married, she decided bench-work wasn't for her and retrained as a chemistry teacher."

"So why is she still teaching?"

Susan shrugged. "As hard as it is to imagine some days, there are still those who teach for the love of it. She's turned down several promotions. She just wants to teach chemistry and be a form tutor. She's bloody good at it too, from what I've observed."

The wide, curved driveway was filled with the best part of a dozen cars, suggesting that not everybody was so bothered about driving home. Susan shrugged. "The house has at least four guest bedrooms and Clare loves hosting. I imagine at least a few people are staying over. Plus Ravvi doesn't drink and Phil's partner is a paramedic, so she may not be drinking." She turned to him impishly. "So no need to get your notebook out, DCI."

Warren grinned sheepishly. Message understood.

The party was even more impressive once they got inside. The house had a huge living room and dining room, both of which opened onto a kitchen big enough to serve a small hotel. French doors led into a large spacious conservatory and, as if that weren't enough space for the hundred or so revellers, the conservatory opened into a marquee with a dance floor and DJ. Gas-powered heaters kept the marquee nice and toasty.

Warren immediately recognised Clare from the school Christmas party and she greeted him like a long-lost friend, taking the proffered bottles of wine and adding them to the already groaning drinks table.

"You have a lovely home and I must say I'm impressed with the marquee."

She flapped her hand dismissively. "Between you and me, I'll be glad to see the back of it. Mark uses it for corporate entertaining. He was going to have it taken down last week, but I said 'I've put up with it for the past month, I want to at least get something out of it!' It'll be gone by the time I go back to school and I can finally see the back garden again."

After accepting a glass of wine each, Susan took him around the party, reintroducing him to largely the same people he'd met two weeks before. By ten o'clock the party was in full swing, with the DJ playing an eclectic mix of tracks that kept the dance floor heaving.

At a quarter to midnight, the revellers left the cosiness of the marquee and went into the impressive garden. The DJ was streaming BBC radio over the speakers and everyone raised a glass as they counted down to midnight. Then, as the unmistakeable chimes of Big Ben rang out fireworks exploded into the air. As he kissed his wife and then took hold of the nearest hands for the singing of "Auld Lang Syne" Warren reflected that perhaps the next year would be better.

* * *

Sitting in the back of the cab some time after 3 a.m., Warren decided it was a good job that he hadn't been called out. Without intending to, he'd drunk a fair bit more than he'd planned. Susan, for her part, had fallen asleep the moment the taxi had pulled away from the house.

Looking out of the window, he watched as a group of scantily dressed twenty-something girls wobbled and giggled their way down the road. His thoughts turned dark. New Year's Eve was the biggest party night of the year. How many young women fitting Richard Cameron's tastes were walking home alone right at this very minute? And where was Cameron? Was he cruising around in whatever vehicle he now drove looking for victims? At Warren's suggestion the traffic police, busy looking for drink drivers, had all been given a copy of Cameron's photograph and asked to keep an eye out for anybody suspicious. It was a long shot, but maybe the predator would be unable to resist the temptation of so many young women out and about.

Regardless, Warren knew that for the next few nights he would be sleeping with one ear open, waiting for a call to tell him that another young woman hadn't made it home.

NEW YEAR

Chapter 58

Much to Warren's surprise and relief, the first two days of the new year passed by relatively peacefully. No new reports came in of either missing young women or dead bodies. Unfortunately, the briefing notes emailed to him were similarly uneventful with no significant new leads. Traffic continued to plod away at the CCTV analysis but there was nothing to report as yet.

Warren and Susan had made the effort to go to church on New Year's Day, before driving out to a local carvery for a Sunday lunch. After a brisk, bracing walk followed by steaming hot chocolate in a quaint country pub, the couple headed back home.

Before settling down for the evening Warren phoned the hospital to check on the progress of Melanie Clearwater. The nurse answering recognised his voice and informed him that she was stable, but the ward would be closed to visitors for at least another twenty-four hours.

The following day was a bank holiday, since the New Year had fallen over the weekend. Warren and Susan spent the day in the traditional manner: queuing to get into B&Q in Cambridge, then painting the spare bedroom. By early evening, Susan had settled down to plan for the coming week and so Warren phoned the hospital again.

This time, the ward nurse put him through to Melanie's consultant.

"Ah, Chief Inspector. Melanie has made considerable progress. Her temperature is down and she is quite lucid. In fact, she is quite stressed about not being able to speak to you. Strictly speaking, the ward is under quarantine for the next twelve to twenty-four hours, but I am somewhat concerned that Melanie is making herself ill through worry."

"I see," said Warren, wondering where this was going.

"With that in mind, I have gained permission for you to enter the ward as long as you are prepared to follow our strict infection protocols."

"Of course." Warren felt a rush of excitement. At last, some progress. Calling to Susan to let her know where he was going, he phoned Tony Sutton. The DI was enthusiastic.

"At last, progress on something. I feel as though I'm banging my head on a bloody brick wall here."

Warren was sympathetic, but declined an offer to meet at the hospital. He had a feeling that the doctors and nurses were going out on a limb to smuggle him into the ward and he didn't want to abuse that.

Arriving at the hospital, he was escorted to a staff locker room where he was issued with a set of surgical scrubs fresh out of a sealed packet and a hairnet. After stripping to his underwear and donning the sterile garb he was shown how to clean his hands and forearms as if he were about to go into surgery.

Finally, he was ready. Warren had made certain to take a digital tape-recorder with him to get a full and complete record of what she said and as he reached her bed he turned it on, placing it on the bedside table. This time her speech was less halting than the previous visit; her colour was still pale but a faint hint of pink highlighted her cheeks.

As before, she was confident that she had recognised her attacker, although she couldn't now give any details beyond that he was white and probably in his thirties. She couldn't recall his hair colour or any distinguishing marks. He had approached her on Truman Street two days before the attack, offering her five hundred pounds if she would accompany him to a birthday party.

She admitted that she wouldn't normally take such a risk, but she couldn't afford to turn down five hundred pounds. Another girl had made a note of the man's licence plate, but Melanie couldn't remember who.

Moving on, Warren asked if there was anything unusual about the job.

"It was a bit weird, but I've done worse. The man drove me to a bed and breakfast over on Gravel Rise. You can hire rooms by the hour and the owner has a problem remembering faces." It was probably useless, he knew; nevertheless, Warren made a note of the address and decided to send a couple of officers around to question the owner.

"When we got there, there was an older man waiting. The bloke who paid me said that the old man hadn't had any for a while and that he had to cum. He was really insistent about that. A bit odd, I thought, taking such an interest. I did wonder if he would stay and watch, but he didn't. He left the room. He also insisted that I use a condom."

Clearwater sniffed. "I always do if I don't know them. It's safer, innit?"

Warren wasn't quite sure how simply knowing a client would protect her from any diseases that he might have, but said nothing.

"So what happened then?"

"Well, we sat down and discussed the state of the economy — what do you think bloody happened?"

Warren shrugged an apology. It had been a silly question on the surface of it, but he had to be certain.

"Were there any... problems?"

"No. The old guy was a bit out of practice and it took him a while but he managed it in the end."

"So you don't think he could have been angry?"

Clearwater shrugged. "He seemed pretty satisfied."

"What about the younger man, the one who set it up?"

"He came back in again and asked if he had cum. Bloody obsessed he was, even looked in the wastepaper basket to check I wasn't lying. Guess he'd have wanted a refund if I hadn't performed as expected. I think the old guy was a bit embarrassed. Then he told me to get my clothes on again and said he'd call me a cab to take me back to Truman Street."

"So he didn't drive you back?"

She shook her head. "They never do. Guys will do anything when they're all horny, then as soon as they've shot their load they get all repulsed and don't want to know any more."

Warren looked down at the brief sketch of events and decided to see if he could fill in any details.

"So, starting from the top, let's see what else you can remember. Can you be more specific about the date and the time of this first meeting?"

She shook her head, clearly frustrated, and Warren was quick to reassure her.

"Don't worry. You said that there was another girl around. We'll interview her." He almost winced at the white lie. Despite their best efforts they hadn't been able to track down anyone who had seen Melanie getting into the client's car.

"Do you remember anything more about the men's appearance?"

Again, she shook her head. "The younger man was about thirty and white. The older guy was fifty or sixty with grey hair. That's all I can remember."

"Clean-shaven or bearded?"

She shook her head.

"Did you hear either of them use a name?"

Her brow furrowed under the bandages as she tried to remember. "No… not that I remember. It was weird, though. I did get the feeling that they might know each other. I mean, really know each other."

"Why was that?"

Again she shrugged. "I can't remember. It was just how I felt at the time."

Warren could see that she was starting to tire again. Besides which, he could see that she wasn't going to be the most reliable of witnesses. Any halfway decent defence lawyer would tear holes in her leaky testimony.

"Moving on to the night you were attacked — tell us what happened."

Again, the young woman's testimony was sketchy and full of holes.

"I was standing on the kerb a few metres down from the alley. I had my back to the pavement and was looking at the road, waiting for clients. I didn't hear him approach. I think he came through the alley? Anyhow, he called my name and I turned around and saw him. I recognised him immediately.

"He asked how I was and if I wanted to earn some more money. I'm not sure how it happened but we suddenly seemed to be standing in the alley where no one could see us. He had his wallet out and I remembered how much he'd paid me before…" At this, her voice began to shake. "I can't remember any more. Everything goes kind of hazy."

Warren let her compose herself.

"You've done well," he reassured her. "There are several promising lines of inquiry here and I'll make sure the team gets everything that you've told me. In the meantime, if you can remember anything else you can get me on this number."

As he put his coat on he noticed the huge bunch of plastic flowers. They were the only ones on the bedside table and he felt a wave of sorrow pass over him. It said something when the only person who actually cared that you were in here was your pimp. Warren fought off the sadness. He'd seen the way that Yvonne Fairweather had looked at the young woman. No, make that two people who cared that you were in here. On impulse, Warren picked up her hand and gave it a reassuring squeeze, rules be damned. She squeezed back, smiling slightly. Make that three, he decided.

TUESDAY 3RD JANUARY

Chapter 59

Thirty-eight years old. Twenty-four hours ago he had been thirty-seven. Warren stared at himself in the mirror. The face staring back was the same as the one that had looked back yesterday; yet it felt older. So much older. Why? The dark brown hair still had no traces of grey, the features still sharply defined. Perhaps it was his best mate's card — younger by two months, he made some sort of joke every year along the lines of "no matter how old I get, you'll always be older". Or perhaps it was Susan teasing him that he could now no longer claim to be in his mid-thirties, he'd have to start describing himself as late thirties.

Ageing didn't used to bother him. He could never understand why so many of his friends became morose as they passed into their thirties. It wasn't as if life were slipping him by, with nothing to show for it: happily married with his own house, a good education, plenty of friends and the rank of Detective Chief Inspector — not a bad place to be for a man of his age. What, then? Why was this year so different? He wasn't even forty and was in robust health. All the statistics suggested he wasn't even halfway to the grave yet.

Maybe that was it. In the past few weeks, he'd gazed upon the bodies of four young women, struck down in the prime of life, and buried a woman his heart had thought would live for ever. So much death. No wonder he was in such a downbeat mood.

Downstairs the doorbell rang. Reflexively, he glanced at his watch. Twenty past eight. The hour's lie-in had been a small birthday present to himself. Susan had only just left for school; the teachers were having a training day so she'd enjoyed the lie-in with him, giving him his present and a little taster of the treat he could expect when he got home from work tonight.

Swapping his towel for a dressing gown, he hurried downstairs, the doorbell ringing for the second time. Opening the door, he apologised to the delivery man standing in the cold, the icy blast of air turning his freshly showered skin to goose bumps. The Parcelforce worker grunted and handed over the electronic clipboard for him to sign, before passing across the large package.

Taking it into the kitchen, he flicked the kettle on then studied the parcel. It was large and soft, clearly some sort of clothing. The neatly handwritten label on the front was addressed to him, with "Angleterre" below the postcode. The top right of the package was covered in several euros' worth of French postage stamps, plus a delivery label from an international parcel firm. The postmark was blurry, but with a bit of squinting he made out "Les Orres, Hautes-Alpes". Warren smiled at his detective work. Jeff had mentioned that he and Felicity would be spending the New Year skiing in the Alps with another family.

Using a pair of scissors from the junk drawer, Warren carefully opened the package to reveal a thick black padded ski jacket and a birthday card.

'Something to keep you warm the next time you get called out. Happy Birthday. Lots of love from Felicity, Jeff, Jimmy, Sammy and Annie. xx'

Warren was stunned at the generosity of the gift and its thoughtfulness. He knew nothing about skiing or the clothes one wore, but it was clearly expensive. Hell, the postage alone must have been a small fortune. He knew the couple could afford it, but still…

The kettle clicked off and Warren poured himself his first coffee of the day. The brew was too hot for his taste, so he jogged back upstairs and got dressed whilst he waited for it to cool. A quick wrestle with a comb — he knew it was time for a haircut when his hair started misbehaving after his morning shower — and a squirt of the new aftershave Susan had bought him and he was back downstairs, the coffee now just the right temperature. Forcing himself to eat a banana, he gulped his coffee down, slipped on his new jacket and, after a quick once-over in the mirror to admire it, he left for the office, grabbing the box of cakes he'd bought for break-time.

The CID office was in full swing when he entered, only the Christmas decorations a reminder that the world was just return-ing from a major party season. Various colleagues wished him a happy birthday as he entered his office. Placing the cakes on top of his filing cabinet — he knew from prior observation that if he put them anywhere near the coffee urn, the early-bird gannets would polish them off before the rest of the office got a look-in — he logged onto his computer.

The holiday season had reduced the volume of email somewhat, with much of the make-work and gossip absent. Nevertheless, he spent the better part of an hour filing and deleting rubbish — it seemed that not even Christmas and New Year were reason enough for the force's health and safety committee to rest. He moved the latest guidelines on the need for "electrical safety testing of personal electronic devices brought into the workplace" to the folder marked "crap to read when bored".

The sharp rap on Warren's door was a welcome distraction. At his bidding, DC Gary Hastings entered, the light in his eyes and his visible excitement making Warren's pulse speed up.

"Sir, we've found a connection between Sally Evans and Carolyn Patterson."

* * *

The area around Gary Hastings' workstation was crowded with most of the team members working the murders.

"I was reviewing the CCTV from the sports centre on the night that Carolyn Patterson was abducted," Hastings was explaining, "trying to identify people coming and going at about the same time she did. At around the time Carolyn Patterson's boxercise class entered the bar a group of lads in their twenties and thirties also entered."

With a click of the mouse, he zoomed in on a picture showing three men with kit bags and wet hair walking through the door. Two of the men were wearing matching tops, although the logo over the left breast was too small and the still image from the video too blurry for Warren to make out the details.

"Meet Middlesbury Sports and Leisure Centre's over twenty-one men's football team, currently sitting third in the local amateur league. They train on Mondays and Thursdays and finish at the same time as Carolyn Patterson's boxercise class. Their star centre forward, absent the last couple of weeks for obvious reasons — one Darren Blackheath."

"Nice work, Gary. Do we know if the two groups socialised at all in the bar?" asked Sutton, patting the young DC on the shoulder.

Hastings nodded and it was clear that there was more.

"I spoke to one of the bar staff, who helped me identify them and he said that a couple of the girls in the boxercise class actually did the class out of convenience, because their husbands or partners were playing football at the same time. The night that Carolyn Patterson disappeared there was more mingling than usual between the two groups — the girls from boxercise were having an early Christmas drink because their class was finishing. Unfortunately, he doesn't remember if Carolyn Patterson spoke to the footballers or stayed with her friends."

"What else have you got, Gary?" Warren could feel the young detective was bursting to share even more.

"The team have a website — just somewhere to share their match reports and fixture lists, post pictures and include links to news articles. That's where I found Darren Blackheath's name. The website also has an archive — guess whose name I stumbled across in match reports about two years prior to this season?"

"Alex Chalmers," breathed Warren, already one step ahead.

"Bingo. They also have a Facebook page — completely open. Both Blackheath and Chalmers are 'friends' of the page. The club's 'wall' is quite busy with members posting lots of news and gossip. It seems that Alex Chalmers was a regular player, a useful right back apparently, until about two years ago when he broke his leg. From what I can piece together he couldn't work or play football for several months, by which time, by his own admission, 'the beer and fags' had got him. He hasn't played since."

"So he and Darren Blackheath knew each other back then — the question is, are they still in touch now?" mused Warren.

"The answer to that is 'yes'. Chalmers is still an active member of their Facebook page and, judging by his posts, regularly watches them play and goes out drinking with them."

Chapter 60

Gary Hastings' discovery was more than enough excuse to open Warren's birthday cakes, he decided, and the whole team sat in the main briefing room sipping coffee and brainstorming.

"The question is, how significant is this link and how are these two related to Richard Cameron?"

The question was an open one and causing much speculation.

"Well, I think it's safe to say that Richard Cameron isn't the team's latest signing, so how is he a part of all of this?"

"And what about Gemma Allen and Saskia Walker? Do we know if either of these two women used the leisure centre or had any link to Blackheath or Chalmers or Richard Cameron for that matter?" asked Tony Sutton.

"We know that Saskia Walker was a keen jogger. We should check out the membership records — see if she used the gym or took any classes," suggested Warren.

Gary Hastings, acting as unofficial note-taker, jotted the suggestion down.

"What about Gemma Allen? We didn't find much evidence in her flat to suggest that she was into exercise. And even if she was, she lived on the other side of town and didn't drive. There are far more convenient options for her if she wanted to go to the gym," Karen Hardwick pointed out.

"Check out Gemma Allen at the same time as Saskia Walker. Karen, can you contact her close friends and mother and find out if she used the leisure centre? Also run the names of Blackheath, Chalmers or Richard Cameron by them, see if they ring any bells."

"The football team train on Monday and Thursday evenings. We should check what they have by way of CCTV footage on those days for the past few months; see if any of our victims crop up and have any contact with the team. We may even see them talking to Chalmers or Blackheath, which would certainly firm up any link," suggested Tony Sutton.

"That's a good idea, but could be pretty labour-intensive. See how much footage the centre has — if any — and I'll see if I can persuade the super to sign off on the extra manpower from Welwyn," Warren decided after a few moments' thought.

"What shall we do about Chalmers and Blackheath? Should we pull them in for questioning?"

"Not yet. We don't have enough to go on for an arrest and if they are in contact with Richard Cameron, we don't want to spook him. With what we've got so far, they'll never admit to anything. If we can get them bang to rights, maybe they'll tell us where Cameron is. Let's keep an eye on them though — we don't want them disappearing."

With that, the meeting broke up, the different officers rushing off to pursue their different leads. Only Tony Sutton remained, sitting in his chair, his slice of cake untouched in front of him.

"If you'd told me there was a link this time yesterday, I wouldn't have believed you. We'd all but eliminated Blackheath. There's only that business with his alibi that causes us problems. Chalmers

I can see, perhaps, although it seems a bit sophisticated for a low-level thug like him. What bothers me is how the hell could two young lads — in their teens when Cameron went down — hook up with him as he strikes again? And why? How does it work? Do they kidnap the girls and he shows them how to get away with it?"

"I agree, Tony. It's a bloody strange business. Of course, this link between Blackheath and Chalmers could just be a coincidence. In which case, we still need to work out how Richard Cameron came to know these women. It wasn't random chance. He stalked them; he knew their routines.

"I've been reading over the previous cases from the Nineties. The similarities are remarkable; leaving aside the DNA evidence and even the methods, with the condoms and the rubber gloves it's the same MO. He followed those three girls. He researched them; learnt their routines. They were joggers, snatched off the street on their regular runs in the most secluded part of the route. He sedated them, pulled them into the back of his van and drove them to a secluded spot. The only difference is that after he'd raped them, he left them alive.

"Of course, that cost him. The final victim was able to help the police. Maybe he's learnt from his mistake. That rubber mask that he wore was unusual back then — the one he's wearing now is ten-a-penny, made in China. The rubber is used in all sorts of products, including the Halloween masks sold in the pound shop."

Sutton rubbed his eyes wearily. "What we need is some sort of link between Cameron and these two. Perhaps they met on the Internet? We know that Cameron visited bondage sites — maybe they hooked up through them? If and when we bring them in, we should impound their home computers, have IT look for any links."

"Good idea. In the meantime, we should get IT to keep on looking at Cameron's computer and see if he joined any forums. That PC has been a goldmine so far."

"I agree, guv. But one thing still worries me a little — how could a man twelve months out of prison, who'd only ever done the most basic level courses in IT, use a PC in such a sophisticated manner?"

Warren sighed. "Yet another thing I'll be asking Darren Blackheath and Alex Chalmers when we pull them in."

Chapter 61

The remainder of the morning was a mixed bag in terms of progress. Phone calls to the leisure centre revealed that Saskia Walker was a casual gym user. She had a pass, but no membership. The centre didn't keep records on gym usage for individuals, but it was reasonable to assume that she didn't use it more than three times a month, otherwise she would have probably signed up for the more cost-effective unlimited usage package. It was impossible to say if her preferred gym nights included Monday or Thursdays.

Unfortunately, there were no records at all of Gemma Allen using the gym. Her friends said that she wasn't one for exercise and had little or no interest in football or any other team sports, nor had she mentioned any acquaintances who played sport that she might have gone to support out of loyalty.

A query about CCTV footage revealed that the centre stored the tapes for their half-dozen cameras for twelve months before wiping them. Even limiting the search to Mondays and Thursdays for an hour either side of the two-hour training session would be a mammoth task.

Consequently, the appearance of DS Richardson at Warren's door just before lunch was extremely welcome.

"It's a stretch, sir, but I think I know how Sally Evans and

Carolyn Patterson were kidnapped." Detective Sergeant Margaret Richardson was a middle-aged mother of two whose former role working with the traffic division had made her the ideal choice to lead the team searching CCTV and traffic-camera recordings on the nights of the kidnappings.

"Tell us what you've found, Mags," instructed Warren, following her to her workstation.

"Sally Evans went missing at 6 p.m. — right in the middle of the rush hour. Unfortunately, there were no cameras covering the back alley where she was waiting. The best we could come up with was a scan of the roads surrounding the area. As you know we found several dozen vehicles, including Darren Blackheath's, that could conceivably have taken a detour down that alleyway and stopped for at least a couple of minutes. We prioritised that list by putting certain classes of commercial and public vehicles to one side, figuring that the perpetrator was most likely to be using a private vehicle. We prioritised the list still further, by downgrading vehicles that made that same journey at the same time on at least eight out of the preceding ten workdays."

Warren nodded his acceptance of her tactics. It made perfect sense. Middlesbury might be a small town, but it still had a pretty busy rush hour. Furthermore, the town stood at the junction of several equally congested A roads and experienced commuters often chose to go through Middlesbury rather than take a substantial detour. Tracing all of those drivers in a short time would tax the resources of the unit and so prioritising the workload was essential.

"That reduced the list to a more manageable number and so we started running the licence plates. But it seems we whittled it a bit too much and found nothing.

"And then Carolyn Patterson happened. As soon as you identified the Middlesbury Sports and Leisure Centre and the approximate time, we did the same thing. That job was bigger, since the time window was much wider and there are several busy residential roads with cars coming and going — not to mention cars picking up and dropping off users of the sports centre.

"To save time, we cross-referenced the two long-lists and picked up three vehicles on both. One belongs to an elderly couple in their eighties. CCTV footage from the car park shows that car coming right up to the centre and an old man getting out. He returns a few minutes later with a teenage girl. I'm guessing granddad picking his granddaughter up from the tae kwon do class that finished about then."

"Sounds reasonable," agreed Sutton, who had wandered over to join them.

"The second vehicle appeared at 21:25 and picked up another woman from boxercise. However, we ran the registration through the DVLA and found their home address. There's a CCTV camera around the corner from their house and sure enough the car was seen seven minutes later. According to our calculations, it's four point two miles by the most direct route so the car averaged thirty-six miles per hour. That includes three traffic lights and two roundabouts all in thirty zones. I showed the route to one of our fast-response drivers and he reckons that's pretty quick driving even late in the evening with all of the lights on green; definitely a bit of a boy racer.

"Even if they were able to subdue and get Carolyn Patterson into the boot of the car in sixty seconds, the average speed would have been forty-two miles per hour. If it took two minutes, that's over fifty. In both cases the car would have probably triggered at least one of the four speed cameras on that route. On top of that, we picked up his car near Sally Evans' workplace every working day for the past month, at pretty much the same time give or take a couple of minutes. No deviation on the day of the attack."

"Good enough for me," Warren stated and Sutton nodded.

"So that leaves one vehicle, appearing on both lists. I have to confess, sir, both times I moved it over to the lowest priority list since you see them everywhere. Besides which, closer inspection reveals it isn't the same vehicle both times. The licence plate varies by one letter.

"But then Constable Robson, who was assisting me, asked, 'Why would a post van be out collecting letters at nine-forty in the evening?'"

* * *

"Say that again, Sergeant," asked Warren, although he was pretty sure he had heard her correctly the first time.

"A Royal Mail postal delivery van drove past a traffic camera at 21:41 hours, about three quarters of a mile south-west of the sports centre. The same van went past another camera to the west of the centre earlier in the evening at 19:56 hours. As best we can tell it didn't leave that area during that time."

"Now that is bloody weird. What about this second van?"

"Another van, same model, same year but slightly different index was in the vicinity of Sally Evans' workplace on the night that she disappeared. Fortunately, the traffic-camera software allows for dirt on the plate or bad lighting and flagged it as potentially the same vehicle. It was photographed at 17:56 hours on the high street just east of the alleyway—" she pointed to a location on a printed map circled in red "—then again at 18:04 hours by this camera, three quarters of a mile further on. The mean traffic speed calculated by averaging ten vehicles either side of the van was approximately thirteen miles per hour, meaning the van should have covered the distance in about three and a half minutes. Those twenty cars are picked up in the same formation at the second camera at about the expected time; the van doesn't reappear until later. There are four and a half minutes unaccounted for. Time enough perhaps to detour down the alleyway, pick up Sally Evans, then turn around and rejoin the road."

"OK, that's a good theory, but surely there's another possibility: he's a postman — he could have been emptying a postbox. I'm sure four minutes or so is plenty of time for him to pull over, open the postbox, empty the mail and then pull back into the traffic if it's busy."

Margaret Richardson smiled wolfishly. "Already ahead of you on that one, sir. There are no postboxes in that vicinity. Second, even assuming that he had taken a detour after finishing his route nearby — popping into a newsagent for a paper, perhaps — he had no business being in that area at that time. Last collection up that end of town is 16:45 hours. Whatever that post van was doing in the area at that time, it wasn't picking up mail."

Warren looked at Tony Sutton, who was looking as shell-shocked as he felt.

"A post van. Who would have thought? They're like buses and bin lorries — part of the furniture. Who would ever notice them?"

"And even more importantly," mused Warren, "who do we know who works for the post office?"

Chapter 62

Middlesbury central sorting office was just to the east of the centre of town. A large, functional affair, it served Middlesbury and most of the surrounding villages. To the right of the lobby a small queue of people waited to pick up parcels. To the left an enclosed but unmanned reception desk with a bell served as gatekeeper for the large double-doors marked "Staff Only" and a cargo-lift, similarly signed. Swipe-card readers provided access to both of these.

Warren and Tony Sutton rang the bell. Eventually a middle-aged woman wearing her hair in a bun and a Royal Mail uniform entered through a door behind the reception desk.

"If you have any queries about parcels, you need to speak to that desk. This is for visitors only."

The line was practised and well worn; she was clearly used to self-important members of the public trying to avoid waiting their turn.

Warren flashed his warrant card. "We're not here to pick up a parcel. I wonder if we could speak to the person in charge of your vehicle fleet, please."

The woman blinked in surprise. "Oh. I suppose that would be Mr Carroway. Let me see if he's in today." Picking up a phone on the desk, she dialled a three-digit number.

A few seconds later, after explaining who the visitors were, she cupped the mouthpiece. "May I ask what it's about?"

"A minor traffic incident," Warren lied smoothly.

After a few more seconds, she hung up. "He'll be down in a moment to pick you up. In the meantime, could you sign the visitors' book, please? You'll also need to wear these visitor badges. Please return them to Reception before you leave."

Warren signed the pair of them in as North Herts Police, purposely leaving "nature of business" blank. The two men accepted the badges and hung them around their necks on bright red lanyards. At that moment, the doors to the right of Reception opened.

Angus Carroway was a short man, with a shock of bright red hair and a pale, freckled complexion to match. Middle-aged, he had the remains of a Scottish accent. After introductions, during which Warren stuck with the line that they were investigating a minor traffic incident, the fleet manager led them through the double-doors into a maze of corridors. A rattling noise permeated the fabric of the building.

"That's the automated sorting machines. Believe me, it's a lot noisier on the main floor."

Finally, they emerged into a huge, enclosed garage. A number of loading bays were occupied by a variety of vehicles, from the familiar small red vans to large, articulated trucks — some with Royal Mail livery, others with Parcelforce. A dozen or so men in red polo shirts were busy loading the vehicles, either by hand or pump-truck. At the far end, open shuttered doors revealed the road outside, an icy wind blowing fat, wet snowflakes through the opening. Nevertheless, the garage stank of diesel fumes. Carroway led them to a steel and wooden door to the right of the garage, marked "Fleet Manager".

Inside, the office was a cluttered affair, the large wooden desk a mess of in-trays and pieces of paper jostling for space with a vintage-looking desktop PC. A full-height, steel-framed bookcase against the far wall was filled with dozens of red and blue A4 folders, each with its spine neatly labelled with what looked like a registration number and vehicle description. A small window behind the desk provided the only natural light. A much larger window overlooked the garage area from which they had just come. To the left of the room a connecting door led into a small anteroom, in which a young woman was sitting at a far tidier desk, using a hands-free telephone headset and tapping away at a more modern-looking computer. There was only one visitor chair in Carroway's office, so he reached through to the anteroom and borrowed hers.

With the three of them settled, Carroway leant forward. "So what can I help you with, officers?"

As the person in charge of the Royal Mail's fleet of vehicles in the local area, Carroway had probably had numerous dealings with the police. A traffic violation by any of his drivers would naturally come across his desk first, as the police tracked down the person responsible. However, he would almost certainly have been dealing with the traffic division. It was unlikely that he had much to do with CID.

Warren pushed across the clearest images of the two suspect Royal Mail vans taken from the CCTV footage examined by Mags Richardson and her team. The vehicle registration numbers were clearly visible.

"Are these two vans part of your fleet?"

Carroway glanced at the images; he clearly knew the registration numbers of his fleet off by heart. "Yes, they are both part of the local fleet that I manage."

He licked his lips nervously, Warren noted. He remained silent, waiting for Carroway to fill the void.

"Have they been involved in some sort of incident? Nothing was reported in the log or spotted by the mechanics."

"We're more interested in their whereabouts over the last few weeks. This van—" he pointed at the picture of the vehicle spotted near the leisure centre "—was spotted on CCTV at half past nine in the evening on Thursday the eighth of December, near the Middlesbury Sports and Leisure Centre. This is a local delivery van, I believe. Isn't it a bit unusual for it to be out so late at night?"

Carroway squirmed in his seat. With the blanket coverage in the local media of the recent murders, he had to recognise the date in question.

"This van," Warren continued, "was spotted up near the high street on Friday the second of December at about 6 p.m. Over an hour after the last pickup for the post boxes in that area. Is that normal?"

Carroway looked like a rabbit caught in the headlights. Suddenly, he got up, crossed the office and closed the door to the anteroom. Sitting back down, he took a deep breath.

"If I tell you something, can I rely on your discretion? This could very well cost me my job."

"I can't promise anything, particularly if any laws have been broken. However, we are not in the habit of causing trouble unnecessarily," replied Warren cautiously.

Carroway sighed and massaged his temples; his face had turned a pale, sickly colour.

"I always knew this would happen," he mumbled to himself.

Pointing out of the window and into the garage, he gestured to the various vehicles parked in there.

"Middlesbury is the regional depot for the local area. As such, we maintain the various vehicles that service the area. As you can probably imagine, demand for deliveries fluctuates throughout the year and the volume of letters being delivered each year is reducing all the time. So it isn't unusual for many of our vehicles to remain unused at any one time. We have nine red delivery vans in total. At peak demand, immediately before Christmas with very bad weather, when we wouldn't have the bicycles out, we need up to eight on the road at any one time, plus a spare."

Warren had an inkling of where this was going, but said nothing, letting the man continue. He did so reluctantly. The look on his face was one of a man clearly signing his own P45 and resignation letter.

"Posties don't earn very much and the overtime isn't what it used to be. Some of the lads do a bit of business on the side to help ends meet, you know, a bit of building work on the weekend, a bit of kitchen-fitting. A couple of the guys have kids at uni and they help them move house at the beginning of term. They don't do enough to justify buying a van and it costs a fortune to hire one, so I help them out."

He started speaking quickly, trying to justify his actions. "It's not like it costs the Royal Mail or does any harm. They fill up the tank before they return it and it's not as if they're using it for anything it wasn't designed for — what's the difference between sacks of letters and parcels and sacks of builder's sand or a flat-pack fitted kitchen?"

"And, presumably, you take a small commission for your trouble?"

Carroway blushed. "Yeah, a few quid."

"So how does the system work, then?" asked Tony Sutton.

"Well, it's pretty much under the radar, as you can imagine, just a few trusted lads. The keys to all of the vehicles are kept in that lock-cabinet there—" he nodded to an open gun-metal key cabinet attached to the wall "—but the key to open it is in the bottom of this pencil pot. If one of them wants to borrow a van, they pop in when it's quiet — and help themselves. They usually stick a few quid in the honesty jar in the desk drawer."

Tony Sutton smirked at the irony of an "honesty jar" under such circumstances, but said nothing.

"It's not a big deal and they know not to abuse the system. It's just helping out a few mates. It doesn't do any harm."

The whining tone in the man's voice was starting to grate on Warren's nerves.

"Either way, can you tell us who borrowed these vans on those dates?"

Carroway shook his head, helplessly. "Sorry, I don't keep records." He smiled humourlessly. "I'd be — what's that phrase? — 'hoisted by my own petard'. It's all done on trust."

Warren was starting to feel his patience wearing thin with this little creep.

"Then perhaps you could give me a list of those included in your little circle of trust."

Carroway groaned quietly, but he clearly knew when he was defeated. Picking a pen out of the pot, he tore off a sheet of paper and, with a look of concentration, wrote down a list of eight names.

"I can't promise that there aren't one or two others that have heard about the system and joined up informally, but these are all the ones that I know about."

Warren and Sutton looked at the list, before looking at each other with a grim smile. Fourth name on the list — Alex Chalmers.

Warren and Tony Sutton stood outside the closed door of Carroway's office. The noise from the diesel engines and the workers shifting parcels easily drowned out their conversation. Through the window, they could see Carroway slumped at his desk.

"So it looks as though Alex Chalmers had access to a van whenever he needed one. Bloody clever set-up — who the hell takes any notice of a post van?" said Tony Sutton.

"And it supplied Darren Blackheath with a perfect alibi. He could drive into that alleyway in that ridiculous car of his and wait for Sally Evans calm as you please, then they stuck her in the back of the post van and drove her out," continued Warren.

"Reckon we'll have to get a warrant to impound the vans for forensics. At least we know why the victims all had that cardboard dust on their clothes. The inside of those vans are probably covered in it. Forensics will have a field day; even if they can't find any trace from the victims in the back, they'll be able to match soil and mud from the tyres to the dumping spots." Sutton was looking excited.

Warren was looking less so however, as he walked over to one of the vans parked by the side of the garage. Walking around the vehicle, he squatted down by the back wheel, looking under the wheel arch.

"Don't get your hopes up too much, Tony. Take a look at these wheels — what do you see?"

Sutton crouched down beside him. He saw it immediately.

"They've been cleaned. Bloody things look practically factory new."

Standing up, the two officers surveyed the bright red van. In the lights of the garage, it positively gleamed.

Walking back to the fleet manager's office, Warren entered without knocking.

"Those vans. How often do you clean them?"

"Three times a week. We have a lad who does them with a power hose to earn a bit of extra money."

"We'll need to speak to him."

Chapter 63

Speaking to Robbie Cartwright wasn't as straightforward as Warren had hoped. First of all they needed to wait until his father arrived as a responsible adult.

Pat Cartwright was a short, balding man in late middle age. Shaking both officers' hands, he sat in one of the visitors' seats in Carroway's office. The fleet manager was now bending over backwards to help the police, probably still hopeful he could avoid losing his job. However, after finding some extra chairs, he'd been sent to stand outside like a naughty schoolboy.

"We found out that Robbie would have Down's syndrome when Molly was six months pregnant. Fortunately, Robbie is on the milder end of the spectrum. He's physically healthy and he went to a mainstream comprehensive school. The thing about Robbie is he has a real work ethic. We've always been open with him about his condition and he's determined to overcome it. When he was at school, they used to send him home with extra reading and maths practice. When I finished his homework with him for the evening, he'd go upstairs and badger his older brother to carry on practising. He finished school with GCSE passes in English, Maths and Art and then went to the local tech college to do a workplace skills course."

"So how did he get the job at Royal Mail?" asked Tony Sutton.

Pat Cartwright smiled. "They've been bloody good to him here. He came here on work experience placement a couple of years. They started him off doing routine jobs, like cleaning the sorting office floor, sweeping up scrap paper and elastic bands. He also became the office tea boy, I suppose you could call him. He's always had a pretty good memory and he learnt how everybody in the general office likes their coffee and tea. He's got his older brother's charm and everyone loves him. When his course finished, they took him on. He's only on minimum wage, but he's earning his keep."

Cartwright looked sad, glancing out of the window at where his son was waiting, chatting to a couple of postal workers. "My wife and I realise that with all the medical advances these days, there's a good chance he'll outlive us. His brother and the rest of the family have always promised they'll look after him, but the more independent he is, the better. We hope in a few years' time for him to move into his own flat and to live independently, with a minimum of supervision. This job will help him do that."

"So what about the vehicle cleaning?"

"Well, they can only offer him so many hours a week working inside. He's always been mad about cars, absolutely obsessed with them. He used to love cleaning my car with me on a Sunday morning and his attention to detail is bordering on the fanatical. The old boy who used to wash the vans here left last year and so they gave the job to Robbie. He loves it. It really makes him proud. Mr Carroway tells him that the Royal Mail vans are like the Royal Mail posties — they're the bit the public see and a clean van is like an ironed uniform. He's really taken him under his wing."

The older man looked worried. "Look, I hope there isn't

a problem, officers. It's just that Royal Mail have been really good to Robbie, Mr Carroway in particular. I'd hate for him to lose this job. With the way the economy is at the moment, it's hard for anyone to get work these days, least of all somebody with Robbie's challenges."

Warren smiled reassuringly. "No problem at all, Mr Cartwright. We're just doing some routine enquiries and Robbie might be able to help us with a few questions. It won't have any effect on his job and, as I said when we first met, he is not in any trouble at all."

Reassured, Pat Cartwright stood up and called his son into the office.

Robbie Cartwright was a short man in his early twenties, with a full head of blond hair, which his father ruffled as he came in. He looked worried when Warren and Tony Sutton introduced themselves, but after reassurances from his father relaxed.

"So how many days a week do you clean the vans here, Robbie?" asked Warren.

"Three times, Mr Jones. Tuesday evenings, Thursdays and Saturdays. I use the big hosepipe."

"You do a pretty good job, Robbie. Whenever I see the vans they are always gleaming and clean. We should get you to come and clean some of our police cars."

The young man smiled shyly.

"Do the vans get very dirty on their runs?" asked Tony Sutton.

"Sometimes. Especially if it's been raining. They splash through dirty puddles and I have to clean underneath them. Mr Carroway says it's really important to do that in winter because the salt on the roads can make them rust. You should make sure you clean your car regularly as well, or it might get rusty," he advised.

"Thank you, I'll have to remember that," said Warren seriously.

"Thinking back, have any of the vans come back unusually dirty? Perhaps with more mud than normal. Maybe the wheels were very covered in mud?"

Robbie thought for a moment, then looked at his feet.

His father frowned, clearly recognising the change in his demeanour.

"Robbie, answer the question."

"Sometimes they come back more muddy than normal. The wheels and the bits above the wheel are all covered," he mumbled, still not looking up.

"What aren't you telling us, Robbie?" asked his father. "Remember these are policemen. They need your help."

"Sometimes they come back really dirty. The man driving them told me to make sure I cleaned them extra well, especially the wheels, and gave me a ten-pound note to do a really good job."

"Robbie!" His father sounded shocked. "It's your job to clean the vans. You shouldn't be taking money off someone just to do it properly."

The young man stared morosely at his feet. "Sorry," he mumbled.

"We'll talk about this when we get home," his father admonished.

Warren and Tony Sutton exchanged glances.

"Robbie, can you remember when this happened?"

Robbie shook his head, still not meeting anybody's gaze. "About a week ago. And before Christmas."

"Can you remember who it was that asked you?"

"Don't know his name. I see him around sometimes."

"Do you think you'd recognise him if you saw him again?"

Robbie nodded his head, finally looking up.

"Are you going to arrest me?"

Warren shook his head, trying hard not to smile. "No, you haven't done anything illegal. But you should be careful taking money off strangers. They might be up to no good and get you into trouble as well."

"Listen to the man," said his father reprovingly. "I don't want to hear about you taking money off people and getting yourself locked up for helping them commit a crime."

Suitably chastened, the young man nodded.

Rising to his feet, Warren stepped outside the office where Angus Carroway stood waiting.

"Do you think it would be possible to have a printout with photos of all the members of staff that work here?"

Carroway thought for a moment. "It should be possible. Andrea, my assistant, has access to personnel records. I'll see if she can help."

It took only a few minutes for Andrea, the young woman in the adjoining office, to access the list of employees and send their headshots to the colour printer. There were several sheets, each containing twenty photos in a four-by-five grid.

Leafing through them, Warren verified that Alex Chalmers' photograph was amongst them. Placing the sheets in front of Robbie, he told the young man to take his time. After going through the sheets three times, the young man's answer remained the same.

The man who paid him was not on the list.

Chapter 64

Back at the station, there was more news awaiting them. A team of door-knockers had revisited houses close to where both Gemma Allen and Saskia Walker had disappeared and when prompted at least a couple of witnesses at each location had recalled a Royal Mail postal van parked nearby. None of them had thought to mention it when questioned the first time, confirming how easily overlooked the vans were.

Warren and Tony Sutton arranged a briefing with Superintendent John Grayson to discuss their progress and their next steps.

"It's a damn shame that Robbie Cartwright couldn't identify who slipped him that tenner. Maybe he can do it in a line-up. Those photos were pretty old and Alex Chalmers has a completely different haircut now," said Warren.

"Nevertheless, there's been some good work here. Now you just need to work out how this damned Richard Cameron fits into all of this. What's your next step?"

"We're drafting a search warrant for those Royal Mail vans as we speak; we'll get Forensics to give them a good going-over. Hopefully Robbie wasn't quite as thorough with the hosepipe as he could have been. We don't have a registration number for the vans seen near Gemma Allen or Saskia Walker, so we're going to have to impound the whole fleet."

Grayson winced. The Royal Mail were not going to be happy about having their entire fleet of delivery vans impounded and no doubt he'd get pressure from above to resolve it quickly. Thank God it wasn't the week before Christmas...

"We're also about to bring in Darren Blackheath and Alex Chalmers for questioning. We may even be able to arrest and charge them. The main thing is to try and get them to give up Richard Cameron to us."

Grayson frowned slightly. "I agree that Alex Chalmers is a definite; it's too much of a coincidence that these Royal Mail vans have been seen in the area of both attacks. However, this Darren Blackheath is a bit more of a stretch. He seems to be part of this largely through circumstance." He raised one hand, marking off each point with a finger. "He happens to know Alex Chalmers and presumably Carolyn Patterson; we can't prove his alibi at the time of the attack; he has a dropped charge of rape and he is the boyfriend of the first murder victim. The CPS will never let us charge him on that basis."

"I see what you are saying, but I still think it's enough to bring him in for questioning and to hold him for a period of time if necessary. It's vital that we do so if we are bringing in Alex Chalmers, because if we leave Darren Blackheath free he may well contact Richard Cameron and tip him off. We can't risk that."

After a few moments' consideration, Grayson nodded his agreement. "OK, we'll do it your way. Bring them in and as soon as the warrants are prepared I'll arrange for them to be signed and then somebody can go and give the Royal Mail the good news."

Leaving Grayson's office, Sutton muttered to Warren, "I notice we're doing it 'your way' again. I wonder who will carry the can for this if we're wrong and who will take the credit if we're right?"

"Yeah, well, such is life, Tony. Look on the bright side though. That little weasel Angus Carroway is going to have some explaining to do when his bosses at the Royal Mail want to know why all of their delivery vans are impounded in Welwyn."

* * *

Arresting the two suspects was a simple and smooth affair. Alex Chalmers finished his shift at exactly 1 p.m., heading out of the sorting office into the biting wind. Pausing only to light a cigarette, he slipped his headphones in, hunched his shoulders against the snowflakes and started walking, seemingly oblivious to the world around him. He almost jumped out of his skin when Warren tapped him on the shoulder; flanked either side by two burly detective constables on loan from Welwyn. His only protest as he clambered into the back of the unmarked Audi was that he had missed his morning smoke break and they wouldn't let him finish his cigarette in the car.

Darren Blackheath was manhandling a new tyre onto an old Ford when Tony Sutton appeared at his side. He placed the tyre down, making no move towards any of the dangerous-looking tools within arm's reach, and followed the three officers to their car. The young man looked tired and worn-down. Sutton couldn't tell if he was a guilty man resigned to his fate or an innocent man still too grief-stricken to care.

Both men were taken to Middlesbury CID, but processed separately and installed in interview suites at opposite ends of the building. Warren was confident that neither man knew that the other was present.

As soon as Alex Chalmers was safely tucked away, Warren contacted Karen Hardwick. Wishing her luck, he told her to proceed with the next stage.

Four miles away, Karen Hardwick rang the bell of the shabby house, an officer from the domestic violence unit by her side. After a few moments the door opened. Katie Oliver was even bigger than before; it couldn't be long before she gave birth. Today, no amount of make-up could conceal the split lip.

"Hello, Katie, do you mind if we come in? It's important." The young woman nodded silently.

Less than thirty minutes later, Karen Hardwick was on the street again, mobile phone pressed to her ear. Inside, her colleague from the domestic violence unit was helping Katie Oliver pack a suitcase.

"Good news, guv. Katie Oliver confirms it. Alex Chalmers has no alibi for the dates in question — apparently he's out who knows where several nights a week and she can't account for his whereabouts. And if you need another reason to hold him, you can finally charge the bastard with assault and ABH."

Chapter 65

Alex Chalmers was in a combative mood by the time Warren and Tony Sutton joined him in the interview room.

"What's this crap all about? I've done nothing wrong. You've got nothing on me."

Tony Sutton ignored his bluster.

"Where were you 9.30 p.m. on Thursday eighth December when Carolyn Patterson went missing on her way home from the Middlesbury Sports and Leisure Centre?"

"I already told you before. I was having a night in with my missus. Ask her." He folded his arms triumphantly; however, there was a slight tightening of his eyes.

Sutton ignored him. "What about 6 p.m. or thereabouts on Friday second December?"

"Again, I told you. I was with the missus. In case you ain't noticed, she's more than eight months pregnant. Fit to burst any minute. In fact, the sooner you hurry this along, the better. I'd hate to miss the birth." He smirked, but his cockiness was forced. The man was clearly worried about something.

"How about Saturday seventeenth December? Or a week later, Friday the twenty-third?"

"I don't know. I'll have to check my social calendar."

Warren leant forward. "We know that you weren't with your girlfriend, Mr Chalmers. I suggest you have another think."

Chalmers stood up abruptly. "This is bullshit. You haven't got anything on me. You said yourself, I'm not under arrest, I'm just 'helping you with enquiries' — well, I've decided to stop helping." He addressed this last statement directly to the PACE recorder sitting on the table, then raised his middle finger to the ceiling, presumably towards whatever non-existent video-camera he thought was recording the session for posterity.

"I'm off home to look after my pregnant girlfriend."

"Sit down, Chalmers. We're not done yet."

Warren's voice was low, barely raised, but it had the desired effect. Chalmers paused on the way to the door.

"She won't be there." He pointed silently at his lip.

Chalmers got the reference immediately. He paused. Warren could almost see the thoughts whirling around the man's mind. With no other way out, he resorted to his favourite strategy. A sneer appeared on his lips.

"Oh, that's what this is all about? A little revenge from Katie." The man was clearly fabricating on the fly. Warren almost wished there were a camera in the room; Chalmers clearly had no idea how much his innermost thoughts were reflected in his face.

"Well, that's no good, it's my word against hers. And this—" he pointed towards his lip "—was self-defence." His voice turned whiny. "You know what pregnant women are like. They're all full of hormones and shit. They fly off the handle at the smallest thing. She was threatening me with a knife, one of the big ones from the kitchen. I didn't want to hurt her, but we wrestled and she caught her face on the cupboard door." He smiled broadly, trying to look magnanimous. "Anyway I didn't want any fuss and

I forgive her, so I decided not to call the police. She doesn't need the stress, what with the baby and all that.

"She's clearly still upset. She's trying to cause trouble. I'm a good father. I'm in every night looking after her, so she's my alibi and she knows that. Like I said, it's her word against mine and no jury in the land will convict me on that. I had nothing to do with those girls' deaths. You're just fishing cause of some bullshit allegations from years ago. You ain't got nothing else, or you'd have arrested me and charged me."

He sat back, his face smug.

Warren looked at Sutton, who sighed theatrically, his expression clearly saying, "Where do we begin?"

Warren started. "You don't know much about juries. Let me paint you a picture. This is what they will see. Photographs of a heavily pregnant young woman with bruises on her arms, and her chin and a split lip. They will then see her boyfriend, a big tattooed thug. The neighbours have already called the police once, claiming that you were beating her. We'll apply to the court to have permission to submit the previous allegations as evidence of bad character and, of course, we'll get Carolyn Patterson's mum on the stand to give evidence regarding the bruises that she saw.

"They won't see a young woman trying to get revenge by causing trouble for her boyfriend. Oh, no. What they'll see is a brave young woman who was terrorised by her violent boyfriend into giving him a false alibi, who finally plucked up the courage to do the right thing and admit she was lying."

Warren leant back in his chair. "Tell us what you were doing on those nights or we'll charge you and you can take your chances with a jury."

Chalmers stared at them, trying to maintain a poker face, but his darting eyes and the beads of sweat gave him away. Finally, he came to a decision.

"It's bullshit. If that's all you've got, then screw you. I wasn't doing anything on those nights and you can't prove anything. If you have nothing except me not having an alibi, then charge me and we'll see what the court says."

He leant back, arms folded. It was his last desperate ploy and on the face of it a good one. A lack of alibi was circumstantial at best and, even with his past history as an abuser, the principle of "no smoke without fire" wasn't yet enough to convict a man in an English court of law.

Tony Sutton glanced over at Warren, who nodded slightly.

"You have a good job at the post office, yes?"

The change in direction threw Chalmers off balance. "Yeah, it's OK, I suppose. A bit crap in weather like this," he tried to joke.

Sutton smiled, but he didn't look amused.

"Well, I suppose that when the weather gets really bad and you have loads of parcels, they let you put away the bicycles."

"Yeah, of course."

"What would you say if I told you that every time one of those young women disappeared, a Royal Mail postal delivery van was spotted in the area at the same time?"

Chalmers shrugged, the confusion written clearly across his face.

Warren took over. "Tell me about your little agreement with Angus Carroway and the keys to the delivery vans. He tells us you've borrowed a van quite a few times."

Chalmers squirmed in his seat. Warren could see the man trying to work out the implications of what Warren had just accused him of. Not wanting to give him any time to fabricate an answer, he pressed on.

"Tell me, how did you and Darren Blackheath hook up with Richard Cameron?"

It was like a slap across Chalmers' face. His eyes widened in horror as he clearly recognised the name of the man the papers had dubbed the "Middlesbury Monster".

"Oh, no. No way."

Warren and Tony Sutton watched in fascination as the man in front of them crumbled. All of his cockiness disappeared and he seemed to shrink in on himself.

"OK," he croaked, "I admit, the alibis aren't real. I'll tell you where I was on those nights, but it isn't what you think."

* * *

Thirty minutes later, Tony Sutton and Warren Jones emerged from the interview room. The two men had a lot of information to process. Warren's head was spinning and he couldn't decide what to believe and what it meant. A few moments later a beaten and defeated Alex Chalmers emerged, held firmly by the station's custody sergeant.

"You remember that bit at the beginning where I said that he had the right to a lawyer and that he didn't have to answer anything?" Warren asked. Sutton nodded. "Silly bastard should have listened."

Chapter 66

It was time for another brainstorming session as Warren shared the day's developments so far.

"So basically, Alex Chalmers has been out dealing in stolen goods and using the postal delivery vans to move large items around." Karen Hardwick sounded incredulous.

"That's what he claims. He admitted it when he thought we were going to charge him with the murders. However, there's a fly in the ointment. He swears blind that whilst he was not in the house on the nights of the murders, he hadn't borrowed a van. In fact, he made the exact same point that we did — why would a postal delivery van be out and about at half-nine at night? He reckons he only borrowed them in the afternoon after he finished his shift." Warren raised his palms in surrender; he knew it was a big coincidence.

"So, assuming that we believe him, the van was being driven by somebody else those nights?" asked Gary Hastings. "And what about Darren Blackheath?"

"We haven't questioned him yet — he's still cooling his heels downstairs. Chalmers admits that they are friends but swears that Blackheath has nothing to do with his fencing operation."

"Could Blackheath have got access to a delivery van through him?"

"Anything's possible, but Chalmers claims not. He also claims not to have any knowledge of Richard Cameron."

"Although I don't think that's much of a surprise," Sutton grumbled.

"Right, we need to check out both men's stories. Let's see if we can find somebody willing to vouch for Chalmers on the nights in question. I'll leave it to you, Tony, to figure out how to get hardened thieves to incriminate themselves by admitting they were fencing stolen goods with Alex Chalmers on the nights in question."

"Thanks, guv," grumbled Tony Sutton.

"We should also take a look at the rest of the names in Carroway's motor pool and see if any more of them have form or any links to Richard Cameron. And check the CCTV at the depot — maybe there's footage of whoever borrowed the van.

"In the meantime, let's look at this from another angle. I can't believe it's a coincidence that a post van was seen at every scene. What does that mean? How can that be linked to Richard Cameron? Take a few minutes, have a coffee and get your imaginations going, everybody."

As everybody filed out of the room, Warren closed his eyes briefly, half listening to the babble of conversations. He tuned them out, trusting his team to thrash their way through any suggestions, testing them for plausibility before bringing them to him.

"I'll say one thing, Chief, this is definitely a birthday you'll remember." Tony Sutton patted his boss' back in sympathy.

Warren chuckled, despite himself. "Yeah, when people ask me how I spent my thirty-fifth birthday, I'll be able to tell them I spent it hunting a serial killer in an office full of Christmas decorations as the snow came down outside."

Sutton snorted. "Thirty-five, my arse. We're detectives, no point trying to lie about your age." He looked out of the window at the blustery blizzard. "Looks as if it's going to settle. It's a good job you've got that nice new coat."

"Yeah, Susan's sister sent it to me from the Alps, would you believe?"

"Bloody hell. Got a few bob, have they? What was the postage like?"

"Too much, you don't want to know…" Warren's voice trailed off. Sutton opened his mouth, but closed it again immediately as Warren raised his hand.

Sometimes it just struck you. Like a puzzle with all the pieces when the final pattern suddenly started to become clear. Warren was reminded of the dream he'd had the night that Melanie Clearwater was attacked. A half-dozen pieces seemed ready to click into place and for a moment Warren was paralysed with indecision. What to do first? Leaping to his feet, he pulled out his mobile, hurrying into the main office and at the same time calling over his shoulder to Tony Sutton.

"We've been barking up the wrong tree. Completely. We've been so obsessed with finding a link between Blackheath, Chalmers and Cameron and tying them to their victims that we've completely missed what's under our nose."

* * *

Warren startled Gary Hastings, who was deep in conversation with DS Kent.

"Gary, do you have any enhanced images of the team tops that the football team were wearing?"

"Nothing enhanced, but some of them are clearer than others." Opening a folder on his PC revealed a series of thumbnail images from the leisure centre's CCTV footage.

"See if you can work out what the logo is on their left chest. Bring up the best image you have on the screen."

As Gary Hastings complied Warren dialled Susan on her mobile phone. Just as he'd hoped, his wife was at home. Unfortunately, she was busy preparing Warren his favourite meal — a meal that he had forgotten all about. Her voice was decidedly chilly by the time Warren admitted that he couldn't promise to be home at a decent hour. "Channelling the spirit of Bernice" was how Warren privately thought of it. Nevertheless, she agreed to his request.

Turning to DS Kent, Warren asked him to look through the interview files. He needed full confirmation of something that he half remembered, before he could put all of the pieces together.

"Got it — it's their team sponsor," said Gary Hastings, pointing out the logo. "But if you want a better image than that, it's splashed all over their website and Facebook page."

At that moment Warren's mobile beeped — a text message with an attached photo from Susan.

"There you are, sir — World Wide Parcel Logistics." A bright yellow logo, comprised of a stylised, wire-frame globe and a sweeping arrow with an envelope giving the impression of mail being rushed across the globe, all sitting upon a pedestal composed of the letters WWPL with a trademark sign.

Warren opened the photo message on his phone; the same logo was affixed to the parcel delivered to him just that morning. The parcel delivered to him by Parcelforce — the Royal Mail's parcel delivery and courier service.

Without being asked, Gary Hastings opened a new webpage, following the link from the Middlesbury Football Club's homepage. Clicking on 'About', he scanned the page.

"World Wide Parcel Logistics is a European-based company, specialising in the delivery of mail and packages of all sizes throughout the European Union and beyond. The majority shareholder is Royal Mail, which has delivered WWPL mail in the UK via its existing Parcelforce delivery network since 2008."

"Click on the link marked 'Depot Finder'," instructed Warren, his heart pounding.

Hastings typed CID's postcode into the pop-up box.

Red push-pins denoted the locations of WWPL depots across a map of the East of England. Centre of the map, less than one mile from CID headquarters, was the nearest WWPL depot: based at the Royal Mail sorting office.

DS Kent appeared at Warren's elbow, a piece of paper in his hand. "Good memory, sir. Cameron's son, Michael Stockley, works for a logistics firm. Care to guess which one?"

"WWPL?"

"Bingo."

Chapter 67

Warren instructed Tony Sutton to round everybody up, Detective Superintendent Grayson included, in the briefing room in ten minutes. He wanted everybody to examine his theory before they started making arrests. In the meantime, Warren phoned Yvonne Fairweather.

"Constable, are you with Melanie Clearwater?"

"No, I'm in Stevenage."

Warren swore, then apologised.

"However, one of my colleagues was due to meet her this afternoon, now that they've reopened the ward. She might still be at the hospital."

"Is there any way you can send some pictures over for Mel to look at, to see if she recognises them?"

"Sure, if you text them to me, I'll forward them on."

It seemed to take an age for Warren's handset to upload two good quality images over the mobile network. As it did so, he paced his office. If his hunch with the photos was right then it added yet another layer of complexity to the story. There was great potential here for a world-class screw-up, he realised, with all of their hard work destroyed through carelessness. The killer had expertly covered his tracks. Most of the evidence was still circumstantial; they had to make certain that everything was in place before they made their arrest.

Finally, Warren's phone rang; he didn't recognise the number. "DCI Jones?"

"Speaking."

"It's Fatma Mehmet from the vulnerable persons unit." She sounded irritated. "I wish you'd given me some more warning before that stunt you just pulled."

Warren's breath caught in his throat. "Did she recognise either of them?"

Mehmet snorted. "You could say that. The poor girl's beside herself. She recognised them both."

* * *

The team were back in the briefing room, yet again.

"So basically, it's been Michael Stockley helping his father all along?" summarised Karen Hardwick.

"No, I don't think so. I don't think Richard Cameron has anything to do with it. Melanie Clearwater just confirmed the last piece in the puzzle. A few days before she was beaten up and left for dead, Michael Stockley picked her up and took her to a bed and breakfast where she had sex with an older man she has identified as Richard Cameron. Looking at the date, it was probably his idea of a birthday treat for the old man. Stockley was apparently obsessed that his father reached climax, even going so far as to check the waste bin for a used condom. What I think happened then was that he took the condom and stored it in a refrigerator, then used it to plant his father's semen at the scene of his next rapes and murders. That would explain why the technician spotted such a big drop in sperm motility. They can only survive for a short time without being properly stored and frozen."

"So where's his father in all of this?" asked Gary Hastings.

"My money's on dead. I reckon if we take the sniffer dogs out to one of their far fields we'll find evidence of a freshly dug hole. Richard Cameron would provide a convenient scapegoat for all of this, letting Stockley carry on raping whilst we chase after the ghost of his father."

"So when do we bring him in?"

"Any moment now. We're preparing the warrants as we speak and the Crown Prosecution Service is going over our evidence before we arrest. We can't afford for him to go free on a technicality. Who knows what he might do?

"DI Sutton is over at the depot leading the search of his office; Stockley finished work a few hours ago. He has all sorts of equipment that he needs for the attacks, yet we haven't found a trace of it at the farmhouse. He must be storing it somewhere. Tony found a locker key taped to the bottom of a drawer in his desk and he's checking all of the staff lockers to see which one the key fits."

Gary Hastings smirked slightly, but restrained himself from saying anything.

Warren's phone rang and he glanced at the caller ID. "That's him now. Tony, what have you found?"

Warren's face became grimmer and grimmer as the call went on. Eventually he told Sutton to return to the station, before hanging up.

"He's identified the locker, but it's empty. Worse than that, he says that the vehicle forensics team down at the postal depot have been discreetly bringing in the delivery vans and impounding them as they finished their morning runs. They're missing one. It looks as if somebody in Angus Carroway's unofficial motor pool has helped themselves. If he has taken his rape kit and he has got himself a post van I think we have to assume he's getting ready to strike again."

* * *

The atmosphere in the CID room was positively crackling, a new sense of urgency permeating the room.

As yet, there were no missing person reports, but that meant nothing, Warren knew. At this very moment, Michael Stockley could be murdering and raping another innocent young woman.

"Traffic reports that all units are on the lookout for Royal Mail delivery vans and that they are using automated number plate recognition, but coverage is patchy. If he sticks to the back roads as he did before we'll never pick him up."

Warren felt helpless, his mind whirring. How could they stop the man? He could always issue a warning to the press but that would take some hours before it made it onto the bulletins. Frustration burned at him. He wanted to stand on top of the building with a megaphone and tell all young women to lock themselves inside then ask the whole world to be on the lookout for a stolen postal van.

The look on Tony Sutton's face as he entered the office broadcast the same frustration. He shook his wet hair vigorously. "It's really coming down out there, and starting to settle. Maybe the snow will stop him?"

"Or maybe the snow will help him cover his tracks," countered Warren, glumly.

DS Kent poked his head around his office door.

"Sir, a young woman, blonde hair, has been reported missing."

Warren's stomach lurched. Five long strides and he had the headset pressed against his ear. As he listened to the details the sickness in his gut grew.

"The report's a fresh one. She's probably been gone less than thirty minutes," he broadcast to the office. "A twenty-four-year-old office worker, Jemima Duer. She normally walks to the bus stop at five-thirty each day and catches it to her flat, but her dad has been picking her up for the past few days. She waits for him at the corner of Corporation Street and the high street. He arrived a few minutes late today and she wasn't there. Her phone's going through to voicemail and her co-workers claim she left at the usual time."

"I'll get onto traffic, see what cameras we've got there," said DS Richardson.

"Even if we get images of him picking her up, they're going to be minutes old," cautioned Sutton. "If we're lucky they'll show which direction he's going, but once the van's outside the town boundary, we'll be lucky if a patrol car picks them up by chance."

"We need to get smart, try and work out where he's heading."

Warren strode over to a massive laminated paper map of Middlesbury and the surrounding villages stuck to the briefing-room wall. Taking a whiteboard marker, he put a cross on the point where Corporation Street and the high street met.

"There are no CCTV cameras overlooking where she catches the bus or was waiting for her old man to pick her up," Margaret Richardson called across the room, "but one on the junction of the Cambridge road and the high street has what appears to be a Royal Mail delivery van at 17:36 hours."

Tony Sutton located the junction and drew a large arrow angled up the road, heading roughly north. He glanced at his watch. "That was twelve minutes ago, guv. He's got a big lead."

"Well, let's not let him extend it too much. If he follows past form he'll be wanting somewhere secluded and woody to do what he needs to do, then dump her. That means he has to be travelling somewhere north. Keep trying to track him. I'm going to call in the cavalry."

The cavalry in question was Hertfordshire and Bedfordshire's Mobile Armed Response Unit. Within moments of Warren's call, they were en route, racing north from their base at Welwyn Garden City. It would take them several minutes to reach Middlesbury. During that time, Warren knew that he had to come up with some better directions for them.

"We've got it travelling north on the A506, six minutes ago," sang out Margaret Richardson from her workstation. "Good news is, he's travelling well within the speed limit. Conditions are poor and I guess he doesn't want to risk attracting attention or having an accident."

"That means he's heading towards Cambridge. There are loads of potential dumping spots on the way." Tony Sutton's local knowledge was far superior to Warren's so he let his deputy wield the pen on the large map.

"We're still trailing behind him. He could be going anywhere up there. Armed Response have no chance. There must be some way that we can track him."

"Sir, that's it!" yelled Gary Hastings, almost falling off his chair in excitement. "It's a Royal Mail delivery van. They must have anti-theft and tracking devices, like GPS."

"Brilliant, Gary. Time for Angus Carroway to redeem himself," said Warren, snatching up his phone.

It was the work of seconds to call the Royal Mail's sorting office. Where they were met with nothing but voicemail.

"Shit! They've finished for the day."

Warren's heart sank.

"Hang on, those articulated lorries run all through the night," said Tony Sutton. "I'll bet they have tracking. It'd be crazy if they used a different system for the vans."

Gary Hastings was already on the Internet, searching for one of the Royal Mail's central depots. "Try this number, sir. It's one of their main hubs and this number should be working until midnight."

This time, the call went through. It took a few seconds for the bemused operator at the other end of the line to understand what he was asking for, but then he was transferred to the regional logistics manager, Simon Bourne.

"Yes, all of our vehicles are GPS tracked, using the same system. If you give me the licence plate number of the van you want, I'll be able to pinpoint it in a few seconds."

Those few seconds seemed more like minutes, before Bourne triumphantly announced a fix.

"OK, I have the van travelling at an average speed of thirty-eight miles per hour north-westerly on the A506. Its current co-ordinates place it three point seven miles north of junction twelve."

"That's brilliant, Simon. Can we get you to hold on the line, whilst we direct the response units in?"

"Absolutely, I'm not going anywhere." Suddenly finding himself assisting in a police car chase had clearly livened up the late shift.

Margaret Richardson had now moved her laptop over to the map wall and was maintaining an open channel with Welwyn, relaying GPS information from Simon Bourne to central Control.

Suddenly, her radio crackled with a message from Control.

"Bad news. A lorry has jackknifed on the A1 just south of the Middlesbury exit, blocking all north-bound carriageways. The armed response units are snarled up in the traffic. They are going to be delayed by at least ten minutes."

Warren swore.

"Get Essex on the phone, see if they can spare anyone." Turning back to the open speaker phone to Bourne. "Where's the van?"

"Still heading north, same speed."

"Tony, where do you think is the most likely spot?"

Sutton puffed his cheeks out. "Christ…" he muttered under his breath. He stared at the map for a few more seconds, before drawing a big cross.

"Barrington Woods. It's the first wooded area that they come to. It's secluded enough for what he wants to do, especially in this weather, but popular with walkers. She'll be found in a couple of days, which seems to be what he's aiming for. Keep blaming the old man."

"Sir, Essex on the line, they're sending an armed response unit, but it's in the far east of the county. It's going to take some time in the traffic."

"How long until he gets to Barrington Woods, Tony?"

Sutton looked at the map. "At his current speed, he's probably about ten minutes from the edge of the woods. Presumably he will then have to travel some distance into the forest, either by car or on foot. We need to be there within the next twenty minutes if we want to stop anything happening to her."

Warren noted his use of the word, "we". His mind was working in the same direction as Warren's. It was a breach of protocol and he'd have a lot of explaining to do if things went wrong. But then he'd have a lot of explaining to do to his conscience if another young woman was killed when he might have been able to stop it. He made his mind up.

"Grab your coat, Tony. Let's see how good that advanced driver's course was that we paid for you to go on."

Chapter 68

Sutton opted to sign out the station's unmarked Audi. The car was powerful, with four-wheel drive, ideal for the weather conditions. Just as important, Sutton drove a similar model Audi himself and felt comfortable behind the car's wheel.

By now the snow was coming thick and fast, a thin, wet layer already settling on the road. The conditions would only get worse as they left the town — something Susan had called the Urban Heat Island effect when Warren had commented on it one day.

Warren was still wrestling with his seat belt when Sutton exited the station's car park, the car's wheels spinning slightly in the snow before the traction control kicked in. Warren hit the button that activated the car's two-tone siren and blue flashing lights hidden behind the front grill. They'd decide if such a noisy arrival was appropriate when they were closer to their destination. For the time being, Warren just wanted everyone out of the way.

He held on tight to the door handle as Sutton jumped a set of red traffic lights. Sutton's faith in the power of blues and twos to get Joe Public to shift out of the way and not do something silly was a lot greater than his, Warren noted. Christ, he hated high-speed pursuit driving.

After a few more red lights and a brief jaunt the wrong way

down a one-way street at forty miles per hour, they joined the A506.

In the passenger seat, an increasingly pale Warren juggled his mobile phone, the car's radio and a road atlas. If there was one thing he hated more than high-speed driving it was reading in a moving vehicle. But his personal discomfort was a trivial concern. He just prayed he wasn't sick — even if he could bribe Tony Sutton to keep quiet, there was an open radio-link.

Warren's stomach lurched as Sutton swerved into the oncoming lane to overtake a line of more sedately moving cars. The car's powerful engine roared as Sutton down-shifted to squeeze more acceleration out of it. The needle flicked past eighty miles per hour. Up ahead the massive headlights of a lorry loomed increasingly large. The line of traffic on their left-hand-side stretched endlessly ahead of them.

The lorry's air horn blared. In response, Sutton reached over and toggled the lights and siren. Warren's fist tightened on his seat belt. "Um, Tony..." he started.

"I'm on it, guv," he muttered as he racing-changed up to fifth gear. The glare of the lorry's headlamps now filled the windscreen, angling downward as the driver started to apply his brakes, shifting the huge vehicle's centre of gravity forward. That was all they needed, worried Warren — another jackknifed lorry.

At the last possible second, the line of traffic to the left came to an end and Sutton threw the Audi into the newly opened gap. The car fish-tailed slightly, buffeted by the close passage of the lorry, its four-wheel drive struggling to grip the slick surface.

Warren let out a breath as the car righted itself.

"Sorry, guv. I'm used to driving on my own, forgot to take into account the extra weight."

Warren just nodded, not quite trusting himself to comment.

The radio crackled. "Bourne says he's turning left off the A506 onto the B1198 a single-lane side road that should lead him alongside Barrington Woods. There is a dirt track about a mile and a quarter past the turn-off, which leads into the woods proper. The smart money is on him turning up there."

"Roger that," replied Warren. "We are approximately four minutes from the turn-off, making good progress."

"Three and a half minutes," corrected Sutton.

"Three and a half minutes." *Assuming we aren't killed first*, he added silently.

By now the traffic was thinning out and Sutton could race along the carriageway as fast as he wished without having to perform any more death-defying overtaking manoeuvres.

Finally, the exit for the B1198 and Barrington Woods loomed up ahead. Sutton down-shifted and left the main road at speed.

The radio crackled into life again. "Sir. We have a problem. The van has not, repeat not, turned up the dirt track. He's still on the side road, travelling at thirty miles per hour. We're trying to work out where he is heading."

Forcing his discomfort to one side, Warren flicked on the map light, locating both cars on the road map on his lap. Immediately, he could see an even bigger problem.

"He's travelling almost due west. That means he is travelling away from both our armed response unit and Essex's."

"We're already on that, Sir. Detective Superintendent Grayson has contacted Cambridgeshire. They're sending a unit now, although it's questionable how much sooner they'll make it."

They now had armed response units from three counties involved in the chase. We'd better have something to show for it at the end of this or he'd be paying the deployment bill out of his pension pot, thought Warren ruefully.

"OK, next best guess for a dumping spot is Livingstone Forest." Gary Hastings took over the radio.

Warren located it.

"There is a turn-off three miles from where he is now, assuming he stays on the same road. Dirt track, little more than an access road by the looks of things."

Warren could just about make out the faint brown marking in the dim glow of the overhead map-light. The whole area seemed to be tree-covered with a few small clearings, bisected by a river, although Warren had no idea how accurate or up to date the map was.

He opened the Google maps app on his smartphone. No 3G signal. He cursed.

"Good try, boss. But don't worry, if we keep at this speed and he doesn't go any quicker, we'll intercept him about thirty seconds after he makes the turn off."

Then they'd just need to decide what the hell they were going to do against a man with a shotgun, worried Warren. He'd give anything for a bulletproof vest right now. In fact, if he was being absolutely honest, he'd give anything for the comfort of his duvet, safely pulled over his head...

Both men saw the pair of eyes at the same moment, Warren stamping on an imaginary brake pedal even as Sutton cursed mightily and stood hard on the Audi's brakes.

Warren had once asked Susan if she knew why deer and other animals chose to stand in the middle of the road and simply stare at an oncoming car, rather than get out of the way. She'd put it to her students as an informal homework. The most convincing answer came from Francis in year seven who said it was because cars don't have visible limbs and the deer's brain is programmed to recognise typical predator shapes. Its hard-wired instincts simply haven't evolved to deal with two glowing lights heading towards it. Let alone two glowing lights flanking blue flashing lights emitting a piercing, whooping noise.

This nugget of knowledge was absolutely no use to the two men as the deer loomed nearer. The creature wasn't the biggest deer Tony Sutton had seen, but he knew that it was more than big enough to write off their car if they hit it. If its huge head and antlers penetrated the windscreen it could very well decapitate them both.

In desperation he yanked the wheel to the right; it spun easily through his hands, confirming that the car had lost its traction on the icy road. He felt the drumming beat of the car's anti-lock braking system rapidly disengaging then re-engaging as it fought to re-establish grip on the road.

The car slid sideways, beginning a slow pirouette. Warren's last thought before impact was of Susan, waiting patiently at home as she kept his birthday meal warm.

Chapter 69

"DCI Jones, come in, please. DI Sutton, what is your status?"

Gary Hastings fought down an increasing feeling of panic. The radio hissed. The last sound the team had heard was a violent series of curses, followed by a loud sliding noise then a deafening bang, before the radio went silent.

He turned to Karen Hardwick. "Get an ambulance to their last-known position."

Suddenly the static was interrupted by Warren's voice, shaky but calm. "We're OK. Repeat, we're OK. We're in a ditch, no injuries."

The whole team let out a breath of relief.

Gary turned to Karen. "Keep the ambulance en route anyway — we don't know what state Jemima Duer is in. But tell them to hold back until they get the go-ahead — we don't want them wandering into a live fire zone." He cursed himself for not having thought to order medical back-up before.

The deer had made its mind up at the last moment, leaping over a low hedge into the field beyond. The Audi had continued to spin, ending up on the wrong side of the road, sliding backwards. With a deafening crunch, it came to rest against a large tree. For a few seconds, the silence had been overwhelming as the engine stalled and the powerful jolt knocked the car's electrics offline, silencing the sirens and killing the radio.

"Sorry, guv," muttered Sutton, still dazed with shock.

Warren shook his head. "We're still in one piece, Tony. Are you fit to drive still?"

"Yeah, but I don't know if we're getting out of this ditch any time soon."

"See if you can get the engine back on and the power back," ordered Warren as he toggled the radio's on-off switch. It took three attempts to restart the engine, by which time the lights were back on and the radio was working.

Most of the warning lights on the dashboard remained off, so Sutton slipped the car into first gear and gently pressed the accelerator. Mud sprayed off the back wheels as the stranded car struggled to find grip in the muddy ditch.

Shifting the car into reverse, he depressed the accelerator again, before shifting back into first. The change in the car's position was enough for the front wheels to find purchase on the icy tarmac and with a loud sliding noise the car hauled itself back onto the road, the smell of burnt rubber permeating the car. The road was narrow and it took more than a three-point turn for Sutton to manoeuvre the car in the correct direction.

The radio burst into life again. "The van has stopped. Repeat, the van has stopped. About a quarter of a mile from the turn-off, in an open clearing. Cambridgeshire ARU report that they are still ten to twelve minutes out, with Essex about five minutes behind."

Warren looked at Tony; Jemima Duer's life was now measured in bare minutes. No words were necessary. Moving quickly, but cautiously, the Audi headed off again. Leaning over, Warren switched off the lights and sirens.

* * *

Jemima Duer, Jem to her friends, felt nauseous. The lurching of the vehicle as it bounced along what she guessed was a dirt track mingled with the sickly sweet smell of the rag around her throat.

Her last memory was of a blurred figure approaching her out of the shadows as she waited on the darkened corner for her lift home. She was busy updating her Facebook status on her phone and barely glanced up until she felt the strong arms wrap around her, smelt the solvent-soaked rag and the world around her faded away.

The front of her face still felt numb, but she could taste blood in her mouth. Running her tongue around her gums, she could feel the fragments of at least one broken tooth. Her brain was still fuzzy, but adrenaline was doing a good job of clearing the clouds that seemed to envelop her mind.

The van gave an even bigger jolt and she felt herself lifted bodily off the metal floor before crashing back down again. Her head thumped against the wheel arch. Was this why the rag was no longer tied to her face?

Moving her arms, she was amazed to find them unbound. Without pausing to question why her attacker hadn't taken the trouble to bind her more securely, she yanked the stinking cloth off her neck and tried to kneel. Another bounce from the van sent her sprawling on her back again. Taking deep cleansing breaths of the cold, fresh air, she felt her head clearing more, the sickness in her stomach slowly abating.

The van lurched to a halt, the rear briefly lit red by spillage from the brake lights. Cold fear clutched at her insides. She frantically looked around the back of the van for a weapon, something to defend herself with against the madman who had snatched her. Like everybody else in Middlesbury, she'd read the newspapers and followed the news bulletins and was under no illusions what was going to happen to her.

A big black kit bag lay beside her. Ripping the zip open, she rummaged inside. Packages of what appeared to be rubber gloves and a role of tape were of no use to her, but at the bottom of the bag she suddenly felt something long, and cold and metal. What was it? A tyre iron? Some sort of wrench? Pulling it out, she couldn't believe her luck. She wasn't a particularly religious woman, but if this wasn't a sign from God, she didn't know what was.

Turning to face the van's rear doors, she aimed the shotgun at what she guessed was head height, placed her fingers over the triggers and waited for the monster to come and get her.

* * *

Michael Stockley clambered out of the van, breathing the cold night air deeply. The snow was coming down heavily now and he was confident that in a few hours his tyre tracks would be completely obliterated. The ground was so frozen, he might not even need to pay the disabled kid to clean the van more thoroughly.

His heart pounded with excitement and he felt his engorged penis throb; the two Viagra he'd taken an hour before had kept him hard throughout the drive. Crunching through the snow, he yanked the rear doors open.

His step back was instinctive as he raised his arm and closed his eyes in a futile defence against the shotgun blast. There was a quiet click and a squeal of frustration. Stupid bitch hadn't disengaged the safety, he realised as he stepped forward, grabbing the shotgun's barrel, cold even through his gloves. The girl had fight, he'd give her that, he thought as he tried to yank the gun from her. She held on tight as they wrestled for control. The chloroform mask must have come off in the back of the van. He'd have to take that into account next time, maybe tape it on or perhaps tie her hands, although he prided himself in being able to subdue his victims and get them into the back of the van in less than a minute.

He was starting to win, his superior strength and the fact that he was standing giving him the advantage. Suddenly, as if realising she was about to lose, his victim snapped her right foot out. The impact against his swollen penis was excruciating and he felt all of the wind driven out of him. Ironically it was the sudden application of all of his body weight as he staggered backwards that finally allowed him to rip the shotgun from Jemima's grasp.

With no other options, she jumped off the tailgate and ran past the groaning monster. She had no plan, she just headed for the treeline, hoping to lose herself in the woods. Her back tingled as she imagined him bringing the shotgun to bear, slipping off the safety catch — why hadn't she thought to do that? she berated herself — and blasting a hole in her.

She'd taken barely a half-dozen paces before she stumbled, catching her foot on a root, hidden from view by the snow. She crashed to her knees. Scrambling back to her feet, she staggered another two paces, but it was too late. She felt a rush of wind beside her head then an explosion of light, followed by darkness.

* * *

Stockley stared down at the young woman, breathing heavily. A thin trickle of blood on her left temple, black in the dim moonlight reflecting off the snow, marked where he'd hit her with the solid wooden stock of the shotgun. She was out for the count, but he wasn't going to take any more chances. Reaching down, he hoisted her over his shoulder and carried her back to the van in a fireman's lift. She was light, barely seven stone, he estimated. Nothing for a man who'd spent the early part of his working career hauling sacks of letters and parcels around the Royal Mail depot and more recently heaving bales of hay with his father on their farm.

Laying her insensate body on the tailgate of the van, he picked up the chloroform-soaked rag. The solvent was highly volatile, evaporating rapidly, and he decided to play safe, taking the glass jam jar of chloroform out of the kit bag and resoaking the rag, before retying the sodden cloth around her face.

Suddenly the area was bathed in dazzling bright lights. Cursing, he dropped the jar, spilling its contents down the front of his jacket.

"Police! Step away from the van," came a loud voice, the command repeated by a second voice. Squinting, he could just make out the shadows of two figures, stepping out of the car. Shading his eyes from the glare, he ignored the instruction, reaching into the back of the van, where he'd leant the shotgun.

* * *

Turning onto the dirt track, Sutton had doused the headlights.

"Approaching the clearing," Warren had whispered into the radio, before muting it. The thickening snow muffled the sound of the car's tyres and deadened the quiet thrum of its engine. As they eased towards the clearing, the sparse moonlight reflected off the snow, dimly illuminating the area. Up ahead, the glow of headlights marked their target. As they entered the clearing the two men could make out the form of a man bent over the tailgate doing something to what appeared to be another body. The red glow from the van's tail lights illuminated the shadowy forms, hopefully destroying his night vision.

"Ready?" breathed Warren softly.

"Ready," replied Sutton, flicking on the Audi's powerful main beams and hitting the flashing blue lights.

It had the desired effect, the startled form jumping in surprise.

"Police! Step away from the van," roared Warren, his command repeated by Sutton, as the two officers leapt from the car.

Warren had taken two paces before he realised what the man was doing.

"Gun," he shouted, throwing himself backwards.

To his right, Tony Sutton did the same, ducking behind the car's open door.

A deafening boom shattered the night and glass rained down on Sutton's head.

"I'm OK," he shouted over the ringing in his ears.

Warren risked a peek through the side window of the door he was sheltering behind, hoping that the glare of the lights would render him invisible. Stockley was dressed in black from head to foot and was pacing towards the car. His stride was confident. He knew that neither officer was armed. If they had been, they'd have shouted, "Armed police". He had the gun; he had the advantage.

"Give it up, Stockley. It's over," shouted Warren. In the light he had seen the outline of the gun. It was a shotgun of sorts, presumably the one that Stockley had once upon a time owned a licence for. He tried to remember what the licence had said.

A double-barrelled shotgun, he recalled. Warren thought back to his firearms training years before. British police officers were not routinely armed — mainly because British criminals weren't routinely armed — and so the course had been very theoretical, a basic crash course in different types of guns and what to expect. They hadn't even fired one. From what he could remember, a double-barrelled shotgun had two cartridges, fired one at a time. To reload you had to break open the breech and insert two new cartridges. Stockley had fired one. To take out both officers, he would need to either reload so that he had two full barrels, or he would have to fire one cartridge, then reload.

"Don't be silly, Michael. You know you'll be in a world of shit if you shoot a police officer," Sutton called in desperation.

"Oh, yeah, what are you going to do? Lock me up for longer? Stick me in a cell with no TV?" His voice was slightly slurred, but he was clearly rational.

The fact was, they had nothing to bargain with. Stockley had killed four young women, possibly a fifth and probably his own father. He was probably looking at a whole-life tariff. Even if his defence team convinced the judge that he was not guilty by reason of insanity, he would probably die in Broadmoor, locked away in the secure hospital for society's protection. Killing two police officers wouldn't add anything meaningful to that sentence and might just give him a chance to escape.

He didn't seem to be making any move to reload yet as he walked towards the car, angling towards the passenger side, clearly aiming to take out Warren first. Hidden behind the door, his mind racing, Warren frantically tried to think of a way out of the deadly situation.

* * *

Stockley walked towards the car, his finger tight on the trigger. He'd never shot at a human-sized target before, but he imagined it was probably easier than hitting a rabbit. He stumbled slightly. The chloroform soaking his jacket was making him feel a little light-headed. Nevertheless, he was fully aware of his surroundings and was confident that he'd make it.

He knew that his plans for the girl were ruined, but he still had over twenty thousand pounds in cash and a pocket full of shotgun shells. He'd have to ditch the delivery van — a shame, it was a ruse that had served him well; those bright red vans, a true British icon, really were invisible. That wasn't a problem. Parked half a mile away, concealed by a dense copse of trees, was an old white Transit van, almost as unnoticed by the general public as the post van. He'd paid cash for it a week ago and as long as the building firm the cloned licence plates belonged to kept the tax and insurance up to date and he didn't get pulled over or flashed by speed cameras, the diversion should work.

The police officers had called him by name. He was certain they couldn't recognise him under his mask, which meant they'd figured out his true identity. A pity — he'd enjoyed the news stories blaming his father for his misdeeds. Poetic justice really — after all, it was his father's fault that he was the way he was. Something passed down in his genes or maybe he'd been infected by him directly, like a virus, when the bastard had made his fumbling, drunken advances all those years ago.

It wasn't his fault. He knew that; he'd come to terms with that a long time ago and it had been confirmed by that kind, loving Reverend Harding. For the past week the two men had sat up late, the priest confirming that in modern interpretations of scripture the sins of the father would not be visited on the child. As long as he truly repented then Jesus would forgive him and would not hold him accountable for that which he had no control over. Of course, the well-meaning vicar had no idea that Stockley was speaking, not in the abstract, but in literal terms. That he had in effect become his father. That journey had been completed two weeks ago when he'd sunk the wooden hand axe into the back of the old man's skull and pushed him into the freshly dug pit in the farthest field on the farm.

Regardless, he had no intention of stopping now. He had the resources to continue what he was doing, fulfilling the desires passed on to him by his father indefinitely. And if and when the time came for him to answer for his crimes — well, he had the shotgun and, failing that, the bottle in his pocket. He'd answer directly to God and ask for forgiveness for himself and his father. There was no way he would stand before a jury of his peers, to be locked in a cell for the rest of his life.

He carried on stepping towards the car. He didn't know which police officer he was about to kill first; he presumed that the pair were those two damned detectives, Jones and Sutton. He looked forward to killing them, remembering the smug look on Jones' face as they'd stared each other down during that first encounter at the farmhouse. He'd backed down then, unable to afford to be arrested for resisting arrest. Then there was that small, pig of a man, DI Sutton, who'd sneered contemptuously during each encounter. It didn't matter which one he shot first; they both needed to die.

The chloroform was making his head fairly buzz now, and he took shallow breaths. One more step. He stumbled slightly, but corrected himself. He started to lift the shotgun.

* * *

Crouching behind the driver's door, Tony Sutton watched helplessly as the man advanced towards the passenger side of the car; it was clear that he intended to shoot Jones, then continue around the car and finish him off also.

Two cartridges. He'd fired one already. Sutton had caught a glimpse of the gun before he'd thrown himself behind the car — it looked like a double-barrelled shotgun. That meant he had one left then he had to reload. How long would that take? The problem was that unless he was a lousy shot, that one bullet would almost certainly kill Jones. Even if Sutton disarmed him afterwards, it would be cold comfort. He glanced over at Jones, who raised a single finger. One. He'd done the same calculation.

Sutton turned his attention back to the approaching figure, stumbling slightly in the snow and weaving from side to side. His voice had sounded slurred. Was he drunk? High on drugs? Either way it was their only advantage.

The two detectives had only known each other since the summer and had really only become friends in the past few months, but their minds were working as one tonight. A single nod from Warren was all it took.

Sutton leant forward to the central console. The car was fitted with standard police lights, complete with a choice of sirens. The one Sutton chose was a deafening blare, designed to move cars out of the way by basically scaring the shit out of their drivers.

It had the desired effect, the shotgun discharging harmlessly into the trees as Stockley leapt in surprise.

That was Warren's cue. He burst from behind the door, throwing himself forward. Immediately he realised his mistake. Both his mistakes, in fact. First, he wasn't as quick over the snow-covered underbrush as he thought he would be. Second, a skilled shooter like Stockley could reload a shotgun very, very fast, especially when he already had the cartridge in his free hand and only bothered to load one barrel. And with Warren at such close range and getting closer, he wasn't even going to need to aim. Warren was still the better part of ten feet away when Stockley snapped the breech closed and started to raise the weapon one-handed.

The snowball wasn't particularly good, but, as anybody who had been ambushed would tell you, the surprise factor was what really counted. Sutton's snowball hit Stockley squarely on the side of the cheek. Instinctively he spun to his left, from where the projectile had come.

Warren dived forward, more of a stumble than a rugby tackle if he was honest, and slammed his head into Stockley's midriff. The two men crashed backwards in an ungainly heap. Warren immediately grabbed at the arm holding the shotgun, rolling on top of it. He felt the barrel digging into his ribs and prayed that Stockley's finger was nowhere near the trigger. Using his free arm, he punched the inside of Stockley's elbow. The man grunted in pain and Warren felt the arm go loose.

If he thought that was the end of it, he was sorely mistaken. With a guttural shout Stockley swung his free hand around in a wild haymaker, connecting soundly with Warren's left ear. Warren rolled onto his back, stunned.

Stockley knew he had no choice; the gun was gone. Letting go, he pulled his numbed arm from underneath Jones' insensate form and scrambled to his feet. Before leaving, he delivered a final kick to the man's ribcage before turning and stumbling off into the woods.

* * *

Lying on his back, Warren sent a prayer of thanks to Felicity and Jeff for their thoughtfulness. The thick padding on the coat had turned a potentially bone-crunching kick into something less.

"Guv!" Tony Sutton skidded to a halt next to Warren.

"I'm fine, Tony. Check out Jemima. Get an ambulance down here and let the armed response units know the score."

Sutton nodded and scrambled back to his feet, jogging over to the slumped body next to the delivery van. Taking one last deep breath, Warren rolled to his feet. He looked longingly at the shotgun, but left it where it was. Tempting as it was, he wasn't a licensed firearms officer and he'd find himself on a murder charge if he used it.

As he'd wrestled with Stockley on the ground Warren had caught the sweetly pungent odour of the chloroform that he'd spilled down his front. After Professor Jordan's initial suggestion that some sort of sedative, perhaps chloroform, had been used to subdue his victims, Warren had looked up the chemical on Wikipedia. It was extremely volatile, meaning it evaporated really quickly. That was why it was so good as an inhalant. It also meant that over time it would evaporate away. Warren remembered from school that evaporation happened faster at higher temperatures, but he had no idea what effect the evening's freezing temperatures would have on the evaporation of chloroform.

Regardless, it was an advantage that he intended to exploit. Stockley had sounded slurred and seemed slightly uncoordinated. Was it the effects of the chemical? Would that last until the armed response units arrived? Or would it wear off enough for him to implement the back-up plan that Warren was sure he must have? The man was clearly deranged, an evil sexual predator controlled by his urges. If he escaped their net, how long would it be until he struck again?

Ignoring Sutton's shouts, Warren headed into the woods.

* * *

Stockley crashed through the trees, his breath labouring and his head spinning. It was like being drunk. He stumbled again, falling to his knees. He wobbled as he stood up and had to hold onto a tree branch to regain his balance. Somehow he reoriented himself and started again.

Up ahead he heard a rushing noise. It took a moment for his befuddled brain to fully comprehend what he was hearing, and then he felt a surge of relief. It was the river, his pathway to the small grove where he'd concealed the Transit van. All he had to do was get to the bank, turn left and follow it for about three hundred yards until he came across the dirty old coat he'd found in the back of the van and hung from a branch as a marker.

Emerging from the trees, he saw the glint of water. The noise was much louder than he remembered from a week ago, the recent rain and snow having increased the flow substantially. The river was ancient and had cut a deep channel into the land, the banks as high as fifteen feet in places. It wouldn't do to fall into it and he didn't trust his balance, so he kept away from the edge.

Turn left, he remembered dimly. His legs seemed to be working on their own now, disconnected from his brain as he placed one foot in front of the other. Suddenly he felt his stomach lurch and he stumbled to his knees throwing up violently. Nausea came over him in waves. Nevertheless, he pushed himself to his feet. Look for the coat, he commanded himself, look for the coat.

The coat. What was so significant about a coat? He stumbled again, face first into a pile of snow. The sudden shock of the cold startled his brain into alertness. The coat. Of course, he'd spilled chloroform down it. No wonder he was feeling so ill. His fingers were numb, their co-ordination all gone, but somehow he managed to unzip the front of the jacket. Squirming on the ground, like a snake shedding its skin, he worked his way out of it and rolled over. He gasped at the fresh air, before grabbing another handful of snow and rubbing it into his face.

Already his head was clearing, the cold air and freezing snow chasing away the cobwebs. He scrambled to his feet, shivering. The coat was an expensive, all-weather sort and so he'd only worn a light sweater underneath. His head was covered in a thin bather's cap to stop any hair getting on his victim and he wore latex gloves — neither of these provided any warmth and he knew that he had to get to the van as soon as possible. He prayed the warm-air blowers worked.

Turning to the left again, he resumed his trek.

* * *

Following Stockley hadn't been hard. He'd left a trail of destruction and footprints visible to even the poorest of trackers. Warren picked his way rapidly through the trees, following the trail, pausing every few paces to listen for signs of an ambush. Away from the glow of the vehicle lights, Warren's eyes had soon adjusted to the dim moonlight and he could see reasonably clearly.

Just how badly affected by the chloroform was Stockley? Breathing in the fumes from his soaked jacket had clearly had some effect, but how long would it last? Would it get worse with time, or would it wear off? Had the man still got the presence of mind to remove the coat? If he had, how long until he overcame the effects?

Warren paused again, leaning against the trunk of a tree. His hands were so numb with cold that he couldn't tell if the tree had the roughness of an oak, or the smooth papery bark of a silver birch. His new jacket was fantastic, but he'd forgotten the gloves and woolly hat that he kept in his old one.

After a few more paces, he stopped again, listening carefully. In the background he heard a dull roar — there was a river running through this part of the woods, he recalled from the map book. But what sort? The book hadn't really given any indication; it could be a small, meandering brook, a rapidly flowing stream, or a gushing river for all he knew. It sounded as if there was a substantial amount of water rushing along, but he acknowledged that alone in a darkened forest, on the trail of a murderous rapist who'd demonstrated that he had no compunction against killing police officers, his mind could be exaggerating the sound.

He resumed his careful passage, the sound of the river getting louder. Up ahead, the light filtering through the trees started to take on a different quality, brightening and then, almost without warning, Warren found himself in the open.

The rush of the river had become a dull roar. Looking to his left, Warren spotted a lone figure, picking his way carefully along the narrow border between the riverbank and the tree-line. He didn't appear to be wearing his coat anymore, but still seemed to be wobbling a bit.

How long would it take him to recover fully? Warren didn't know, but he knew he couldn't let that happen. He had to take his chances whilst the man was still off balance and not thinking clearly.

Ducking back into the tree-line and hoping that the noise of the river would mask his approach, Warren moved as quickly as he could, travelling parallel to the river. Stockley seemed to be moving with a definite purpose now; he looked like a man with a clear destination in mind. Moving a little further into the woods, Warren drew alongside the man. Suddenly Stockley stopped and turned, looking into the woods. Warren froze. Stockley reached up and started tugging at something hanging in the trees. He clearly hadn't spotted Warren.

Then, to Warren's puzzlement, Stockley started to *put on* what he'd pulled from the tree. A coat? What on earth was a coat doing hanging from a tree? There was no way the man could have foreseen what was going to happen to the coat he was wearing, so why was one hanging there. Coincidence? Warren couldn't accept that. What then?

A marker, Warren realised. Some way of knowing when he'd walked far enough along the riverbank. Moving slowly, so as not to draw attention to himself, Warren turned on the spot, searching. Finally he saw it, moonlight reflecting off the mirrors in its headlamps. Stockley's means of escape.

* * *

Stockley wrestled with the coat that he'd found in the back of the Transit van. He wasn't a large man, but the previous owner had clearly been small, maybe even a woman or child. It didn't help that he could barely feel his fingers and he was shivering so violently that he thought his teeth would break.

Barely a dozen metres away, concealed by the trees, sat his salvation, its keys already dangling from the ignition, the doors unlocked. A pretty safe gamble, he'd decided, out here in the middle of nowhere. He wanted to get in, start the engine and race down the dirt track that led to freedom, but he knew that he was close to hypothermia. He needed the jacket.

All of a sudden he heard the thrum of a helicopter above and a bright light shone down upon him.

"It's over, Stockley. You're surrounded by armed police. The helicopter above has thermal imaging. There's no escape. Come quietly, nobody needs to get hurt." Warren stepped out of the tree-line, barely twenty feet from Stockley.

The appearance of the helicopter had surprised Warren almost as much as it had Stockley; he hadn't thought the helicopter flew in this sort of weather. Regardless, he decided to capitalise on the moment. The most important question was — had it been dispatched to supply support for the armed response units? Or was it here because the ARUs were still delayed?

Either way, Warren had seen no evidence yet of any armed back-up, so it would seem that, even with the helicopter hovering above, he was still on his own. But there was no need for Stockley to know that...

"Give it up, Michael. There are trained snipers surrounding the area — you know you can't escape."

He was right, Stockley realised. It was over. Unless he did something about it, the next step was his arrest and then that was it. Prison. He shuddered at the memory. Visiting his father in there had left him with nightmares. The cold grey walls and solid steel doors. The smell of disinfectant everywhere that still couldn't quite overcome the smell of fear, of hatred, of despair. Every time he'd left the prison, he'd thrown away the clothes he was wearing and stood underneath a scalding shower until the hot water ran out.

He'd made his vow long ago. What would it take to make them shoot him? If he attacked that bastard Jones, would they put a bullet in his head? End it for him in a millisecond?

No, probably not, he realised. They'd aim for the body, the centre-mass. Maybe he'd be dead, maybe not. Maybe he'd be paralysed, incarcerated not just in prison, but in his own body as well. And maybe they'd not even shoot him. Weren't they encouraged to use non-lethal weapons like TASERs these days? Fifty-thousand volts of excruciating agony, then on with the cuffs.

No, it would have to be by his own hand. He reached into his trouser pocket, surprised to find the bottle intact. Pulling it out, he gripped it numbly between thumb and forefinger and started to unscrew the lid.

Warren stood in the tree-line, waiting for Stockley to make his move. Where the hell was the armed response team? he asked himself for the thousandth time. He cast his gaze around the woods surrounding him, desperately searching for his back-up. Nothing. But then would he see them anyway? Dressed in matt-black, like some sort of twenty-first-century ninja, they could be standing three metres from him, with Stockley square in their infra-red sights, and he would be none the wiser.

Stockley was also looking around, like a rabbit caught in headlights — or a deer for that matter, thought Warren ruefully. The man reached inside his trouser pocket and Warren tensed. Expecting a knife or other weapon, he was not expecting to see a small bottle.

Warren watched as he struggled to unscrew the cap. What was he doing? The cyanide, he realised; the man was going to kill himself. A surge of anger ran through Warren's blood. *Not on my watch*, Warren vowed.

The man was a killer; he had to answer for his crimes. He had to stand in the dock and face his victims' families as justice was handed down. Then he had to spend the rest of his life in prison. No way was he going to take the easy way out.

Without really formulating a plan, Warren raced forward. Concentrating on getting his numbed fingers to unscrew the bottle's cap, Stockley didn't notice Warren's movement until it was too late. Warren rammed into him, knocking him to one side. The bottle flew out of his grip, landing in a pile of snow a few feet away. Warren was holding onto Stockley's lower body with all of his might, trying to stop the man from scrambling free to retrieve the bottle. Not for the first time in his police career, Warren wished he'd extended his self-defence training beyond the required courses. A working knowledge of judo would come in useful right about now.

Fortunately, Michael Stockley was no martial artist either and the best he could do was batter away at his opponent's body, trying to find a spot where the coat's padding was thinner.

For his part, Warren simply hunkered down and took the blows; where the hell was his back-up? He'd be black and blue in the morning, but his attacker couldn't get enough of a swing to do any real damage. The coat that Stockley had tried to force himself into was restricting his movement, whilst the biting cold and lingering effects of the chloroform robbed him of his strength.

Finally, Warren decided to seize his chance. Relaxing his tight grip on his assailant's ribcage, he pushed back, lifting his head. He felt the crown of his head connect solidly with Stockley's chin and he fancied he could hear the clack as his teeth snapped together. Warren let his grip go completely now and Stockley reared backward, widening the gap between them as Warren had hoped he would.

Reversing direction, Warren snapped his head forward, slamming his forehead into Stockley's nose full force.

The satisfying, crunching, squidging noise was definitely worth the bruise Warren would no doubt be wearing in the middle of his forehead for the next fortnight. As Stockley collapsed back, with a deep groan, Warren scrambled over and grabbed the bottle of cyanide. Without pausing, he threw it overarm into the rushing river below.

"No!" shouted Stockley, watching his last chance to control his own fate spinning end over end into the void below. He knelt, covering his face with his hands. A quiet sob racked his body.

"It's done, Michael. It's all over. Come quietly — there's no need to make any more of a fuss." Warren fought down his revulsion for the man in front of him and tried to sound sympathetic.

It wasn't easy. The man before him was a monster of the worst kind. A sick predator who had ended the lives of a string of young women for nothing but his own sexual gratification. Unbidden, the faces of five young women swam before his eyes: Sally Evans, Carolyn Patterson, Gemma Allen, Saskia Williams and last of all poor Melanie Clearwater. She'd survived, but at what cost? And then there was Jemima Duer; Warren hadn't seen a photo of her, had no idea what she looked like. He prayed that he could say hello to her in person, now that it was all over — to know that they'd saved at least one of this animal's victims.

But what about Stockley? Warren had been acting instinctively when he'd tried to stop him from taking the cyanide, but what had he accomplished, really? The man had destroyed so many lives, not only those he'd killed, but their loved ones as well — yet he would survive and live out the rest of his days. He would almost certainly spend those days in prison or a secure institute, but so what? He'd have access to TV, books, probably even the Internet eventually. Every day he'd wake up and live that day until he went to bed, ready to do it all over again. How was that fair? Warren thought back to the tear-stained face of Gemma Allen's mother. "How is that right?" she'd asked through her tears. Warren hadn't been able to answer her then — he still couldn't answer her now.

Reaching behind him, he was relieved to find the plasti-cuffs he kept in his back pocket still there. He tossed them to Stockley.

"Put those on, Michael, then let's get you some warm clothes and hot coffee."

Stockley stared at the cuffs lying on the snow before him.

Suddenly, in a burst of speed that Warren would have thought beyond him, he leapt to his feet.

"Never!" And with that he hurled himself past a frozen Warren, towards the rushing river below.

Epilogue

Warren sipped gratefully at the freshly brewed coffee poured for him by Assistant Chief Constable Mohammed Naseem. It was barely forty-eight hours after the climactic events in the forest and, despite technically being on sick leave, Warren had been writing up report after report. More than once he'd considered switching the sling from his left arm to his right arm and claiming that he couldn't write properly. Unfortunately, the paperwork wasn't going to go away and he might as well get it done with.

Now, with most of the administration completed, he had been summoned to the ACC's office to give his side of the story. No police investigation ever went completely smoothly and the fact that Stockley had managed to kill so many victims was guaranteed to provoke condemnation from some quarters, so the force was determined to rebut any allegations of poor detective work immediately.

That wasn't the only reason, of course, that Jones found himself face to face with his boss. The rumours were that Naseem fancied himself as something of a novelist and that one day he would parlay some of the more interesting cases to have come across his desk into fiction. Whether it was true or not, Naseem was known to be an appreciative audience and Jones was actually rather looking forward to telling the tale.

"Thanks for coming in, Warren. Of course, I'd have completely understood if you had felt you needed more time to deal with what happened." He gestured at Warren's bruised and battered face and his sling. Warren smiled at the white lie.

"Hell of an ending, Warren. Of course, the circumstances were horrendous and I don't think anyone could have expected you to stop him."

Warren nodded; in his mind's eye he again saw the mother of Gemma Allen as she asked how it was fair that Stockley would live, when her daughter was gone.

Naseem shook his head in sympathy. "Between you, me and these four walls, I think a hell of a lot of us believe that an ice-cold, watery grave is a fitting end for a bastard like Michael Stockley. There is nothing else in our system that will ever adequately punish him enough or bring justice for his victims."

Warren nodded. Tony Sutton had suggested much the same as he had wrapped his shivering boss in a blanket and awaited the arrival of the ambulance, that fateful night.

However, forty-eight hours after the event, Warren wasn't so sure. Who was he to pass sentence out in the woods, with nobody else to argue his decision with? To horribly misquote Churchill, the adversarial justice system was the worst type of system, except for all the others. Deep in his heart, below the moral certainty that all policemen needed to do the job, Warren knew that he was only a facilitator of justice, not its arbiter. Morally, Warren knew that allowing Stockley to kill himself through inaction was no different from pushing him into that river himself. It was up to a jury of twelve peers to be swayed by arguments both in favour of and against the defendant. He had no right to make life or death decisions. Did anyone? Not even the family of those victims had that right, he felt. Perhaps one might argue that the killer's victims might have that privilege, but, until somebody figured out how to communicate with the dead, that remained nothing more than a philosophical debating point.

For him to assume that responsibility, out in the woods on his own, would place him on the same moral plane as Michael Stockley and that wasn't somewhere that Warren wanted to be. He didn't feel that he could cope with the burden of guilt that passing such a sentence would leave him with. Would he ever sleep again?

For that reason, Warren was glad that Sutton had arrived when he did. His desperate lunge to grab a falling Stockley had strained and torn ligaments in his shoulder and the pain had threatened to overwhelm him. A few more seconds and he would have had to let go whether he wanted to or not. As it was, his saving of the twisted killer and rapist had garnered him a mixture of admiration from those who were impressed by the lengths he went to or dismay from those who regarded it as an opportunity lost.

"So why don't you take us through the whole story, Warren? I hear that Stockley is admitting everything." Naseem had settled himself down, cradling his cup of coffee, and was clearly looking forward to the tale.

Warren grunted. "You could say that. We can't get him to shut up. Of course, he claims no personal responsibility and that we aren't the ones who should be judging him."

Naseem raised an eyebrow. "How so?"

"As far as Stockley's concerned, it was the fault of his father; he claims that his father passed on something in his genes that meant he was wired wrong — claims it's all his dad's fault and had he not been so wicked et cetera et cetera. He also claims that as it's not his fault, he won't be punished for his actions by God."

Naseem rolled his eyes, clearly expressing what he thought of that. "Then I guess we'll just have to punish him on God's behalf. Leaving that aside, what sort of influence did his father have on him?"

"Pretty significant, it would seem. He found out a lot about his father's crimes during the court case and later through his own research. He emulated his father's methods, not only to implicate him but because they were so effective."

"And this wasn't the first time he's done this?"

"No, he says it started when he raped a jogger in a park in Bristol back when he was at university. He learnt from his father's mistakes and nearly killed the woman with an overdose of chloroform to stop her coming around. Nevertheless, he pulled it off and the crime remained unsolved.

"It seems that this episode woke him up and he voluntarily committed himself to drug rehabilitation and counselling. He admitted whilst he was in therapy that he had strong, inappropriate sexual urges and blamed them on his father, but claims to have been sufficiently vague that the therapist didn't make the connection with any crime, assuming that he was talking hypothetically.

"The therapy had some limited success, but fast forward four years and Michael is working in Reading. He loses control again. Again, he gets away with it. But he says that he felt revulsion for what he had become and started to blame his father. Moving back to the family farm, he underwent counselling again, this time with a local priest, and was advised that he should seek to reconcile his relationship with his father to move on."

"Bloody amateur."

"Exactly. It was the worst thing that he could have suggested.

God only knows what he picked up from him. We know that he shares his old man's phobia of prison — that's why he carried that small bottle of cyanide; whether or not Cameron had any influence over his son or aided him directly, we'll probably never know. The shrinks reckon he really does believe that his urges weren't his fault. He's successfully managed to shift all the blame, mentally, onto his father."

"So I guess using his father as a scapegoat for his own actions makes a kind of perverted sense."

"Exactly. He even planned his father's death, figuring that with Cameron seemingly on the run, he would be able to continue to indulge himself and let his father take the fall."

Naseem shook his head in disbelief. "Surely he knew that it couldn't last for ever. What were his long-term plans?"

Warren shrugged. "That we don't know. We're not sure he really knows. We found a notebook with jottings and observations about his various victims; presumably that was how he planned his attacks. There were some vague scribblings in there that indicated he might have been eyeing up some other potential targets, but they are too ambiguous to identify the women he was stalking. I don't suppose it really matters now."

"No, I don't suppose it does. Besides, what would we do if we could identify them? Can you imagine how those poor women would feel if we told them?"

Warren nodded; he'd had similar thoughts himself.

"So how did he select his victims? Not all of them were at that sports centre."

"Stockley has a long association with the football team and Alex Chalmers knew him through the Royal Mail, from years back. When Royal Mail bought into World Wide Parcel Logistics,

Stockley moved sideways into WWPL. The depot shares offices with the Middlesbury sorting office and so he stayed where he is. Workers at the office are so used to seeing him around that he pretty much has the run of the place. I believe that he found out about Angus Carroway's little vehicle-hire business and helped himself. Robbie Cartwright didn't recognise his photo because technically he isn't a Royal Mail employee and so doesn't appear on their staff database. It never occurred to me to ask for a printout of everybody that worked in the building."

Naseem shrugged. "Why would it?"

"Anyway, Alex Chalmers asked if he could get WWPL to sponsor the team. They did and Stockley started coming along to some of the games. He was never a football player himself and so he doesn't appear on the fixture lists or anything.

"According to the Reverend Harding and Cameron's probation officer, Stockley has always had problems making friends, but the team was happy to have him along. A cynic might point out that you welcome your sponsor with open arms, especially when he always gets the first round in." Warren indicated that it didn't matter.

"Nobody at the sports centre knew of his connection to Richard Cameron of course and he kept it that way. As he socialised with them he met Darren Blackheath's girlfriend Sally Evans and Chalmer's then-girlfriend Carolyn Patterson.

"Looking back on it, people we've interviewed say that he was always a bit weird around them, and women in general. A bit too attentive to them, perhaps. But nothing too extreme, and you don't want to offend the team sponsor by asking him not to be so nice to your girlfriend."

"Reading the report, Alex Chalmers stopped playing over two

years ago — surely Stockley wasn't planning to rape these poor girls back that far?"

Warren shook his head. "Very doubtful. We think that his father's release last year was the action that caused everything to fall into place. Maybe something happened; there are suggestions that his father abused him as a child. He won't say and obviously we can't ask Cameron — we found him buried in the farthest field with an axe in the back of his head, just like Stockley told us. Regardless, when he decided to choose his targets, it was obvious for him to go after women that he'd been somewhat obsessed with."

Naseem placed his empty coffee cup on the desk and leant back in his chair.

"So, what about the other victims?"

"Saskia Williams had been a casual gym user for years. No direct link to the football team, but they could have crossed paths. Gemma Allen was just very unlucky. She worked in the Costcutter around the corner from the sorting office where staff would go for a paper or whatever. Physically, they both fall into both father and son's preferred type. Blonde, slim to average build, twenties and pretty — a bit vague, but line up their photos and you can see the similarities. Interestingly, you can also put a photo of Angie Cameron — Stockley's mother — in that group."

Naseem grimaced. "Let's leave that one to the psychologists, shall we? What about his last victim, Jemima Duer? How is she, by the way?"

"Physically, she's fine. Tony Sutton got the chloroform rag off her before she suffocated fully and kept her warm until the ambulance arrived. She was unconscious from a blow to the head, but escaped serious injury. Psychologically though... time will tell. Again, she simply seems to have caught Stockley's eye on several occasions as she waited for the bus. He worked out her routine, which stayed essentially the same even when her dad started picking her up."

"So tell me, what was it that finally made you realise that it was Stockley and not his father?" Naseem now looked excited; this was what he was most interested in.

"It's hard to say, but something that always nagged me was his confession to having given his father a false alibi for the nights that Sally Evans and Carolyn Patterson were taken. He said that he panicked and so claimed that his father was asleep in bed. That matched his father's alibi, of course. However, if you think about it, if Cameron really was giving us a false alibi and his son made up one, then what were the odds that they'd give the same one? Especially since they both implied that he had 'gone to bed early', in other words it was a bit unusual. I figured that there must have been some sort of agreement between them, which meant that Stockley was at least guilty of conspiracy, if not an active participant.

"Of course, we know now that Stockley was slipping his old man a sleeping pill on the nights he needed to go out. We found an old pot of prescription tablets going right back to when his mother was ill. That opened my mind to the possibility that Stockley was less than honest, although at the time I hadn't really thought it through.

"Something else that bothered me was how an older man who entered prison with little education in 1998 could use a computer in such a sophisticated manner. He even erased his Internet browsing history. I spoke to his probation officer and he said that Cameron did basic literacy and numeracy courses as part of his rehabilitation, but as a sex offender was taught only the most basic computer skills — he had no access to the Internet.

"What we now believe was that Stockley set up the computer and knew his father's password and used his account to surf for porn and plan the attacks. He erased the Internet history to stop his old man realising what he was doing — assuming that he even used the computer. He might even have known that we would be able to trace his surfing history even with the cleared browsing history and so did it to make our discoveries seem more authentic."

"Well, he's certainly a crafty bastard, I'll give him that," mused Naseem.

"Then there was the matter of his slipping up and leaving a sample of semen with both Gemma Allen and Saskia Williams after he'd successfully left no traces previously. Bad luck or fatalism, perhaps, but it niggled me. Then I had a conversation with Melanie Clearwater, the prostitute attacked and left for dead. She remembered being picked up by a younger man as a treat for an older man, who she thought may be related to him. He was very insistent that the older man had a happy ending, so to speak, even to the point of checking the wastebasket afterwards. At the time, I thought we might be dealing with a separate attacker and so didn't immediately join the dots."

"But you were open to the possibility that Stockley was guilty of at least something?"

"Yes, but he muddied the waters quite successfully in the beginning. He knew about Darren Blackheath's past problems with the law and he was also aware of Alex Chalmer's reputation for hitting women. He guessed that we would follow those leads — no smoke without fire and all that."

"And the Royal Mail van and Angus Carroway's little vehicle-hire operation just pointed the finger even more clearly. Bit of a gamble though — surely there was a risk that we would follow it back to him?"

"Calculated risk, I suppose."

"So, is he insane?"

"That's beyond my pay-grade, sir, but in my opinion he's one sick bunny."

The two men sat for a moment in contemplative silence.

"Well, you did well, Warren. There will be lessons to be learnt as always and a few voices asking why we didn't do things differently, but twenty-twenty hindsight is a wonderful thing.

"From a personal perspective, I'd rather my officers were a little less inclined to go running into a darkened forest after a serial killer without back-up. But all's well that ends well, I suppose."

Warren said nothing. The grapevine suggested that ACC Naseem had run into his own fair share of darkened forests when still on the beat and he was grateful that he didn't have to endure another earful about his rather rash decision. Susan had gone ballistic when she'd picked him up from the hospital that night, and the following day he'd received another dressing-down from Bernice.

"On a more serious note, you were very lucky, Warren. Your carelessness by the river could have cost you your career." Warren blinked in surprise. Naseem continued, his eyes crinkling slightly.

"Apparently the cyanide bottle didn't break when you threw it away. I can downplay your heroics in the forest and DI Sutton's over-enthusiastic driving style; however, the Chief Constable is an obsessive fisherman and Forensics reckon there was enough poison in there to wipe out half the trout in the river."

Acknowledgements

Phew, that 'difficult second novel' wasn't as difficult as I feared! And again, that's in large part down to my wonderful family and friends who help and encourage me in everything. Whether they proof-read drafts, gave me their thoughts on extracts that I sent them or just said something really interesting that I shamelessly pinched...

As always, there are too many to list you all, but a few stand out. Again, my father and Lawrence proof-read the complete manuscript, corrected my grammar and gave me their thoughts. My favourite lawyers Dan and Caroline gave me sound legal advice and an insight into custody procedures. I am also extremely grateful to Crime Scene Investigator Lee Robson from Essex police, who's description of the procedures and day-to-day working practise of the folks in white suits has been invaluable. I apologise sincerely for any errors or artistic liberties taken to advance the story.

And finally, a big thank you to Father David Barry who not only double-checked the authenticity of a key chapter, but also helped make my little sister's wedding such a perfect day!

As always, the support and friendship of Hertford Writers' Circle has been wonderful and I appreciate the fact that nobody reported me to the authorities for turning up each month with a new description of a grisly murder…

And finally, the editorial team and staff at CarinaUK and Harlequin, in particular Helen, Lucy and Victoria for their hard work on this and The Last Straw.

I hope you enjoy reading it as much as I enjoyed writing it.

Disclaimer:

The town of Middlesbury, Middlesbury CID and all characters featured in this book are entirely fictional and not intended to represent any real-world individuals or organisations. It is also important to stress that whilst Hertfordshire and Bedfordshire Constabularies are real organisations, they are not in any way affiliated to this book and the way that they are represented in this book is entirely imaginary.

Dear Reader,

Thank you so much for taking the time to read this book – we hope you enjoyed it! If you did, we'd be so appreciative if you left a review.

Here at HQ Digital we are dedicated to publishing fiction that will keep you turning the pages into the early hours. We publish a variety of genres, from heartwarming romance, to thrilling crime and sweeping historical fiction.

To find out more about our books, enter competitions and discover exclusive content, please join our community of readers by following us at:

 @HQDigitalUK

facebook.com/HQDigitalUK

Are you a budding writer? We're also looking for authors to join the HQ Digital family! Please submit your manuscript to:

HQDigital@harpercollins.co.uk

Hope to hear from you soon!